Robert Sims grew up in Melbourne, going straight from high school to a job with the *Herald & Weekly Times* in Flinders Street. This was to involve stints as a reporter at *The Sun*, 3DB radio, the *Sydney Morning Herald* and the *Papua New Guinea Post-Courier*. He took a career break from journalism to complete a degree in politics and philosophy. After that he spent more than 20 years in London working for Independent Radio News and ITN. While writing *The Shadow Maker* he did freelance radio work with the BBC. Robert and his wife and two young sons divide their time between London and Melbourne.

Robert Sims

To Dave,
cheers, Rob

ROBERT SIMS

THE SHADOW MAKER

ARENA
ALLEN&UNWIN

This is a work of fiction. Names, characters, places and incidents either are the product of the author's imagination or are used fictitiously, and any resemblance to actual persons, living or dead, business establishments, events or locales is entirely coincidental.

First published in 2007

Copyright © Robert Sims 2007

All rights reserved. No part of this book may be reproduced or transmitted in any form or by any means, electronic or mechanical, including photocopying, recording or by any information storage and retrieval system, without prior permission in writing from the publisher. The *Australian Copyright Act 1968* (the Act) allows a maximum of one chapter or 10 per cent of this book, whichever is the greater, to be photocopied by any educational institution for its educational purposes provided that the educational institution (or body that administers it) has given a remuneration notice to Copyright Agency Limited (CAL) under the Act.

Arena
an imprint of Allen & Unwin
83 Alexander Street
Crows Nest NSW 2065
Australia
Phone: (61 2) 8425 0100
Fax: (61 2) 9906 2218
Email: info@allenandunwin.com
Web: www.allenandunwin.com

National Library of Australia
Cataloguing-in-Publication entry:

Sims, Robert, 1950- .
  The shadow maker.

  ISBN 978 1 74175 173 4 (pbk.).

  I. Title.

A823.4

Set in 12/14.5 pt Adobe Garamond Pro by Bookhouse, Sydney
Printed and bound in Australia by Griffin Press

10 9 8 7 6 5 4 3 2 1

Some sit in darkness, and in the shadow of death:
prisoners in misery and irons

Book of Psalms

1

Philosophers have pointed out that hell exists in this world, not the next. To observe the ranks of the damned we need only look at ourselves, for we comprise both the devils and the souls in torment.

Although this subtlety would have been lost on the woman facing a man across a cheap hotel room, she was about to experience her own version of it, for the man was there to engage in an act of inhuman depravity.

The room was furnished with no more than a double bed, a bedside table, a wardrobe and a wooden chair. There was no carpet on the floor and no curtain on the window, just a blind patting against the window sill, warped by more than a century of sun and rain. The only light came from the flickering flames in the fireplace – strange in such uncomfortably hot weather. Not that it bothered the woman. She wasn't fazed by the man's need to act out a fantasy, or, for that matter, by the mask, manacles and neck shackles he was placing on the bed. This encounter was part of the anonymous life she'd chosen by default – the series of mistakes that had led to this night and to this room. Her purpose was business, that was all, or so she thought as she removed her clothes. His tense attitude she put down to impatience.

When he put on the mask and took hold of her she pushed him away.

'Back off,' she told him. 'Money first.'

He stood there, not responding, just staring at her.

'I told you,' she said. 'Bondage is extra.'

Then he said something in a quiet voice, and she realised, with a sense of panic, that she'd just made the biggest mistake of her life.

She turned to grab the spray can in her handbag, but he hit her from behind with a glass ashtray from the mantelpiece. The blow stunned her, and she felt her ribs crunch against the metal base of the bed as she dropped to the floor.

The woman regained consciousness with a piercing headache. There were points of pain in her ribs, and a dull throbbing in her groin. The room was in total darkness, but she could feel the breeze from an open window and hear the drone of cars zooming past at high speed. There were smells of drains and petrol fumes and also a strange odour of burnt flesh. Then she remembered. He'd cruised to a stop where she was standing on a corner by the casino and after he'd picked her up they'd driven to a hotel beside the freeway. That's where she was lying now. But why was it so dark?

He hadn't paid the extra money, she remembered both that and the way he'd come after her in the mask. He must have hit her from behind and she'd fallen against the bed, but afterwards – a blank. It wasn't the first time she'd been caught. More than once she'd been left with cracked ribs, and by the feel of it that's what she had again.

Along with the pain came the humiliation. Under her body she could feel the scattered contents of her handbag pressing into her skin – lipstick, tweezers, a broken perfume bottle, a piece of foil for inhaling crack. The spilt components of her life.

Groaning with the pain, she propped herself up against the bed, her chains clinking as she moved. So that's how it was. He'd acted out his fantasy on her unconscious body. The weight of the manacles dragged on her wrists, and the metal shackles pressed down on her neck. But how much damage had he inflicted? After knocking her senseless he must have chained and raped her, and – what else? She raised her hands nervously to her face and felt a gritty texture on her cheeks. She put her fingers to her nose and sniffed something like soot or ash. At first she thought her face had been disfigured then realised there were no wounds on her cheeks. So where did the burnt smell come from? Tentatively she moved her fingertips to her eye sockets. That's when she started screaming.

2

The desk sergeant looked up as a young woman walked through the lobby of Melbourne's police headquarters.

'Good morning, Van Hassel,' he said. Then he raised an eyebrow at her pale turquoise linen suit. 'Very arresting,' he added.

'That sounds like a hint to slap the cuffs on you,' she laughed.

'I can think of worse ideas.'

She smiled and breezed past him to the lifts, looking cool and crisp in defiance of the heatwave. Despite her composure, she gave the impression of a woman who strove hard to win. Her face and physique were in keeping with the Australian ideal of athletic good looks, and her short blonde hair was swept back.

Detective Sergeant Marita Van Hassel – Rita to her friends – was arriving for another day of work with the Sexual Crimes Squad. As usual, she came with a sense of energy and purpose. It was more than a job to her, it was a daily challenge. It was also an opportunity, a career path.

She'd been assigned to Sex Crimes seven years ago, thanks to the recommendations of a senior officer at the Police Academy and her honours degree in psychology. It hadn't taken long to impress the head of the squad, Detective Inspector Jack Loftus, with her intuitive grasp of crime scene analysis and an assertiveness that had to be channelled. He decided she was the type who needed fast-track development, and three years ago she'd been selected by the Australian Bureau of Criminal Intelligence to train as a profiler. That meant a part-time return to studies in subjects like forensics, behavioural science and pathology. It also meant a three-month visit to the FBI Academy at Quantico in Virginia. She still had a year to go on the course, but once she was fully qualified she'd move up to the Intelligence Data Centre, perhaps with a post in the Behavioural Analysis Unit. Until then she was still a squad detective – albeit one who possessed profiling skills and a small, glass-panelled office to focus on them, as well as a desk in the squad room.

Once upstairs she cleared a space on her desk and started sorting through her case files. Her in-tray had accumulated a drift of paperwork and, with another court appearance pending, she wanted it out of the way. The mood around her was subdued. Officers sat at their work stations tapping at keyboards, shuffling through reports or mumbling their way through routine phone calls. Some were nursing hangovers. No doubt most of them wished they were somewhere else, preferably by a shaded pool outside. That said, the office was quarantined from the hot March day by tinted windows, air-conditioning and fluorescent strip lighting. Like so many other workplaces, its design was neat and functional, right down to the grey filing cabinets and the drab roller blinds.

When the paperwork was under control, Rita logged on and transferred a set of evidence notes from the server to the hard drive of her computer. There were no other pressing chores, so after checking her emails she strolled over to the coffee maker.

'So how's your love life, Rita?' came a voice from behind her, as she got her espresso.

She turned to greet Erin Webster, a fellow detective sergeant with the squad.

'Detached. How's yours?'

'With a two-year-old driving me nuts, non-existent, despite the holiday,' said Erin. 'Your ex is still your ex then?'

'Definitely. And he's not moving back in.'

'Why not? I thought you two were good together.'

Rita thought for a moment. 'Because he appeals to my worst impulses.'

Erin laughed. 'But that's what makes you interesting.'

Erin Webster was Rita's closest friend inside the police force. As well as being a colleague she filled the role of confidante – a woman to share gossip and moral support in a male-dominated environment. A fellow graduate from the Police Academy, Erin had employed a different work method to Rita to gain promotion, one that came naturally. Her looks helped. A boisterous competitor to the core, she had copper-coloured hair and a wholesome face with hazel eyes. These she highlighted, though her freckles she tried to hide. They made her look *cute* – not an image she wanted. Physical prowess and out-scoring the boys were what counted. And an appetite for fun. As a career strategy it had its rewards. Those who won her favours usually put in a good word for her.

'I can see we're due for another wine session,' she said.

'Thanks for the warning,' joked Rita, before the shrill ring of her mobile broke into the conversation.

It was Detective Senior Sergeant Wayne Strickland. 'This is a bad one,' he said. 'Put everything on hold. I want you down here as soon as possible.'

The sombre tone of his voice as he gave her the name and location of the hotel he was calling from told Rita it wasn't a good time to ask questions. Swallowing her coffee, she quickly farewelled Erin, grabbed a notepad and ran downstairs to her car.

3

When Rita arrived at the crime scene the hotel parking lot was already taped off, and half a dozen squad cars and patrol vehicles were slanted at untidy angles out front. Uniformed officers stood around, eyeing the passers-by.

The Duke of York hotel was a classic Victorian building with high gables and turrets. Sandwiched between a corner garage and a used car dealer, the place had seen better days. The paintwork was peeling, slates were missing from the roof and there were weeds in the spouting. The nearby concrete pillars and graffiti of the freeway overpass completed the tawdry aspect.

Rita lifted the yellow tape, spoke to a uniformed officer at the entrance and hurried up the stairs. Walking down a passage on the second floor, she took in heavy wooden doors and framed lithographs mildewed with age. The place was redolent of cheap, anonymous vice.

The crime scene investigation was well underway when she reached it. Evidence techs were busy dusting for prints, measuring distances and bagging anything that might be relevant. In front of the fireplace, chalk circles were drawn around two small, ugly stains on the floor. A police photographer bent over them, camera flashing. Beside them lay a poker. The rest of the fire irons stood in a rack on the hearth, where ashes and charred wood littered the grate. A dented fire screen had been moved to one side. There were more stains nearby, next to chains and manacles that hung from the metal bedstead. A red handbag sat on the bedside table, and underneath a chair was a pair of red stilettos. The contents of the handbag were strewn across the floor. A detective constable squatted on his haunches, taking notes.

From the next room down the passage Rita could hear raised voices, one of them Strickland's. She went and stood in the doorway. The man Strickland was interrogating must be the proprietor, she guessed. He was braced backwards in a chair by the window, his eyes bloodshot and his balding head glistening with perspiration as he tried to fend off the questions. He wore a singlet which barely covered his paunch, and baggy shorts. Another officer, Bradby, watched, arms folded.

'Look, mate, it's not my business what the girls get up to in the rooms,' said the publican.

'Wrong,' said Strickland. 'And I don't believe you anyway. You allow the place to be used by prostitutes – in fact, you charge them entrance fees.'

'Dunno where you got that idea from.'

'From the woman who's just been mutilated on your premises,' snapped Strickland, his anger in danger of boiling over. Like the publican, he looked like he'd got up in a hurry after an early morning call. He wore no tie, and he was unshaven. 'How'd you like to be on the receiving end of that?'

Bradby glanced across at Rita and shrugged.

Strickland leant in closer, glaring at the publican.

'You're a whore-bludger, aren't you? This is an illegal brothel.'

'Shit, go easy. I just run a pub.'

'Then you're a liar. I'm arresting you for being a liar.'

'You can't do that.'

'Can't I? Then we'll call it obstructing a police officer.'

'Look, I told you I didn't see the bloke she was with. But I did get a look at his car parked out front.'

'What type of car?' said Strickland, straightening up.

'One of those little Mazda drop-tops.'

'An MX-5?' put in Bradby.

'Yeah – a black one.'

'And did you see the numberplate?' asked Strickland, but the only response he got was a shake of the head. 'Well what time was it?'

'They got here about one-thirty. I heard the car leave around three. I assumed they were both in it.'

'Not that you'd give a damn,' said Strickland in disgust. Then he saw Rita at the door and beckoned her over. 'I want you on board for this one.'

'Okay,' she said. 'Where do you want me to start?'

'With the victim,' said Strickland. 'According to her ID, her name's Emma Schultz. She's twenty-five and lives in Coburg.'

'When can we question her?'

'The doctors reckon this afternoon. At the moment, she's out of it.'

'Then I'll take a closer look at the crime scene first, make some notes.' Rita turned to the publican. 'Do you know the victim? Has she used this hotel before?'

He hesitated before answering. 'Yeah, I suppose so.'

'How often?'

'Half a dozen times.'

'So she's a regular,' said Rita.

'I don't want to say any more,' said the publican, 'till I've spoken to my lawyer.'

'Sure, if that's how you want to play it,' said Strickland. 'We'll have another go when we've charged you.'

But Rita interrupted. 'Wait. I need to know about the fire.'

The publican looked at her irritably. 'I don't know what the hell was going on there,' he said, ''specially in this heat. The fireplace is supposed to be for decoration.'

'Then why isn't there a smoke alarm?' she asked.

'It's an old hotel, if you hadn't noticed. A lot needs doing.' He was getting more defensive. 'But I don't expect customers to rip up the fittings and set fire to them. And don't ask me about her bloody chains. That's nothing to do with me.'

Strickland gestured to Bradby. 'Get him out of here.'

As the publican was manhandled from the room, Strickland turned to Rita. 'This is as sick as it gets,' he sighed. 'It looks like this poor hooker got brought here by a customer who bashed her, put her in chains, lit a fire and used a red-hot poker on her eyes. You're the expert, so tell me what sort of psycho could do this?'

'I can begin a psychological evaluation once we've questioned the victim,' she said, 'if that's what you want.'

A flinty look came into Strickland's eyes – patronising. 'We'll make that decision when we've been to the hospital.'

As Rita weighed up his answer, she became aware of the traffic thundering over the freeway just outside. She thought fleetingly of the thousands of motorists caught in the familiar flow, unaware of the backdrop of savagery they were passing.

The sound of Strickland's mobile broke her reverie.

'Yeah?' He listened for a few moments. 'Good,' he said and clicked off the phone before pocketing it. 'They've done a vaginal swab. The bastard had unprotected sex with her. We might be able to nail him with a DNA profile.'

4

Rita soon decided that Strickland's optimism about the DNA was misplaced. With her notes and diagrams from the crime scene spread on her desk, she sat back and gazed vacantly across the squad room. This attack was different from anything she'd worked on before in both its method and its cruelty. And looking through the database of physical abuse records, she could find only one case file that was comparable. It detailed a series of mutilations, rapes and murders attributed to an unknown perpetrator dubbed 'the Scalper' because he cut his victims' hair. Although she'd looked at the file before, she had no first-hand knowledge of the investigation, coinciding as it did with her stint at Quantico a year ago. The brutal assaults had begun, escalated and abruptly ended within a matter of weeks. Now it was virtually a cold case.

There was one odd similarity – the offender's car had been identified as a black Mazda MX-5. But with nothing in the way of MO to link this new attack to the Scalper, and with no other obvious candidate in the database, the probability was that a new offender had struck, and the existence of any DNA on file would be down to sheer luck. Without it he would be difficult to trace, unless the victim could provide some lead to his identity. That seemed unlikely given the initial report from the patrol car officers. All they got from the victim, apart from uncontrollable hysterics, was that she had no idea who he was. Perhaps she would come up with something when she was questioned more closely.

As she sat there pondering, one of the squad's hard men heaved into view, Detective Sergeant Derek Higgs. He came over and leant on her desk.

'Strickland's given me the job of hitting the town tonight and interviewing street pussy,' said Higgs. 'So whatever you can find out from the blind hooker, anything about this prick, will be greatly appreciated.'

'Okay,' nodded Rita, though she didn't really need to be told how to do her work.

Higgs was an old-school cop – blunt, opinionated and the most streetwise in the squad, with a reputation for taking shortcuts to get results. He was jowly, sharp-eyed and a chain-smoker, and his clothes bore a permanent aroma of stale tobacco. Although he shared the same rank as Rita, he was fifteen years her senior, and while her cerebral methods and rapid rise baffled him, there was no animosity between them.

'It won't be easy,' he added. 'Her recall could be completely fucked. So take it slowly.'

'Thanks for the advice,' she said.

'No sweat. I'm off for a beer.'

Emma Schultz lay in a hospital bed propped up by pillows, her ribs strapped, a wad of bandage and surgical tape covering her eye sockets. She was conscious now, but heavily sedated, which was just as well. Her mother sat beside the bed, gripping Emma's hand, tears streaming down her cheeks. Along with being traumatised by the attack on her daughter, she had been shocked to learn that Emma was a prostitute. Emma's arrest sheet and medical record revealed charges for shoplifting and drug possession, and she'd been hospitalised before with beatings. Yet until today, the mother had been none the wiser. Behind the tears, there was a pleading look in her eyes as she watched Rita questioning her daughter about her movements the previous evening – when she'd left home, how she'd travelled into the city, where she went – a portable mini-disc recorder rolling across the answers.

'You must be completely honest with me, Emma,' Rita said gently. 'It doesn't matter what you did, but I need to know everything if we're to catch this man.'

'I scored some crack in Chinatown,' said the girl in a slow monotone, her voice thick from the medication.

'And what did you do next?'

'I went down an alley and sat in a doorway.'

'Is that where you took the drug?'

The girl nodded. 'I heated and inhaled it.'

'What time was this?'

'About ten-thirty.'

'Good. Every detail helps.'

Rita worked on maintaining professional detachment as she went through her list of questions. Strickland remained silent. The last thing Emma Schultz needed to hear was a male voice. Reminding herself to breathe calmly, Rita paused between each question.

'Where did you go from there?'

'I took a slow walk around the block, but there was no action on the street.' Emma squeezed her mother's hand. 'So I went to a club that's usually good for business.'

'Which one?'

'A Greek joint – Plato's Cave.'

Rita raised her eyebrows at Strickland but he shook his head, as if warning her not to get distracted. Just the mention of the nightclub sent a chill through her. Only six months ago she'd arrested owner Tony Kavella for running a vice ring that used date-rape drugs on its victims, mostly young models. The girls were lured to an isolated villa along the Great Ocean Road with a promise of auditions for a movie company. Instead they were drugged, beaten and gang-raped by underworld thugs, who filmed the assaults and paid Kavella for the privilege. The victims kept quiet through sheer terror and the threat that videos of their ordeal would be released on the internet. Several associates were jailed but Kavella walked free from court, his involvement not proven. His evasion of justice was a sore point, but Rita had been told to accept it and move on.

After a pause, she continued. 'Is that where you picked up your client?'

'No,' said Emma. 'It was quieter than usual. A couple of blokes bought me champagne cocktails, but they weren't in the market so I left.'

'How late was that?'

'After midnight, about twenty past.'

'So where did you go?'

'I just walked towards Southbank and watched the flame show along the river, so it must have been one o'clock. I went over the bridge and was standing near the casino when a car pulled over.'

'Was it a sports car?' asked Rita. 'A black Mazda MX-5?'

'That's right. He was driving with the top down.'

'Did you get a look at the numberplate?'

'No,' said Emma. 'I was too busy checking him out.'

'Perhaps you'd seen him before somewhere,' said Rita. 'At the club, for example.'

'It's possible. He was definitely a regular punter.'

'How do you know?'

'He was ready for action and completely cool with it. I never guessed he was a wrong 'un.'

'What do you mean by *cool*?' said Rita.

'The way he acted – laidback, confident. And the way he dressed – black jeans, silver T-shirt, silver glasses – the reflecting sort, mirror shades.'

'Was there a design on the T-shirt?'

'A picture of Ned Kelly – the one in the mask.'

'At any stage,' said Rita, 'did this man mention his name, or where he lived or worked – or any location?'

'No,' came the flat response.

'How old was he?'

'About my age,' said Emma, 'or maybe a bit older. Early thirties at the most.'

'I need to know more about his appearance,' Rita pressed her. 'Anything distinctive.'

'There wasn't anything. He had dark hair. It wasn't short or long, just neat, like the rest of him. He was clean-shaven, okay build, average height – and seemed like a nice, normal guy.' Emma sighed. 'Until we were on the way to the hotel.'

'What happened?'

'I offered him sex in the car for seventy bucks, but he wanted a private room, so I said for another thirty we could use the Duke of York. On the way he asked if we could do role-playing. I told him bondage would be an extra hundred, and he said no problem. I just didn't spot what was coming. After I paid at reception and took him upstairs to the room I noticed he was carrying a laptop case. While I stripped, he opened it and took out a mask and chains and put them on the bed. Then he looked around and said something really weird – that the place was perfect but he wasn't ready for it. He asked me if I had matches. I did, so I handed them over. Then he started ripping up a stack of old hotel magazines and shoving them in the fireplace, and he found all these wooden coat-hangers in the wardrobe and put them on top of the paper and lit it. I asked why we needed a fire in the middle of a heatwave, and he told me we had to play by the rules. I said, "Rules of what?", and he said, "The cave". I don't have a clue what he meant.'

'What did he do next?' asked Rita.

'He switched off the light,' Emma answered. 'Then he got undressed and laid his clothes out at the foot of the bed, and that's when the shit happened. He put the mask on and grabbed me. I pushed him off and said I wanted my extra hundred bucks. He told me I was a prisoner. He said the first one fought him off that night, but not me. I was going to be defeated. It was freaky. I went for the Mace in my handbag but he hit me before I could get to it. I fell against the bed and felt my ribs go – then I was out of it.'

'Did you ever see his eyes?' Rita wanted to know.

'No. He kept them hidden behind the glasses, then the mask. I never got a really good look at his face.'

'The mask,' said Rita. 'What sort was it?'

'Like those ancient theatre ones.'

'Ancient, as in Greece or Rome?'

'Yeah, that's it – bronze coloured.'

'All these details are good,' said Rita. 'They'll help us track him down. Is there anything else you remember?'

'No, not till I woke up and felt what the bastard had done to me. Tell me, please, I've got to know – are the doctors going to be able to save my sight?'

Rita swallowed hard and couldn't answer. Strickland looked away and the girl's mother bowed her head, weeping again. The doctors hadn't broken the horrific news to their patient. They wanted to keep her calm and sedated for as long as possible, to help with her recovery. They hadn't told her that her eyes had been burnt and gouged out – and that she would never see again.

5

A uniformed constable nodded gravely to the two detectives and closed the door of Emma's private room before resuming his seat on a nearby chair. As they walked from the ward, Rita flipped through her notes before shoving the pad and mini-disc recorder in her pocket. Something was bugging her, and Strickland knew what.

'Okay,' he said. 'Spit it out.'

'Are we going to question Kavella?'

Strickland sighed and rubbed his eyes. It had been a long day. 'Look, I want to go after him as much as you.'

'Then we've got a perfect excuse,' Rita insisted. 'Emma was at his club. Her attacker even mentioned "the cave". Surely that's no coincidence, and we know Kavella's into designer violence, organised rape. For God's sake, did you know he was selling tickets to that vice ring he was running?'

'I know you take the injustice personally because you were the arresting officer. The girl was at his club, yeah, about an hour before she was picked up on the other side of the city. Where's the connection?'

'She could have been followed.'

'It's possible. But you know as well as I do we've got to be careful. At this stage we're only justified in checking out the club's customers.' He pressed the button for the lifts. 'We can't make a move against Kavella without evidence or his lawyers will have us for harassment. It's as simple as that.'

They rode to the ground floor in silence, but the lift doors opened on a clamour of voices.

'Oh, no,' said Strickland. 'The dingo pack.'

Journalists. They'd invaded the hospital's reception area – radio reporters, photographers, newspaper hacks, a couple of camera crews – and it was too late to avoid them. Among them was someone who was more unwelcome than the rest: TV crime reporter Mike Cassidy. He winked at Rita as the media scrum converged on the two detectives.

'I'll do the talking,' said Strickland from the corner of his mouth.

The arc lights came on and the cameras flashed – along with the questions.

'Is it true a woman's eyes have been put out?'

'Is she a prostitute?'

'Has anyone been arrested?'

Strickland held up his hands, 'Okay, okay. A brief statement, that's all.' He waited for the microphones to jostle into position. 'I can't give many details at this stage, so let me just confirm a woman has been the victim of a vicious attack in the early hours of this morning. It's one of the most sickening I've had to deal with in more than twenty years on the force. And yes – she's been permanently blinded as a result. As you'll appreciate, she's traumatised and heavily sedated. We've just come from talking to her. As yet she's unable to identify her attacker but she's given us a description which we'll make public later.'

That brought another barrage of questions.

'Does that mean there's a maniac on the loose?'

'What are the police doing to catch him?'

'Is he likely to strike again?'

'Let me assure you,' said Strickland firmly, 'the investigation is already well underway and we're doing everything in our power to track down the assailant.'

Then Mike Cassidy asked, 'Is that why Detective Sergeant Van Hassel is here? Has she been brought in to profile the attacker?'

Strickland glared at him and gave Rita a sideways glance. He was fully aware of the history between them.

'Detective Sergeant Van Hassel is part of the team working on the case. And it's clear that profiling can give valuable insights when we're trying to trace anonymous offenders. But at this point in the investigation, she'll be concentrating on basic detective work, like the rest of my officers. And that's all I've got to say. No more questions. Our press office will issue further details.'

As the journalists began to disperse, Strickland drew Rita to one side.

'I'm going back up to the ward. I want uniform clear the media's banned from going anywhere near the victim.' He leant closer. 'What I want you to do is put the heavy word on your boyfriend.'

'We split up months ago.'

'Whatever. Just tell him to back off. We've got enough to worry about without him doing a beat-up.'

She watched Strickland go back into the lift and deliver a stern jerk of the head as the doors closed. This was a chore she could do without.

She caught up with Cassidy as he was trotting down the steps outside the hospital entrance, his cameraman beside him.

'Thanks for nothing, Mike.'

The two men stopped and turned.

The cameraman grinned but Cassidy waved him on. 'See you back at the office.' He waited until the other man was out of earshot. 'Nice to bump into you too, Rita. I've missed you chasing after me.'

'In your fantasies,' she said. 'What were you trying to pull back there?'

'Lighten up. It was a valid question.'

He said it without a trace of deceit. It reminded her of how disingenuous he could be, and why their relationship had survived only a few stormy months. Like many journalists he was plausible and witty. On top of that he possessed the chiselled good looks of a professional charmer, which in a sense he was. She'd fallen for his brazen approach, along with the handsome profile and the dark eyes with their hint of danger. Even now she only partly regretted it. If nothing else, their time together had been worth the entertainment value alone.

He turned on a lopsided smile. 'I get it,' he said. 'Strickland is still needling you for being a woman on the make. He told you to have a go at me.'

She sighed. 'Well, you've given him more ammunition. And he wants me to curb your tabloid approach. So what am I supposed to do?'

'Tell him to fuck off.'

'I certainly will not.'

'Then tell him I'm uncooperative. That I'm ready to hype the story – and I'll only reconsider over a drink with you.'

'And what's that supposed to achieve?'

'It'll achieve a drink for a start.' Cassidy chuckled. 'And it might make me reconsider the virtues of gutter journalism. It'll also give you the chance to explain why you dumped me.'

'That's easy. Your lack of ethics.'

'But I'm a reporter. Ethics is a grey area.'

'Not when it comes to cheating on me with that lawyer.'

'It was research. I was working on an exposé.'

'Exposing your cock in the process.'

'Come on, we're both adults,' he protested. 'It was a big exclusive.'

'Not so *big*, as I remember.'

'Very funny.'

'And anyway, it proves my point. You'd sell your soul for a scoop.'

He shrugged and leant back on a railing of the disabled access ramp. 'Only with global TV rights.'

She tried to look at him with contempt, but couldn't help smiling. 'Which would make you a global arsehole.'

'Good to see your sense of humour's intact,' he said.

'Exactly what my friends said when I went out with you.'

'Your girlfriends were jealous you'd got me into bed. I was an impressive catch.'

'It's the size of your ego that's impressive,' she laughed. 'They wanted to arrest you.'

'On what charge?'

'Perverting the course of justice.'

He conceded the point with a grunt.

Around them moved the daily traffic of the hospital – visitors going in and out, kids with their arms in slings, old people in wheelchairs. Rita stepped aside for a woman with a pram.

'Look, Mike, seriously,' she said, 'I can do without the coverage.'

'Well, well. What a surprise. Rita Van Hassel, publicity shy.'

'I'm not even fully qualified as a profiler.'

'Pull the other one,' he said. 'You've been profiling cases for more than a year. I remember the tedious hours of homework.'

'It won't help me do my job.'

'Tell it to the other boys and girls.'

'What do you mean?'

'It's too late, mate. The TV cameras were rolling. The snappers were grabbing shots of you. See it from the hacks' point of view – a criminal profiler who also happens to be a sexy blonde. That's too good an angle to miss.'

'Oh, shit.' She scuffed the ground with her heel. 'Like I said – thanks for nothing.'

Rita found Strickland in the hospital car park, his face reflecting a mood of futility.

'Well she's a write-off,' he said at last, his cigarette smoked to the butt. 'As a witness, I mean,' he added uncomfortably.

'I'll question her again tomorrow,' said Rita.

'She won't be able to identify him. This is gonna come down to forensics.'

'So what do you want from me?'

'Follow up what evidence we've got,' he said, grim-faced. 'But I think your ex has got a point. Start doing a profile as well. I know it's early but I've got a feeling we're in for the long haul on this.'

'Okay. She's given me enough to work on.'

'Good. Anything that'll narrow the field.' He dropped the cigarette butt and ground it under his heel. 'Time to start the donkey work.'

6

Mike Cassidy's TV channel headlined the story on its early evening bulletin.

A newsreader introduced the segment:

A young woman is being treated in hospital after falling victim to a horrific attack in which she was blinded. The twenty-five-year-old, who is believed to have a conviction for prostitution, has not yet been named by police. The attack took place in a hotel room overnight. A team of detectives is hunting the man who carried out the assault. Reporter Mike Cassidy is at the scene.

Rita winced inwardly as Mike's face filled the screen.

The full details of what happened in the hotel behind me have not yet emerged. What we know so far is that the woman checked in to a second-floor room after midnight, apparently to engage in sex with a male client. Sometime later the encounter turned violent. Among other injuries inflicted in a savage assault, the victim's eyes were deliberately put out. The man leading the police investigation, Detective Senior Sergeant Wayne Strickland, has expressed his disgust at the sadistic act.

Now Strickland was on the screen, and Rita heard again his brief statement of that afternoon.

Let me just confirm a woman has been the victim of a vicious attack in the early hours of this morning. It's one of the most sickening I've had to deal with in more than twenty years on the force. And yes – she's been permanently blinded as a result.

The camera cut back to Cassidy.

> This evening she remains under intensive care in hospital. Although she can't identify her attacker, she's been able to give detectives details of his appearance. A short time ago, police issued a description. The man they're hunting is in his mid twenties or early thirties, white, clean-shaven and of medium build with dark hair. He was wearing a silver Ned Kelly T-shirt, black jeans and a distinctive pair of silver-rimmed glasses with mirror lenses. He drives a black Mazda MX-5 convertible. Any member of the public with information should contact police or ring Crime Stoppers. And while detectives are hoping to make an early arrest, they're also preparing for what could be a difficult investigation by drafting in a criminal profiler.

Rita groaned on hearing Strickland's words used out of context.

> Detective Sergeant Van Hassel is part of the team working on the case. And it's clear that profiling can give valuable insights when we're trying to trace anonymous offenders.

Rita's face appeared on the screen as Cassidy summed up.

> It's an indication of what the police are dealing with. Somewhere in the greater metropolitan area this evening a dangerous predator is on the loose. Women working in the city's sex trade have been warned to be on their guard. The implication is obvious. Unless there's a quick breakthrough, this maniac could strike again.

As Van Hassel's close-up appeared on the TV screens, an ironic cheer went up around the squad room, accompanied by wolf-whistles. 'Who's the cheesecake?' 'Nice crime bust!'

'Get knotted,' was her response. The attention was unwelcome – though she was pleased to see that she looked professional on camera – now that her name, face and reputation were associated with the case. This left another bone to pick with her ex-boyfriend, but that would have to wait.

Rita was concentrating on a vital piece of information Emma Schultz had given them. According to Emma, she was the attacker's second target of the night, after the first one had fought back and managed to break loose. Assuming the account was correct, the first victim was a crucial witness. So where was she? Rita was doing a running check on police reports, the emergency services and the hospitals, but so far not a single case of attempted sexual assault had emerged. A few domestic incidents had been reported in the past twenty-four hours, though none was consistent with the facts of the investigation.

With the line of inquiry getting nowhere, she phoned the police forensic services centre. Her call was put through to a crime lab scientist, Dale Quinn.

'Hi there, Van Hassel, so they've put you on the hooker mutilation, eh? I'm in the middle of processing the evidence bags.'

'What have you got so far?' she asked.

'There'll be DNA from the semen and perspiration we got. He sweated a lot – not surprising given the circumstances. I've also got sets of fingerprints off the poker, chains and ashtray, but I've checked and his prints aren't on record.' Quinn cleared his throat. 'The substance we recovered from the floor was corneal and vitreous tissue. There were burnt traces of it on the tip of the poker. So that's what he used – *after* he'd had sex. There were traces of semen on the grip.'

'What about the hooker's stuff?'

'That's what I'm examining now – the contents of her handbag.'

'Anything significant?'

'You mean aside from the crack, the can of Mace, strawberry-flavoured condoms and lubricant?' said Quinn. 'There's a mass of receipts, coins, cards, cosmetics – the usual female clutter. Why don't you drop by in the morning? We'll have it done by then.'

'I might do that,' she said.

Rita put down the phone and resumed her series of checks, but there was still nothing coming up. Eventually she sat back and watched her fellow officers going off duty, listening to their banter and laughter as they headed to the pub to put the frustrations of the day behind them. They'd spent hours in the company of some of the lowest forms of urban life as they'd interviewed known sex offenders, or trawled through the files for more suspects. It had been depressing and unrewarding. There was already the shared sense of a difficult investigation, with no obvious leads. The longer that went on the more pressure Rita would feel to come up with psychological insights into the perpetrator.

Erin Webster came over, pulling on her jacket.

'Found your witness?' she asked.

'No.' Rita grimaced. 'And you – any joy?'

'What do you reckon?' said Erin. 'Since lunchtime I've been stuck in an interview room questioning suckholes with a history of violence. Not one fits the bill. Tomorrow I'll do more of the same, and I'm not looking forward to it.'

'Think of it as broadening your social life.'

'Broadening my arse, more likely. I've got a feeling the guy we're after isn't on file, and the investigation will be a sticker.' Erin sighed. 'Which is where you come in, of course.'

'And I might as well get started,' said Rita, as she stood up from her desk, 'while it's still fresh in my mind.'

'You off to your cubby-hole?'

Rita nodded at the reference to the small, converted storage room that the head of the squad had assigned to her to use as an office, study and squad room retreat. It was in there that she did her profiling work.

'By the way . . .' Erin grinned. 'Nice pose on the box.'

'Bloody Mike,' said Rita. 'He set up Strickland with a trick question then edited the answer. He's still pissed off that I dumped him.'

'He wants you back,' said Erin. 'Men can't take rejection. Makes them schizo.'

'Maybe you should be the profiler.' Rita reached into her bag as her mobile started ringing. She checked the caller ID. 'Speak of the devil.'

Erin whispered, 'See ya,' and headed for the lifts.

'Hi!' said Cassidy. 'Did you catch my lead story?'

'*Story*'s right,' Rita replied. 'It was full of fiction.'

'Don't be like that. It's modern journalism – informed opinion from a correspondent with authority.'

'Putting you and authority in the same sentence is like finding a whore in a church.'

'Tut-tut,' said Cassidy in mock reproof. 'Not very charitable – but the sort of comment I should expect from a sinful Dutch Protestant.'

'Is that more of your informed opinion?'

'Absolutely. I've observed your foibles intimately. I know what you're like in bed.'

'Shut up, Mike.'

'You're also driven and career-obsessed. You need me around to lighten you up and stop you being so hard-edged.'

'How thoughtful of you to act as my therapist,' said Rita, 'when I'd mistaken you for a sleaze-bag.'

'No problem,' said Cassidy. 'Which is why I've phoned – to see if we're still on for a drink.'

'I've got work to do – as you've pointed out to about a million people.'

'Oh, well,' he said. 'Career before carousing.'

As she hung up, Detective Sergeant Higgs loomed up. He was on his way to a red-light district.

'Your boyfriend's done my team a big favour,' he said.

'He's my ex,' Rita corrected. 'But what's the favour?'

Higgs gave a cruel smile. 'The street snatch will be scared shitless now. They'll fall over themselves to cooperate.'

7

For a police office, Rita's glass-panelled room had a slightly cloistered feel to it. Along with the desk, computer gear and grey metal filing cabinets stuffed with printouts and case files, there were stacks of academic magazines and shelves of scholarly books. Psychology, criminology and forensic science rubbed shoulders with texts on art, mythic symbols and philosophy. The range reflected her depth of interest as well as the demands of her specialised work – something she could take too seriously at times, to the detriment of her personal life.

As Rita sat amid the comfortable clutter, poring over glossy crime scene photos, police statements, the medical report and her own notes, she was already jotting down the sequence of events and the first broad outlines of a profile. The crime was horrendous, but it presented her with the kind of challenge she liked to deal with. She had to look at the act of blinding and traumatising the victim as an expression of personality. The sexualised nature of the violence pointed to a deviant whose sadistic fantasies were extremely rare. Unless his DNA was on file, the unknown suspect would not be easy to trace, and she'd have to call on all her expertise to focus the investigation and help track him down.

She turned to her laptop and began drafting the crime sequence.

TIMELINE (Summary – timings approx.)
21.00: Emma Schultz leaves her flat, takes a train into the city and walks the streets without picking up any clients.
22.30: She scores some crack cocaine in Chinatown and inhales it in a back alley.

23.00: She walks to a regular pick-up haunt in the Greek precinct – Plato's Cave nightclub.

Rita paused. It was barely three months since the club's owner, Tony Kavella, had eluded a guilty verdict on a series of sex crimes. No matter what Strickland said, if there was a second chance to get him she wasn't going to miss it.

She took a deep breath and resumed.

00.20: Emma leaves the club after drinks with two men, and walks the streets again.
01.00: She crosses the river and is standing near the casino when a client pulls up in a car.
01.30: Emma and her customer arrive at the Duke of York hotel.
01.40: In the hotel room, the client produces bondage equipment, lights a fire and puts on a mask. When Emma resists he hits her with a glass ashtray.

Rita glanced at her copy of the medical report before continuing.

01.45: The offender manacles his unconscious victim to the framework of the bed and shackles her neck. He rapes her violently, as indicated by bruising to the inner thighs and vulva. He also achieves full penetrative sex, as indicated by the vaginal swab. His final act, according to the initial lab report, is to put out her eyes with a hot poker.
03.00: The offender leaves, making no attempt to conceal or tidy the crime scene.

Rita scrolled back and read through what she'd just written. Deciding it was sufficient as a guideline, she opened a fresh file on her laptop. From her perspective the crime was an expression of the offender's social background and personal psychology. Her job as a profiler was to pin down what he was revealing about himself – his mind trace. Only then could she evaluate what type of sex attacker he was – whether he was deliberate or spontaneous, whether he was calculating or mentally ill.

She resumed.

OFFENDER PROFILE (Preliminary)

White male. Mid 20s to early 30s. Articulate. Intelligent. Affluent – smartly dressed & drives a sports car. Single, or committed to an unrewarding relationship/marriage. Socially and sexually competent, but needs to dominate. In his work role, this man is in a position of authority. He issues orders and expects to be obeyed. As well as exerting power over others, he imposes a high level of self-control on himself. The resulting pressure is relieved by the use of prostitutes. If he is defied, it can also be released as physical and sexual violence. His family background was oppressive, with an overbearing father and a passive mother. In a social context, he has overcome the negative influence of his upbringing to establish his success, although he still carries an enduring sense of resentment. It is possible that he has vented aggression on prostitutes before, but he has now moved to a more intense phase by inflicting an injury unnecessary to the sexual act (burning out eyes). This would seem to fulfil a revenge or punishment or empowerment fantasy. This offender has crossed a psychological line and will strike again.

Rita was reading through what she'd formulated when the head of the Sexual Crimes Squad, Detective Inspector Jack Loftus, knocked on the door and walked in.

'Strickland says he's got you working on a profile,' he said. 'How's it going?'

'Just getting started,' she said, swivelling around to face him.

Loftus was more than her boss – he was also her mentor. At twenty years her senior he had the experience to recognise flair and intelligence when he saw it. That always deserved a helping hand. Her ability to maintain fierce concentration for hours on end was one of the reasons he'd chosen her for the profiling role. And even though it intimidated some of her colleagues, he also saw her intellect as a valuable attribute. Another reason – which he didn't discuss with anyone – was her dark imagination, rooted in a disrupted and unhappy childhood. Before she'd started the course in profiling, he'd asked her if she could cope with focusing so closely on damaged minds. She'd replied flatly, 'We're all damaged, Jack.' That's when he knew she was the right choice to be a profiler. It was clear she had her own demons — and you needed a few on board to do battle with the devil.

As well as admiring her policing abilities, he also found his protégé attractive. It wasn't an issue, because a stable marriage, large family, Catholic guilt and no free time ensured he made no attempt to make their relationship anything other than strictly professional.

This was probably just as well, because the attraction was mutual. Rita saw Loftus as a man of depth, who managed to steer his own course through the jargon and the regulations while still being respected. While there was something world-weary about him, like a man who carried too many burdens on his shoulders, or had put in too many years with what he called the Human Depravity Squad, behind his heavy-lidded eyes was a mind full of insights only partly blunted by cynicism.

'I don't want you to feel you're under time pressure with this,' he said.

'What's your point, Jack?'

'We should work the case and see if it bottoms out before factoring in a profile. I don't want premature assumptions to impact on the investigation.'

'Then let's hope we catch this guy quickly.'

'Why do you say that?'

'Because the man who carried out this attack needs to inflict extreme violence on women. If we don't stop him he's likely to do it again sooner rather than later.'

Loftus didn't say anything. He shoved his hands in his pockets and sat back on the edge of her desk.

'You've gone pensive on me,' she said.

He didn't reply, but got up from the desk and peered at the clutter of items tacked to her pin-board. An A4-size sketch in black pencil caught his eye. It was a picture of a man standing alone under a streetlamp at night. The image was unremarkable except for one thing. The look in the man's partly shadowed eyes was too intense, ferocious even, psychotic. At the foot of the page was the inscription *Hell is otherness*.

'This is new,' he said. 'Where's it come from?'

'An agent I studied with at Quantico. Thought I might find it instructive. It was drawn by one of the serial killers he interviewed.'

'What's "Hell is otherness" supposed to mean?'

'Well, this particular killer suffers from a dissociated personality...'

'Remind me.'

'It's the pathological coexistence of more than one centre of consciousness in one mind.'

'Multiple personalities.'

'Yeah. And he's in a psychiatric prison undergoing therapy. So one way of reading it is this man's personal hell of dissociation.'

'No,' Loftus shook his head. 'The guy in this picture's alone.'

'Interesting,' she said.

'Don't try to play the shrink on me,' he said sternly, catching the analytical tone in her voice. 'The guy's alone and apart – that's the message.'

'Then perhaps it's what we all feel at times – the hell of alienation.'

'Maybe, or what some of us see as the inevitable fall from grace,' he sighed. 'Anyway, back to the case in hand. Strickland's told me about the victim's taste in nightlife. I don't want you getting any ideas about paying a call on Tony Kavella.'

Rita looked at him unconvinced. Then she took a deep breath and said, 'He's a career criminal, a diagnosed psychopath. And he's instigated violent sex attacks before.'

'Don't even go there. He's out of bounds. Unless there's solid evidence against him, steer clear of Kavella.'

'The victim was a regular at his club,' argued Rita. 'And the offender made a reference to "the rules of the cave". That has a nasty ring of familiarity. Kavella could even be taunting us with another round of sadistic sex games, after getting away with it before.'

'First, that can't be proven in court,' Loftus replied. 'Second, he's got lawyers like a school of sharks. And third, you're making it personal when you should be exercising objectivity.'

'But –' she persisted.

'No evidence, no move on Kavella,' said Loftus, walking to the door with a warning glare. 'Plato's Cave is more dangerous than you can possibly know.'

Rita watched him go with a puzzled look on her face. There was something he wasn't telling her. Loftus had access to information that senior officers kept to themselves, so there was no point in trying to guess, nor was there any point in dragging out her work any longer. The day had drained her. She logged off, and went to the ladies to freshen up, her face in the mirror regaining some of its glow with a touch of make-up.

She rode the lift down to the ground floor and nodded to the desk officer as she crossed the lobby.

'Cheer up, Van Hassel,' he said. 'It's us against the bastards.'

'Yeah, but they play dirty,' she laughed. 'And they outnumber us.'

8

Mike Cassidy's crime report was broadcast again on the late news bulletin. He stood at the counter of a Southbank wine bar, surrounded by fellow journalists, and assessed his own performance on the overhead screen. It was authoritative, no matter what Rita thought, with just the right note of alarm.

One of his colleagues agreed. 'Nice scare story.'

'It's all in the delivery,' said Cassidy.

Not everyone watched the news report as a detached observer.

One man viewed the story with a vivid image in his mind. He didn't try to imagine what the girl in the hospital was going through, or how her family was trying to cope. Their ordeal was beyond his concern. Nor did he try to reconcile the tragic consequences with the events of the night before – the naked body in chains, the flickering flames, the shadows. What fascinated him most was her transformation from prisoner to she-devil, and how she'd been tamed. The TV report mentioned none of this.

Yet it did predict there would be more to come. Were the police simply guessing, or did their profiler have a special insight into the dynamics of the game that was up and running? It would be a challenge to get close to her and find out. But not now. It was time to switch off. He picked up the remote control and turned off the television. Then he got up, shrugging off any feelings of involvement, picked up the bronze-coloured mask beside him and put it away.

9

Crime lab scientist Dale Quinn was an enthusiast who enjoyed his work, wore his hair in a ponytail and talked too fast. Rita listened intently as he rattled off his findings.

'The bondage equipment is top of the range, imported, and not some cheap back-street product,' he was saying. 'We're talking quality fetish gear, Donner-und-Blitzen brand, made in Germany with proper serial numbers. Only a handful of shops around the city stock it and they charge top dollar. I'm surprised they were left at the crime scene.'

'Me too,' said Rita. Her morning visit to the forensic services centre was already pointing to contradictions in her preliminary profile of the perpetrator.

'Chrome steel chains, manacles, shackles – and in mint condition,' said Quinn. 'At a guess, all recently purchased with tender, loving fantasy. If they were mine I wouldn't abandon them.'

'Sometimes I worry about you being vacuum-sealed in here with your imagination.'

'Admit it, Van Hassel, these shiny chrome objects have a lurid appeal.'

She smiled. 'I'll admit to an urge to see you bound and gagged. But in the meantime I've got to work out why he left such a messy crime scene.'

'Did your bondage freak beat a hasty retreat?'

Rita shook her head. 'No, he was in the room for nearly an hour and a half.'

'Ah, that's interesting.'

'Why?' she asked.

'That's just long enough for the fire to burn out.' Quinn gave a satisfied nod. 'We recreated the paper and coat-hanger effect.'

'Nice one.'

'Thank you.' He appeared to enjoy her approval. 'By the way we've got three sets of prints off the manacles – his, hers and partials from someone else.'

'The first intended victim . . . We've got to find her,' breathed Rita. 'Anything else?'

'Yeah, I'm saving the best till last.'

He held up what looked like a key card or credit card. It was made of black laminated plastic with silver lettering. There were no numbers or codes on it, just two words: PLATO'S CAVE.

Rita stared at it, her spine tingling at the thought of the net closing in around Tony Kavella.

'What am I looking at?' she asked.

'At first we thought it was a smartcard with a chip, the kind used as a security pass, that sort of thing. But were we surprised – it's not smart, it's a bloody genius!' He gave a grin. 'The technology and software embedded in this card are cutting edge, heavily encrypted, worthy of military security, and we can't even begin to crack it. And only the attacker's prints are on it, not the girl's.'

'But it was found among the contents of her handbag.'

'Well, not quite. Her things were scattered between the bedside table, the bed and the fireplace. This card was lying just under the foot of the bed.'

'Right where he put his clothes,' said Rita. 'It could have fallen from a pocket.'

'That's more likely than a street hooker possessing space age technology.'

There was a new urgency in Rita's voice. 'We know Tony Kavella's spent a lot of money on a new system with an impenetrable firewall. The card could be part of a program he's developed. You've got to decode it.'

Quinn shook his head. 'We don't have the hardware, the computing power or the expertise.'

'Well, who does?'

'The top expert in the field is a young professor out at Monash University. His name's Byron Huxley. He's your best bet. If you sign for it you can take the card with you. We can't process it any further so he's free to handle it.'

'Thanks,' said Rita. 'I'll use it as my calling card.'

10

Rather than heading out to the university in one of Melbourne's south-eastern suburbs, Rita decided to touch base at the office. She noticed the morning newspapers lying on the desks as she walked into the squad room. They'd picked up from where the TV news bulletins had left off. The headlines took their cue from Mike Cassidy's report.

SEX PREDATOR ON THE LOOSE
POLICE FEAR MORE MUTILATION ATTACKS

As Rita sat down at her desk she wasn't sure if the coverage would help or hinder the investigation. She didn't have much time to think about it. Strickland strode up and slammed a newspaper in front of her.

'What the fuck is this?'

The rest of the room fell silent.

'The last thing we need is your boyfriend stirring the shit. I've got reporters all over me like flies.' Strickland's face was flushed with anger. 'I'm having to call a press conference to deny this garbage about a serial offender. What the hell are you playing at?'

She took a deep breath, willing herself to stay calm. 'First of all, he's not my boyfriend. He's my ex-boyfriend.'

'Don't piss me around,' he shouted. 'What did you tell him?'

'To back off, like you asked me to –'

The rest of her sentence was cut off by Strickland thumping the desk with his fist. 'Not very convincing then, were you? From now on I don't want you to say a damn thing to the media! I don't care if they're boyfriends, ex-boyfriends or one night stands! I've already got them queuing up for interviews with my *attractive young profiler*!' He smacked the newspaper aside in disgust. 'So let's get it straight. Your job is to support the investigation, keep your mouth shut, and let your senior officers do the talking. Understand?'

'Yes, sir.'

'I hope you do. Otherwise you'll be butting your head against more than just macho attitudes,' he said, leaning across the desk towards her, his jaw thrust forward. 'You're a smart detective, Van Hassel. Smart enough to have university degrees. But I don't think you're a team player. And that makes you the wrong sort of cop.'

She folded her arms defiantly. 'There are only two sorts,' she snapped. 'Smart cops and dumb cops.'

Strickland straightened up, his face still full of aggression. At first she'd read his obvious resentment of her as cultural. The tall poppy syndrome. She was too young, too educated and had been promoted too fast. Then, after she'd heard him warning his junior officers, 'Never get married!' she'd pigeonholed him as a common garden variety misogynist. But as she came to know him better she decided he was more complex than that. Middle-aged and brittle with thinning hair, a jowly expression and a tendency to emphasise how tough he was by talking out of the side of his mouth like Humphrey Bogart, Strickland was blunt and not an impressive manager, though he had a cachet among the boys. Yet his gruff exterior concealed a man of intelligence and sensitivity. He was more than a solid detective. He was astute. He was also literate – in a quiet moment Rita had once caught him reading T.S. Eliot's 'The Waste Land', though he'd scowled and put it away as soon as he saw her. In his own way, Strickland was perceptive and unorthodox in his thinking. He just hid it well to fit in.

'I know you disapprove of my approach as psychologically crude,' he said. 'You think I'm unsubtle. But what counts is results. And you don't get those with criminal profiling. At best it's of peripheral use, at worst it's a gimmick – little better than fortune-telling. It doesn't solve crimes.'

'I never said it did,' Rita protested. 'So I take it you've changed your mind about me starting a profile on this case?'

Strickland paused, but clearly decided to be politic. 'The top brass tell me to use profiling when appropriate. Let's just say I've ticked the box on this one.'

'I've always accepted it's just one of many investigative tools. Another way of analysing behaviour.'

'Sometimes I get the impression you're analysing *us* as much as the criminals.'

'Maybe I should. I'd start with assessing the level of paranoia.'

Strickland shook his head disdainfully. 'Wrong,' he said. 'You're proving my point about playing a lone hand.'

'I put in the hard slog like everyone else. And that's on top of the profiling, the intelligence data work and my study.'

'That just makes you another ambitious woman who wants to be a career detective. Doesn't score any points with me.' Turning away he added, 'And for Christ's sake, get a life.'

As her fellow detectives turned back to their work, Rita picked up the phone and punched in the number of Mike Cassidy's direct line at the TV newsroom. The call was answered by a woman who said he was out of the office working on a story.

'Can I take a message?' she asked.

'Yes. Tell him he's a complete prick,' said Rita before slamming down the phone.

She waited for her breathing to return to normal then checked if any reports of sexual assault had emerged, but there were still none. She went over to the water cooler, filled a plastic cup and swallowed the contents in a single gulp.

Then she hit the filing cabinet beside her with her fist.

'Fuck,' she said through clenched teeth, then sighed and leant on the cabinet. This wasn't how things were supposed to go.

She stared out the window, beyond the parks and river, her gaze moving to the wall of skyscrapers. What was it with men? Why did they feel the need to give women such a hard time? What galled her most was the arrogance of it – both her ex-boyfriend and her boss assuming they had the right to judge her character, and both getting it so wrong. In their different ways they had both accused her of being cold and distant. Their aim was to zero in on her self-doubt. In doing so, both men were revealing their own inadequacies. And that only made her more determined to do things her way.

She knew she was driven. And maybe Cassidy was right. Maybe it came from her Dutch Protestant background. But hard-edged – no. That was simply her refusal to suffer fools gladly. And if she expected a lot from others, she expected even more from herself. That too came from her upbringing.

Her thoughts were interrupted by the broad-shouldered bulk – built up over years of long-distance swimming – of Detective Senior Constable Kevin O'Keefe. He'd been assigned to work with her on the case. His meaty hand rested on her back in a gesture of reassurance.

'Which one of the bastards do you want me to deck?' he asked quietly. 'Strickland or your ex?'

'Thanks for the offer,' she chuckled. 'How about a double decking?'

'No sweat. Just say when.'

'It's a deal,' she said, leading the way back to her desk. 'In the meantime, we've got work to do.'

O'Keefe dragged a chair over. 'Okay, boss,' he said. 'Bring me up to speed.'

That's what Rita liked about him – no fuss, no attitude, just ready to do her bidding. He was a plodder, and at times lethargic, but once motivated he was dogged and relentless, with the forward thrust of a juggernaut. It made him one of the easiest detectives to work with.

'You've looked at what we've got so far?' she asked.

'Yep,' he answered, and rubbed his left eye with a thick, hairy knuckle. 'I reckon we're looking at long odds with this one. We'll need a break with the evidence. Who's chasing the car?'

'Bradby,' said Rita.

'That'll keep him busy,' said O'Keefe. 'The MX-5's the most popular sports car in the world, and there are plenty of black ones around. What are *we* working on?'

Rita sat back and called up a checklist on her screen. 'Our top priority is tracing the first intended victim. I've checked with hospitals, medical centres, counselling services – all the contacts I've got. No woman's reported a sex offence, or even an assault. But I'm convinced the attacker got up close and virtually had the chains on her before she fought him off. That means, if nothing else, she should have defensive injuries to her hands or forearms. It also probably means she doesn't want to report being attacked.'

'You want me to do the rounds with the hospitals again?'

'Yes, but this time just ask if a woman's been treated for those sorts of injuries, even if she says they were accidental.'

'Okay,' said O'Keefe. 'Anything else?'

'These.' She passed him glossy photos of the bondage gear. 'As you'll see from the lab report they're imported from Germany and only a few outlets stock them. We need to know where he did his shopping.'

'Hmm, sex boutiques.' He raised his bushy eyebrows. 'I might do a bit of browsing myself.'

'Don't *you* start, you haven't got time,' she said. 'Any browsing you do will be for a bronze-coloured mask. The other item we need to source is the Ned Kelly T-shirt. It's unusual.'

'What about the sunglasses?'

'They're last on the list. I know the type; it's a designer brand and available at any decent shopping centre.'

'So while I'm occupied, what'll you be working on?' asked O'Keefe.

'This.' From her jacket pocket, Rita lifted a small clear plastic bag containing the Plato's Cave card. 'It's hi-tech and encrypted. I've got to find out if Emma Schultz can tell me anything about it.'

11

A uniformed constable sat outside Emma Schultz's room flipping through a men's health magazine. He stood up abruptly as Rita approached.

'Any problems?' she asked.

'No, not really,' he answered. 'I had to shoo away a few journalists. The only other visitors were a pair of hookers, apart from half a dozen delivery people with flowers.'

'You didn't let anyone in?'

'No, and I questioned the street girls, friends of the victim, but they don't think they know the man who attacked her. I've also taken the details of the florist orders, just in case they're relevant.'

'Good work,' said Rita. 'Email them to Kevin O'Keefe in Sex Crimes. He'll check them out.'

She went into the room to find Emma much as she'd left her the day before, propped on pillows, sedated and still in ignorance of the full extent of her injuries. On shelves around her were lots of flowers in vases. Emma's mother was still there, exhausted and red-eyed, but out of tears. As Rita greeted both women, Mrs Schultz handed over a photo of her daughter, as had been requested of her. It was a studio portrait, a head and shoulders shot, showing a young woman with a girlish smile, rosy-cheeked, bright-eyed.

Rita reached out to take Emma's hand. 'Is there anything else you've remembered about the man who attacked you?'

Emma made herself more comfortable as she thought about it.

'I remember he was clever,' she said.

'In what way?'

41

'Some of the things he talked about in the car, you know, just making conversation on the way to the hotel. Stuff I didn't understand.'

'Such as?'

'Computers, how they're changing the world. Technical stuff.'

'Did he give any examples?' asked Rita.

'When I told him computers would never replace sex, he said they were already improving it. I thought he was talking about internet porn, but he wasn't.'

'What *was* he talking about?'

'Cyber sex games, he reckoned. He didn't explain, just flashed a card at me. That's when we arrived at the hotel.'

Rita paused and took the plastic evidence bag from her pocket.

'I've got something here we recovered from the hotel room,' she said. 'It looks like a credit card, it's plastic and it's black with silver lettering on it. Just two words are embossed on it: Plato's Cave.'

'That'll be the one he had; it's certainly not mine,' said Emma. 'You think he stalked me from the club?'

'I don't know yet,' Rita answered. 'But it's beginning to look that way.'

She sat in her car, tapping the rim of the steering wheel with the black plastic card in its bag. The silver lettering shone in the sunlight, and those two gleaming words – Plato's Cave – glinted back at her like a provocation. Tony Kavella had escaped retribution more than once, but the last time was the one that grated the most.

It was Rita's perseverance that had finally cracked Kavella's vice ring. She got one of the girls who had been promised a movie audition to talk. Others followed. The villa was raided, the videos recovered, and all the men stupid enough to be caught on tape were seized. Kavella was taken into custody at his club, but his lawyers were already there. They successfully argued he had no case to answer on charges of abduction, conspiracy, blackmail and a list of counts relating to organised vice. Although his customers got heavy prison terms, he walked free from court. There were no witnesses to implicate him and no uncontested evidence to connect him. He'd mocked her best efforts to put him behind bars and was still banking the profits of his crimes. She wanted another chance to break him. His drug and vice business was thriving, and the small, glossy card seemed to be compelling proof that Kavella had gone hi-tech with it. Loftus had said, 'No evidence, no move on Kavella.' Well now the evidence was in her hand.

'Fuck it,' she said, and called the squad room.

O'Keefe answered and she told him how the attacker had flashed the card at Emma Schultz and talked about cyber sex games.

'You want to go after Kavella, don't you?' he said.

She took a breath then said, 'Yes. Let me talk to Strickland.'

He put her on hold and left her listening to the recorded voice of the police service going through its self-promotion spiel.

As she waited for Strickland to pick up, Rita watched a middle-aged couple grappling in the hospital car park and hoped she wouldn't have to intervene. They were swearing at each other in a mixture of English and Serbian. The woman had her arm in a sling but it didn't stop her bouncing a can of Coke off the man's head. He slapped her once, twice, then stormed off, cursing her, the world around him and the sky above.

When her call was finally picked up again it was Strickland on the line.

'This better be important. I'm five minutes away from talking to the media thanks to your ex-boyfriend's efforts. What have you got?'

'A strong lead. A hi-tech connection to the Plato's Cave nightclub. Is there any reason now I shouldn't question Tony Kavella?'

Strickland blew out a heavy sigh. 'How should I know? I haven't had time to look at the evidence. I'm too busy dead-batting this morning's headlines. Make your own judgement call,' he said and then hung up on her.

Rita clicked off the phone and gave a grunt of satisfaction. In effect, Strickland had just given her the go-ahead.

12

The midday sun glared over the city traffic, inflaming drivers and scorching pavements, as Rita pulled over in front of the nightclub. The main entrance was a polished metal door with an iron ring, chained and padlocked. A small brass plate bore the club's name. It was so discreet it went unnoticed by the stream of daytime shoppers passing by.

Plato's Cave straddled a sleazy borderline area where Melbourne's Greek precinct merged with Chinatown. Its neighbours to the left were the Acropolis Cafe and a Greek emporium, and to the right a Chinese pharmacy and a sex supermarket. Above the shopfronts rose the original Romanesque facade of the brick Victorian building, the date 1887 inscribed in stone amid the flaking paintwork. The club's bar and dance floor occupied the cellar – a dim and sweaty cavern reeking of stale tobacco and illicit liaisons. But Kavella conducted business from an air-conditioned office on the first floor, reached by back stairs from a narrow lane. This was where Rita headed as she got out of the car, a tremor of anticipation in her step.

She walked down the lane through baking sunshine and the smells of spicy chicken. When she reached the stairs she found someone standing on the bottom step, smoking a cigarette. Despite the heat of the day, he was wearing a black suit, with the jacket buttoned over a white shirt and a precisely knotted tie. His shaved head glistened like oiled leather. He was slim and sinewy and his face was Asiatic, though his eyes were hidden by sleek, black sunglasses. She tried to brush past him; he refused to budge.

'If you don't mind,' said Rita, trying again to get past him.

One of his hands shot out, cat-like, and grasped her firmly around the throat. 'Who you?' he asked.

Rita tried to jerk out of the hold but his grip was strong. 'Let go,' she said through clenched teeth.

'Maybe. Maybe not. I press little more and you unconscious.' Grinning now, the sun reflecting off his numerous gold fillings. 'How you like that?'

'How you like to be arrested?' she replied.

Instantly his grip relaxed and his hand was back in his pocket. 'You cop?'

'Detective sergeant.'

'Okay. I sorry. You not troublemaker. What you say, officer – no harm done?'

She stroked her throat, wanting to punch him, but instead mimicked him with a 'Who you?'

'I the Duck. Quack, quack,' he said, taking off his sunglasses with a flourish. 'Maybe you hear of me.'

'Maybe,' she replied.

In fact she'd read the intelligence data file on him. He was a Vietnamese hitman with a military and martial arts background, not to mention a trail of bodies left behind him in south-east Asia. He was proficient in the use of guns, knives and his bare hands. His official status was political refugee, but he was currently employed as an enforcer for one of Melbourne's biggest heroin smuggling gangs. 'The Duck' was his anglicised nickname, though the name on his passport, probably an invention, was almost as disconcerting – Duc Hung Long. According to the file he liked to boast that he was.

'And since when have you been a bouncer for this dump?'

He ignored her question, flicking away his cigarette and putting his sunglasses back on. Then he stood aside and gestured up the stairs. 'You come in now. The Duck escort you.'

Rita shook her head, gesturing back at him. 'You first.'

He shrugged and trotted briskly up the stairs ahead of her, a mobile phone suddenly appearing in his hand, presumably to text message her arrival.

The Duck wasn't the only one who looked out of place. As Rita reached the upstairs office she almost collided with a smartly dressed middle-aged Chinese man, who glanced at her briefly as he pushed past. She recognised him immediately as Victor Yang, a Triad gang leader who ran his own drugs and vice enterprises. What was he doing here on rival turf?

Tony Kavella's voice called out to the Duck: 'Show Mr Yang out.'

The Duck did as he was told, leaving Rita to stroll through the door.

Tony Kavella was sitting in a big leather chair behind a chrome and black desk, tapping at a laptop. A nest of new computer screens glowed alongside. It was clear that he'd gone hi-tech and upmarket since the last time she'd been here. Around him the office was cool and spacious, with white walls, a white marble floor and tall yucca plants in white glazed pots. Classical bronzes stood on marble stands and there was tinted glass in the arched Victorian windows. It looked like an interior designer's idea of the setting for a cultivated businessman.

Kavella looked up as Rita entered the room.

'Fuck me,' he said, immediately dispelling any notions the new decor might suggest. 'So you're the cop who's come calling.' He didn't get up. Just slouched back in his swivel chair. 'You here for business or pleasure?'

'Not pleasure, sadly,' said Rita. 'Since I haven't got an arrest warrant.'

That brought a sour chuckle from Kavella's lips, and a deadly gleam to his eyes. The eyes of a psychopath, she reminded herself.

She'd profiled Kavella in detail and there was no doubt about his psychopathic personality. The son of a greengrocer, he had developed into a high school bully, though was smart enough to qualify for university, where he'd started a classics course at the behest of his aspiring but indulgent Greek mother. Impatient and ambitious, he dropped out after cornering the campus market in soft and hard drugs. A natural standover man, he didn't indulge in drugs himself, but enjoyed the power it gave him over others. Casual violence came easily and helped him expand his connections into the city. The nightclub became his base and his legitimate front, from where he established his reputation among those on both sides of the law as a slick and intelligent operator. Yet although his mind was razor sharp, he had not developed a conscience and could inflict pain and brutality without hesitation.

Now, as he lounged back and propped his shoes on the desk, he looked totally at ease with his success. There was a certain dangerous charm about him too, his dark good looks combined with a hypnotic gaze and seductive manner. Along with the computers and upmarket decor, he'd also smartened up his appearance, adding to her suspicions. Gone were the beard, moustache and shoulder-length hair of their last encounter; he was now clean-shaven and neatly groomed. She saw it as a mask to conceal his true identity just as, when trouble arose, he managed to conceal himself behind a phalanx of lawyers, accountants and portfolios.

Something else was new as well. Directly behind his desk was a steel door where no door had been before. It led into the adjoining property. On the wall beside it was a security keypad with a slot for a smartcard. What expansion of his criminal business did it conceal? Perhaps the crime she was investigating.

'No warrant, huh?' he said. 'So you must be appealing to my better nature.'

'Let's not get into the realm of fantasy,' said Rita. 'Mind if I sit down?'

'Be my guest,' said Kavella, waving a hand at the upholstered leather chair just vacated by Victor Yang.

As Rita sat down, she tossed the black Plato's Cave card onto the desk in front of him. 'Recognise that?' she asked.

Without taking his feet off the desk, Kavella reached over, picked up the card and removed it from the clear plastic evidence bag. He studied it for a moment, turned it over twice, then looked at her with no expression.

'Can I keep this?' he said, deadpan.

'No,' said Rita, observing him closely. 'It's police evidence.'

He shrugged, tossed it back at her, and gazed through the tinted windows at the sheet of sunlight glaring from the building opposite.

'So I take it the card is yours?' she asked.

'Take it, leave it, stick it up your arse,' he replied, stretching back with his hands behind his head. 'Do what you like. I'm saying nothing till I know what this is about.'

From her jacket pocket Rita drew out a photo of Emma Schultz and flicked it across the desk as if it were an ace in a poker game. Kavella raised a sceptical eyebrow but pulled his feet off the desk and leant forward in his chair.

'Recognise her?' snapped Rita.

He let her wait for the answer, then said, 'Of course I do. The blind prostitute in the news. What's she got to do with me?'

'She was here at your club less than an hour before she was picked up and attacked.'

'So what?'

'Your calling card was left by the attacker.'

'That card?' he asked, pointing at the one on the desk.

'Yes.'

A flicker of a frown passed over his forehead, before disappearing. It was enough to convince her that something was worrying him.

'What is it, Kavella? More of your nasty games catching up with you?'

'Don't flatter yourself, Van Hassel. You know fuck-all about fuck-all.' Despite attempts at self-control, his nostrils flared with anger. 'There's only one thing obvious here – that you're on a fishing expedition. Wouldn't surprise me if you're wearing a wire.'

'If you're this touchy, something must be bothering you.'

'*You* bother me with your psycho-babble diploma. But as for this . . .' he gestured dismissively at the card and photo, 'you're just trying to set me up.'

'Now why would I want to do that?'

'Because you can't get me legitimately. Because your last attempt ended in failure. Because you want to impress the men who push you around at work and treat you like a pair of tits on a stick.'

Rita felt the bile rise within her. He'd done this to her before, while she was interrogating him after his arrest. Needling her, baiting her, till she lost her temper. It didn't happen often, but this man could do it. Partly because of the obscene crimes he'd committed and partly because he could recognise her frustrations.

'I read about you recently in *Police Life* magazine,' he went on. 'All that bullshit about profiling, studying with the FBI, a woman with a golden future in the force. Boy you must piss off your fellow cops.'

'Let's get back to the prostitute,' she said angrily.

'Let's not. Let's stick with you and whether I should put in a complaint of harassment,' said Kavella.

'You've got no grounds,' said Rita.

'I could think of something.'

'I'm being civil, you shit,' she said, immediately regretting it.

'That's more like it.' His jaw came forward with contempt. 'You should lose your cool more often. Makes you seem less like a cold-blooded bitch. Maybe you're worth a grudge-fuck after all.'

Rita didn't say anything, but the look in her eyes was enough.

He dropped the smile abruptly. 'Look. I don't want to piss around anymore. This woman is nothing to me. And as for the card, it's not mine.'

'I don't believe you.'

'That's your problem,' he said.

'Yours too, if I come back with a warrant,' Rita countered.

'You'd be wasting your time, yet again. I'm telling you the card is from somewhere else.'

'Another Plato's Cave?'

'Why not? I didn't invent the name. It's been around for a few thousand years.'

'Yes, but yours has the underworld connections. Hardly surprising a vice case should lead me straight here.'

'Surprising or not, you've picked the wrong cave, Van Hassel. You've begun your descent into the underworld in the wrong place.'

He picked up his phone, ignoring her.

She watched him send a brief text message, and a moment later Kavella's right-hand man, Brendan Moyle, was at her side.

Rita tensed.

Moyle was thick-set and intimidating. A former debt collector, he didn't hesitate to use violence. He liked to get up close when he inflicted pain and had served time for knee-capping a man with an ice pick.

'Remember our old friend?' said Kavella.

'I don't see a friend,' answered Moyle. 'But I can smell something.' He pushed his face close to Rita and sniffed loudly. 'It's rotting fish.'

It took all Rita's self-control to avoid reacting.

Moyle laughed.

Kavella remained stony-faced. 'We're done,' he said. 'For now.'

It was an implied threat and a taunt, but she couldn't let herself be provoked. She stood up, collected the card and photo, and walked out. Anything else and she'd be suspended.

13

Walking away from Tony Kavella's office, Rita felt certain that he was assuming a more powerful role in the city's criminal elite. She'd seen first-hand that he was expanding his influence and reinventing himself with an image makeover, while equipping himself with expensive hi-tech resources. It was entirely possible that Emma Schultz was a casualty of his new initiatives.

As soon as Rita got back to the squad room, Strickland appeared beside her.

His face was tight, but he spoke quietly. 'Looks like we're both in for a carpeting.'

'What do you mean?' she asked, though she had a sinking feeling that she'd just overstepped the mark.

'We've been summoned to a meeting in Nash's office. I get the feeling we've trodden on somebody's toes.'

This was all she needed, thought Rita, as she headed for the lifts and the office of Superintendent Gordon Nash.

'Is this about today's headlines?' she asked Strickland, feigning ignorance.

'Could be.' His worry lines were in sharp relief. 'Maybe Nash has seen a tape of my presser.'

'How did it go?'

'It just went.'

They rode up three floors in the lift and then walked down a long corridor towards Nash's office.

'Whatever it is, he sounds pissed off.' Strickland gave a heavy sigh. 'One way or another, you seem to have ruined my entire day.'

•

Nash sat at his desk with his hands clasped and his sharp eyes staring over the rims of his glasses. To Nash's right sat Jack Loftus. To his left was Detective Inspector Jim Proctor from the Organised Crime Squad. Behind him leant two of his detectives. Strickland and Rita stood in front of the desk like truants before a headmaster. There was a feeling of inquisition, and Rita was suddenly aware of being the lowest-ranking officer in the room, not to mention the only woman.

Nash looked down at the report sheets spread in front of him, frowned, took off his glasses and waved them impatiently. 'This case you're working on – the blind prostitute – are you getting anywhere with it?'

'We're narrowing the field,' answered Strickland carefully.

Nash's gaze focused on him. 'And what exactly does that mean?'

'While we're waiting for the DNA results, we're getting through a lot of interviews, eliminating potential suspects. As you know, we've only got a vague description to go on. We're also chasing what leads we've got – the car, T-shirt, bondage gear, and so on.'

Nash knew the sound of evasion when he heard it. 'So would you say you're making progress?'

Strickland hesitated, sensing a procedural pitfall in front of him. 'It's early days yet, but I'd say we are. The DNA should make all the difference.'

'Let's hope so. The longer this goes on, the longer we have the media on our backs. And that's just the first cock-up in your investigation.'

Strickland swallowed hard and said nothing. He stood rebuked. Nash was more than just a high-ranking officer, he was also an accomplished bureaucrat and an expert at internal politics. Assigning blame was part of his expertise. The cold-hearted stare over his steel-rimmed glasses had curtailed more than one career.

Nash turned his unsmiling gaze on Rita and said, 'Which brings us to a cock-up of monumental proportions. What on earth possessed you to go barging in on Tony Kavella?'

'I was following a lead,' she said, puzzled. 'I'm sorry, but I don't understand what the problem is.'

Nash answered with a sigh of irritation. 'The *problem* is that Kavella's out of bounds. He has been for three months. Since his acquittal, in fact. That's how long the Taskforce Nero surveillance operation has been in place.'

'Surveillance?'

'You've jeopardised that entire investigation. A huge amount of work and police hours could now be wasted. And worse still, if you've alerted Kavella, he may actually achieve what we're trying to prevent.'

'I don't understand,' said Rita feebly.

'He's putting together an alliance of rival organisations on a scale we've never had to deal with before. A sophisticated partnership of criminal gangs – diversified through drug smuggling, distribution, counterfeiting, tax fraud, illegal immigration, money laundering, extortion. It's an extremely clever move in the wake of Melbourne's underground wars, given their high body count. And it poses a huge threat. Get the picture?'

Rita had a sudden feeling of nausea, realising she'd committed a career-wrecking blunder. She wanted to believe it wasn't her fault – that she wasn't to blame because she'd been told nothing of the surveillance. But in her heart she knew she'd been too eager to go after Kavella again. Revenge had clouded her judgement.

'I'm sorry,' was all she could think to say. 'I didn't know about the operation.'

'Of course you didn't,' said Nash brutally. 'It was on a need-to-know basis. But in any case there are procedures to follow before questioning a suspect. Professional discipline must always come before inspired guesswork.'

Like Strickland, she stood rebuked. But she knew that last comment – about guesswork – had a malicious undertone. It was personal, and she knew it. Nash set no store by criminal profiling and disapproved of her psychological training. To him it was a distraction and, more to the point, foreign to the process of real police work. In his opinion she was being indulged as a woman and pampered because of her academic background. Unfortunately, he wasn't alone in that view.

'Did you check with your senior officer before you went barging in?' he barked.

The question was loaded. Nash was giving Rita the chance to pass the blame onto Strickland, knowing that whichever way she answered it would be held against her. Fuck it, she thought. It was too late to undo the damage, so she might as well stand her ground. Besides, she wasn't prepared to grovel.

After an apologetic glance at Loftus she looked Nash in the eye and said, 'It seemed like a good lead. I made my own judgement call.'

Nash threw his steel-rimmed glasses onto the desk in a gesture of disgust, but Rita continued, almost abrasive now. 'If you're worried about Kavella, you can relax. He has the same opinion of me as you.'

'And what's that?' asked Nash.

'That I deal in psycho-babble.'

'So you don't think he's been alerted?' he asked, his voice still harsh, but clearly more concerned with the continued viability of the operation.

'Like you, he thinks I'm on a revenge mission.'

Proctor leant forward in his chair. 'This is very important, Van Hassel. We haven't been able to bug his office or do long-range eavesdropping. He's got electronic defences in there, so he assumes he's being watched. But did he give any hint of suspecting a major operation's being mounted against him?'

'Just the opposite. He's more confident than ever.'

Proctor turned to Nash and said, 'Maybe it's not blown after all.'

'I don't like playing hunches,' said Nash, then turned to Jack Loftus, who'd sat through the proceedings with a long-suffering look on his face. 'What do you reckon, Jack?'

Loftus took his time answering, scratching his ear and shrugging.

'She ought to know,' he said at last. 'She's got a degree in it.'

Nash sat back, unconvinced. 'I must say I'm in a quandary. Kavella will be seeking feedback on our reaction, possibly right now. If I discipline her, he'll suspect we're onto him. But if we let Sex Crimes focus on him, he'll batten down the hatches and the surveillance operation will be a waste of time, money and resources.'

Proctor folded his arms. 'Maybe there's an alternative way to deal with this.' He was a different species of cop to the others in the room. He was tall and patrician, with a steady gaze and an air of being permanently at ease. His professional detachment was legendary – no one had ever seen him flustered – and he tended to view crimes as intellectual puzzles. 'Maybe we can turn Van Hassel's headstrong behaviour to our advantage.'

Nash was doubtful. 'What are you suggesting, Jim?'

'That she's *not* disciplined, and that her line of inquiry is officially ruled out, for all to hear, in Jack's briefing this afternoon. That way Kavella gets the feedback we want.'

'What feedback?' Rita asked impatiently.

'From the police detectives who are in Kavella's pocket,' Proctor explained.

An abrupt silence followed, as if he'd let slip unmentionable information.

Morale had already hit a new low with the disbanding of two squads at Melbourne police headquarters amid headlines such as ROUGH JUSTICE and DIRTY ROTTEN COPS. The reputation for beatings and drug deals was thanks to overzealous interrogations and the jail sentences for detectives doing business with gangland figures. The murky image of cops operating on both sides of the law in the city's underworld wars was something no one wanted to revisit.

Nash sighed. 'What are you doing, Jim? The more who know about your unit's remit, the more it risks being compromised.'

'Van Hassel's now in the loop,' Proctor replied. 'So I'm suggesting we use her. Instead of spooking Kavella, she may be a way of forcing his hand.'

'Wait just a minute,' butted in Loftus. 'I don't want her used as a cat's paw. Kavella's far too dangerous.'

'Calm down, Jack,' said Proctor. 'I'm talking disinformation, not provocation.'

'But there's history between them and he doesn't need further reminding. We know he's killed before to settle a score.'

Proctor ignored him and turned to Rita. 'What exactly was the lead you were following today?'

'A smartcard embossed with the name Plato's Cave,' she said, taking it from her pocket and handing it to him. 'I spoke to the victim, Emma Schultz, again this morning. She said the attacker showed her the card and talked about cyber sex games. In light of her visit to the club, and Kavella's track record in organising sexual sadism, I decided to question him.'

'There's clear logic there,' conceded Proctor, turning the card over in his hand. 'And Kavella's response?'

'He told me to stick it up my arse, but didn't immediately deny the card was from his club.'

'What's it for, precisely?' Proctor wanted to know.

Rita shrugged. 'The crime lab can't tell us, other than to say it's some sort of super-smartcard. It's heavily encrypted.'

Proctor sat back, rubbing his chin. 'It's quite possible you've stumbled onto something we've failed to pin down in three months' work. We know he's invested in a big hi-tech system housed next to his office. He bought the adjoining building from Victor Yang – it used to be a Chinese laundry. Then he reinforced and soundproofed the walls and, apart from fire escapes, sealed the exterior entrances, with access only from his premises. He got planning permission for office suites, but what he really uses it for, we don't know.'

'I saw a connecting door,' put in Rita. 'Steel-plated.'

'Exactly. It's his private fortress, and we can't get into it with listening or tracking devices or phone taps. But you've managed to get close, and in his face at the same time. I think we can take it further.'

'If you're thinking of entrapment,' Nash warned Proctor, 'I refuse to sanction it.'

'I'm thinking more of encouragement – spur him into action to give himself away. And for all we know, Van Hassel is right about Kavella's involvement in the mutilation; he's capable of it. Our separate investigations may have reached common ground.'

'What sort of encouragement?' asked Nash.

'The Delos Club. She could drop the name in front of him, sometime in the near future, when their paths cross again.'

'But we don't know where or what the Delos Club is,' pointed out Nash.

'We know it's pivotal,' argued Proctor. 'A secret meeting place, perhaps. We've got it on tape three times in conversations between Kavella and other gangland figures. If it's a genuine club, it's not listed as such. The word "Delos" pulls up about a million results on a web search, but other than learning the island of Delos was Apollo's birthplace, we're none the wiser. What about you, Van Hassel? Can you shed any light? You know how Kavella's mind works better than most.'

'He's a psychopath,' she answered. 'He likes toying with people, including their heads. Symbols and emblems are what he's into, and don't forget he studied classics for a while – look at the name of his nightclub.'

'I don't want a profile,' said Proctor. 'I'm asking for ideas.'

She paused, before continuing. 'The island of Delos was the headquarters of the Delian League in the fifth century BC when the Greek city-states united against the Persians. It became the basis of the Athenian Empire. I'd say the Delos Club is the code for the association he's forming.'

'My God, it fits,' Proctor breathed. 'He's empire building.' He faced both Nash and Loftus squarely. 'And I think Van Hassel's just proven her value to my op.'

'That remains to be seen,' said Nash, as he turned his cold gaze on her again. 'And don't forget, young woman, I've got you in my sights.'

14

'Calm down, Van Hassel,' said Loftus. He had asked Rita to accompany him back to his office. 'They're just following procedure.'

She paced up and down, swearing – a delayed reaction to the ticking off she'd received from Nash.

'Procedure, my arse!' she said. 'You know as well as I do it's only an excuse.' She stopped pacing and stood at his window, looking at the city skyline. 'What it's really about is resentment. They won't accept what I do.'

'Give them time.'

'Time for what?'

'To get used to the idea of profiling.'

Rita shook her head in exasperation. 'It's like waiting for a new primate to evolve. I haven't got the patience.' She pulled a frond off his potted fern and began to shred it.

'They'll come around,' Loftus said wearily. 'But in the meantime patience is something you're going to have to learn. For the sake of your career.'

'Maybe it's just the wrong career.'

'There's nothing wrong about it at all,' he said, 'if you'll just leave the politics of the job to me. And perhaps you'll listen to me the next time I warn you not to do something. That move on Kavella – you did clear it beforehand with Strickland, didn't you?'

'He was under pressure at the time. He was just about to go into a press conference.'

'So you let him off the hook instead of yourself?'

'What's it matter? It's an attitude I'm up against.'

Loftus sighed. 'I admire you, but your sense of honour might be misplaced.'

She turned and looked at him sharply. 'I always do what I think is right.'

'That's fine up to a point, but don't add to the obstacles in your way. And you bloody well keep me informed if Proctor decides to enlist your services.'

She turned back to the window, plucked another frond from the plant. 'Are you lecturing me, Jack?'

'No, just giving you good advice,' he said irritably. 'And leave my fern alone.'

She huffed and folded her arms. 'So what am I supposed to do?'

'First of all, I want you to go and cool off.' He looked at his watch. 'You've got half an hour. Then I'm holding a fresh briefing in the squad room. Thanks to you and Strickland, this case has turned into a can of worms that's now my personal responsibility. Apart from anything else, I don't want it going off the rails.'

As detectives gathered for the briefing, Rita pulled over a chair to sit next to Erin.

'You look pissed off,' said Erin. 'Want to tell me about it?'

'No,' answered Rita. 'I want you to deliver on your promise.'

'What promise?'

'Wine. Lots of it.'

'When?'

'Tonight. Jimmy Watson's Bar. I'll ask Lola to come as well.' Lola was Rita's best friend. 'We're overdue for a blow-out.'

'I can do threesomes,' agreed Erin. 'I'll have to check if the couch commander can look after Tristan, but it shouldn't be a problem.'

The chatter in the room tapered off when Loftus entered and started adding items to the whiteboard. Rita could tell he was psyching himself up to deliver the briefing.

He cleared his throat and turned to face his detectives. He had a printout of Strickland's crime report in one hand, a pen in the other. Behind him was a wall map of the city and a noticeboard with duty lists alongside a display of crime scene photos. 'I've pulled some of you off other investigations for obvious reasons,' he said.

'The attack on the prostitute's not only vicious, but thanks to the media it's a high-profile case. However,' he took a deep breath, 'I don't want that to distract you. There's more likely to be a stuff-up if we go charging off in search of a quick bust. If you've got the impression people are breathing down your neck, ignore it. Any pressure for a result will be dealt with by me – personally – from now on. I'm talking internal *and* external pressure.' He shot a look at Strickland. 'Including the press.'

There were nods of appreciation. Loftus was generally admired by his squad members.

'You may have got wind of another problem over one particular line of inquiry.' The expression on his face was stern. 'As far as I'm concerned it was a glitch that's been resolved, and I want this investigation back on track.'

The officers shuffled and exchanged looks, wondering exactly what the glitch was. Rita shifted uncomfortably, then glanced around, trying to gauge if any of her colleagues knew what Loftus was referring to. If so, did they represent a pipeline to Kavella? Just the thought of more corrupt detectives in the building was depressing.

But as at any briefing, everyone was being careful and observant, trying to second-guess allusions. Some sat on chairs, arms folded, their faces wearing customary frowns. Others sat back casually on desktops, legs outstretched. Two or three sipped coffee from plastic cups, notebooks at the ready. Apart from an air of heaviness in the room, it could have been any other meeting in any other office.

Loftus dumped the crime report on top of the desk in front of him and waved his pen at them.

'Now, although I'm overseeing the case, it will be run by Detective Senior Sergeant Strickland,' he said, beckoning Strickland over. 'He'll bring you up to speed on the details and tell you what your assignments are.'

Strickland peeled himself away from the ranks of detectives and stood in front of them with a hard stare. As always, his presence commanded respect, at least among the men. The women were more ambivalent. As their senior officer they had to defer to his judgement – as the alpha male of the squad they had to tolerate him.

'Even though the man we're after is an anonymous client of the victim,' he began, 'and there's only a rough description of his age and appearance, we've got a few other things to go on. First there's his DNA. If we're lucky and he's on file, we'll know once we get the results back from the lab. We've also got his prints, but no match so far.' He straightened his shoulders. 'Next is his car. We haven't got a number, or even a partial number, but we've got the make and model – a black Mazda MX-5. It'll be slow and methodical work because there are so many of them and we've got no descriptive details to narrow the field. But we've been this way before, thanks to the Scalper case, so some of the groundwork's already been done. Even so, we're going to have to continue tracking each one of them down, and if nothing else pans out it might end up as our best lead. Senior Detective Matt Bradby's team is checking with car dealerships and going through the list of owners.'

He paused and let his eyes move over their faces. 'Other leads we're chasing are the Ned Kelly T-shirt and the German bondage gear. Senior Detective O'Keefe's out pounding the streets at the moment, trying to find out where they were bought. And we're still trying to trace a key witness – a woman who was apparently this maniac's first target, but managed to fight him off. If any of you hear of a likely candidate let me or DS Van Hassel know. And although we've drawn a blank so far, we'll continue with an appeal for witnesses around the casino. It's just possible some punter saw something. There's enough of them around late at night. We'll also keep pulling in known offenders who fit the description, even if it's just to eliminate them. DS Erin Webster's in charge of that happy task. Finally, DS Higgs and his crew are out questioning street prostitutes. He's made it clear we're not interested in vice, we just want to nail this offender. They're scared after the news reports, so they're cooperating. The obvious problem is they have a large client base and therefore a large suspect pool.'

He gave Loftus a reluctant sideways look, then went on. 'I agree with what Jack says about not rushing to get a result. Having said that, we all know the first seventy-two hours of any investigation are crucial, and if there's no breakthrough within the first five days we're looking at a long haul. So I just want to remind you, the clock is ticking. Be thorough, but be efficient.' He turned back to Loftus again. 'Jack?'

'That's a good point,' said Loftus. 'And it reminds me we've got someone on our team who can help with that very thing. Most of you have worked with Detective Sergeant Van Hassel on different cases over the years and know she's a damned good investigator. But you're less familiar with the role she's currently developing.'

All heads in the room turned to look at Rita, who swallowed thickly and straightened up, wondering what the hell Jack was about to say.

'I know there's a lot of scepticism about criminal profiling, but I'm convinced it's a valuable asset to certain types of investigation. This could be one of them. Now, despite some popular misconceptions, the profiler's role is not to perform the magic act of identifying the offender. It's far more pragmatic than that. When a case is in danger of getting bogged down, a profiler can conserve our resources and energy, telling us where *not* to look, for a start, and where not to waste our time. A profiler can also give us a fresh focus if his or her analysis finds a connection that isn't obvious. DSS Strickland has asked DS Van Hassel to put together a profile on our mutilator-rapist. Although she's only at the preliminary stage she's already come up with some insights into his background. But I'm going to let her tell you about that,' he said, indicating for Rita to come up to the front. 'She can also give us a few broad impressions of who we're looking for.'

Rita pulled herself up from the chair, with an encouraging pat on the back from Erin, and moved over to stand in front of the whiteboard. As she faced her fellow detectives their collective doubt was plain to see. Yet there was also an attentive curiosity among them. Jack had given her the floor because it offered her a captive audience. It was time to make her pitch.

'My role isn't to tell you how to investigate this case,' she began. 'I'm not here as another supervisor or monitor or – God forbid – some sort of psychic. So for a start I want to set aside all that bullshit. I know the methods we use as detectives to work a case. They're the right methods. That's how we solve crimes. And in most investigations there's no need for profiling at all. It only comes in to play when the odds are stacked against us – when we're hunting an elusive type of criminal, a predator who has no apparent link to his victim. That's what we're dealing with here, and with any luck we'll catch the bastard by following up straightforward leads or evidence. But like Detective Inspector Loftus said . . .' and she paused to highlight the point, 'when there's no clear lead, that's when profiling comes in. It can be used to *prioritise*.'

One of the detectives cleared his throat. It was Strickland's protégé, Bradby, who said, 'I think we understand the principle. But isn't there a danger we can get blinkered and miss out on other things?'

Rita had dealt with this objection before and was ready for it.

'That would only happen if we treat a profile as the main piece of evidence. We mustn't – because it isn't. It's an extra element, that's all. And, sadly, profiling only gets sharper the longer a case drags on and the more attacks an offender commits.'

'And in this case?' asked Bradby. 'You think that's what we're looking at?'

Everyone knew what he was referring to – her ex-boyfriend's TV news report and the front page stories that followed.

'Today's headlines about a serial attacker were based on no information whatsoever,' she said firmly. 'It was sheer tabloid fiction. As far as we know, this was his first such offence, although it was his second attempted sex assault of the night. But going on past patterns, and data on this type of crime, this offender won't be content with a one-off rape and mutilation.'

This was greeted with some low groans.

'I'd say he'll attack again soon unless we stop him,' she continued.

'What else can you tell us?' asked Strickland dourly.

'The man we're looking for would seem much like one of us. He's in the same age group as many of us here – mid twenties to early thirties. He's articulate, respectable-looking, drives a sports car. He's also intelligent and au fait with the latest computer technology, quite possibly working in or dealing with the hi-tech sector. Whatever work he does, he's in a senior position. Also like us, he has to endure constant stress. But this man is unstable – which isn't as obvious as it sounds. We've all questioned criminals who can lie through their teeth without losing their composure – many of them psychopaths.

This offender isn't like that. If he's defied, he loses it. He's also a regular customer of prostitutes.' She turned to Strickland. 'That's as much as I can say. The rest is too speculative at this stage.'

Her comments brought a muted response from her colleagues – a mixture of quizzical stares and murmurs of acknowledgement. The jury's still out, she thought. As she resumed her position beside Erin, Strickland echoed Loftus's moral support – or at least pretended to.

'I think that proves we can get some valuable input from profiling,' he said, before addressing Rita directly. 'In fact, I'm going to ask you to go through the interview tapes we've already got – just to double-check he hasn't slipped through. You might spot something we've missed.'

Rita nodded her agreement, then he went on. 'One point though – the hi-tech connection. For the benefit of the other officers could you explain how you arrived at that?'

'His comments to the victim,' she said, then added carefully, 'and an encrypted smartcard he left at the crime scene which we're yet to decipher.'

'Okay. Good,' said Strickland, nodding with something like approval, before turning back to his team. 'Let's keep that in mind. We'll also continue with checks on any security cameras that might have picked up the car. Nothing's turned up at the casino, but we tracked down the owners of two Mazda MX-5s coming off the CityLink in the right timeframe. Unfortunately one was a private female nurse on a night call, the other was a middle-aged businessman who didn't match the victim's description – though what he's up to in a sports car in the early hours sounds like funny business to me.' That got some chuckles. 'I think that brings us up to date.'

'There's just one other thing,' added Loftus. 'You'll see from the crime report the victim left the Plato's Cave nightclub about an hour before she was picked up and attacked.' His words provoked a reaction, laced with cursing and swearing, to which Loftus raised his voice. 'Yeah, well we'd all like to take another crack at Kavella, but this isn't the occasion. At this stage we haven't established a connection with the club. Although the smartcard mentioned by Van Hassel has got Plato's Cave printed on it, the card appears to prove nothing either way. It may be just a coincidence, so I'm telling you now: this is not – repeat *not* – a line of investigation. And Plato's Cave stays off the agenda or you'll answer to me. We've got enough on our hands without that litigious creep distracting us. So let's get on with it.'

As they dispersed, chairs scraping, voices grumbling, Loftus moved over to Rita.

'Thanks, Jack,' she said.

'For what?'

'For dropping me in it.'

'No sweat,' he said unsympathetically. 'Anyway, you more than handled it. If profiling's going to play a significant role we've got to beat the drum a bit.'

'Is that what I was doing?'

'Yes. And you've also given the case a little more focus.'

'Maybe.' Unconvinced, she changed the subject. 'And now there's a general health warning against Plato's Cave, what do I put in my report on Kavella?'

Loftus gave a weary sigh. 'You don't write it,' he said, lowering his voice. 'Is there any chance of finding out more about the card?'

'Yes, but I want to look my seductive best.'

He fixed her with a suspicious stare, before relenting. 'Okay, I'll bite. What are you talking about?'

'The crime lab says there's a young cybernetics professor at Monash who might be able to help,' Rita replied. 'I'll go out there tomorrow. What do you reckon, Jack – you think I can charm him with my academic prowess?'

Loftus just shook his head. 'I've had enough to think about today.'

Rita's work was over for the day, and all in all it had been a bad one, thanks to internal politics. She took the lift down to the basement car park, cursing her miscalculation over Kavella and wondering if her career in the force would soon be blocked by Nash. As she approached her car she could see a figure leaning against it. Strickland. He was smoking a cigarette. He straightened up when he saw her coming, an embarrassed look on his face, the look of someone wrestling with an apology.

'How'd it go with Loftus after the meeting with Nash?' he asked awkwardly.

'I got another lecture,' she said, giving him a sour stare.

'Shit.' He dropped the cigarette and ground it with his heel. 'One way or another we've all chewed you out today.'

The belated sympathy didn't impress her. 'I'm surprised you noticed.'

'I might be a hard bastard but I try to be fair. You don't deserve what you got from Nash. But that's not what I wanted to say.' He looked at her squarely. 'I owe you a favour for what happened in there with Nash. You could've fed me to the wolves.'

This was unexpected – Strickland admitting he was in her debt. Rita wasn't quite sure what to say. 'Well, I wasn't being noble. They just got my back up,' she said eventually.

'Doesn't matter. I appreciate it anyway. Just wanted you to know.'

He glanced away, uncomfortable with himself. It was something she hadn't seen before.

'Okay,' she said. 'And maybe you can drop the macho bullshit occasionally.'

'No chance of that.' He started to walk away. 'I'm still a hard bastard.'

15

'Mike's great company when you're out on the town,' Rita was saying. 'But that's not enough, is it?'

'My God! You need to ask?' said Lola, looking at her in amazement.

Rita and Lola Iglesias had been friends since their late teens. They'd met at a seminar on the psychology of cultural icons. Rita was setting out on her degree course at a time Lola was exploring screenwriting as an option. She'd become the arts critic on a women's magazine instead. Their temperaments were as divergent as their careers. It's why they clicked. Each found the other highly entertaining and a little mad, but there was also deep mutual trust. Family pressures, relationships, break-ups – they always had each other to talk out the crisis with and provide a lateral perspective and creative advice. They were to each other what no woman should be without.

'He says I'm sinful and hard-edged.' Rita was a little drunk. 'But I doubt he can sustain a relationship. He's unreliable.'

'No wonder, with all that Irish blood in his veins.' Lola's family was from Ecuador. 'Even worse, he's a journalist. They're brilliant at partying but useless at commitment.'

'I just can't deal with his lies and his egocentric attitude,' Rita continued. 'He's like a little boy.'

'Tell me about it,' said Erin feelingly – her son was going through the terrible twos. 'Boys are born with high levels of testosterone. It makes them so demanding. And when they grow up they think with their dicks.'

Lola flicked her hand at the general surroundings. 'In fact, so much in life's hormonal. Like PMT – or fucking in elevators.'

That got a laugh, since she'd once been caught at it.

'Oh my God, you'll never guess,' Lola went on. 'I'm getting flowers at work. And I don't have a clue who's sending them.'

'Make the most of it,' said Erin, reaching into her handbag for cigarettes, a plastic rattle falling out in the process. 'Secret admirers are good for two things, champagne sex and five-star room service.'

Erin's foray into wife- and motherhood was relatively recent, preceded by a time in which she drank hard, swore loudly and slept around. An impressive tally of male colleagues had tried to keep pace with her alcohol intake and promptly fallen prey to her provocations and sturdy physique. In the end one of them – an inspector in the uniform branch – got her pregnant and married her. With a hyperactive toddler, the marriage was under strain. In public Erin joked about it. In private she threw crockery at the wall and wondered if her husband was screwing someone else.

'I used to get flowers,' she said wistfully. 'Now I've got piles of nappies and a man who grunts at me while he watches the footy.' Erin emptied her glass. 'Another bottle of cab sav?'

The other two nodded and she got up and made her way towards the counter.

They were drinking at the wine bar that had become their regular haunt. Its mood was reassuring. Oak casks behind the bar. Dusty wine bottles on the shelves. Vases of freesias. And in the small back garden where they were sitting, tables shaded by the leafy lacework of ferns and bamboo.

'So how was your day?' asked Rita.

'Tedious,' said Lola. 'The magazine sent me to interview a self-satisfied bitch with a size six figure and legs up to her neck. Yet another C-list celebrity turned crime writer.'

'You're kidding.'

'It's the market. No-talents cashing in on what's become the biggest mainstream genre.'

'Wasn't it always?' asked Rita.

'No. Thrillers used to be cheap pulp written by middle-aged alcoholics for semi-literates. And no one tried to be clever about it.'

'Shakespeare was a crime writer.'

'There you go – not listening to me again!'

'His best plays are psychological thrillers – *Macbeth*, *Othello*, *Hamlet*.'

'Do I *look* like I believe you?'

'I could even argue Hamlet's a flawed and reluctant detective who was a forerunner to the heroes of film noir. All the elements are there.'

'Oh, how convincing. Not!'

'Then there's Dostoyevsky,' Rita persisted. 'The greatest novelist of all, and a genius on the psychology of crime.'

'No wonder you're a profiler,' said Lola. 'You keep getting intellectual bees in your bonnet!'

Erin came back with a fresh bottle and sat down purposefully. 'Do you know how nice it is to have a night out and actually have a conversation with an adult? Tristan's gorgeous but the little bugger never gives me a break. When I'm out with him I end up with wine knocked over, every sentence interrupted and stains on my skirt.'

'Sounds like my last date,' said Lola.

Erin refilled the glasses. 'So don't get broody too soon. And in the meantime fuck around.'

Rita shrugged. 'Part of me agrees. The best way to put Mike behind me is to get plastered and get laid.' She drank deeply from her glass, the wine blurring the edges of her thoughts. 'But another part of me thinks about consequences.'

'Listen to me, Rita,' Lola said insistently. 'I love you madly but you have a bad habit of observing your own life. You should get on with living it.'

'Hang on, I'm supposed to be the shrink here.'

'You know very well all women are sex therapists,' retorted Lola. 'And I agree with Erin, you've got to find a bright new hunk. It'll take your mind off everything else.'

Rita laughed. 'When you put it *that* way, how can I disagree?' She gave a wicked smile. 'It so happens I'm meeting a hunk tomorrow morning, a young professor. I've checked out the photo on his website. He's very cute.'

16

Rita hugged and kissed her friends goodbye before they settled into a taxi to go south of the river. She waved them off feeling very different from when she'd met them a couple of hours earlier in a mood of frustration and despondency. Now she was feeling distinctly mellow as she got in her car and decided she was sober enough to drive the short distance to her house in Abbotsford.

Light was softening in the evening sky as she drove past the terraced rows of the old inner suburbs. She turned down a road hooded by the leafy sprawl of plane trees, then into a quiet side street. Home was a compact weatherboard with a corrugated iron roof, a narrow wooden verandah, and a tiny front garden with a couple of hydrangea bushes.

Rita drove her car into the cobbled bluestone alley that ran behind the houses, then stopped, unlocked her back gate and pulled into her backyard, which had just enough room for a shed, an almond tree and a parking space. It wasn't until she was climbing the back step that her senses went on to high alert. Something was wrong. What was it? A sound came from inside her house. It was the static of voices and applause. The TV was on. But she was certain she'd switched it off.

Steadying her breathing, she slid the key into the backdoor lock and silently opened it. After easing the door shut behind her, she stood motionless, listening. Then, over the inane banter of the game show, came the distinct rattle of the venetian blind beside her. The kitchen window was wide open and there were scratches in the paintwork where someone had prised it open.

Reaching out with her right hand, she drew the carving knife from its metal scabbard, crept out of the kitchen, and walked softly down the passage to the open doorway of the lounge. The smell of cigarette smoke drifted in the air. Rita tried to swallow but her mouth was dry.

Focusing her attention, she drew a deep breath, raised the knife and moved swiftly into the room to confront the intruder, but there was no one there. She moved quickly through the rest of the house, and when she was sure it was empty she returned to the lounge, put down the knife and switched off the TV, her blood still pumping fiercely. As her eyes adjusted to the light filtering through the venetian blinds, she noticed a dab of cigarette ash on the coffee table next to her armchair. It lay there like a subtle token of menace.

That night a storm blew in from the west. The air was still humid but the sudden downpour eased the heat. Rita lay in her bath listening to the rain drumming on the tin roof. The sound was comforting but she still couldn't relax. There was too much adrenalin in her system. Her brain wouldn't switch off.

She'd locked and bolted the doors, wedged shut the windows, and collected her police-issue gun which had been stowed in the floor safe. Then she'd cooked herself a meal which she'd thrown out half-eaten. Later she ran herself a bath, lit candles around it and drank some Scotch while she soaked in the soft glow. It didn't work. She couldn't get rid of the tension.

The fact that someone had broken into her home was preying on her thoughts. After carrying out a detailed check through the house she'd realised nothing had been taken by the intruder. The purpose seemed to be intimidation. Her first thought was Kavella and his henchmen, or even a bent cop in his pay. The same tactic – a break-in with no theft – had been used before against the anti-corruption detectives known as 'toe-cutters'. It was a way of delivering a warning to back off. But this felt different somehow. It wasn't just the TV left on and the open window that bothered her. Other things had been moved, drawers opened, papers shifted. The feng shui touches she was testing in her bedroom had been disturbed.

The intruder had been prying through her things, and she realised she'd dealt professionally with this type of blatant intrusion before. The pattern fell under the category of stalker, and it cast doubt on her initial suspicion of Kavella. The observation only increased her sense of unease and left her running one scenario after another through her mind as the candle wax dribbled onto the tiles and the bathwater cooled. Her thoughts beat down on her as steadily as the rain on the roof.

17

The man with the bronze mask lay awake, unable to sleep. He got out of bed, pulled on a polo shirt and jeans, went down to his car and drove towards the nightlife of St Kilda.

It was a scene he was familiar with – when the restaurant and cafe clientele had mostly dispersed. That's when a different mood took over. Along with the after-hours ravers and revellers, the clubs and bars attracted a drift of streetwalkers, junkies and kerb crawlers. By the early hours the roads along the seafront exhaled a dank air of vice. Pushers in the car parks. Hookers in the shadows. Rowdy pavement drunks. It was why he came here. The streets felt lurid and edgy. A place for anonymous pick-ups.

His wheels rumbled over the tramlines as he cruised past the gaping mouth of Luna Park, his gaze prowling through the figures passing by. He was on the lookout for solitary women – the sort that would suit his purposes. He'd found them here before, the hard, desperate street whores. Because their brains were often fried with drugs they were so much easier to bend to his needs. They were halfway senseless already.

He spotted one at a trestle table in the gaudy red and yellow glare outside McDonald's. She was sitting alone, like a human takeaway – fishnets, stilettos, cleavage. A tired leather handbag rested on the table beside her. She was drinking coffee from a paper cup, her eyes busily scanning for customers. He slowed down to pull over, but as she got up and came towards him a police patrol car swung onto the Esplanade behind him. He couldn't risk being stopped or recognised, so he changed gears, eased back onto the accelerator and signalled a left into Carlisle Street. Luckily the police didn't follow him. Lucky for the woman, too. She turned back, disappointed, never knowing how close she'd come to being bludgeoned and maimed.

After the first one he'd got a taste for it. The physical damage he'd inflicted had gone beyond anything he'd done before. It was like an epiphany – he'd been surprised by his own violence and a powerful sense of release. The media coverage and public outrage only served to inflame his need for more of the same. Yet no one could possibly understand why, except perhaps the profiler. That's why he'd visited her home while she was out, to get a feel for her presence, to make himself comfortable in her personal space.

As he'd relaxed in her armchair, smoking, checking out her collection of books and DVDs, watching her TV, he'd sensed a strange affinity. This woman had nothing in common with the prisoners he'd left behind or the she-devils he was hunting or the enemies who were hunting him. Detective Sergeant Van Hassel was a cut above the rest, operating at a higher level, full of insight and empathy. He saw her more in the role of a muse, or an oracle, or even an Amazon – a worthy participant in what was unfolding. In the meantime, the hunt must go on.

He drove past a group of prostitutes leaning by a bus shelter, smoking, beckoning for business. No sale. More than one meant witnesses. Further on he turned into the shadowy side streets around the Botanic Gardens. As he completed the circuit he came face to face with another patrol car, its lights flashing, its officers in the process of arresting a girl and a motorist. The police watched him as he passed by, their eyes reflecting more than a casual interest. Though they let him pass, the encounter was too close for comfort.

He headed back towards the highway, his taste for savagery unsatisfied, the bronze mask still concealed in the laptop case beside him. His first conquest had readied him for more, but tonight was not the night for the next.

18

Rita wore her powder blue trouser suit to work the next morning. It was light and cool in the heat and comfortably hid the holstered .38 on her hip.

Within minutes of arriving at the police complex she was downing a triple espresso, hoping the caffeine would help her brain focus on the clusters of data scrambling across her computer screen. She felt the strain of a bad night's sleep, frayed at both ends by insomnia and a sense that her home had been violated. But she wouldn't report it, for reasons of self-respect as much as anything else. Anyway, with nothing stolen, the break-in was personal rather than criminal, so she decided to tell no one about it, not even Jack, who would probably overreact and slap some sort of curfew on her. She refused to be restricted or intimidated, and instead would become more vigilant and carry a gun. Last night she'd put it under her pillow.

The computer updates told her there was no breakthrough in the investigation. No obvious suspect had emerged, the check on MX-5s continued to draw a blank, and there was still no sign of the key witness, the offender's first intended victim. The DNA results hadn't yet come through from the forensic services lab, though Detective Sergeant Higgs was already compiling a list of regular street clients he wanted DNA-tested. Meanwhile, O'Keefe had tracked down the St Kilda sex shop where the bondage gear had been bought, but the manager could add nothing to the description of the wanted man.

O'Keefe plonked himself on a chair next to Rita's desk.

'No luck yet with the bronze mask,' he said. 'It's not stocked by any of the sex shops.'

'Then Emma Schultz could be right about it being theatrical,' she said. 'Try theatre and costume shops. What about the T-shirt?'

'I still haven't found where it comes from,' O'Keefe answered. 'But that could be a good sign. It's looking more like an upmarket item, from a designer outlet maybe.'

'Good, keep looking,' she said.

'Okay, boss.' He gave her a wily look. 'I hear you hit a dead end with the smartcard.'

'Dead end or dead on,' she answered. 'It could go either way. I'm off to Monash this morning to try and find out more about it.'

'The reason I mention it,' he continued, 'is because I found this on my porn tour.'

He placed on the desk in front of her a pink business card with a name, address and phone number on it. The business name was Plato's Cave.

Rita was taken aback. 'You've found another Plato's Cave?'

'It's a new brothel touting for business,' O'Keefe answered. 'I wondered if there was a connection with your smartcard?'

'I doubt a brothel could afford the technology,' she said. 'But leave it with me. I'll add it to my travel list.'

Rita's mood was more upbeat as she drove around the leafy fringe of the Royal Botanic Gardens, thanks to the caffeine lift and getting out on the road. She was also looking forward to her encounter with Byron Huxley, the hunky professor.

She joined the surge of traffic on the South Eastern Freeway where it followed the course of the Yarra River. With the glare of the morning sun in her windscreen, the wheels drumming smoothly and the needle nudging the speed limit, she headed towards the outer suburbs as she hummed along to the plaintive angst of Chris Isaak wailing from her CD player.

Monash University had a hinterland feel to it. Tower blocks and brown-brick architecture straddled the campus behind maturing gum trees. It was set amid a monotonous sweep of outer suburbs stretching towards the Dandenong Ranges. The surrounding landscape typified the seamless residential sprawl that fanned out from the city, ribbed with a neat grid of streets, homes and gardens.

Rita left the highway, parked and made her way through the knots of students. The place had a drowsy, placid air.

The woman at the faculty office directed her towards a seminar room. The door was open. Rita looked inside. A dozen students sat at computer terminals around a rectangular table. Byron Huxley stood in front of a flipchart, explaining what his students were looking at on their screens.

He was even better-looking in the flesh than in the photo on his website. The young professor was fit, lean and roguishly handsome with his tousled black hair and engaging manner. While his appearance seemed at odds with that of a leading academic, he was completely at ease with his students. In his sandals, Bermuda shorts and Pavarotti T-shirt he could have been the antipodean version of Renaissance man, his briefcase beside him stuffed with scientific textbooks, a squash racquet and a beach towel.

'This is just the beginning,' he was telling his students, 'in the development of neurocomputers. Once we've integrated digital electronics with living neurons we'll have the potential to build cybernetic systems far more powerful than our present silicon ones. We're talking about machines built around living neural networks – living brains, if you like. It's inevitable.'

One student asked, 'Isn't that playing God?'

'Interesting question. Yes – you've spotted the ethical minefield, and that means it's beyond the remit of science. And beyond the scope of this seminar, which has already overrun.' The students started shuffling their folders together and reaching for bags. 'We'll continue from this point next week.'

Rita waited for the undergraduates to file out of the room before going in.

'Professor Huxley?' she asked.

He looked up from the notes he was shoving into the briefcase. 'Yes? Can I help you?'

'I certainly hope so. I'm Detective Sergeant Marita Van Hassel. I left a message.'

'Yes, of course.' He zipped the bag shut. 'We've got a half-hour window while I set up an experiment for the next tute. It means a trip down to the computer lab, if that's all right.'

'Sounds delightful.'

'Only if you're a cyber nut,' he said, smiling. 'Your message mentioned something about encryption. If I crack it do you get to make an arrest?'

'Possibly.'

'I know what case you're working on,' said Huxley. 'I saw you on TV – you're the profiler. So, Detective Sergeant Van Hassel, if you want specific information it's no good being evasive.'

'I can tell you're used to talking to students,' she retorted, causing him to chuckle.

He led her downstairs to a large room crowded with hi-tech machines, computer screens, accessories and heavy duty cabling. The space was cool and shaded from the day's brightness. Thin streaks of sunlight gleamed at the edges of the closed blinds on the windows.

He slung his briefcase onto a desk and dropped into a seat in front of a keyboard.

'Grab a chair.'

Rita sat down beside him, looking around as he logged on.

He glanced at her. 'Welcome to my world,' he said. 'Sorry about the mess.'

'Looks like a cargo hold from *Star Wars*. What exactly have you got down here?'

'A few generations of digital electronics, mainframes, robotics. Various scanners. And rats.'

'Rats?'

'In cages down the far end. We use them for experiments in communication between silicon circuits and biological neurons. Amazing what happens when you implant an array of electrodes into a specific part of a rat's brain. It can learn thought control.'

She shook her head distastefully. 'Great. Like a few other rats I know.'

He laughed. 'Okay, detective, show me what you've got.'

She raised an eyebrow as she handed him the plastic card, though it didn't bother her at all that he was flirting.

'The crime lab's best guess is that it's a sophisticated smartcard,' she said. 'But they thought you might be able to tell me more.'

'Plato's Cave – how very erudite,' he commented. 'Shouldn't you be in the Philosophy Department?' He slotted the card into the wall of electronics that faced them. 'Let's see what it's hiding.'

She watched Huxley lean forward, his fingers nimbly tapping the keys, as moving holograms, geometric graphics and rivers of encrypted data flowed over the screens above him. Every now and then he glanced up, his eyes quickly scanning the test displays, before punching in more commands. Eventually he sat back, put his hands behind his head and gave a nod of admiration.

'Your crime lab's right,' he said. 'It's a super-super-smartcard, certainly cutting edge, with heavily encrypted data.'

'Can you decode it?' she asked.

He shook his head. 'No. But I can give you an educated guess about its use.'

'That would be welcome. It's more than I've got so far, Professor Huxley.'

'Call me Byron. It makes me feel less like a boffin.' He folded his arms. 'What do you know about VPNs – virtual private networks?'

'Aren't they a sort of intranet, for use by a business organisation?'

'You're in the right neighbourhood. A VPN allows external access through intranet portals. It provides remote users with secure access to the internal network. That is, people can use the web to get into it, thanks to cryptographic tunnelling protocols. Are you following me?'

'I think so,' she answered.

'Good. The most crucial aspect of a VPN is security and its authentication mechanisms. These can include a login, a card key, even biometric data like fingerprints or iris patterns.'

'Let me get this straight,' she said. 'Are you telling me this card would let me log in to someone's private network?'

'Essentially, yes. But the card isn't enough. You'd also need all the security components and a computer configured to connect to the VPN before you could get in. Even then, you'd be treading on thin ice.'

'Why do you say that?'

'The card's got more than silicon in there. It's also got a bit of nanotechnology and a micro wireless connection, so I'd guess the login is constantly changing.' He hit the keyboard and the screens froze. 'This Plato's Cave is very private. No one wants you to get in.'

He handed the card back to her.

'Any idea where it was made?' she asked.

'There are a few places around the world where it could've been produced, Melbourne being one. The software firms here are up with the best in the world.'

'Is there anything else you can tell me?'

'Not off the top of my head. But I'll give you a call if something else occurs to me.' He smiled. 'I've got your mobile number.'

There was a glint in his eye as he said it.

19

Rita sat in the cafe at the Campus Centre drinking a strong black coffee and digesting the information Huxley had imparted. Along with his scientific analysis he'd given her a new lead to follow. It would mean knocking on the doors of the best software firms around the city; with any luck, one of them could identify the card's provenance. Of course, there was one glaring flaw with that approach. If Tony Kavella was indeed the customer, the firm would probably deny all knowledge of him, the card and its manufacture, so even if it had been made in Melbourne, there was a good chance it would be a fruitless quest.

She switched her thoughts to Huxley himself. He'd made a good impression on her, not just because he was attractive, but because he'd surprised her with his manner and personality. From a university professor she'd anticipated a dry, even condescending welcome. Instead he was friendlier than she'd expected, more amenable, not pretentious at all.

Her mobile bleeped. She took it out of her shoulder bag. It was a text message from O'Keefe.

T-shirt bought in Bourke St mall. No luck with ID. Still looking for mask.

She smiled to herself. Detective Senior Constable Kevin O'Keefe was doing what he did best, pursuing each objective with plodding tenacity.

Rita put the phone back in her bag, and tried to relax as she sipped her coffee. Around her, groups of students clustered at cafe tables. The place was full of loud conversations – the clamour of burgeoning intellects among the coffee cups and donuts. The scene almost made her feel nostalgic. A decade ago she would have been at home here in the heady mix of idealism and naivety – a convergence of sharp-witted youths, intense young women, and post-adolescent boys. Outside the cafe, students were strolling back and forth from lectures, or heading for the restaurant or the bookshop, bags slung casually over their shoulders. Then a blind girl with a guide dog walked past. It snapped her back into action, like a visual reminder of the urgency of the manhunt.

Rita picked up her bag and walked through the heat and swirling dust towards the car park. Overhead the leaves of the gum trees lashed themselves in the gusts of a northerly and a flock of galahs swerved in pink arcs as they looked for a stable perch. As she rounded a brown rotunda of lecture theatres her mobile started ringing. It was O'Keefe again.

'I've just got into the office, and a hospital's got back to us,' he told her. 'There's a patient with the type of injuries we're looking for.'

'Go on,' said Rita.

'She's a thirty-year-old woman with concussion and wrist injuries.'

'Is she a hooker?'

'No, the complete opposite – a company executive who says she was knocked off her bike. It might be nothing.'

'A company executive riding a bike,' retorted Rita. 'That's dubious for a start. Give me the name and hospital.'

'Kelly Grattan, and she's at Epworth in a private room,' replied O'Keefe. 'By the way, if she's the victim of a hit-and-run, she didn't report it. In fact, there's no report of an accident.'

'Okay, anything else I need to know?'

'The DNA result's come through from the lab,' he answered, 'and like we thought, the offender's not in the database. Strickland's pissed about it. His best hope for a breakthrough just went down the pan. It also means Kavella's in the clear.'

'Not necessarily,' she corrected him. 'I never had him down for carrying out the attack himself. Kavella doesn't leave messy crime scenes with a trail of evidence, he's too clever for that. He's a puppet master, a manipulator. Besides, his prints are on file and there was no match.'

'But you still think he's involved?'

'Officially, no. We've been told he's out of bounds so we follow up every other lead.' She paused as she reached her car. 'That means my next stop is another hospital visit.'

Rita drew the ward nurse aside to ask her about Kelly Grattan. 'When was she admitted?'

'Three nights ago,' answered the nurse. 'Just before nine.'

'What are her injuries?'

'A hairline fracture of the skull, concussion and a head wound that needed three stitches. She's also got two sprained wrists, with lacerations and contusions to both hands.'

Rita jotted down the details, along with Kelly's address in Toorak. 'What treatment has she had?'

'On admission, an X-ray and a CT scan, but there was no sign of bleeding or swelling of the brain. She was injected with a local anaesthetic before doctors sutured the wound on the back of her head. She's on supportive treatment for the fracture, simple analgesics. We've been keeping her in for observation, but she's ready to be discharged.'

'And she claims she was knocked off her bike?' said Rita, tapping her notebook with her pen.

'Yes. But she's hazy about the circumstances because of the concussion.'

'She didn't give any indication that she was attacked?'

'None at all. Is that what this is about, a road rage attack?'

'Possibly,' said Rita evasively. 'Possibly not. One other thing, was she brought here by ambulance?'

'No, she came by taxi.'

She thanked the nurse who pointed out a private room at the end of the ward. Rita walked over, opened the door and went in. A young woman, propped up on pillows, turned from a TV and regarded her with a cool stare.

'Who are you?' she asked.

Rita took in the split lip, the black eye and the graze marks on the woman's chin. Both wrists were strapped, several fingers were bandaged and there was wadding on her skull, but the injuries didn't detract from her self-assurance. She had the air of a woman who was strong-willed and professional, well-groomed with neatly trimmed auburn hair, her face handsome even without any make-up. She wasn't someone who would accept being beaten and mauled. A Gucci handbag stood on the bedside table. Lavish bouquets of flowers adorned the room.

'I'm Detective Sergeant Marita Van Hassel.'

A fleeting shadow moved over the woman's face, replaced by something more composed. 'What do you want?'

'I'm told you're the victim of a hit-and-run,' said Rita, opening her notebook. 'I'm here to investigate.'

'I see.'

'If I could just check a few personal details first,' Rita went on. 'Your name's Kelly Grattan, you're thirty, have an apartment in Toorak, and you're a company executive, is that correct?'

'Yes.'

'Which company and what executive position do you hold?'

'I'm the business administrator at Xanthus.' Kelly pressed the TV mute button with some difficulty. 'That's a software company in South Melbourne.'

Rita wrote it down, underlined the word *software*, and said, 'I haven't heard of it.'

'Well, you will.'

'Why do you say that?'

'Because it's about to hit the computer games market big-time,' answered Kelly. 'And because it's owned by Martin Barbie.'

'Martin Barbie?' repeated Rita. 'The TV star?'

'Yes, there's only one,' said Kelly dryly, 'though it's hard to believe as he pops up everywhere.'

As Rita wrote down the name it seemed to be an exotic addition to her notes. Martin Barbie's face was familiar to television viewers as the host of a reality TV show, and it was common knowledge he'd capitalised on his ratings to float publicity campaigns, sporting events and advertising. He belonged to a special breed – the celebrity entrepreneur. He was a man with an image and the brain to market it. But owning a software firm? He'd kept that quiet.

'I thought he was just a self-promoter,' said Rita. 'I didn't know he was into computer games.'

'You'd be surprised,' replied Kelly. 'He's funnelled his earnings into production companies, diversifying into games software and online services. Believe me, the Barbie media net is expanding. He's unstoppable and incorrigible.' She waved a hand at her bouquets. 'Who do you think sent all the flowers?'

'Very considerate,' said Rita. 'But I need to hear about the hit-and-run incident that put you here.'

'There's not much I can tell you,' said Kelly. 'I only assume I was knocked off my bike, I don't actually remember. One moment I was riding along Toorak Road, the next I was sitting on the footpath with people helping me up and my bike buckled in the gutter. They hailed a taxi and I came straight here.'

'Did you get any of those people's names?' asked Rita.

'Sorry.'

'What about the taxi? Do you remember which firm?'

'I wasn't in any state to notice much.'

'What did you do about your bike?'

'It was wrecked. I just left it there.'

'Where on Toorak Road was this?' persisted Rita.

'I can't even remember that,' shrugged Kelly. 'Somewhere between Chapel Street and Orrong Road.'

Rita put a hand on her hip, not bothering to note this down. 'That's quite a distance. What on earth were you doing cycling at that time of night? It must have been well after eight.'

'Yes, silly of me, it was getting dark. I'd been browsing in the shops, didn't notice the time. I should have driven there but thought the exercise would do me good. How wrong can you get?'

'Not much more wrong than that,' said Rita. 'Why weren't you wearing a safety helmet?'

The question seemed to take Kelly by surprise. 'I should have been . . .' She hesitated. 'I just forgot. Big mistake.'

'Yes,' Rita agreed. 'There's something else I've got to ask. Were you assaulted?'

'What do you mean?'

'Did someone try to molest you – a man, a stranger, with a mask and chains?'

Kelly burst out laughing. 'Absolutely not!'

'Are you sure? After all, you were concussed.'

'I think I'd remember *that*! But if it comes back to me, I'll let you know.'

'You do that.' Rita wrote in her notebook, tore out the page and placed it beside Kelly's handbag. 'That's my mobile number.'

'Thanks,' said Kelly, smiling. 'I'm impressed by the level of police concern.'

'Part of the service,' said Rita. 'When do you get out of here?'

'I've decided to discharge myself as soon as the doctor does his rounds. I've got urgent business to attend to.'

'With Martin Barbie?'

'The man himself,' said Kelly. 'He's due to have a crisis on his hands.'

Rita wondered about the comment. It seemed to have a double meaning. As an afterthought she pulled out the Plato's Cave smartcard.

'Ever seen this before?'

There was a fleeting reaction, something like a brief flicker of recognition in Kelly's eyes, but Rita couldn't be sure.

'No,' said Kelly firmly. 'Means nothing to me.'

20

Strickland's scowl was setting in. It wasn't directed at anyone in particular, not even Rita and O'Keefe, sitting across the desk from him. It was more an involuntary response to a growing list of frustrations.

'So, effectively, you two haven't come up with anything either,' he was saying. 'That means not a single lead has panned out. This investigation is already starting to drag.'

'Look on the bright side,' put in O'Keefe. 'At least it's not headline news anymore.'

'Until the next victim,' said Strickland grimly. 'Then we'll have every hack and his dog on our backs.'

They were sitting in the untidy surroundings of his office, where Rita had just briefed him on her trips to the university and hospital.

'Kelly Grattan's story bothers me,' she said.

Strickland massaged a temple, still scowling. 'But it rules her out as the offender's first victim.'

'Completely,' agreed Rita. 'But it doesn't add up.'

'You haven't even checked it out.'

'That's just it, I can't. Not one aspect of it. She's given me an uncheckable version of what happened to her. I know she's lying.'

'For Christ's sake, women lie out of habit!' Strickland snorted. 'That doesn't mean she was attacked.'

'Sexism aside,' Rita remarked, 'look at it another way. The injuries and timing are consistent with an assault. But if she's got a strong reason to conceal it, she'd come up with just the sort of unverifiable crap I had to listen to. I mean, a woman executive cycling to window-shop at night in Chapel Street! Excuse me, that's bullshit.'

'Okay, okay, she got up your nose with a dicey account,' Strickland conceded. 'But it doesn't make her a victim and, more to the point, it doesn't give us a witness.'

'Maybe she's got amnesia,' said O'Keefe. The other two looked at him to see if he was joking, but they couldn't tell. Then he added, 'Or maybe she's just a businesswoman who doesn't want sex assault on her CV.'

'The way I see it,' Strickland went on, 'is we just keep grinding away. I'll keep Bradby's team looking for the car, Higgs and his crew working the street angle, while you two start checking software companies. And you're gonna check out this other Plato's Cave, right?'

'A new boutique brothel in Collingwood,' Rita explained. 'I'll drop in tomorrow.'

'Fine. But the smartcard could turn out to be the best lead after all. If we pin down its source it might give us a direct line to the offender.'

'Fair enough,' said Rita. 'And I'm going to begin with Xanthus. Even if Kelly's injuries are just coincidence, it gives me a starting point.'

Strickland rubbed his eyelids tiredly. 'Why does this make me nervous?'

'Because you're twitchy?' Rita offered.

'No, because I know what you're like,' he countered. 'You've already got your wrist slapped for going after one prominent target. I owe you a favour, so I'll protect your back as best I can. But if you try to interrogate someone as high-profile as Martin Barbie, you'll stir up a shit-storm beyond my control.'

'Relax,' she told him. 'I'm just doing background checks at this stage, and so far nothing's been flagged up. No MX-5s owned by him or his employees. But something in Kelly's attitude has aroused my curiosity. Barbie's hosting an awards ceremony tonight at Crown Casino and I plan to be part of the audience, no more than that.'

21

A storm crackled in the night sky as Rita parked her car and hurried along the river promenade to the awards ceremony. The tops of buildings gleamed like geometric crystals in the flashes of lightning. And high above the riverbank, reflecting the glare, was the cylindrical tower of the casino complex, rising like a citadel amid a sprawl of clubs, cinemas, gambling halls and theme bars radiant with neon.

By the time she made it into the reception venue proceedings were underway. Rita flashed her badge at a security guard and slipped into the auditorium through a side entrance. There in the spotlight, standing before the podium, was Martin Barbie. He was gazing down over a sea of faces from the advertising industry, delivering the opening address. This was the first time she'd seen him in the flesh, but it was obvious he had presence. Still in his early thirties, Barbie was well-built and broad-shouldered in his tailored dinner suit, his face tanned and chiselled like that of a sporting hero. As a television personality he was supremely polished, as a businessman, sharp and disciplined. But Rita suspected that, more than most, Barbie knew appearances were deceptive. Glamour, charm, the lure of the superficial were his stock in trade. Even his surname was deceptive, an anglicised version of the original. Although he'd been born in Australia, his father was Estonian, with a fierce reputation and a questionable past. In Rita's opinion, it was unlikely that Barbie had emerged from his childhood unscathed.

He'd been invited to speak on the values of modern salesmanship, and no one was more expert at proclaiming the gospel of the media, extolling the virtues of mass communications. Tonight he was in an evangelical mood, despite the fact he was preaching to the converted.

Rita accepted the offer of a chair from a waiter and settled down to listen.

'I feel at home here,' Barbie was telling them. 'I feel a sense of community. A sense of purpose. We share a vision.'

He paused, saw the message was getting across.

'And what could be more appropriate than to gather here, in the middle of a vast entertainment centre. No matter what the palaeo-traditionalists of our society say, it's from places like this we project future lifestyles.'

Heads nodded in agreement above rows of dinner jackets.

'I remember the barrage of criticism when this complex was built. They said it was crass, in bad taste. They opined that the elegant charms of the city were being sacrificed to the vices of the consumer society. Reactionary rubbish. These are the arguments of people who feel nostalgia for an era that produced ice boxes, gramophone records, Bakelite phones, two global wars, and a depression. The sort of people who advocate an authoritarian society. Everybody in his or her determined place. Minimum skills. Limited prospects. Basic income. The economics of intolerance. Well, if it comes to a choice, I'll take the consumer society any day.'

A ripple of laughter.

Barbie gave a nod of appreciation.

'Take a stroll around the amazing facilities of this complex and what do you see? The dynamic of social wealth? Certainly. The tangible rewards of a free market economy? Definitely. Or, as its critics suggest, a temple to mammon? Perhaps. Undeniably it's devoted to the secular – a place where people can shop, dine, party, enjoy a concert, a cabaret, take in a movie, try their luck at the gaming tables. Commerce at every turn. But I'll tell you what you see here above anything else. Something fundamental. Human happiness. People spending money and having fun. Individuals satisfying their needs in a way no earlier society could grant. If that's a consumer paradise, then great. If it's a neon temple to the god of entertainment, why not? After thousands of years of struggle, human beings deserve it.'

A wave of spontaneous applause.

Rita couldn't help being impressed. Even though she objected strongly to his theme, she could see he was delivering it with charismatic flair. That in itself was a rare talent.

Barbie hurried towards his closing remarks, his voice resonating with conviction.

'All of you here tonight play a role in pushing the boundaries of human fulfilment. For all the bad-mouthing it gets, advertising is one of the driving forces of social motivation and development. And more than that. It's art. It's psychology. It's mind games – the semiotics of the future – or to borrow an idea from John Lennon, it's the projection of images onto the blue screen of the cosmos. So congratulate yourselves. Be proud of what you do. The images you manipulate are more than marketing tools. They project reality. They reinvent it. They change our perception of the world. They help open up a frontier of individual freedom unattainable in all the centuries past. Forget Babylon and Byzantium. Forget the British Empire. The past is a place dominated by the hierarchy of indulgence. The self-gratification of elites. In contrast, the consumer society breaks down class barriers and political divisions because it wants access for all. It's global. It's egalitarian. It's a democracy of pleasure. It's also the fast track to the future – and all of us here tonight are helping to shape it.'

The audience leapt to its feet, clapping wildly, each one a believer – all, that is, except Marita Van Hassel. She didn't applaud, but simply observed an almost dangerous enthusiasm. There was no doubting Barbie's ability as a communicator. However she was equally convinced that his message subverted the very notion of civilised values. It left her cold.

Rita walked out of the reception venue by the way she'd come in, leaving in her wake the sort of hero worship that troubled her deeply. When anyone was treated as an idol, her response was to look for feet of clay. It was partly because of her vocation – the deconstructive process involved in profiling – and partly because of her instinctive dislike of mass behaviour. What also bugged her was the self-indulgence of the idol himself.

She'd seen and heard enough for tonight. Her brief observation of Barbie in action had reinforced her decision to find out more about Xanthus, and with no other pressing line of inquiry open to her, she'd start in the morning.

For now, it was time to go home and catch up on some sleep.

22

For a while after his speech Martin Barbie basked in the admiring warmth of his audience, accepting the handshakes and backslapping from the men, and the appreciation in women's eyes. It all served to reinforce his status as a social hero, and that was good for business. It didn't bother Barbie that his heroic posture was a fiction choreographed by the media. In fact it was commercially satisfying. After all, his business was nothing less than the cynical manipulation of mass culture. The adulation of others simply confirmed he was good at it.

As people resumed their seats and the presentation of awards began, he lost interest. A long and repetitive ceremony lay ahead, and he had urgent chores to attend to. As soon as he could he slipped out of the hall, made his way to his car, and drove to where the inner city development merged with the suburbs. He pulled off the highway and nosed the car into the concrete driveway of his small computer company, Xanthus Software.

It was a low smoked-glass building with nothing noteworthy about it, apart from the vaguely sinister look of the chain-link fence fringed with razor wire and studded with security cameras. A uniformed guard sat in a cabin beside the tubular steel gates, which he opened promptly as he recognised the company boss sitting behind the wheel of his Lamborghini. Barbie drove onto the narrow forecourt as the gates closed behind him. Getting out, he strode through reception and climbed the stairs to his office on the first floor.

Two of his software developers were still at work, despite the late hour. Barbie expected nothing less. He was paying them huge salaries to deliver a virtual reality games package in time for a meeting with Japanese executives, and the deadline was approaching. As he checked his email he could hear them arguing. Their nerdish banter irritated him.

'It's important.'

'No it's not.'

'How do you know until I've explained?'

'Just shut up.'

'But I've been reading about brains. Human brains.'

'I haven't got time for this.'

'We've got some spooky stuff in there. Hippocampus, hypothalamus, limbic system.'

'I don't care.'

'And modern humans still have reptile brains inside their skulls.'

'Bullshit.'

'I'm serious, Flynn. It's a biological fact. The structures in our heads evolved over millions of years, from the brain stem upwards. And they're still in there – still functioning. Producing the same thoughts as a snake or crocodile.'

'You're weird, Maynard.'

'I'm just making a point.'

'Which is?'

'Brain chemistry.'

'That's not a point, you dork. That's a meaningless statement.'

'All I'm saying is we're playing around with it, and we don't know the consequences. We're stimulating people's brains electronically without knowing what the neurological effects are.'

'You're not making sense. Who's this "we"?'

'You and me. With this software. Plugging into people's brains through stereoscopic images and synchronised sound.'

'It's a *game*, for fuck's sake.'

'No, it's a computer-generated environment in which people are immersed.'

'Quite right,' said Barbie, interrupting them as he strode into the room. 'And it'll make a fortune for whoever markets it.' Tokyo had emailed the schedule. 'Will the software be ready in time?' he snapped, then stared ominously at the two of them – Bruce Maynard, lanky and sullen; Eddy Flynn, wiry and volatile. Both dysfunctional human beings, but technically the best in their field.

Flynn and Maynard looked at each other, then spoke simultaneously.

'Probably.'

Barbie pursed his lips. Was this a wind-up, or was a multi-million-dollar deal really in jeopardy?

'You don't need reminding how important this project is to me.' He took a deep breath. 'So failure's not an option. Nor are smart-arse comments.'

They slouched on their swivel chairs and gazed up at him with bland expressions – a pair of unresponsive geeks surrounded by their clutter of screens and keyboards and processors and tech toys.

'We're working our bums off for you,' said Flynn. 'For the past ten hours I've been chasing a paper trail because of a bug the test team failed to unearth. I haven't had time to fart.'

Barbie leant over him, unimpressed.

'Listen to me carefully. Timing is everything. Programming directors and software managers arrive from Tokyo this month. It's my window of opportunity to sell this package while it's still hot – before anyone else fills the gap in the market. So I don't want excuses. It's got to be ready on time. Complete. Bug-free. Best-of-breed.'

'Or what?' said Flynn.

'Or I'll have your balls surgically removed and pickled.'

'But there's still an endless amount of diagnostics to do,' protested Maynard. 'Source code testing. Integration testing.'

'Project artefacts,' added Flynn.

'Regression tests. Performance tests.'

'Function point analysis.'

'Code metrics.'

They were playing a game with him and he knew it.

'Unless you want us to ignore the usual benchmarks and quality gates.'

Barbie stood up straight and smiled coldly. 'I want you to get the job done without acting like a couple of propeller heads. Which reminds me – there are supposed to be three of you working tonight. Where's Josh?'

They exchanged a look.

'Well, where is he?' Barbie demanded.

'Out getting pizzas.'

'I'm not paying him to do pizza runs! He's the number one troubleshooter on this software so the game succeeds or fails on his level of input. Next time get the fucking pizzas delivered!' shouted Barbie, adjusting his bow tie. 'And when Josh gets back, pass on my message. Up and running on time – or balls in a jar.' He threw them a look as he walked out the door. 'Code metrics, my arse.'

23

Barbie had been gone less than ten minutes when Josh Barrett returned, juggling a stack of pizza boxes, chocolate fudge cake and coleslaw tubs. He was greeted with looks of despondency.

'What's up?' he asked.

'Barbie wants to castrate us,' said Flynn. 'And Maynard's got a reptile's brain.'

'That's not what I said.'

'And the game we're designing will boil people's heads.'

Josh dumped the food on a desktop among strands of cable. 'Interesting sales pitch.'

'He twists everything,' Maynard complained.

'You're the one who's twisted, arsehole. If anyone's got the brain chemistry of a snake –' said Flynn.

'I was just trying to make the point –' started Maynard.

'The point is you're weird. If you didn't know how to point and click no one would even communicate with you. No wonder you frighten women.'

'Go fuck yourself.'

With a scowl, Maynard picked up his pizza and went to the far side of the room where he could eat in peace and watch the highway traffic through the window.

'See what I mean?' said Flynn. 'No social grace.'

'And what about Barbie?' said Josh as they helped themselves to the food. 'What's his problem?'

'Shitting himself about the deadline.'

'Did you tell him it's sorted?'

'No.'

'Good. Let's keep him guessing.'

Flynn swallowed a mouthful of pizza and frowned. 'You can be a smug bastard at times. Don't forget I'm the system administrator on this. It's down to me if it isn't clear of bugs.'

Josh took a swig of Coke. 'It'll never be clear of bugs.'

'Are you trying to piss me off?'

'I'm trying to get you to loosen up.'

'But the test team . . .'

'A bunch of tossers. The bugs they've found are minor. They can be fixed with patches.' Josh licked his fingers and picked up another slice. 'There's only one important thing the test team's come up with.'

'What?'

'It's not a technical problem, but in a way Maynard's right. The level of input from the eyephones is too high. You should go easy on wearing them.'

'Sometimes I think you're as nuts as he is. What the fuck are you talking about?'

'The game's addictive. Gives you a physical buzz.'

Flynn stared at him dubiously. 'That's priceless from someone hooked on dope.'

Josh shrugged and took a bite of cake. 'You don't have to believe me – but what a selling point. Makes your bugs irrelevant.'

'Yeah,' said Maynard, coming back from the window, spilling bits of pepperoni in his wake. 'I believe you.'

'Big deal,' Flynn sneered. 'You believe in aliens and the Easter Bunny.'

'I've got proof,' said Maynard, then realised he'd said too much.

'What proof?'

'Forget it.'

'No.' This time it was Josh. 'Tell us.'

Maynard shook his head.

'Maynard!' Josh insisted. 'Tell us what you've found out.'

He sighed. 'I went to see Huxley. He did some tests.'

Flynn gave a groan. 'You dipstick.'

But Josh was curious. 'Isn't he the guy you both studied under?'

'Yeah,' said Maynard brightly. 'Professor Byron Huxley. Computer science. Monash University.'

'And he did tests?' asked Josh. 'What sort?'

'Scans. Brain scans.'

'While you were wearing eyephones?'

'Yeah. Goggles and gloves. Me, and a few undergraduate guinea pigs.'

'Jesus,' muttered Flynn. 'If Barbie finds out, you're dead.'

'Sod Barbie,' said Josh. 'The scans. What'd they show?'

'Something weird. The wrong areas lit up. The game stimulates the limbic system – bits like that. Like I was trying to say earlier.'

'You didn't make sense then,' said Flynn, 'and you're not making sense now. I'm surprised Huxley could find any brain at all.'

'Get stuffed.'

'The scans,' Josh insisted. 'What do they mean?'

'They explain why we get such hard-ons when we play. It's not just the images – it's the software itself. It stimulates the sex centres of the brain.'

Josh nodded to himself. 'And that's why it's addictive.'

'Yeah,' said Maynard. 'And that's why I was talking about the reptile brain in our heads. This game turns it on – literally.'

'Maybe that's why it's so hot,' said Josh. 'Maybe that's the real selling point – but Barbie hasn't bothered to tell us.'

He finished eating, stood up and pulled on his leather jacket.

Flynn looked at him suspiciously. 'Where are you going now?'

'Out and about.'

'With Barbie on the warpath?'

'Bollocks to him.'

Flynn shook his head. 'Your crazy streak will stuff you up one day.'

Josh gave him a careless smile.

As usual, he was saying nothing, but still managed to exude a hint of something illicit. It fitted in with what they knew about him, which wasn't much. Josh had come back to Australia suddenly and under doubtful circumstances after a two-year visit to England – something to do with activities in the cybertech underworld. At first they thought he'd learnt his tradecraft as a hacker until it became obvious he was a fully qualified computer scientist. It turned out he'd once worked for the Defence Department in Canberra. They assumed he'd left in a huff or been fired, probably because of his attitude, maybe as a security risk. Too much of the bad boy in him. He drank vodka, lots of it, got chased by women because he was good-looking and irresponsible, and he did deals on the side in hot computer gear. Beyond that, his background was a mystery.

But Flynn was curious. 'Will you be back tonight?'

'Don't count on it.'

'Just where do you go when you're on the prowl?'

'The only place worth being at night.' Josh jiggled his car keys. 'The wrong side of town.'

24

Barbie drove back to the casino complex beset by nagging worries about the software deal. Though he'd sunk millions of dollars into the project, he'd known from the start it was a calculated risk, and each passing day took another sizeable bite out of his diminishing finances. Despite his assets and his image, he was short of ready cash and delving deeper into the pockets of his bankers. Another showdown with the bank in Sydney was looming but he'd handle that when the time came. As he brushed that prospect aside he tried to convince himself there was nothing to worry about. Any doubts about the deadline were nothing more than the nerdish antics of his design team. They were trying it on, that was all, and would deliver the software package on time. He would sell it to the Japanese, forget money hassles forever and become a high stakes player in new media.

With that comforting thought in mind he got back to the awards ceremony in time to present the top honour of the night to the Advertiser of the Year. 'Excellent work. Maximum impact,' he said into the microphone. 'Well done.'

He led the applause as the audience rose to their feet below him in a wave of acclamation. These men and women were all sharp and glamorous operators whose profession was to invent and reinvent glamour. And this was a night when they reaffirmed their role of convincing people about all the things lacking in their lives – such as beauty, health and happiness – so they'd go out and buy them. They stood clapping with enthusiasm and glossy faces above a sea of tables bristling with silver champagne buckets, glasses and the remains of steak dinners, as a team of waiters began clearing away the plates.

A few cheers and whistles rang out with the applause and echoed overhead among the glittering artificial stars that laced the ceiling. Yes, this was what he was good at. This was where he belonged.

Afterwards, champagne glass in hand, he mingled with the guests. The conversation was smart and the laughter boisterous. He drifted around the tables, networking with the executives, absorbing the gossip. But it was mostly the women, with their tight dresses and over-bright smiles, who gravitated around him. With each inviting look and each fresh mouthful of champagne, the night became less formal and his animal urges more imperative.

Doing a final sweep of the hall, he decided there was no woman he could take to bed discreetly so he said his goodnights and rode the elevator up to his private suite. There he threw off his tuxedo, loosened his tie and, phone in hand, stood gazing through the window over the dark expanse of the bay. He took a deep breath and dialled a number.

A woman answered, her voice silky. 'Hello. Can I help you?'

Barbie cleared his throat. 'Yes. Tell me who's available tonight.'

25

Rita's day began with three bronze-coloured masks lined up across her desk, and O'Keefe's thick, hairy finger pointing to one after the other.

'Toy shop, games shop, costume shop,' he indicated. 'Only one's metallic, the other two are plastic, but they all look Greek to me.'

'Yes,' Rita agreed. 'And there's no way of knowing which type the offender was wearing. Emma Schultz can't tell us, that's for sure.'

'So they're not much help, except for ex's,' said O'Keefe, who as well as being a prize-winning swimmer – his achievements were proudly reported in the police magazine, although photos of him grinning above a hairy torso coated with grease were a distinct turn-off – was a champion at claiming expenses. 'I've kept the receipts.'

'They're no good as a lead but they help with the profile,' she reasoned. 'It means the man we're after isn't into simple bondage, he's also acting a part. That's why he used the term "role-playing". It wasn't a euphemism, he meant it literally.'

'But for the investigation, the mask's another dead end?' asked O'Keefe.

'That's right. That leaves us with the card.' Rita cleared away the masks and handed him a photocopy of the Plato's Cave smartcard. 'The crime lab's given me a list of a dozen software firms to check out. We'll do half each. I'll take Xanthus and another five in a cluster nearby. You get the rest.'

'Okay, boss. What about the brothel?'

'I'll pay a call this afternoon.'

•

As Rita drove to Xanthus Software she was beginning to think Strickland might be right. She might have overreacted to Kelly Grattan's bike story. That would mean her focus on the company was based on a false assumption, and unless the smartcard had been produced by the firm, there was no tangible link to the investigation.

Security checks had showed that Xanthus was a small operation with less than fifty on the staff list. When Rita cross-checked the names with police files nothing jumped out at her. Along with an absence of MX-5s, there were no rap sheets for assault or sex offences, but they seemed a sorry bunch – several drink-driving incidents, some minor drug busts, and a drowning off Portsea. But two things interested her. First, for a small company it had a high staff turnover – a sign of intense pressure, if nothing else. And second, of course, the owner: Martin Barbie.

Apart from witnessing last night's performance at the awards ceremony, she'd seen him on television fronting his reality game show. *Gold Rush* was a competition in which contestants eliminated each other by appealing to the lowest instincts of the viewing public. People voted in massive numbers for their favourites, with exhibitionism, vulgarity, cruelty and greed all rewarded, while sensitivity was seen as weakness.

As for Barbie, she was no fan. Nevertheless, she found him intriguing. He was a darling of the media and got nothing but good press. No hint of scandal. No word of inappropriate behaviour. He was a winner. Hugely popular. A cultural icon. Yet he was too smooth to be true. It made her wonder what went on below the surface.

As she drove up to the front gate of the software company, she hoped she'd get to question him at some stage.

The security guard came out of his cabin, leaned down to her side window, and looked at her ID.

'Detective Sergeant Van Hassel,' he said amiably. 'How's life in Sex Crimes?'

'You're an ex-cop?' she asked.

'Yeah,' said the guard, extending a hand. 'Pete Pollard. I saw you on the news.' They shook hands through the window. 'I was a senior constable with the drug squad till the Commissioner shut us down.'

'Nice to meet you,' she said. 'Is the owner here by any chance?'

'Barbie the bastard?' said Pollard. 'No. He just makes flying visits to kick arse.'

'Why do you call him a bastard?'

'Because he's not all sweetness and light like you see on telly,' Pollard answered. 'He can cut you dead with a look, and he treats this place like maximum security, shit-scared of a breach.'

'I see.'

'What are you here for?' Pollard wanted to know.

'Just a routine part of the investigation, visiting all the software firms.' Then she added, 'Have you heard anyone here mention Plato's Cave?'

'Kavella's joint?' He gave her an odd look, which left her wondering if he was one of the former detectives embroiled in the corruption scandal. 'No, not a dickybird.'

The guard went back into his cabin and opened the steel gates. She gave him a nod of thanks as she drove through past the chain-link fence, the razor wire and the closed-circuit cameras.

The receptionist was partly decorative and partly paranoid.

'I can't let you go any further,' she said. 'You haven't got clearance. You haven't got an appointment.'

'Sorry,' said Rita. 'But I don't investigate crimes by appointment. Who's in charge here?'

'That would be the system administrator, Eddy Flynn. I'll page him.'

'You do that.'

Minutes later he strode down the stairs into reception looking flustered, a young man full of focused intensity. Dynamic but distracted. Presentable without being well-groomed – his dark brown curls were untidy, and he needed a shave. Yet there was something watchable about him – not just in the energetic manner, but in the agile physique and the strong, forceful face. With his dark eyes, smooth complexion and full lips Flynn had the looks without the personality. Too abrupt. Insensitive. He was wearing linen trousers, a Ralph Lauren polo shirt and an agitated expression.

'What are you doing on the premises?' he demanded. 'This is a sensitive security area.'

'So I've noticed.'

'Have you got a warrant?'

'I don't need a warrant to question people about a crime.'

'How do I know you're a cop?' he persisted. 'We're working on a multi-million-dollar project here. For all I know you're an industrial spy.'

She shook her head in disbelief. This was getting silly.

'There's my ID and there's my card.' She slapped them onto the reception counter. 'And I'll give you the number of police headquarters. You can check with my senior officer.'

Flynn calmed down a little. He waved away her ID but pocketed her card. 'What crime?' he asked.

'A brutal sexual assault that's left a woman blinded.' When he looked back at her blankly, she added, 'Don't you watch the news, read the papers?'

'Of course not!' he snapped. 'I don't have the fucking time.'

'Okay.' Rita looked around. 'Where can we discuss this?'

'Well you can't go into any of the private offices or technical areas. The R&D floors are strictly off-limits to all outsiders.'

'Anywhere will do,' she sighed. 'It's the human components I'm interested in.'

He looked vaguely confused, missing the irony.

'Okay. Come this way,' he said, leading her into a smoking area behind reception. 'No problem with security in here.'

He shooed away a couple of smokers and they had the room to themselves. It was one of those communal office spaces that were always untidy – plastic chairs and tables, ashtrays, disposable coffee cups, a scattering of computer magazines. There were also vending machines, travel posters on the wall and a view over rhododendron bushes and recycle bins. The air-conditioning blew around an odour of stale tobacco.

She declined Flynn's grudging offer of a drink and he went off and got a can of Coke from one of the machines. As they sat across a table from each other he flipped it open. She placed the Plato's Cave card on the surface between them and watched his reaction.

'What's that?' he said, picking it up.

'That's what I'd like to know,' she replied. 'Is it a Xanthus product? A security smartcard for a customer's new hi-tech system?'

He took a swig from the can and answered, 'This is a games company. We don't produce security hardware for any customers.' He tossed the card back to her. 'You're wasting my time.'

Rita sat back and stared at him curiously. 'Do you have a problem, or something?'

'Of course I bloody do! I'm the poor mug who has to shoulder the responsibility around here. I'm the system administrator.' He drank some more Coke. 'Frankly I'm too damn busy to worry about anything other than getting the project done.'

'What *is* the project?'

'Can't tell you.'

'It's obviously a software product.'

'Obviously.' He fidgeted in his chair. 'I can tell you it's a VR game. I can't say anything more.'

'VR?'

'Virtual reality. There's a shitload of money riding on it, and I'm the poor bastard who has to deliver on time. It all comes down to me.'

She sensed someone who was ambitious and impatient, also highly strung. She wondered whether he was the sort of emotional inadequate who should never be a manager – the type who was capricious, abusive and vindictive and believed the future of the world rested on his shoulders. What he accomplished as a geek he probably lacked as a human being.

She put the card back in her pocket and asked casually, 'Is Kelly Grattan back at work today?'

'No. Why do you ask?'

'I spoke to her at the hospital yesterday about the hit-and-run accident.'

'Well her timing's fucking great,' said Flynn.

'Who works closely with Kelly?' Rita continued.

'Barbie. She's the link between us and him.'

'When you say *us*, who do you mean?'

'In practical terms mostly me, Maynard and Josh – the core team. Otherwise she's up at Barbie's city office head-kicking his accountants and trying to outmanoeuvre him.'

'You don't like her.'

'She's pushy and manipulative – like a lot of women.' He made sure she got the point with an acerbic look. 'More interested in her own priorities than the team effort.'

It was a familiar theme, but her brief meeting with Kelly told Rita it could well be true.

She let Flynn finish off his drink then asked, 'Have you ever noticed anyone following her, anyone showing an unhealthy interest in her?'

'No I haven't.' He crushed the can in his hand. 'Now can I get back to work?'

'Of course,' she said. 'But I'd like a quick word with the other two you mentioned. What are their full names?'

'Bruce Maynard and Josh Barrett. But only Maynard's here at the moment.' He tossed the can into the dustbin angrily. 'I'll send him down, but don't arrest him for being a freak.'

Maynard entered the smoking room like a bad vibe – chewing his lip, hands jittery, his lanky frame clad in tracksuit pants and a Harry Potter T-shirt. He was self-conscious enough to be referred for immediate therapy, but Rita wasn't here to assess personality disorders.

As he sat down she asked him, 'Is your name Bruce Maynard?'

'Yes, what's yours?' he asked her back.

She told him and said, 'I assume you've heard Kelly Grattan ended up in hospital after being knocked off her bike.' When he nodded she continued, 'I'm investigating if she was the target of an attack.'

He didn't respond other than to wring his hands.

She went on, 'I want to know if she mentioned anyone who bothered her. Anyone who made her nervous.'

'Nervous?' He waved his hands around extravagantly. 'Check it out – this isn't an office, it's a pressure cooker! We're all nervous! Everyone here's a basket case.'

There was certainly something wrong here. Even for computer nerds these guys had a few wires loose. Add to that the reactions of the security guard and the receptionist and you almost had a case of group neurosis.

'So, Bruce, what do you think of Kelly?'

'Bloody sure of herself,' he said, his tone resentful.

'How do you get on with her?' she asked.

He blushed, then said, 'She mostly ignores me.'

'Why is that do you think?'

He bit his lip again. 'I have trouble telling her what she wants to know. Technical stuff. I can't put it in simple terms.'

'She loses patience with you?'

'Yeah.' He drummed his fingers on the table. 'But that happens a lot when I talk to women. I get embarrassed.'

'Like right now?'

He dropped his gaze and nodded.

'Okay. That's enough for the time being.'

As Rita got up to leave Maynard said, 'I've seen you on TV. You deal with rape cases, don't you?'

'Yes.'

'Must be mind-blowing.'

'Interests you, does it?'

'Yeah.' He gave her an inappropriate smile.

'Rape isn't about sex, it's about violence.'

'Yeah, I know. Like the guy who blinded the prostitute.'

Rita didn't answer. She just looked at him.

As she drove from the Xanthus premises, Rita wondered if the collective jitters were due to a multi-million-dollar deadline or symptomatic of something worse than corporate angst. She had no way of telling, and no legitimate grounds to probe any further. Her call on the company had produced nothing for the investigation, and now she must concentrate on the other software firms on her list. But as she looked in the rear-view mirror, watching the steel gates close behind her, she had the feeling the guard's remark about maximum security was somehow significant, and that those inside had something in common with inmates. It seemed her suspicions about Martin Barbie's true personality might have substance to them.

26

Martin Barbie peered down through the canyon of skyscrapers to where, far below, moved beetling queues of traffic and swarms of miniature pedestrians. Further along sprouted the antique architecture of church spires, dwarfed by the modern giants of the city. Beyond the office blocks, colonial buildings and shopping arcades, a thin ribbon of tramlines stretched along Collins Street to the horizon of the docklands. Barbie was viewing the panorama of the city from the vantage point of his business suite, occupying the thirty-seventh floor of the bank tower.

The voice of his private secretary came through the desk speaker. 'The satellite link to Tokyo is up.'

'Thank you,' he replied.

He stood beside the plate glass window, his feet just inches from a sheer drop to the street below. Sometimes he felt he was walking on air, or even floating in space – gazing across the gulf to other glass-walled towers that were planted in the sky. He could see them peopled by neat men in neat offices with their rows of desks and screens and potted shrubs – huge buildings that were human filing cabinets, or something more apocalyptic, the hollow mountains of Nostradamus. At night the vision was even more graphic, with the glass interiors glowing, the illuminated masts pointing heavenwards, a dusting of lights as far as the eye could see. There were silent moments when he felt like a lord of the dark, elevated into the firmament where he belonged. It was the nearest he came to a religious feeling.

'Tokyo says Mr Jojima will be ready in ten,' came the secretary's voice again.

'Good,' said Barbie.

His office was different from all those around him. Not a shrub in sight. Just a swathe of carpet between the electronic decks that studded his desk and an interior wall covered in flat-screen televisions, dozens of them, their flickering transmissions from points around the globe. A glass cabinet displayed his collection of TV awards.

'I'll be there in five,' he added.

Despite his personal, business and celebrity achievements, appearances were not all they seemed. In quiet moments such as this, alone with his thoughts, Barbie felt the nausea of self-doubt. It was nagging and persistent, a flaw beneath his gleaming surface, and each new success failed to erase it. And he knew why.

He was well aware of the illusions of the secular world. It had been beaten into him as a child, year after year in his Christian fundamentalist home, whipped into him with a leather belt, so he'd never forget. The metal buckle kept splitting the skin on his buttocks and thighs, his father shouting quotations from the Bible, in the upstairs bathroom that became a torture chamber. The beatings left drops of blood on the white tiles, the wounds cut deep in his memory, reminders of the shallowness of the world. And no series of triumphs could ever expunge them.

Barbie sat in his teleconference suite, conducting his private chat with Tokyo to finalise the schedule for the upcoming visit. The key decision-maker was facing him on the screen, going patiently through a list of questions. Kenshi Jojima's English was flawless, and his expression – even across a video link – was implacable.

'You can assure me,' he was saying, 'that the software will be ready?'

'I can,' answered Barbie firmly.

'And the problems identified in your last progress meeting will be resolved?'

'Yes. My system administrator Eddy Flynn and project manager Josh Barrett are the best in the field.'

'That remains to be seen,' said Jojima with almost lethal understatement. 'But what is more important is the marketing strategy. We shall need convincing.'

He had the stern, unwavering focus of a corporate samurai – a man who made a powerful ally or a ruthless foe. If Barbie were to swing his multi-million-dollar deal, he had to win him over. This man was more than a software expert. He was the company executive who would lead the delegation from Japan, and his team would look at more than the computer game. They would examine the entire cross-media package. If he had any doubts he could veto the deal. So Barbie was choosing his words carefully.

'You know my track record,' he said calmly, but with an assertive edge. 'My last reality TV format is now global. But this computer game will be even bigger. The high-resolution virtual reality and internet tie-ins will make sure of that. But what will guarantee high-profile media interest is the content. Believe me, Kenshi, this product will generate its own publicity in the tabloids, as well as online.'

'You are talking about hype,' said Jojima fastidiously, and Barbie noted the implied scepticism.

'Partly. But with all due respect, the power of the software mustn't be underestimated. You'll know what I mean when you examine it yourself.'

Jojima was silent.

Barbie folded his hands in his lap, breathed in quietly. He knew he was being probed in one of those disconcerting Japanese moments that wrong-footed garrulous westerners. Luckily he knew enough to keep his mouth shut. He didn't mind playing these oriental games of patience. In a way it suited his temperament.

When the moment had passed, Jojima nodded, they exchanged courtesies, and the teleconference was over. But as the screen went blank, a frown darkened Barbie's face.

He keyed in the mobile number of his system administrator and snapped at him when he answered. 'Flynn, give me an update.'

'I'll give you an update!' Flynn snapped back. 'The test team are a bunch of clowns. Where did you recruit these arseholes, Luna Park?'

Flynn's attitude was less than reassuring. It left Barbie worrying about how the software would stand up to scrutiny when the Japanese started testing it. It was a worry he could do without.

The voice of his private secretary interrupted his thoughts. 'Kelly Grattan's on the phone. She says it's urgent.'

He bit his lip and grimaced. This was a call he had been dreading. 'Okay,' he said.

'Putting her through on line three,' said his secretary.

He watched it flashing, his hand hovering over the receiver before picking it up. 'Kelly,' he said, trying to sound matter-of-fact. 'I'm glad you called.'

'I'll bet you are, you bastard.'

He bowed his head. This was going to be tricky.

Kelly Grattan was one of Barbie's most trusted employees. She was sharp, diligent and attractively venal. As the business administrator at Xanthus Software she was also privy to sensitive information. Her salary reflected that. A reward for making sure company data remained confidential. What he didn't know was whether she would keep her mouth shut about the attempted rape. He hoped she was open to negotiation.

'It's obvious we need to talk.' He cleared his throat with discomfort. 'I appreciate it's fairly urgent.'

'More urgent than you think.' The ice in her voice made him wince. 'The police have already spoken to me and –'

'Let me stop you right there,' he interrupted. 'Are you calling on a mobile phone?'

'Yes.'

'Fine. Then don't say anything more about the subject we're discussing. We need to have the rest of this conversation face-to-face. Not here in the office, of course. Somewhere discreet. How about my yacht at the marina?'

'No, I don't think so. I'd feel safer in a more public place.'

'Okay. It's your call.'

She thought for a moment, then said, 'Young & Jackson's pub. The upstairs bar. In half an hour.'

The line went dead.

He put the phone down and sighed. Kelly was out for revenge, but she was still a smart operator. Was she ready to do a deal to forget what happened? Sounded like it. If so, how much would it cost him?

27

It was a short walk of several city blocks, but Barbie was perspiring from the heat of the day as he waited to cross with the traffic lights towards the pub. Behind him rose the Gothic Revival spires of the cathedral. Schoolgirls in uniform milled around its steps. Lethargic shoppers strolled past. On public benches nearby, a group of Aborigines sat despondently. As he gazed at them, he caught the bleakness of their mood. Defeated by forces beyond their control. It bothered him. He looked away, loosening his tie and collar.

As the traffic rolled by the sun bore down like a furnace, making the air shimmer over the asphalt. On the far side of the intersection people sat in the yawning entrance beneath the dome of the railway station, loitering in the shade. In front of them a busker in faded tartans played on his bagpipes. The tune was 'Amazing Grace'. The lights changed and Barbie strode towards the pub.

It wasn't the sort of place he frequented but he'd been here before, years ago, during a student rag week. He and his fellow schoolboys visited the pub as a prank, wanting to get a taste of the seedy atmosphere. The bar had a spit and sawdust feel to it, full of deadbeats and aggressive drunks, and the boys had trouble holding their beer. The night became blurred, and Barbie found himself on the back stairs with a cheap whore. He gave her money and she went with him into the old-fashioned lavatories. In a cubicle, amid the dripping pipes and stained enamel fittings, she went down on her knees and sucked his penis. The experience – his first with a prostitute – was both daunting and exciting. It awakened sexual proclivities that he'd indulged in ever since.

As he walked into the pub he was pleasantly surprised. It had gone upmarket with a complete makeover. Carpets, upholstered furniture, American tourists drinking cappuccinos. He climbed the stairs and found much of the upstairs bar was now a fashionable restaurant. Kelly Grattan sat at a table beneath the pub's most enduring fixture – *Chloe*, a Victorian oil painting of a tantalising nude. In contrast, Kelly was power-dressed in a sharp pinstripe skirt and jacket, and a crisp white blouse. She was wearing sunglasses to hide her black eye, and she'd used make-up to cover her split lip and the graze on her chin. A pair of long gloves concealed the injuries to her wrists and hands.

Barbie sat down opposite her and glanced around the bar to check if anyone had recognised him. No one was paying attention. He turned to her and gave a nervous smile.

She looked at him coldly and said, 'I don't want to discuss what happened. Is that clear?'

He nodded, and she went on, 'You're a complete shit. You know that? No scruples or morals. I'm amazed how corrupt you are.'

There was no point in arguing, but he said quietly, 'What have you told the police?'

'Nothing. *Yet.*'

He brushed a bead of sweat from his cheek and breathed a little more easily. 'So.' He tried to sound forceful but amenable. 'You phoned me before you went to hospital, and you phoned me after. I'm here and I'm listening.'

'No.' She folded her arms. 'You first.'

Barbie liked her style and realised why he'd employed her. Perhaps the best tactic was directness.

'What will it take to keep your mouth shut?' he asked. 'What do you want?'

She gave a bitter grunt. 'That's more like it. We're beyond finesse.' Her gaze didn't shift from his face. 'So, for not going to the police, I want one million dollars.'

His mouth fell open. 'You've got to be joking. A million?'

Just a twitch of the lip – the faintest hint of a smile – before she added, 'And for not going to the media, another one million dollars.'

He stared at her, trying to gauge how serious she was, but her expression was like stone.

'Two million bucks.' His voice was deliberate. 'I can find other solutions much cheaper than that.'

'Before you start making threats, here's something for you to think about.' She bent towards him across the table, the drift of her perfume teasing him as she whispered, 'I've processed a series of emails. Unless I key in a command every three hours, they'll go automatically to the police, the tabloids, the networks, and my lawyers.'

He stroked his chin thoughtfully, already calculating damage control.

She continued, her voice still low, 'And don't assume there's no evidence. I have samples of DNA, stored and ready for collection.'

His shoulders sagged a little, but he didn't say anything. Just turned and gazed out the window. A queue of trams was banked up at the intersection. Passengers clambered on and off. At the kerbside a cop was cautioning a pedestrian. He'd ignored a red light. The pedestrian swore and gesticulated, so the cop booked him. On the far corner, the street musician was still blowing on his bagpipes. Barbie watched it all, the mundane flow of urban life, and knew that she had him beaten. He almost admired her.

'The figure's non-negotiable,' she said. 'But look at it this way. Your reputation's worth a lot more. And your deal with Tokyo will end up making you a billionaire.'

Clever woman. She was flattering him, but she was also right. With his eyes still on the scene below the window, he said, 'When do you delete the emails?'

She opened her handbag, took out a slip of paper and pushed it in front of him.

'This is the number of a Malaysian bank account. When the money's cleared, and I'm overseas, I'll delete them.'

He looked at her heavily, as if to question whether he could trust her.

'You know I can keep a secret,' she said. 'And with adequate financial compensation, there's no need for me to go public.'

He nodded. Game over.

'I'll arrange a money transfer as soon as I'm back at the office.' He pocketed the slip of paper and allowed himself a modest smile. 'It's a rare thing that I'm made to pay for my sins. Considering the price, it's just as well.'

'Sins?' She closed her handbag with a click. 'You're guilty of crimes. And one day they'll catch up with you.'

'Whatever.' He shrugged. 'But we're both too pragmatic to bother with guilt. It's just another control mechanism.'

As they got up from the table she looked at him with contempt. 'Well don't be smug about it.'

28

Rita's visits to the other five software companies proved as unhelpful to the investigation as Xanthus. What set Barbie's outfit apart from the rest was the level of security and the accompanying air of paranoia. She made a mental note to do a follow-up interview with Kelly Grattan, but for now this line of inquiry was over.

O'Keefe had just phoned her. He'd also drawn a blank with his list of software firms and Strickland had recalled him to the office and assigned him to other duties. The hunt for Emma Schultz's attacker was already being cut back. Rita could see she'd soon be joining O'Keefe back in the squad room. She had just one last place to check out – the brothel.

It was one of those substantial, late colonial residences that had once formed part of a terrace. Now it stood in isolation between a wood merchant's and a scrap metal business. The house had long ceased to be residential, but it still seemed out of place in a neighbourhood of wholesale firms and warehouses. With its neat exterior and fresh white paintwork the building had a professional air to it – as if it might belong to a consultant physician or a well-heeled solicitor. Only the gleaming red light over the side entrance told otherwise. That and the discreet neon sign that said 'Plato's Cave'.

Rita rang the bell and waited for the door to open. She guessed she was being observed through a small security camera, and wondered what they'd make of a woman in a charcoal grey suit and dark glasses. She tapped her foot impatiently. The sun was hot on her cheeks and a smell of sawdust rose from the alleyway. When a buzzer sounded she pushed the door open and went inside. As it clicked shut behind her she took off her sunglasses.

She was standing in a small entrance lobby with thick pile carpet, dim lighting and a reception desk. No one was sitting at it. On a small side table rested a Greek bronze of a couple about to engage in coitus. Soft orchestral music played in the background. Next to the reception desk was an archway. Rita walked through it into what looked like a waiting room. The decor was more refined than that of other brothels she'd visited. A mixture of classical chic and restrained vulgarity. More bronzes of naked couples, a wall mosaic of Aphrodite, amphoras with erotic scenes. A gilt chandelier hung overhead and leather sofas stood at right angles, but no customers were waiting for service.

An internal door opened and a woman walked through. She was wearing a professional smile and what looked like a black Versace gown. The dress had a thigh-high slash and a low-cut lace bodice that opened on a plunging cleavage. It was the wrong time of day for such fashion, but then again, it was the right place for it. The woman looked charming and expensive. Self-assured, late thirties, with a strong, handsome face and high Slavic cheekbones. Her eyes shot an appraising glance over Rita.

'How can I help you?' the woman asked.

'I'm here to see the manager,' said Rita.

'I'm the manager. Come into my office,' she said, then turned and led Rita through the door into a businesslike room furnished with office chairs, a computer desk, security monitors and a filing cabinet. In one corner a TV set was on, tuned to a financial channel, and at the far end of the room was a curtained window. The black velvet drapes were drawn.

The woman sat down behind the desk but didn't offer a chair to Rita. Instead she said, 'You're a little earlier than I expected, but that's good.' She folded her hands together and leant forward on her elbows. 'I like what I see so far. Let's see the rest. Take your clothes off.'

Rita stared at her, uncomprehending.

The woman's smile faded at the edges. 'Don't waste my time. Do you want the job or not?' she said curtly.

At this, Rita threw back her head and laughed.

As the woman watched her, the smile vanished completely, her mouth forming into a hard line. 'What's so funny?'

Rita smoothed back her hair. 'Who do you see me as? A Roxanne? Or a Jade?'

The manager frowned. 'I see you as trouble. You'd better just fuck off, honey.'

Rita shook her head, still amused by the mistake. 'I'm not taking the piss. And I'm not here under false pretences.'

'Who are you?'

'Detective Sergeant Marita Van Hassel. I need to ask you some questions.'

The woman sighed irritably. 'Shit. Why didn't you say you were a cop?'

'I was about to, believe me. But making the grade as a professional whore – that's the most flattering thing I've heard in ages.'

'Is it now?' The woman raised her eyebrows. 'Maybe you ought to think about it.'

'Is that a job offer?' said Rita, smiling.

'Why not? We've only been open a month and I'm still recruiting. You could earn a lot more than you do now.' The woman eased herself back onto the chair, smoothing her gown. 'I know what cops earn. I've already got several among my customers. Special discount offer.' She gestured for Rita to sit down. 'An ex-policewoman would be a great addition to my stable. And you'd outsmart your male colleagues a lot easier here. You know a man loses fifty points off his IQ when he looks at a woman's breasts?'

'That explains a few things,' said Rita.

'And by the way, I *do* see you as a Roxanne. Not a Marita.'

Rita gave a grunt and sat down. She was starting to dislike the woman. Too confident – and sharp with it. More like a female lawyer than a successful hooker.

'Okay. You know my name. I assume yours is Kasia Pozarik. That's whose name is on the licence as the owner-manager of this whorehouse.'

'Yes, I'm in charge of what is a completely legal and very profitable business in this town.'

'But you weren't always a businesswoman. Or legal. You've been round the block a few times.'

The brothel owner said nothing, so Rita went on, 'Kasia. Unusual name.'

'Both sides of my family were political refugees from Poland.' Her voice had an edge to it. 'But let's get to the point. What do you want?'

'I'm investigating the attack on a prostitute who was blinded,' said Rita, taking the black Plato's Cave card from her inside pocket and tossing it onto the desk. It lay there like an accusation.

'What's this?' asked Kasia, staring at it suspiciously.

'That's what I want to know.' Rita leant forward, her expression uncompromising. 'Is it one of your cards?'

'Of course not,' Kasia snapped back. 'Of what possible use could it be?'

'An entry card to some of your more illicit rooms,' Rita suggested.

Kasia pulled open a desk drawer, took out a small stack of cards and dumped them in front of Rita. 'These are the only cards I've got. Help yourself.'

They were variations of the pink business card that O'Keefe had collected on his travels. Simple and elegant. Edwardian script printed on the face. Along with the brothel's name and phone number, one version carried the slogan, 'For Greeks baring gifts'.

Rita gazed at it distastefully. 'Don't tell me. You specialise here – in Greek.'

The response was contemptuous. 'It's not called Plato's Cave because we study philosophy. Anal sex is one of our major services.'

Rita sat back and glanced at the black velvet drapes covering the window at the far end of the room. It was a momentary reaction, but an obvious one to the other woman's observant eye.

'Bother you, does it?' she asked.

Rita shot her an indignant look. 'We're not here to talk about me.'

'Maybe not,' replied Kasia smoothly. 'But if there's one thing I've learnt it's how to see inside people's heads.'

Rita lifted her chin and tried to outstare her. 'Well I do it professionally.'

'So do I, honey. And I know a control freak when I see one. The flaky type, who secretly likes to lose it.' She shook her head pityingly. 'A control freak who wants to be subjugated.'

'Enough,' said Rita tightly, putting the card back in her pocket. 'I don't have time to waste on crap, I'm trying to find a man who gouged out a prostitute's eyes. Is he one of your customers?'

'Absolutely not,' insisted Kasia. 'The scumbag who blinded the girl, I want him caught too. But he's not among my clients. No one with a hint of violence is allowed anywhere near my girls – and believe me, with my experience, I can spot the creeps in an instant.'

'Have you read the description of the man we're after?'

'Yes, of course, and he's a bit on the young side for this place. Our clientele is mostly more mature.' Kasia gestured towards the black velvet curtains. 'If you want proof, just take a look through that window.'

Just then the buzzer sounded.

Kasia glanced at the security screen.

'Ah. This must be the job applicant. You'll have to excuse me while I attend to business.' She stood up, walked to the door, then paused. 'Just a friendly warning, in case you open the curtains. Don't blame me for how it makes you feel. Some people see a sort of bliss. Others stare into the abyss of their own soul.'

With that parting shot, she went out and shut the door behind her.

It was a challenge Rita couldn't ignore.

She got up and walked the length of the room to stand before the black drapes. She reached out cautiously. As she drew them aside, she stepped back quickly, before realising it wasn't a window at all, but the reverse side of a two-way mirror.

On the other side was a bedroom. The decor was mostly in burgundy: matching carpet, chairs, bedspread. The lighting was sombre, moody, lamps on the wall. There was a recessed light above the shower cubicle. Filling the wall beside the door was a gilt-framed painting of an explicit sex act. The same act was being performed by the couple on the bed, just a few feet from Rita's steady gaze.

They were both naked. The girl was young, blonde, quite attractive, slim. She was on the edge of the bed – down on all fours. The man wasn't attractive at all. Balding, middle-aged, with a beer gut, he was standing by the bed, thrusting heavily from behind, the girl wincing and gripping the bedspread under the strain.

As she watched, Rita's mouth went dry. It was both obscene and compelling. A physically repulsive man using a pretty girl to indulge in anal sex. Even his ugliness was somehow engrossing. Despite her aversion, she couldn't look away.

29

As Rita walked back to her car, the side streets and alleyways were filled with hot afternoon sunshine and little else. There was no one about. Not even any traffic. The rows of locked warehouses seemed to sleep in the heat, the smell of bitumen rising from the road surface. All so quiet and mundane, as if the place she'd emerged from wasn't real – a dark, fantasy interior that didn't fit with its surroundings.

Her car was parked around the corner of an intersection. She got in behind the wheel, shut the door, switched on the air-conditioning and sat there, doing nothing, just staring through the windscreen. Letting the cool air blow over her face and neck.

After a while she shook herself out of the trance and glanced around. At least there were signs of human activity here. On one corner a milk bar. The subdued ding of its bell followed a customer out the door. It was an elderly woman, weighed down with shopping bags, a scarf over her head, her shoulders stooped, walking slowly away. On the opposite corner, people were sitting at the tables of a pavement cafe, umbrellas shading them, drinking coffee, eating sandwiches, reading newspapers. At one table a man and a woman were chatting casually. Office workers by the look of them, nodding, shrugging, exchanging gossip. And sitting on her own, a teenage girl – the cafe's waitress – sunning herself, smoking a cigarette and looking bored.

Rita relaxed a little. The scene had a drowsy appeal to it, full of the dull normality of the world. A new model BMW drew up beside her. She recognised the man at the wheel. He was wearing a suit, a white shirt and a neatly knotted tie, the picture of respectability.

But in the past half-hour she'd seen his bald head gleaming with sweat, his beer gut wobbling, as he had his way with a prostitute. He looked each way, checking the traffic, then accelerated off, putting distance between himself and the brothel. A moment later his car was out of sight.

Her mobile started ringing, and to her surprise the call was from Detective Inspector Jim Proctor, head of Taskforce Nero, the secret operation set up to track Tony Kavella.

'I need your help,' he said. 'How quickly can you get to Fioretto's Restaurant in the city?'

'Ten minutes,' she said.

'Good. But don't go near the front of the restaurant. We've got a surveillance point on the opposite side of Bourke Street.'

'Okay,' she said, and listened to his instructions on how to approach it.

30

Rita drove fast into the city, found a parking space near the top end of Chinatown, and rushed on foot to an alley that threaded its way to the rear of a fast-food outlet. A panel van with tinted windows was conspicuously out of place at the end of the alley. Its door slid open and an officer she didn't recognise led her swiftly up two flights of fire escape stairs and into a room with a view over the busy street below. Inside the room were Proctor, members of his taskforce, surveillance equipment and a pervasive smell of hamburgers.

'Great, you made it,' he said. 'I've got a job for you if you think you're up to it, but we've got to move quickly.'

'Tell me,' said Rita.

'Let me brief you first,' said Proctor, more animated than usual as he led her through a jumble of cables and listening devices to a front window. Detectives with headphones squatted on their haunches doing nothing.

Proctor pointed through the lace curtains. 'We've got direct line of sight to Fioretto's.' Rita looked through the window to the elegant Italian restaurant on the opposite side of the road as he went on. 'Notice the three stretch limos parked outside? They belong to Tony Kavella, Victor Yang and Paolo Fazio.'

She was beginning to realise what this was about. 'I see.' Three of the biggest names in the underworld were meeting together, the heads of three rival crime gangs.

'Kavella's playing host to the Triads and the Calabrian mafia, our local axis of evil,' Proctor explained. 'He's commandeered the upstairs dining room, while their goons police the downstairs entrance.'

Rita noticed the figure of Kavella's chief lieutenant, Brendan Moyle, looming just inside the door, his eyes scanning pedestrians as they passed.

'I'm assuming you've got a problem,' she said.

'You're damn right,' said Proctor. 'This is an unprecedented criminal summit on neutral turf, as brazen as they can get. It's also a golden opportunity to gain intelligence. We've got all three cars tagged with listening and tracking devices, but we're not hearing a thing from inside the restaurant.'

'Why not?' she asked.

'Kavella's dropped some sort of electronic curtain in the dining room, back and front, a jamming device that blocks our long-range mikes.' Proctor's frustration was showing. 'But this is a unique chance to eavesdrop on them, so I've got to try something. That's where you come in.'

'Go on,' said Rita.

'I want you to gatecrash.'

She looked at him dubiously. 'Won't that be counterproductive?'

'There's a risk of that,' Proctor admitted, 'but it might achieve what I want. In fact, you're the only one who might be able to pull it off. Let me explain. I need somebody to bug the dining room – to plant a short-distance, high-performance digital microwave transmitter. I've already got the receiver in the bistro directly below. It's between the feet of two undercover officers who are busy flirting and pigging out.' He sighed. 'But I haven't been able to get anyone upstairs to plant the bug. It's embedded in this wine list.'

He handed her a leather-bound folder from Fioretto's.

'Exactly *how* am I supposed to get away with what you're asking?' said Rita.

'I'll leave you to improvise the details,' he answered, 'but I suggest a frontal assault. If you can barge your way through the hoods downstairs, and past the lone goon on guard outside the dining room upstairs, I think Kavella will assume you're doing your maverick bit again, especially after the feedback he's got. It wouldn't hurt if you ham it up a bit.'

'You're asking a lot,' said Rita, 'after what you told Jack Loftus about no provocation.'

'If you don't want to do it –' Proctor began.

'I just want Jack brought up to speed,' she interrupted.

'As soon as practical,' Proctor agreed. 'One final thing. Your role is twofold – to plant a bug and drop a stink bomb. I want you to mention the Delos Club, almost as a throwaway line.'

'Won't that spook them?'

'It should certainly get a reaction, which is what I want.'

'And how am I supposed to have heard about it?' she asked.

'It's been blabbed about in public at least once. One of Kavella's henchmen shot off his mouth at a Grand Final party.'

'What happened to him?'

'He retired after being disciplined – had his left hand fed through a meat grinder. Look, in case you're worried, I've got an armed response team in place.'

Rita looked sceptical. 'Is that supposed to put my mind at ease?'

Proctor shrugged. 'It means you're not alone.'

'As long as the bug works.'

'It'll work.'

She shook her head. 'All right. What the hell.'

'Excellent,' said Proctor. 'I like your style, Van Hassel. There's something fearless about you.'

'Only when I don't think about it,' she said.

With the bugged wine list hidden in her shoulder bag, Rita emerged from the hamburger outlet, crossed the street through the traffic, and strode between the stretch limos parked outside Fioretto's Restaurant. As soon as she reached the front door, the bulky figure of Moyle blocked her way.

'No tunnels welcome,' he said.

She looked up into his face.

'I'm going upstairs for a glass of wine,' she said. 'And you're getting out of my way.'

'Make me.'

She pulled out her police radio and spoke into it. 'This is Detective Sergeant Van Hassel. I want all available units to deploy outside –'

'Okay.' Moyle held up a hand. 'One member of the filth's not worth a pinch of shit.'

'Cancel that,' she said into the radio, and Moyle stepped aside, allowing Rita to walk in past two more minders. She trotted up the stairs unhindered, grabbed a glass of wine from a bar tray and, slipping the wine list from her bag, approached the man barring the way into the dining room. It was the Duck.

'Private party,' he told her. 'No one go in.'

She stared at him, glass in hand, the wine list tucked under her arm.

'I tell you what,' she said with more confidence than she felt, 'you let me pass, right now, or I arrest you for obstruction, call for backup and arrest everyone inside this room. Think about it, a full-scale raid, and who'll get the blame?' She let him consider, then added, 'The Duck will be fucked.'

He cocked his head to one side, weighing up the choices. Rita could feel her pulse thumping as she waited to see if the ploy would work. He must have decided that dealing with one cop armed with a wineglass was the most palatable option.

'No worries,' he said with a smile. 'I announce you.'

As he opened the door she followed him through, dumped the wine list on a sideboard and faced the three occupants of the dining room.

'Most sorry,' the Duck told them. 'Uninvited guest.'

'I can handle this – wait outside,' said Kavella, watching the Duck close the door behind him. Then he said to Rita, 'You must be fucking mad.'

She walked towards them and stopped at the end of their table.

'I get a bit mad when an ape like Moyle tells me where I can, or can't, have a drink.'

Despite her racing heartbeat, Rita was relieved that her first task had been achieved unnoticed. The bugged wine list lay inconspicuously amid the flower bowls and serving utensils on the sideboard. She only hoped the bug was working.

'Do we have a problem here?' asked the elderly Yang.

'She's no more problem than a bush fly,' replied Kavella. 'Not even that. No more than a maggot.'

'What we've got here,' put in Paolo Fazio, leaning across the white damask tablecloth, 'is a floor show.'

Paolo was young and slick in a red silk shirt and gold medallion. His family ran an extortion racket in the wholesale supply of fruit and vegetables, with connections to the American mafia, and several politicians at their beck and call. Yang, conservatively dressed in a suit and tie, controlled a lucrative trade in heroin.

'Who is she?' asked Yang.

Paolo laughed. 'She's the cop who nearly put Kavella away.'

'It's just a matter of time,' said Rita, and Paolo laughed some more.

With a calmness that was more acting than real, she sipped her wine and took in the incongruous scene. Here they were, the sole customers in a dining room that was a relic from the Art Nouveau era. High above their heads were leadlight windows and chandeliers hanging from a decorated ceiling, on the walls, wood panelling and Tuscan murals. They were sitting around a table adorned with fine crockery, champagne and gourmet food, and while the ambience was distinctly civilised, the occasion was perfectly evil. It was hard to tell which of the three had the most blood on his hands.

'Maybe Paolo's right,' said Kavella. 'Maybe we deserve a bit of entertainment.'

'Nothing that's bad for business,' warned Yang.

'Relax, Victor, this isn't business, it's personal.' Kavella eased himself back in his chair, his face expressionless. 'She did a profile of me,' he continued. 'So I did a profile of her. You want to hear it? *White female. Age twenty-nine. Single. Obsessive. Lives alone in a two-bedroom house. Unable to sustain relationships. Psychologically disturbed since childhood. Fucked over at the age of seven when father abandoned her. Suffers from Electra complex. Has compulsion to shove father figure's cock up her sexually uptight arse...*'

'You've made your point,' said Rita.

But Kavella kept going. '*Craves submission. Needs to be dominated. Fantasises about rape.*' He paused, then added, '*Destined to have her wish fulfilled, barbecue style, complete with skewers and butchers' hooks. She'll be hung up, like a piece of meat. Yeah, a treat for gang-bangers, three at a time, a pig on a spit.*'

Paolo was laughing again as Rita considered the explicit threat. She put down her wineglass and asked Kavella, 'Is your mother still disappointed at your failures as a human being? Does she still weep at night because her son is a university dropout and moral cripple?'

'My mother is nothing to do with you,' he replied.

'How is Nina these days?' Rita persisted. 'Is she still praying for your soul in the Greek Orthodox church? Does she still curse you for corrupting your younger brothers, Theo and Nikos?'

Kavella stood up, turning to his dining companions. 'Time to get back to business. I'll just show the bitch out.'

Rita also decided it was time to leave, but as she opened the door she paused and said, 'If these are the members of the Delos Club, it hasn't got much of a future.'

Kavella's fist slammed the door shut, preventing her from leaving. An icy silence filled the room. Paolo had stopped laughing and Victor Yang stared at her stony-faced.

'Tell me,' said Kavella, laying a hand on her shoulder, 'where you heard about that.'

'Take your hand off me,' she said.

He moved in closer, placing both hands on her shoulders and breathing into her face. 'You know, I could snap your neck like a twig, and I wouldn't even do time for it.'

Rita swallowed and said, 'You'd be a dead man, and you know it.'

'No one could tell what happened in here, and I've got two perfect witnesses to back me up.'

Hemmed in against the door, his hands pressing down harder, Rita was having to control her breathing, as her hand slid behind her jacket to fumble open the holster.

'So tell me,' Kavella repeated, 'what you've heard about the Delos Club?'

She thought quickly and said, 'It's what I *overheard* from your goons downstairs.'

As Kavella threw a searching look over his shoulder at his two guests, Rita flicked off the safety catch and pressed the barrel of her gun into his stomach.

He lifted his hands and backed away, smiling coldly, knowing she wanted to pull the trigger.

'We're all done here,' he said, resuming his seat at the dining table. 'But next time we'll meet somewhere less public. I'll look forward to that.'

Rita calmed her emotions and holstered the gun. She needed to leave before she changed her mind and shot him.

31

'It worked,' Proctor was telling Rita. 'You stirred up a hornet's nest.'

'And damn near got stung in the process,' she retorted.

'But you didn't,' said Proctor. 'And the only sting at Fioretto's was the one you pulled off. I've now got all three on tape discussing Kavella's blueprint and timetable for an underworld consortium. The information's priceless and I wouldn't have got it without you. We'll launch city-wide raids within a month.'

The debrief was taking place in the comfortable setting of Proctor's club, the two of them reclining in spacious leather armchairs, whisky highballs on a low mahogany table between them, oil paintings from the Heidelberg School ranged on the walls around them. The club, dating from the colonial era, retained the trappings and stiff etiquette of Empire.

'I've got Kavella under twenty-four-hour surveillance,' Proctor resumed, 'but if you're worried I can have an unmarked car posted outside your house.'

'That would only make me uncomfortable.'

'Fair enough, but I promised Jack I'd make the offer.'

'In all your surveillance,' said Rita, putting the Plato's Cave card on the table next to her drink coaster, 'have you picked up any hint about this?'

'No,' answered Proctor. 'But assuming the card's part of Kavella's operation, my bet is it belongs to the hi-tech fortress attached to his club. Some unsavoury characters have been exiting by the fire escape, which makes me wonder what they're up to in there, but none fits the description of the prostitute's attacker.'

'Well, so much for this line of inquiry.' She slid the card back inside her jacket. 'I'd better do what Jack tells me and back off.'

'Have you spoken to him yet?' Proctor asked.

'Yes,' she answered, 'and he ticked me off like I was one of his daughters.'

'Hmm,' nodded Proctor, sipping his drink. 'Some of Kavella's comments got to you, didn't they, like the father figure reference?'

'He'll try anything to control and manipulate, there's nothing new in that. But he's the second person today to accuse me of needing to be dominated.'

'Who's the other person?'

'A brothel madam.'

Proctor laughed. 'I think you can safely ignore both opinions.' He put down his glass. 'You'd be quite wrong to question your personal psychology. I've no doubt whatsoever about your strength of character, not to mention your acting ability. In fact, I'm convinced your skills are wasted in a detective squad. The intelligence you gained for me is like gold dust, and as an undercover operative, you're a natural.'

'Is that a job offer?' Rita asked. 'I've had another of those today too, from the same brothel madam!'

They both laughed.

'I wasn't thinking of my unit,' Proctor continued. 'I wasn't even thinking of the police.' He bent forward, lowering his voice. 'I was thinking more of national security. Your background as a profiler and an experienced detective would make you a perfect recruit, and it just so happens several members of this club hold senior positions with the security services. If ever you want to make the switch, let me know.'

Rita was smiling to herself.

'What is it?' asked Proctor.

'I was just thinking,' she said, picking up her drink. 'It's not such a bad thing to have a few father figures around.'

32

More than a week had passed and the investigation seemed to be getting nowhere. The hunt for Emma Schultz's attacker had produced no breakthrough. The fingerprints had still gleaned no matches, and nor had the DNA. The car was proving a fruitless and time-consuming lead, while the questioning of known offenders, prostitutes and their clients had failed to yield any likely suspects. No links had emerged to the bondage gear, the smartcard or software producers, and tip-offs from the public about the identity of the man in the Ned Kelly T-shirt had only wasted police time. As the lines of inquiry petered out, detectives were being reassigned to other cases. The sense of urgency and the departmental pressure for a quick result had dissipated. This corresponded with a lack of coverage in the media. The story had become last week's news.

Rita made another visit to the crime scene in a vain attempt to get fresh insight into the offender's mind. All it produced was a stilted conversation with her mini-disc recorder. As she crossed the lobby of the police complex, Strickland emerged from a lift, frustration creasing his face. Without breaking stride he shuffled a cigarette from a packet into his mouth and beckoned for her to come outside with him.

'God I hate smoke-free environments,' he said, lighting up the instant they reached the front entrance. He inhaled deeply, like a diver surfacing. 'Used to be great when we could smoke where we liked. Fucking bureaucrats.'

They went through the thick stone pillars at the entrance and walked a little way along the front of the building. Strickland nodded at a few of the fellow smokers loitering on the steps – men from another squad, officers in shirtsleeves, holstered guns on their hips, standing with that watchful nonchalance peculiar to cops.

Eventually he stopped at a discreet distance and said, 'Don't suppose you've got anything new to add?' When Rita shook her head he glanced at the recorder in her hand. 'That part of your anatomy?'

'I use it when I'm on my own at a crime scene. It's better than trying to formulate notes. I sit quietly and record anything that comes to mind.'

'Something you picked up from the Yanks?'

'From a profiler at the FBI. Sometimes it helps. Today it just felt like I was talking to myself.'

'I know the feeling.' Strickland sighed; something seemed to be needling him. 'I say: "We're here to catch ratbags and lowlifes." They say: "You're here to maintain core values."'

'Ah,' said Rita. 'Another strategy meeting.'

'Yeah, all bullshit, Nash presiding. It's all "ethical objectives", "proactive initiatives", "lateral thinking".' He took a heavy drag on his cigarette. 'I come out wondering what the fuck I'm doing here.'

Rita couldn't help smiling at his discomfort. 'Welcome to the twenty-first century.'

'Well it sucks,' he said. 'It's not enough to be a good cop anymore. You have to be aware of "sociometric factors".'

'Sociometric?' she said. 'Not a word I'd expect you to know.'

'As a matter of fact, I don't.'

Despite his irritation, the day itself breathed out a soporific calm. The odd cottonwool cloud hung motionless in a sky of intense blue. Leaves hung limp on the roadside trees. The afternoon sun gleamed on the metal tramlines running down the centre of the road as a thin line of cars moved lazily through the heat shimmer trembling above the asphalt. A queue of police vehicles was parked along the kerb where a dozen recruits were being instructed by a supervisor in the art of traffic policing. From the playing fields opposite came the resonant smack of bat on ball, accompanied by the competitive cries of schoolboys poised in their cricket whites. Behind them rose the bluestone structure of their venerable grammar school.

The peace of the day was abruptly interrupted by a screech of tyres followed by a crunch of buckling metal and shattering glass.

One car had slammed into the back of another and skewed across the road. The two drivers got out and started shouting at each other.

'Arseholes,' said Strickland.

The shouting died away quickly when, to the motorists' alarm, a dozen uniformed cops surrounded them.

'What a dumb place to have a prang.' As the traffic began to jam up behind the collision, Strickland blew out some smoke and turned to her. 'Okay. Let's look at where we are on the prostitute case. More than a week on and what have we got? The DNA doesn't help at this stage – the attacker's profile isn't on the database. Same with the prints. That means we've got a new offender.'

'Or one who's never been caught,' Rita put in.

'Yeah. And you've checked out all the interview tapes?'

'That and observed interrogations. I haven't spotted anyone who fits the crime.'

'Same with the make of the car. All the Mazda owners we've checked seem to be in the clear.'

'It bothers me we've been through the same exercise before with Mazda sports cars,' said Rita. 'The fact that it's exactly the same model and colour, a black Mazda MX-5, strikes me as more than coincidence.'

'So what? In dozens of other cases we've been looking for the same type of Holden or Falcon or Toyota. What's your point?'

'It wasn't just any other case. It's got an almost identical offender profile.'

'Right. You're talking as a profiler now.' Strickland took a deep breath. 'But the Scalper was a rapist and murderer who chopped off women's hair. You're not suggesting there's a connection?'

'No, no.' She shook her head. 'I haven't got any evidence of that. But it's a coincidence that's bugging me. Two psychosexual predators who mutilate their victims and drive the same car. It's like having two parallel cases.'

'Have you compared the DNA?'

'Of course. Two different people.'

'Well you've just shot down your own theory.'

'Don't rub it in.'

'I'm not having a go at you. Maybe what you've stumbled on is one of the great flaws of profiling. Projecting patterns that aren't there.'

'Gee, thanks.'

'Or maybe you're scratching around for a way out of a dead-end case.'

'That's exactly what a profiler's supposed to do,' she said sharply, 'especially when the most obvious line of investigation has been vetoed.'

He nodded uncomfortably. 'Plato's Cave. I must admit it would be nice to get Kavella in an interview room again. Pity we have to tiptoe around that creep.' He finished his cigarette and flicked the butt into the ornamental shrubbery. 'Shit happens.'

Back in her office, with no more evidence to follow and nothing new to add to the profile, Rita decided to resume her online browsing. An internet search for 'Plato's Cave' pulled up more than twenty thousand results. Of the couple of thousand linked to Australia, she'd got through about half, much of them drawn from philosophical or political articles. But as she ploughed on through them, one caught her attention, an academic group called the Plato's Cave Fellowship.

It was based at Melbourne University, where Rita had graduated in psychology. The fellowship was attached to the Philosophy Department, a place she'd never ventured into. But now she realised part of her education was lacking. She had a general understanding of Plato's importance but only a vague knowledge about the significance of his cave. As a profiler, she couldn't ignore the reference. What she needed was a brief, informed summary. Luckily there was someone she could visit, someone who might throw some light on the case by giving her a quick analysis of Platonic themes. It was the sort of thing he was good at. And he was someone who had nothing to do with case files or criminal psychology or internal police politics.

33

Rita sidestepped the shoppers darting along the narrow city lane of Little Collins Street and turned into a pedestrian alleyway lined with coffee shops and salad bars doing a brisk afternoon trade. She picked her way through customers sitting under awnings and walked into an old arcade.

It was like stepping into a bygone era. The tall, arched passageway with its tiled floor and gilt decorations had been built in the late 1800s and retained a quaintness at odds with the overblown malls that were its near neighbours. Its rows of boutiques included old-fashioned toyshops, family jewellers and tearooms. Rita's heels tapped the tiles as she walked past the display windows until she reached the cramped, dusty premises of an antiquarian bookseller. The tinkle of a bell sounded as she opened the door and went inside.

The first time she'd come here had been on one of her earliest assignments in the Sexual Crimes Squad. A member of the public had made a formal complaint about the bookshop, claiming it had hard-core pornography in its window. Rita had been dispatched to investigate, and discovered that the offending material was a shelf of nineteenth-century erotic art, with explicit engravings on show. She'd also found that the alleged pornographer, Dirk Hendriks, was an urbane and intelligent Dutchman in his seventies. Instead of cautioning him she'd simply suggested he remove the books and pictures from the window. He'd done so immediately, albeit with a risqué twinkle in his eye, before inviting her to share some herbal tea. Her acceptance had marked the beginning of a friendship.

Though his hair was white and his face was lined with the wrinkles of experience, Hendriks seemed younger than his years. Along with a refined maturity, there was a sprightliness about him, characteristic of a man who enjoyed life, even if he'd witnessed its worst aspects. One of the reasons Rita enjoyed his company was their shared birthplace. Hendriks had grown up in Amsterdam during the Nazi occupation, emigrating to Australia in the 1950s. Rita often dropped in on him to drink tea, listen to his observations on European culture, and hear his stories set around the canals of *de Walletjes* – Amsterdam's historic red light district. Hendriks was more than a good conversationalist; he was a link to Rita's lost heritage.

The musty smell of the old books closed in on her as she shut the door. For once Hendriks didn't emerge at the sound of the bell. The place seemed deserted.

'Mr Hendriks,' she called out, but there was no answer.

Although just yards away from busy city streets, the shop had a hush to it. With its stock of ageing publications, manuscripts, scrolls and parchments it seemed to belong to history rather than the present. The layout was also disorientating, the interior a miniature labyrinth stretching through three levels with a cast-iron spiral staircase running from the upper floor down to the basement. Everywhere were shelves stacked with thousands and thousands of old books. The most valuable and rare were locked away in glass cases. The rest, many of them leather-bound and the worse for wear, lined a maze of narrow aisles wide enough only for one person to pass at a time.

Rita poked her head into the oversized cupboard where Hendriks catalogued his stock and brewed his tea, but there was no one there. While she waited for his reappearance, she climbed the spiral stairs to the next level. Up here was where the antique erotica resided, along with volumes of lithographs depicting legends and the supernatural, and a section containing the classics. She often browsed here, feeling the bindings, sniffing the vellum. Rita loved books and these had a strange, evocative appeal – the remnants of past mindsets, lost cultures. She ran her fingers along the spines of textbooks from the Victorian era until she saw the one she wanted – an illustrated copy of Plato's *Republic*. Opening it, she leafed through the pages until she found what she was looking for, an engraved print of the cave. It was stark and sinister, a monochrome vision of hell, with a graphic scene of prisoners chained underground amid flames and grotesque shadows, their limbs and necks shackled.

The image jolted her. With a flash of recognition, Rita realised she was looking at a duplicate of the Emma Schultz crime scene. Now it all fell into place – the offender's remarks about role-playing and the rules of the cave, the way he called Emma a prisoner, even the bronze mask. The ancient symbol of Plato's Cave was the template for Emma's attack. It was a staggering insight into the crime, but what did it mean for the investigation? She needed time to think about it, although one subtle difference struck her immediately. Emma had been manacled, whereas the cave figures wore leg-irons. Too much of an encumbrance perhaps? Plato's prisoners weren't targeted for rape, after all.

The dinging of the doorbell told her Hendriks had returned. She took the book with her as she climbed back down the stairs to greet him.

'Ah, what a pleasant surprise,' he said, kissing her on both cheeks. 'I didn't see you arrive. Too busy chatting with the lady who runs the witchcraft shop. Are you here for tea?'

'Actually, I'm here to buy this book.'

He put on his glasses and peered at it. 'Not in your usual range.'

'It's to do with a case I'm working on.'

'You're investigating Plato?'

She smiled at his dry humour. 'In a way, yes. I'm here to pick your brain as well.'

'Sounds serious. We'll definitely need a herbal infusion. What's your choice today, my dear? Camomile? Ginger and lemon?'

'Jasmine, if you've got some.'

'Of course.'

Hendriks brought her a canvas chair to sit on and Rita waited between bookcases pungent with the scent of archival dust. He emerged with china cups, handed her one, and sat opposite her.

'So?' he asked. 'Why Plato?'

'He may be relevant to a crime I'm working on,' she said, stirring her tea. 'And I need you to put him in context.'

'Surely you studied some philosophy at university,' said Hendriks.

'Not really – apart from an idiot's guide for psych students. We covered Plato in about ten minutes.'

'That's a crime in itself,' Hendriks observed.

'Remind me, how significant is he?' Rita asked.

The bookseller sipped his drink as he collected his thoughts. 'How significant? A true hero of humanity. A superstar in the golden age of the ancient world.'

'Good,' she said. 'I knew I'd come to the right man.'

'Anyone today who values knowledge over ignorance, or seeks excellence, or strives for political justice, owes something to Plato. In cultural terms he was arguably the greatest of the classical Greeks.' He paused and placed his cup carefully on a shelf beside a set of obsolete almanacs. 'What's interesting, from your perspective, was his starting point, which was one of the worst crimes in the history of civilisation. We're talking about the year 399 BC. That's when the authorities in Athens ordered the execution of Socrates, the wisest man of his time. Plato was appalled. Like a courtroom reporter, he wrote an account of the arrest, trial, imprisonment and death.'

'And went on to write dozens of books.'

'Yes, prose dialogues. He was a writer and thinker ahead of his time,' said Hendriks. 'He also founded the world's first university – the Academy. Not the least of his achievements. His most famous pupil was Aristotle. Among his other feats he conducted political experiments, laid down principles for Utopian governments, wrote the first account of the legend of Atlantis and handed down a body of work whose key questions still challenge us today. The British academic Alfred North Whitehead described the entire tradition of western philosophy as a series of footnotes to Plato.'

'And you obviously agree.'

'Of course – and he gave us so much more. Our language of ideas, our concepts of mind, body and soul, our pursuit of the good, the beautiful and the true; all these were inspired by Plato. He was an intellectual genius.'

Rita placed her cup on the floor, picked up the copy of *The Republic* and patted the worn cover. 'I know this is considered his masterpiece,' she said, opening it to the picture she'd found and passing it to Hendriks. 'But this is the particular bit I need to know about.'

He adjusted his glasses and stared at the page. 'His most famous image,' he nodded. 'The myth of the cave.'

'Tell me what it means.'

'Plato is relating a dark allegory. It tells of people trapped in an underground chamber where nothing is real but echoes and shadows.'

'Like a parable?' asked Rita.

'Yes. It illustrates our common plight. Prisoners from birth. Deep underground, chained in a rigid position, seeing only the wall in front of us but not the fire at our backs. Mistaking shadows – appearances – for reality.'

'But where is it?' asked Rita.

'You're in it right now.'

She looked around uncomfortably. 'This bookshop?'

Hendriks smiled at her confusion. 'No, I think of it more as an occult chamber from the past. The cave is everywhere.' He tapped the picture in the book. 'What you're looking at is the human condition.'

'A pretty sad condition.'

'Exactly. It's our lack of enlightenment. And to find the truth we must break our chains, climb out of the cave and see the sunlight,' he said, closing the book and handing it back to her. 'I mentioned Atlantis before. That's another of his stories that still has people guessing. It's now part of New Age religion, but in a way it's the opposite of the cave. Let me explain it this way. Plato describes Atlantis as an earthly paradise – a place of amazing wealth, technological wonders and perfect order. But it was a heaven on earth that couldn't last. Human nature got the better of it and Atlantis was destroyed. Like the cave, it's an arcane symbol. Plato was challenging us to build a better world.'

Picking up her shoulder bag, Rita extracted the Plato's Cave card and held it out. 'It's this particular arcane symbol I'm worried about. And I'd love to know what it means.'

Hendriks studied the card carefully, turning it over in his hand. 'How fascinating,' he said. 'Where does it come from?'

'A violent crime scene. It was left there by the perpetrator.'

Hendriks shook his head. 'I'll tell you what it means,' he said gravely, returning the card to her. 'But it's something you know already. You're hunting an intelligent man who is also mad.'

Rita nodded and the conversation gradually moved on to other things. Then she finished her tea and got up to pay for the book. Hendriks patted her arm affectionately. 'You've shared your time with me. That's payment enough,' he said, then added with a frown, 'It worries me – the things you have to deal with.'

'Human nature.'

'But you see it at its worst,' he said, walking her to the door. 'I hope you're looking forward to a relaxing evening in pleasant company.'

'No. I'm on my own tonight. Soup, salad, and a bit of light classical reading.'

34

A steamy heat had settled on the night and Rita opened her windows wide in the hope of getting a hint of breeze into the old weatherboard house. But it was sticky and still, with no movement at all. Wearing only a T-shirt and shorts, she curled up in her armchair, the whirr of an electric fan straining against the humid air, the dramatic tones of *Carmina Burana* playing softly around her. From the open window beside her drifted the cloying scent of the honeysuckle that smothered the end of her wooden verandah. Within reach was the highball she'd mixed, and on her lap rested *The Republic*.

After reading the introduction Rita dipped in and out of the text to familiarise herself with the themes. She found herself agreeing with much that Plato had to say, with his focus on justice and knowledge, and his belief in a supreme Form of the Good. She was less enthusiastic about his idea that governments should be run by philosopher-kings. This struck her as unlikely and impractical, though it must have been revolutionary stuff twenty-four centuries ago.

When she reached Book Seven of *The Republic* she slowed down, reading and rereading the strange and mysterious passage she needed to get her head around. The speaker was Plato's old mentor, Socrates:

> 'Imagine people living in a cave. They inhabit an underground chamber far away from the opening to the outside world. They have been confined there since childhood, with their legs and necks chained. Their heads are also shackled in place and all they can see is the wall in front of them. Imagine a bright fire burning further up the cave behind them. Between the fire and the prisoners

there is a roadway with a low wall beside it, like the screen at a puppet show.'

Rita reached for her drink as she visualised the scene, swallowing a mouthful of chilled malt whisky.

'Imagine there are passers-by on the other side of the wall, carrying objects in the shapes of men and animals. As you would expect, some of the travellers are talking, while others are silent.'

She skipped through an exchange between Socrates and his friend Glaucon, who agreed that the only realities for the prisoners were the shadows on the wall and the echoes of the voices, then read:

'Let us suppose that one of the prisoners is released. He is suddenly forced to stand up, turn around and walk towards the firelight. All these actions cause him pain and the flames dazzle his eyes. It leaves him incapable of discerning the objects of which he used to see the shadows. And suppose someone tells him that he was watching a series of phantoms, but now he is closer to reality. Would he not be bewildered?'

Rita got the point about the difference between illusion and reality. In the following pages Plato hammered it home as the prisoner was dragged out of the cave and into the blazing sunlight. Blinded and confused at first, he was eventually able to see and understand the real world. But if he were to return to the cave, he would be blinded again, this time by the darkness, and what he told the other prisoners about his experiences would be incomprehensible to them. They believed only in their illusory world of shadows and echoes.

Rita shuddered at the theme of blindness. Emma's attacker seemed to have followed the cave's imagery to the letter, and it was likely that his next victim would suffer the same fate.

As she read on, Socrates ended the story on a hopeful note:

'In each human being is the capacity for knowledge. But just as it is impossible to turn the eye from darkness to light without turning the whole body, so must the whole mind turn away from the world of appearances. Only then can we see reality and the brightest light shining from it – which we call goodness.'

Rita closed the book and drank the rest of her highball, crunching the ice cubes between her teeth. It seemed obvious that the image of the cave had inspired the crime she was investigating, but what could possibly connect an ancient philosophical text with rape and mutilation? Somewhere there was a link, and she had to find it.

35

The compulsion had its own relentless logic. It was beyond reason, and yet was driven by an almost clinical rationality. It was a fantasy on the borderline of consciousness, a secret desire too dangerous to act upon under normal circumstances. But it never quite went away, merely subsided, or became hidden – like an encrypted program in his mind, or an attachment waiting to be reopened. Or worse still, a virus that could be contained but never deleted. And when his conscious mind was weak – from stress or stimulation, or when he was overtired but hyper – that's when it emerged. The worst time was in the early hours of the morning, when thoughts were random, sleep was elusive, and the darkest moods were the most intense. When morality was a fiction invented by a cruel and ruthless society, and all that mattered was power and the thrill of exercising it. The compulsion was irresistible then.

It was after three in the morning now and even the cheap bars and more sleazy restaurants were closed. The lights along the seafront shone their tawdry haloes into a steamy mist rolling off the bay. Homeless drunks squabbled on the foreshore under the limp fronds of palm trees. There was little traffic about, just an occasional car swinging erratically along the curve of the Esplanade, or slowly cruising towards the backstreet hotels with their flickering neon signs. He'd come here, restless and compelled by his need and excited by the danger.

He heard her footsteps first, the loud click of heels in the silence. Then her shadowy figure appeared, moving past the darkened pubs and shopfronts. She paused under an awning, looking towards where he sat in his car. As she walked over, he wound down the window.

She bent forward, her face close to his. 'Looking for business?'

Did she do bondage, he wanted to know. The answer was yes, and she got into the car.

He drove past the pier, the shuttered kiosks and then the rickety hulk of the amusement park – its lights out, paint peeling from the woodwork. Turning into a street by the marina, he parked beside an apartment block and she took him up to her rooms on the second floor. Once inside, he opened his laptop case and handed her the money. She was young and thin-faced with an obvious drug habit, but attractive enough to look at. She said her name was Nadine. He didn't care.

She led him into the bedroom. It was girlish and cosy – strangely incongruous with a street pick-up. A Chinese lantern hung above the bed, which was covered with a brightly coloured quilt. A teddy bear sat beside the pillow. There were soft rugs on the floor and lace curtains draped the windows. A dressing table was cluttered with cosmetics and personal treasures – framed photos, china ornaments, a brass candlestick. Among the jumble was an overflowing ashtray and a syringe. A peculiar mixture of innocence and vice.

As she dimmed the lights, he watched her, aroused by his anticipation of what was going to happen. The woman took off her clothes. Her body was thin and pale with small pointed breasts. There were tattoos on her hips and a metal ring through her navel. He wondered how old she was.

'Ready?' she asked, attaching leather and metal bondage equipment to the bed.

'Instead of dimming the lights,' he said, 'can we just have candles?'

'If that's what you want.'

She collected half a dozen candles from around the flat, lit them and switched off the bedroom lights.

He stripped off and stood there naked, penis erect. Then he put on a bronze mask.

She picked up a condom and gave him a perfunctory look.

He shook his head. 'No.'

'You've gotta be kidding.'

He spoke quietly, teeth clenched. 'Didn't you hear me?'

She folded her arms. 'No protection, no fuck.'

He took a deep breath and surrendered to the moment. She didn't have time to cry out. With one movement he lifted the brass candlestick and bludgeoned her across the left temple. The blow concussed her and she dropped to her knees, sagging onto the floor, unable to focus. He picked her up and put her on the bed, face up, strapping her into the bondage restraints. As she lay there, dazed and incapacitated, he climbed on top of her. Then, in a low crouching position, with all the force of his thigh muscles, he started penetrating her violently.

When he was finished he got up, still perspiring from the effort, and went to her kitchen. He rummaged through the drawers until he found what he needed – an instrument to inflict her necessary mutilation. His motive was trivial, but his actions were methodical and extreme. He turned her head and she groaned faintly. Her stupor dulled the pain as he inserted the thin serrated knife through her ear socket. Her blood trickled over his hand as he forced the blade in deeper, piercing the eardrum. He repeated the incision in her other ear, but this time the blade partially severed her carotid artery. The wound was internal, and the arterial flow poured down her throat as her brain went into total unconsciousness. Finally, he sliced off her ears, tossing them onto the floor.

When it was over, he sat on her bed, feeling drained but exhilarated. He didn't view what he'd done as monstrous but, on the contrary, as eliminating a monster – and in some primeval way, it was liberating, like a process of unbecoming. Decompressing his sense of self and throwing off the person he'd become. Venting the violence embedded in his character. He looked down at the serrated knife on the floor between his blood-stained feet. It seemed innocuous now.

Getting up, he looked at the woman spread-eagled on the bed, her unseeing eyes staring at the ceiling. She wasn't dead yet, but she had only a few seconds left. Her head wounds were seeping into the quilt. Blood was leaking from her mouth, though much more of it was flooding into her lungs. When the terrible gurgling sound stopped, he knew it was over. He sighed. That hadn't been his intention.

36

Rita was eating breakfast in her local cafe, a cup of coffee, croissants and her laptop lined up on the table in front of her. She couldn't get Plato's dark allegory out of her mind. There was something haunting about the image, shackled prisoners trapped in a fiery cave, nothing real but echoes and shadows. This was more than philosophical symbolism, it seemed emblematic of hell. Her mind became immersed in it as she began rethinking the profile of the offender.

Her thoughts were interrupted by her phone ringing, Strickland on the line.

'Nash wants me to bring him up to speed on the hooker case,' he said. 'Have you got anything new to tell me, anything at all?'

'Yes, I know what the attacker was doing with the chains, mask and fire, and why the victim was blinded,' she answered.

'Tell me.'

'It's not bondage he's into, it's role-playing. He was re-enacting a scene from the fourth century BC, something described by Plato in his book *The Republic*.'

'Why would someone base a brutal rape attack on Greek philosophy?' asked Strickland.

'Why indeed?' Rita replied. 'Why identify with any symbol? Why name your nightclub Plato's Cave?'

'I don't need a debate, Van Hassel, I need something coherent to say to Nash.'

'I'm making the point that all behaviour has a purpose. If we find out *why* our perpetrator turned the cave scenario into a psychotic fantasy, we should be able to pinpoint him.'

'Okay, Nash might swallow that,' Strickland grumbled. 'Anything else?'

'I've found another Plato's Cave,' she told him. 'It's an informal fellowship, an academic group at Melbourne University and I'm about to check it out.'

'No shit,' he said. 'That'd be a turn-up for the books – a lunatic philosopher.'

'He wouldn't be the first,' said Rita. 'After the university I want to backtrack a bit. Kelly Grattan's story about a bike accident still bothers me. I want to tackle her again.'

'You've got a point,' Strickland agreed. 'If she really was the first target she's a vital witness. If not, we need to be certain. Do a follow-up interview and find out for sure – without getting us sued for police harassment.'

As Strickland hung up, she opened her laptop, went online, found the university website and clicked on the appropriate page. The fellowship appeared insignificant, nothing more than a faculty club for undergraduates, providing an excuse for indulging in talk and drink. The website was full of notes from past gatherings, the venue for the next, essays, anecdotes and intellectual jokes.

She scrolled through them but stopped when she came to the 'Quote for the week' – a one-line comment chosen by the fellowship's founder and chairman, a Phillip Roxby Ph.D. Rita found the choice more than a little resonant. It was a quote from Nietzsche:

> 'God is dead: but considering the state the species Man is in, there will perhaps be caves, for ages yet, in which his shadow will be shown.'

Rita wanted to know more about Roxby.

A further search of the website pulled up a page with an official outline of his career. He was thirty-two, came from Adelaide, and had been to Oxford as a Rhodes Scholar. From there he'd gone to the US where he tutored at Berkeley for several years before returning to Australia. He currently held the post of lecturer in Greek philosophy. The page also listed a number of books he'd published on Plato and the Pre-Socratics, along with articles he'd contributed to various journals.

It was all very worthy and formal and didn't tell her much about the man. But a wider internet search threw up something far more interesting – a note on a radical student website. It listed alternative biographies of academics, including one under the epithet 'Caveman Roxby'. The comments it contained were far from flattering, describing Roxby as autocratic and manipulative, claiming his attention to female students was more than professional. He was also accused, in true Platonic tradition, of being contemptuous of democracy. According to the website's profile, he'd created the Plato's Cave Fellowship as a private fiefdom for the nurturing of his favourite students and the exclusion of the rest. Most telling of all was a paragraph on his personal life:

> To his salivating acolytes Dr Roxby is a charismatic highbrow. They make the mistake, highlighted by Plato himself, of being fooled by appearances. They fail to look behind the oratory, the designer clothes, the fast cars and city penthouse. While on the surface he displays the elements of an enviable lifestyle, underneath he hides the sensibilities of an unreconstructed caveman. All was revealed during his stint at Berkeley. While there he was promoted to senior tutor, made a tidy bundle from online publishing, socialised freely with his Californian students and married one of them. He fathered a child. Then it went bad. Divorced on the grounds of mental cruelty, the court denied him access to his offspring and issued a restraining order to stop him intimidating his ex-wife. After finding evidence of sexual and psychological aggression, the judge described him as 'intellectually brilliant, but emotionally dark' – not something you'll find mentioned in the university handbook.

The vitriolic comments sketched a disturbing portrait. Rita wondered if it was exaggerated. One way to find out. She'd meet him face-to-face.

Curiosity, as much as anything else, coloured her thoughts as she drove to the university. She parked in a street where she'd often parked during her undergraduate years. Then she crossed the road to the Melbourne University campus and followed the leafy byways and brick paths among the faculty buildings. Students with bags of textbooks and lecture notes sauntered through the archways. Another jogged past bouncing a basketball. There was an aura of calm – even in the sunlight on the walls of Tasmanian freestone. The old clock tower chimed the hour as she walked through the cloisters of the Faculty of Law, passing the camellia trees in their secluded grass square. She crossed the paved court to the Old Arts building, opened the door and went inside.

Roxby's room was in the Philosophy Department on the first floor. She climbed the stone staircase with its worn wooden banister and paused in front of the students' noticeboard. In front of her were the tutorial lists: 'Does God Exist?', 'Topics In Formal Logic'. There was also an offer of 'Free Meditation Classes'. Next to it was an invitation to a meeting of the Plato's Cave Fellowship at the end of the month, its subject for discussion: 'Mind Games'. Rita had a feeling that's what she was about to engage in. She walked up to Roxby's door, read his name on it, and looked up through the window over the lintel. Through it she could see the glare of the strip lighting, and the slowly rotating blades of the overhead fan – signs that he was in.

She knocked on the door.

She heard a shuffle of papers, then a voice with a soft, modulated accent.

'Come in.'

She stepped inside and closed the door behind her. Roxby looked up from the computer screen he was working on, a bland, accommodating smile on his face, no doubt the one he used for greeting students. Rita couldn't assume the radical website was accurate in its assessment – after all, he might just be the victim of student animosity – yet there were immediate signs of psychological wear and tear – worry lines around his eyes and furrows above his eyebrows. He was a man with ordinary looks and an average figure. Only his piercing blue eyes stood out in an otherwise unremarkable face.

'How can I help you?' he asked, his voice smooth and honeyed.

Rita walked up to his desk and stood there, looking down at him. 'Dr Roxby?'

'Yes, just as it says on the door. And who are you?'

'Detective Sergeant Marita Van Hassel, from the Sexual Crimes Squad. I'd like to ask you a few questions.'

The expression on his face hardened. 'I don't understand.'

'You may be able to help with police inquiries.'

He stared up at her, suspicion creeping into his eyes. Then he sank back in his chair, regaining his composure with a fatalistic shrug. 'I confess.'

'To how many crimes?'

'How many have you got?'

'A rape and mutilation.'

He sat up straight. 'I withdraw my confession. But you'd better take a seat.'

She pulled over a chair and sat down, looking around. Philosophy books lined the shelves, along with framed photos from Oxford and Berkeley. There were no family pictures at all. The floor was stacked with essay folders, and a jumble of discs filled a rack beside a laser printer.

'Of course, you're working on the blind prostitute case,' he continued. 'I've seen your picture in the news. So what exactly brings you here?'

'Plato's Cave.'

He shook his head, as if bewildered.

'The fellowship,' she said. 'The one you're chairman of.'

'Pardon my ignorance, but what are you talking about?'

She took out the card and placed it carefully in front of him.

Roxby picked it up, gazed at it and frowned. 'So, let me guess. This was found at the crime scene.'

'Yes.'

'Then I can happily eliminate your line of inquiry. It's got nothing to do with the Plato's Cave Fellowship.'

'You're sure of that?'

'We don't produce plastic cards. Absolutely not.'

She fixed him with a look, trying to be more forceful than she felt. If he was telling the truth, then he was right – this was another dead end in the investigation. But something about his reaction bothered her. A certain cavalier attitude. A surface confidence that seemed to hide something nastier – just as the Caveman Roxby description claimed. Despite the grim smile on his lips there was a dull torment in his eyes. She had an urge to ask him about his divorce. But that would be pushing it.

Instead she said, 'So what's your fellowship about?'

Roxby blew out a heavy sigh. 'We're just a bunch of windbags who get together once a month to indulge in wine, cheese and flights of philosophical fancy. We exchange a bit of banter on our website. But we put nothing on paper – or plastic. And as far as I know, we don't commit rape. We only mutilate the English language.' That glibness again. 'I suggest you try other establishments of the same name,' he said, handing back the card.

'Such as?' she asked.

He saw the gleam in her eye and realised his mistake. 'There must be others out there.'

'You wouldn't say that unless you already knew.' She folded her arms and observed him closely. 'So tell me. How often do you visit them?'

He said nothing at first, then gave a smile that was empty of humour.

'Okay, okay.' He raised his hands in mock surrender. 'There's another Plato's Cave in this town. Its name popped up when I was setting up the fellowship's website. And yes – I've visited it. And why? Not just because I like to explore the dark night of my psyche. No. But because the goddamn name intrigued me. A nightclub using one of the most powerful symbols of philosophy. How could I ignore such a sublime irony?'

'Obviously, you couldn't. But how often?'

'Three or four times in the past couple of years.' He smoothed back his hair. 'That's all.'

'When was your most recent visit?'

'Several months ago.'

'Are you sure it wasn't last week?'

'Of course I'm sure,' he insisted.

She couldn't tell if he was lying, but he was certainly uncomfortable.

'While exploring your dark nights,' Rita went on, 'did you pick up any fellow travellers?'

'What do you mean?'

'You know precisely what I mean, Dr Roxby. The nightclub's a glitzy pick-up joint, with dope and vice girls on tap. Men go there for drugs or sex or both,' she noted. 'What's your preference?'

He averted his eyes to contemplate the photos of his academic past, without answering.

Rita softened her tone. 'I'm not here to expose your private life or damage your reputation. What we discuss is confidential, including your personal proclivities, but I need you to answer my questions.'

'Okay,' he breathed out. 'I may have sampled the available talent, so what?'

'Did it extend to bondage?'

He hesitated. 'How shall I put it? There was a range of experience, but it was consensual, mutually beneficial and socially harmless.'

'So that's a yes,' she interpreted. 'And did it include role-playing?'

'No.'

'You didn't re-enact a scene?'

'No.'

'You didn't recreate a theme that appeals to you?'

'What theme?'

'The one that gives its name to your fellowship – the cave.'

'Of course not!'

Rita fixed him with a steady gaze. 'Have you met the club's owner, Tony Kavella?' she asked.

'I met him once, yes.'

'Did he invite you to sample anything more exotic than the girls in the bar?'

'No, he didn't,' answered Roxby. 'We had a brief but charming conversation about the golden age of Athens, after which he told the barman to serve me free drinks. That must have been a year ago, long before his arrest, trial and acquittal.'

'Very chummy,' she commented, but other than underlining a sleazy side to his character it didn't really take her any further.

'What about the new brothel called Plato's Cave?' she asked. 'Have you sampled its wares?'

'Never heard of it.'

'What car do you drive?'

'A Porsche. How much more of this grilling?'

'I'm nearly through,' she smiled. 'Who are the members of the fellowship? And how many?'

'Apart from me, there are thirteen students,' he said, relaxing a little. 'Eight girls, five boys – the brightest of my current flock.'

'How old are they?'

'The oldest is twenty-one, the youngest is seventeen and she shines like a precocious star among the rest of the first-year intake.'

'Starting young,' Rita observed, deciding she'd questioned him enough. She was about to stand up to go but, as an afterthought, she paused and said, 'What does it mean to you, exactly? Plato's Cave?'

'Are you asking for a free tutorial?'

'I'm asking for a straight answer.'

'How fascinating,' he said. 'A police detective demanding a straight answer to a philosophical question.'

'You find that absurd?'

'I find it a strange paradox. But if you insist.' He leant on his elbows, hands clasped together. 'Very well, the myth of the cave,' he began. 'The most famous passage Plato ever wrote, telling of prisoners chained underground since birth . . .'

'Yes, I've read all that,' she interrupted. 'But what do you think Plato's saying?'

'He's describing the human predicament. We're all prisoners of the cave. And we're all deluded.'

'So you'd say it's a pessimistic vision?'

'Not entirely. If a prisoner can shake off his bonds and emerge from the cave, he'll see the light of truth. Then he has a duty to return and try to enlighten his fellow creatures.'

'What does *that* mean?'

'There's the moral perspective. Maybe a message for you. Having attained virtue, if you want it to triumph, you must come to grips with the law of the jungle. Leave the light behind, and plumb the depths of the pit. Descend the chasm of human ignorance, stupidity and obscenity.'

'That sounds like *your* interpretation. But was it Plato's?'

'He was saying you can't trust reality. It's all in the mind.' Roxby tried to smile at her, but again his eyes betrayed him. 'Nothing is what it seems.'

37

Rita walked back to her car and put in a check call on Roxby's vehicle registration. She found out he drove a Porsche, just as he said – a midnight blue Cayman S model, with a price tag nudging $150,000. The car alone would rule him out as a suspect, though she decided to keep an open mind about him.

Next she phoned Xanthus Software and asked to speak to Kelly Grattan.

'She doesn't work here anymore,' the receptionist told her. 'She left last week.'

Rita hadn't expected that. 'Put me through to the system administrator, Eddy Flynn,' she demanded.

When Flynn picked up, he asked abruptly, 'What do you want now?'

'I want to know where I can reach Kelly Grattan.'

'So do I!' he shouted. 'She dropped us in the shit and vanished.'

'What do you mean?'

'She never came back,' Flynn complained. 'She cut a severance deal and pissed off overseas, nobody knows where.'

'When was this?'

'The same day she checked out of hospital.'

'Did she give any reason?' asked Rita.

'Apparently she put the squeeze on Barbie, claiming she was under too much pressure. What a joke!'

'Did Barbie tell you this?'

'No, it was Josh – the project manager.'

'Can I speak to him?'

'No, you can't, he's supposed to be finishing a fourteen-hour diagnostic. Get him when he's not on company time. I've gotta go.'

Flynn hung up, leaving Rita feeling frustrated. She was angry that Kelly couldn't be questioned again, and even more convinced that Xanthus was worth probing further. At least she knew where to focus next. If Josh Barrett knew something about Kelly's sudden departure, she'd start with him.

38

Josh Barrett was losing patience. Flynn and Maynard were becoming increasingly aggressive.

'The trouble with you,' said Maynard to Flynn, 'is you can't think outside the square.'

'Fuck the square,' said Flynn.

'You can't see beyond the box.'

'Fuck the box!'

Josh adjusted his headphones, ramped up the volume of the Rolling Stones and began to round off his marathon diagnostic. The pressure of the job was bad enough without pointless tantrums adding to it. While those around him got sucked into whirlpools of stress, Josh tried to rise above it. Urgency only made him go faster, with the energy of a hyperactive kid. But it was an energy that left him impatient with fools, bad technology and childish behaviour.

'Benchmarking,' he heard Maynard shouting at the top of his voice. 'A paradigm shift.'

'Shift it up your arse!' Flynn shouted back. 'And stop spouting American jargon at me!'

Josh increased the volume on 'Wild Horses' and tried to concentrate.

'You call it jargon because you're ignorant!' Maynard continued, his eyes bulging, his face flushed as he rocked sideways in his chair. 'You're in denial!'

Flynn threw a mouse pad at him. 'Autistic hoon!'

At last, just as Josh had had enough, he wrapped up his day's work.

'Thank God!' he declared, ripping off his headphones, logging out and pulling on his jacket.

'What's your fuckin' problem?' asked Flynn.

Josh rounded on him. 'Is this a software company or a kindergarten?'

'You can fuck off, too,' replied Flynn.

'Fine. That's what I'm doing,' snapped Josh, striding through the door and heading off to his car.

The steady flow of the traffic was a relief after the tantrums of the office. As he waited at a set of lights, the cool breeze of the air-conditioning on his neck, Josh let his mind wander back to his brief fling with Kelly Grattan. With neither of them big on commitment, it had only lasted a few weeks and had ended months ago, but he still looked back on it nostalgically. Beneath Josh Barrett's brash and reckless personality was a well of sensitivity.

As the lights changed, he wheeled the car into a right-hand turn towards home. He needed to get the workplace mania out of his system with a shower, a snack and a relaxing smoke.

An hour later, he felt no better. The pressure and sleep deprivation were taking their toll, and the hash wasn't working – not the way it was supposed to. Instead of a mellow feeling, it was sending a blade of paranoia cutting through Josh's thoughts. As he sat on his sofa, an afternoon soap on the TV, his feet on a coffee table, helping himself to cheese and olives, he became convinced things were going off the rails at Xanthus. Kelly's fast exit and the big pay-off she'd collected were among the warning signs, along with the level of deadline stress and the edge of panic in Barbie's behaviour. If the deal with Japan fell through, Josh would be out in the cold.

The more he smoked, the more his doubts darkened into a heavy mood of pessimism. The sense of an impending crisis lodged in his mind and the dope was intensifying it.

'A shit-storm's coming,' he said to himself, and there was nobody to disagree.

39

Rita stood at Josh Barrett's front gate. It led to a two-storey Victorian terrace house, white and in mint condition, with wrought-iron lacework fringing the upstairs balcony and downstairs verandah. The metal pillars and railings were also painted white, while the black and white ceramic tiles of the steps and paving sported a row of potted palms. It spoke of professional affluence. Parked outside was his metallic grey Saab.

She opened the gate, walked down the path and knocked on the door, banging the brass knocker. No one answered. From what Flynn had said, Josh must have been working since midnight, but surely he wasn't asleep mid afternoon. Then she thought, if so, too bad. The general attitude at Xanthus had left her feeling less than considerate, and she resumed hammering with the brass knocker, more insistently, the sound echoing down the hall.

At last she heard footsteps approaching, and the door was flung open by a barefoot young man in a tropical shirt and jeans.

'Yes?' he demanded, his face flushed, hair adrift, eyes not quite focused.

'Are you Josh Barrett?' Rita asked him.

'I am,' he answered. 'Who are you?'

'Detective Sergeant Marita Van Hassel. I'd like a word with you about Kelly Grattan. Can I come in?'

He was too startled and stoned to respond, so she brushed him aside and went down the hall. He caught up with her in the front room, the air thick and pungent with dope.

'This isn't convenient,' he tried to protest. 'What's going on here?'

Rita ignored the question. 'You worked closely with Kelly?' she demanded.

Josh hesitated. 'Yes.'

'Very closely?'

'We've seen a fair bit of each other.'

'Have you really?' said Rita, her cheek muscles tightening. 'Socially?'

'Maybe we have,' he said, still confused. 'I don't see what you're getting at.'

'Like to assault women?'

Josh stepped backwards as Rita stepped menacingly towards him.

'Of course not!' he shrilled, pushing his glasses back to the bridge of his nose. 'I don't know what happened to her.'

'But you know she wasn't knocked off her bike.'

'Of course I do,' he stammered. 'She doesn't ride a bike.'

'Thank you for that. I knew she was lying.' She dropped her hands to her hips and looked him up and down. 'So you're the third man in the core team at Xanthus?'

'I know what *I* do,' retorted Josh. 'But what's your special field – police intimidation?'

'Only when I'm in a bad mood.' She looked down at his ashtray. 'And if you're not careful I might be in the mood to bust you.'

Josh winced as if he'd swallowed something hard. The banging on the door had obviously interrupted him, and in his haste to ditch the remains of the joint he had spilt ash and knocked over the olive jar.

'Okay, can we just chill out here,' he said, overarticulating his words. 'What would put you in a good mood?'

'If you regain control of your faculties,' said Rita, 'and answer my questions.'

'No problem. I'll make some coffee.' Josh clumsily tidied up the telltale mess. 'You're right, I need to clear my head.'

She followed him into the kitchen, where he grappled with the percolator, then stared at her with renewed perplexity. The hash seeping into his bloodstream was giving him an oblique feedback on his predicament.

'This scene's a bit surreal,' he admitted. 'And I'm famished. Fancy an omelette?'

'I'm fine,' she said. 'But if you've got the munchies, go ahead.'

'Thanks.'

She was in no hurry, so she sat on a stool at his breakfast bar while he got a frying pan onto the stove and smashed eggs against a mixing bowl, covering his fingers in globs of yolk.

'Oh, for God's sake,' she said, getting up. 'Let me do it.'

Josh watched while Rita expertly cracked and beat the eggs.

'Want anything in your omelette?' she asked.

'Yes,' he said, pointing to the fridge. 'I want cheese and onions and bacon and mushrooms . . .'

'I get the picture,' she interrupted, adding the ingredients before switching the mixture to the stove.

With the omelette sizzling in the pan, she waited until he had drunk a mug of coffee before saying, 'Now, I know you're still a bit stoned, my dear Mr Barrett, but if you can concentrate, I need to ask some questions.'

'Fire away,' he said, 'but as you're cooking me lunch, you can call me Josh.'

'Okay, Josh. I have reason to believe Kelly Grattan was the victim of a crime.'

'What crime?'

'Assault and attempted rape.'

'Rape?' The colour drained from Josh's face. 'My God.'

He looked unnerved – a flurry of emotions passed across his face.

'When did you last see her?'

'Nearly two weeks ago.' He fumbled for a bar stool and slid onto it. 'The day before she ended up in hospital.'

Rita was watching his expression closely. 'Now I've got to ask you this formally. Did you hit Kelly Grattan?'

Anger flared in his eyes. 'No!'

'Did you sexually assault her?'

He beat the breakfast bar with his clenched fist. 'Of course I didn't! Kelly and I are . . .' He hesitated.

'What?'

'Friends.'

'You have a relationship?'

'Depends on your definition.'

'Sex.'

'Yes, but . . .'

'Tell me.'

'There was no pressure, no commitments, and we kept it to ourselves.' Josh shook his head. 'No one at Xanthus knows and it ended months ago.'

'Why did it end?' asked Rita.

'We both moved on,' he shrugged. 'You wouldn't ask if you knew her reputation.'

'Enlighten me.'

'She's known as a man-eater,' explained Josh. 'But I didn't mind being gobbled. Sorry, bad joke.'

'I spoke to Flynn earlier,' she went on, serving him the omelette. 'You told him Kelly put the squeeze on Martin Barbie because of stress.'

'I assumed it was stress, but a sex assault makes more sense. She'd want to keep it quiet.'

'And the pressure on Barbie?'

'I found that out when I accessed a confidential instruction to the accountants,' Josh explained as he tucked into his meal. 'Barbie was talking about a seven-figure payout to Kelly. He called it *compensation*.'

'Did he now?' Rita reflected, gazing through the kitchen window at the sunshine streaming into a neat little garden with flowerbeds, rosebushes and a plum tree. A butterfly floated past. 'So what's your impression of your famous employer?' she asked.

'If that's a formal question, then I'd say he's a demanding boss but pays well and hires the best in the field.'

'And off the record?'

Josh brandished a forkful of food. 'What do you call someone who owns a Lamborghini, a bayside mansion, a trophy wife and maintains a wholesome, good-guy image while lacking all morals and screwing around?'

'What would *you* call him?'

'A slime-ball.'

'Thank you, Josh,' she said, climbing off his kitchen stool. 'Your input has definitely helped my inquiries.'

'It has? How?'

'I believe Barbie's seven-figure compensation payment to Kelly was hush money to cover up a brutal crime.'

'For God's sake, you won't let on who told you?'

'Don't choke on your omelette,' she said with a smile, 'I'll keep it confidential.' She shouldered her bag, feeling she'd made some progress. 'But you've given me reasonable grounds to question an icon.'

40

Jack Loftus watered his office fern while he listened to the case for questioning Martin Barbie.

'The investigation's hit a wall,' said Strickland, arms folded, Rita sitting beside him. 'No leads, no fresh clues, we've run out of likely offenders to interview and none of the MX-5 owners who've been contacted is an obvious candidate. There's plenty of forensic evidence – but no suspects.'

'What about the smartcard?' asked Loftus.

'Professor Huxley reckons it gives access to a virtual private network,' answered Rita. 'But we can't trace its manufacture, and we can't link it to Kavella, or anyone else for that matter.'

Loftus put down the china watering can, a present from his grandchildren, and turned to Strickland. 'You're convinced the offender really attacked another woman before blinding the hooker, and it's not just a figment of her coke-addled brain? I don't want to stir up unnecessary crap by chasing phantoms.'

'She was coherent, Jack,' sighed Strickland. 'And the only woman who's emerged as a potential first victim is Kelly Grattan. She's clearly a liar and a possible blackmailer who's done a runner overseas.'

'I did a few checks,' put in Rita. 'Kelly put her apartment on the market and booked a one-way ticket to Singapore, without leaving any contact address or phone number. The agents can't even get in touch by email. They have to wait for her to call them.'

Loftus sat down behind his desk and looked Rita in the eye. 'And you want to treat a television star as a suspect because . . . ?'

'Not a suspect, Jack,' she objected. 'But someone who can shed light on a line of inquiry.'

'Our only current line of inquiry,' added Strickland. 'But I've already got my knuckles rapped because of this case, so I'm passing the buck on this one to you, Jack.'

Loftus grunted, rubbing his brow.

'I won't be heavy-handed, I promise,' said Rita. 'I'll treat him with the respect and awe he deserves.'

'Okay,' said Loftus. 'But if you can't substantiate any of it, you back off immediately. Got it?'

'Yes, Jack.'

'And how do you plan to approach Mr Barbie?'

'I'll catch him on set tomorrow.'

As Rita headed back to the squad room her mobile bleeped. The text was from Lola: *Need to talk asap. Am at Fed Square. Call me.*

Well, she was overdue for a lunch break, thought Rita as she took the lift down to the ground floor, walked outside and jumped on a passing tram. Once seated, she pressed call-back on her phone.

'It's decision time, okay,' Lola told her, 'and I want your advice.'

'I'm already on a tram heading your way,' Rita said.

'Oh my God, public transport!' shrieked Lola. 'That's true friendship!'

They met in a cafe in Federation Square. Above them rose the glass, steel and zinc architecture of the atrium, flanked by shops and art galleries, the afternoon sun streaming high overhead.

'So what's this about?' asked Rita, sharing a glass of wine and a gourmet salad with her friend.

'I've found out who's sending me flowers,' answered Lola, 'and you'll never guess!'

'Russell Crowe.'

'No, he's married. You just don't keep up with showbiz gossip!'

'One of the Wiggles.'

'Behave yourself, this is serious.'

'Okay,' shrugged Rita. 'I give up.'

'A woman!' Lola clapped a hand over her mouth in shameful delight. 'And a hot one at that. She's asked me on a date, so what do I do?'

Rita wasn't sure what to say. 'Does it make a difference that she's hot?'

'Of course it does!' said Lola emphatically. 'But she's also got class – a fashion photographer on her way to do a calendar shoot in the Whitsundays.'

'Lola, you're not a lesbian.'

'No, but I'm always in the market for new offers, and this one's very flattering. She wants to fly me up to Hayman Island for a champagne dinner. To say no would be like turning down a free gift from Tiffany's.'

'Tiffany's wants to get into your purse, not your pants!'

As Rita ran a hand through her hair in exasperation, the ringing of her mobile provided an excuse to escape the subject. To her surprise, the call was from Professor Byron Huxley.

'I hope I'm not interrupting your work,' he said.

'Not at all,' she told him. 'I'm at Fed Square with a glass of pinot noir and a friend who's having a shopping crisis.'

'I'm just up the road at an education conference,' he went on, 'but we've adjourned for the day. Mind if I join you?'

'Okay, though I'll have to get back to the office soon. Had any further thoughts on the smartcard?'

'I'll tell you when I get there,' he said.

As she hung up after giving him the cafe details, Rita wondered what exactly was on Huxley's mind, but Lola was demanding attention.

'Shopping crisis – very funny!' she said. 'Now without being smart, tell me what harm there'd be in accepting a dinner invitation.'

But Rita was too distracted. 'How do I look?' she asked.

'You're ignoring me!'

'Can we set aside your Sapphic fantasies for a moment? I need to know if I'm presentable.'

'You look fucking great,' Lola said impatiently. 'Like a blonde babe ready for action. Why do you need to know?'

'We're about to be joined by a bit of a hunk.'

Huxley turned up looking more city executive than academic in a sleek-fitting business suit. Somehow it accentuated his youthful good looks.

'Here he comes,' said Rita, as he approached through the galleria.

'That's a professor, you've got to be kidding me!' said Lola, with a hefty nudge. 'If you don't jump him, I will!'

'And disappoint your lady-love?'

'This is more like it,' said Huxley, as he reached their table. 'The conference was a form of slow torture.'

Rita introduced Lola. Huxley shook her hand firmly before sitting down and beckoning the waiter. 'Glasses of red all round,' he said.

'I mustn't go back drunk,' Rita warned him.

'Oh, relax,' said Lola. 'You're off-duty in a couple of hours, and half the cops are alcoholics anyway.'

Huxley chuckled.

'That's rich, coming from a member of the media,' retorted Rita, before turning to Huxley. 'Not to mention the drunks wandering the groves of academe.'

'We have the occasional doctorate toppling over a lectern,' Huxley admitted, as the waiter served the wine. 'But that's in the Arts Faculty. In science we're strictly sober.' He raised his glass. 'Cheers!'

They clinked glasses and laughed.

'You can lecture me anytime,' Lola told him, making him blush.

Rita changed the subject. 'You were going to tell me more about the smartcard.'

'Yes, I took a more leisurely look at the data and schematics I downloaded from the card,' said Huxley. 'I'm sure it's a VPN key, as I suspected.'

'What's that, and is it something I should have?' asked Lola.

'A key card for a virtual private network,' answered Huxley. 'Something no woman should be without for remote access to a mother network with highly sensitive data. Anyway, I'm convinced this particular one is Australian-made, probably here in Melbourne, with a level of encryption that can't be cracked but could be bypassed.'

'How?' Rita wanted to know.

'It depends on the authentication components,' explained Huxley. 'If it's a two-factor process, such as a key and a login, you've already got one of them – the card. With the right laptop it might be possible to shoulder-surf the second, and hack your way in.'

'But first I'd need to know whose network I was hacking into,' Rita suggested.

'Yes, and I've no doubt this card connects to top-secret information. We're talking government, industrial or commercial secrecy.'

'What about criminal?' asked Rita.

Huxley sat back. 'If that's the case, I'd be very worried about the data being protected. But if the card was made for gangsters, they had to hire experts to produce it.'

'We've approached the top dozen software firms in Melbourne,' Rita told him, 'but they all deny knowledge of it.'

'Well, you've covered the right ground, so either it was made interstate or one of the firms is bound by confidentiality and is lying to you.'

'Will you two stop talking shop?' demanded Lola. 'Or I might as well go back to my preview.'

'What preview's that?' asked Huxley, smiling.

'A new exhibition at the National Gallery.' Lola nodded across the atrium. 'Fashion from the 1960s – psychedelic, see-through and topless.' She leant forward. 'Works for me.'

Huxley gave a reflex glance at Lola's cleavage and blushed again, making both women laugh before Rita ticked her off. 'Stop teasing.'

'Never,' said Lola, downing the rest of her wine. 'Not even when I've got a Zimmer frame!'

Sunlight gleamed from the fractal facades of the architecture as they crossed the square to the intersection.

'I just can't get used to the design of this place,' complained Lola. 'Too much metal and glass, like a set from *Star Trek*.'

'I like it,' said Huxley. 'It's all geometrical logic.'

'Oh, you'll get on brilliantly with Rita,' groaned Lola, as she hailed a cab. 'You can tickle each other's intellectual fancies.'

As Lola jumped in a taxi, Rita told Huxley, 'Don't mind Lola, she can see sex in a tractor catalogue.'

'I like her too,' he said, adding coyly, 'and *her* surface geometry.'

'Down boy,' said Rita. 'That's Latin dynamite in D&G casing.'

'You're right,' he conceded. 'Beyond my expertise.' He gave her an amused look. 'But what a learning curve.'

'I've got to get back to the office,' Rita said, with just a hint of regret. 'But I think I'll walk off the wine.'

'Do you mind if I walk with you?' he asked.

She pretended to think about it, before saying casually, 'If you like.'

As they crossed the bridge over the river, Huxley slung his suit jacket over his shoulder and loosened his tie. 'If you need any further help with the smartcard, don't hesitate to call me,' he offered.

'Thanks, I might take you up on that.'

They picked their way through pedestrians and skateboarders zigzagging around the theatre complex, then strolled past the moated gallery hung with posters for the *Art of Bollywood* exhibition.

'Do people call you Rita?' he asked.

'My friends do,' she answered. 'So can you.'

'Thanks,' he said, pleased. 'I'm afraid "Byron" doesn't shorten very well, so that's what I'm stuck with.'

'Your parents must be romantics.'

'It's worse than that. Apparently I was conceived in Venice at a palazzo once graced by Lord Byron.'

Rita laughed. 'Unusual programming for a computer scientist.'

'"How little do we know that which we are!"' recited Huxley, quoting the poet. '"How less what we may be!"'

'Now that's my territory,' she said.

As they continued strolling along the shaded avenue, with trams clanking past and homeward-bound commuter traffic getting heavier, Rita realised they were edging towards something deeper than friendly conversation. But where it would lead, she didn't want to guess.

'Psychology and behavioural science are total mysteries to me,' admitted Huxley. 'And as for profiling, it sounds like probability theory mixed with voodoo.'

'The majority of cops would agree with you. But you're right, the intuitive element is essential.'

'Anyway, your visit last week fascinated me,' he said as they stopped at traffic lights. 'It still does.'

When he smiled at her, Rita noticed something intriguing in his eyes, something more than natural enthusiasm – a Byronic quality, perhaps. It drew her in, made her wonder what his passions were, apart from cybernetics.

They resumed walking and she asked, 'What exactly fascinated you?'

'A number of things,' he said evasively, before he stopped again and bowed his head. 'Look, I'm sorry, I'm not usually indirect, so I'll tell you straight out. What fascinated me was you. That's really why I phoned today, but if I'm making an arsehole of myself, tell me and I'll shut up.'

She couldn't help laughing, not just from amusement but with relief that their mutual attraction was out in the open.

He looked embarrassed until she put a hand on his arm and told him, 'You don't have to shut up. I'm flattered, really.'

'Thank God for that.'

They were standing outside the dark stone fortress of Victoria Barracks, fronted by regimented palm trees and antique cannons.

'So I wouldn't be pushing it if I phoned you again and asked you out to dinner?'

'That would be great,' she said. 'But for now I've got to get back to work.'

'Me too. I was supposed to go straight back to campus and chair a faculty meeting instead of acting like a love-sick adolescent.'

'You got your priorities right. Lord Byron would be proud of you.'

Before she went to bed that night, Rita phoned Lola and told her what had happened.

'I knew it!' said Lola. 'He couldn't take his eyes off you.'

Rita grunted. 'Despite your best efforts.'

'Don't be a bitch, I was just testing his resolve. You two are seriously made for each other.'

'That's unlikely. We haven't even been out on a date.'

'Don't be so formal,' Lola complained. 'What do you think this afternoon was – research?'

As she lay in bed, Rita recalled the encounters of the day with a sense of bemusement. The warm attention of one academic, Byron

Huxley, stood in stark contrast to the hostility of another, Dr Phillip Roxby. Their personalities, along with their characters, were poles apart. Then there was Josh Barrett, computer whiz and pot-head, in a category all of his own. Unfortunately for him, he'd be working through the night again in the paranoid company of his colleagues at Xanthus. Rita had added to Josh's stress levels, of course – but at least she'd cooked him an omelette.

41

It was five a.m., but the fluorescent strip lighting still gleamed along the first floor of the Xanthus building. The three members of the core team pulled off their visors and gloves and looked at each other with tense, caffeine-fuelled stares. The work was almost done.

They'd been button-mashing non-stop through the night, hardly pausing to eat, stretch or urinate, as they ran the final diagnostics on the complex programming and subroutines of the game. The visuals, sound design and artificial intelligence all stood up to the test, whether it was played on a PC, a game console or virtual accessories. From a technical point of view it was a state-of-the-art package – high performance, interactive and fully explorable. On top of that – like an algorithmic gateway – it opened up another dimension in video gaming. Wired into the product was a Xanthus-designed system of autostereographics – in effect a new generation of realism. When hooked up to VR it delivered natural 3-D perspectives and rich, fully fleshed-out imagery, immersing the player in an alternative world. Context became environment. Storyline turned into experience. In other words, the game felt real.

All three knew they'd created something special. Reams of printout surrounded them after a last trace for bugs – but the logic, syntax and run-time were all sufficiently error-free. The software was ready to be released.

Josh Barrett clicked the bones in his neck and got up.

'It's done,' he said flatly.

'I'm not so sure,' said Flynn. As system administrator the final call was his, and he wasn't ready to make it.

'I've had enough!' said Maynard, throwing down his visor and kicking petulantly at the piles of paper. 'I don't care what you say. My brain's fried and I'm going home.'

Flynn scowled at him. 'That's right. Go back to your teddy bears and comics. Run home to Mummy.'

Maynard snatched up a handful of discs and hurled them at Flynn, who ducked just in time as they went scything through the air to clatter across the office.

'Drongo,' Flynn commented, straightening up.

'Go piss up a rope,' said Maynard, pulling on his jacket and getting tangled in the sleeves as he did so. 'And don't expect me back today. I'm having a sleep-in.'

He stomped off without a backward glance, still wrestling with his sleeves. For good measure he kicked over a chair. A moment later the door banged behind him.

'He's got a point,' said Josh. 'We should be celebrating, not fighting. The job's done. We've cracked it.'

'That's easy for you to say,' Flynn snapped, sitting hunched on a swivel chair. 'But the buck stops with me on this. I want to do a final walk-through in the lab. Gonna join me?'

Josh shook his head. 'Give it a rest. You'll burn yourself out. We're overtired already.' He picked up his canvas bag and slung it over his shoulder. 'I'm going to smoke a joint, crash out and forget the game. You ought to do the same.'

Unlike his two colleagues, Flynn couldn't stop working. Although egocentric and volatile, professionally he was a perfectionist, as brilliant and creative with software design as he was emotionally erratic. Through willpower, ability and an intolerance of failure, he'd advanced through university and postgraduate research to become a bit player in a global industry. That's where he was now – in charge of Barbie's wet software dream. Game on.

Though Barbie was obviously a flake when it came to technology, he had stumbled onto something unique when he'd bought Xanthus Software. The struggling firm had devised an innovation that increased the sensory impact of virtual reality. Technologically it was a breakthrough. In marketing terms, it was a potential goldmine. It was new and it was hot. All it needed was a game to be designed around it. The challenge was one reason why Flynn had agreed to develop it – the other being the extremely high salary. There was also the kudos. While Barbie stood to reap huge financial rewards, Flynn would make his name in the hi-tech marketplace. The success of the game would launch his reputation. His future would be guaranteed and he would be able to pick and choose between offers from international corporations. The possibilities were stunning.

So too, of course, were the penalties of failure. And with competition so intense, one miscalculation could make all the difference. In this city alone there were ten other video gaming outfits. Some of the biggest had set up shop in Melbourne – Atari, Infinite Interactive, THQ. The prize was a slice of a worldwide business worth $30 billion the previous year – over $10 billion more than the box office total pulled in by the whole of the movie industry around the planet. When the stakes were so high, just one error – software, timing, contractual – could sink a deal. Then someone else would snatch the breakthrough, and Barbie's dreams of hitting the jackpot would be flushed down the commercial toilet, along with Flynn's shot at personal glory and a hefty success bonus. He could kiss goodbye to his job, his salary, his expensive apartment. It would be back to postgrad research at the university – a prospect that made him shudder. That's why he went on working – alone, determined, beyond tiredness, his brain wired on ambition.

He went down to the basement, let himself into the VR lab and stood for a moment on the concrete floor amid a jumble of cables, piping, screens and computer decks. It was like an electronic dungeon, a dim, subterranean level – very appropriate considering the game's content. When he'd powered up the studio, he loaded the latest version of the program, stripped off his clothes and pulled on a lightweight bodysuit studded with sensors. Then he strapped himself into a metal frame, slipped on a pair of gloves, adjusted his headset and logged on to the game.

For a moment he stood in total blackness, suspended between two universes – the real and the hyper-real. In a strange way, the more Flynn visited the latter, the less respect he felt for the former.

It was like taking a psychedelic drug. The real world began to look dull and clumsy while the virtual realm became more vivid and addictive. The effect didn't bother him. After all, this was the future, the new frontier. As the twenty-first century unfolded, more and more people would choose to inhabit virtual reality as they escaped the drudgery of daily existence. The buzz of gameplay would become the stimulant of the masses.

In the pure blackness a control pad illuminated in front of him. He reached out with a virtual finger and touched a virtual button. The audiovisuals clicked into life. It was intense and it was exhilarating. Flynn could congratulate himself. The end result of so much hard work was worth the effort.

He could take much of the credit for the logic and architecture of the game, but he'd been ably assisted by Maynard and Josh, and a whole team of software engineers, 3-D graphics artists, background modellers, visual FX programmers, audio mixers, AI specialists and virtual environment designers. Barbie himself had also played a key role in the overall construction. He'd come up with the original idea and insisted on viewing each stage of its development like an overseer. More often than not his presence was irritating, but he knew what he wanted. And here, at last, they'd delivered it – a game of gods, heroes and monsters – Barbie's hard-core vision of the Underworld.

That's where you started – deep underground in the Kingdom of Hades. The aim was to climb to freedom. You did that by slaying monsters at each level, acquiring new powers, recruiting allies from among the damned or the deities, and – if you made it all the way – attaining divinity on the slopes of Mount Olympus. Barbie seemed to see it as a personal metaphor. To Flynn and his colleagues the interpretation was more basic. In single-player mode it was an epic quest in the sword and sorcery genre, combining mythic themes, gladiator sports and primal fantasies. When played against others online it turned into a team-combat race. On top of the startling realism of the experience, there were other selling points. It was a first-person shooter fully explorable in real-time 3-D, where players could follow branching storylines, enhance their fighting skills and create customised avatars to help in the ascent. There was also its freedom of choice. Gamers could tackle each new challenge in any way they wanted because there was no single or right tactic to get results. With its glossy visuals and realistic death animations, it was destined to join the top rank of hack'n'slash adventures, automatically getting an adult rating for its blood, violence and erotic imagery.

Flynn took a deep breath to prime himself for action.

He was ready to enter the Underworld.

He reached out to the virtual control pad and pressed Start.

With a vertiginous rush he was transported into the wild, alien landscape of the game. He found himself on a narrow ledge deep below the surface of the earth, where naked nymphs were shackled to rocks. Against the cliff face moved the shadows of demonic guards. Overhead towered a precipice, criss-crossed by steep paths leading to the Palace of Hades. The jagged surfaces were lit by the crimson glow of lava and burning sulphur. At his feet yawned the dark chasm of the abyss.

Wielding his sword, he upended a guard and cut his head off, black blood oozing from the convulsing torso, then he turned in time to face clusters of spawning demons. He hacked through them as he fought his way along the ledge – limbs, wings, claws and entrails spraying in all directions. When he reached an upward path cut in the rock he escaped to the next level.

He pressed the Oracle button. It triggered the voice of a god:

'I am Ares, god of war. To see the light, you must destroy your enemies.'

Each level produced confrontations with hideous creatures – Gorgons, Harpies, Minotaurs, Furies wreathed in snakes. By summoning heroes to his cause the beasts were dismembered in a flurry of swipes and bone-cracking duels. More insidious were the seductive enemies who plugged directly into the pleasure node – bare-breasted enchantresses, photo-realistic Sirens with soft-textured flesh. These too were dispatched with a cacophony of thuds.

The whole pantheon of classical terror flashed past him in lurid detail as he fought his way higher and higher. Finally, as he burst into the daylight, the splendour of an ancient paradise opened around him – forests, groves, waterfalls, meadows filled with wildflowers – the Elysian Fields stretching towards the luminous presence of Mount Olympus. He stood still for a moment, his feet on the grass, his face glowing in the beams of virtual sunlight, but there was nothing he could think of to worry about.

He pressed Stop.
It was done, finished.

As he pulled off the visor, peeled off the bodysuit and stepped back into the real world, his head was still buzzing with apocalyptic images. The sleek, virtual carnage of the death match would stay with him for hours, like a hypnotic high – just as it would with hordes of tech-heads and gamers, once it hit the shops. What a mind-fuck.

He looked at the wall clock. It was after dawn, but his work was done. Like the others, he could pack up and go home. Try to switch his brain off. Chill out. There was just one thing left to do: phone Barbie and tell him his designer heaven-and-hell was up and running.

42

Rita woke from a good night's sleep to the pleasant memory of Professor Byron Huxley paying court to her against a backdrop of the ivy-clad barracks and the rumble of commuter traffic. She was singing to herself as she showered and towelled off, before focusing her thoughts on the encounter ahead. It was one that promised to be challenging, as well as potentially risky, so she needed to be on her game. She dressed in a dark pinstripe suit, its jacket and skirt tailored to hug her curves, and a thin cream cashmere top. She swept back her hair and sprayed her neck with Ysatis perfume. Now she felt ready, alert and psyched up for the prospect of bearding an alpha male in his lair: Martin Barbie in his TV studio.

Rita stood at the rear of the studio, among the props and the cables, while Barbie recorded his continuity links for the evening edition of *Gold Rush*. As she watched him she couldn't help feeling a sense of excitement. Maybe it was just the environment – the adrenalin-driven ethos of the media with its arc lights and boom mikes. There was a pervasive tension in the air, people functioning under constant hype. But maybe it was more than that. Rita had been in TV studios before and they'd left her cold, with their artificial sets, plastic people and fake emotions. This time, though, watching Barbie in action, she felt the pull of something different. This man, this celebrity, was perhaps the most plastic of them all, yet he was also a challenge, being a media star with a perfect image and a highly marketable face. But did he have dark secrets to hide? She had a strong feeling he was implicated in a nasty crime and had organised a cover-up.

Martin Barbie might be the pin-up of the masses, but for Rita he was a suspect in a crime hunt.

She had to admit that he was good at what he did. Relaxed, witty and personable, he was a sophisticate who wore his black dinner jacket and bow tie like a second skin. He could have been born to live in front of the camera. Equally impressive was his attitude between takes. The abrasiveness of his production staff didn't rub off on him. He was clearly a man with tremendous self-control. In her own case, her self-control was more than a strategy for social success, it also kept a lid on her demons of chaos. So what were Barbie's demons? What was his secret torment?

A little frisson of anticipation went through her at the prospect of delving into his psyche, but she needed to remain detached. She hadn't even met the man and already her feelings were aroused. Something else. It wasn't just his professional skills that she was admiring. She noticed that he was well-built, but not muscular. He moved well, almost fluidly at times. And once, when he smiled off-camera at the make-up girl, there was something wicked and appealing in it. The man had sexual magnetism. It was undeniable.

At last the recording session was over. Barbie got up off his studio sofa as a technical assistant unplugged him and reeled in the wires. Rubbing his neck muscles, he began to walk off the set, before a slim young man in tight denim with a clipboard stopped him and spoke into his ear, pointing at Rita.

Barbie changed course and walked towards her. When he reached her he flashed a professional smile.

'I'm told you want to speak to me.'

'Yes,' she said, watching him carefully. 'It's about Kelly Grattan.'

There was a momentary flicker, but Barbie recovered quickly and started loosening his bow tie. 'And your name is?'

'Detective Sergeant Marita Van Hassel.'

'I wasn't expecting the police here. Was it you who called my private secretary?'

'Yes. She said you had a full schedule, so I thought I'd try to catch you on the off-chance.'

Barbie nodded slowly then suddenly lost his stern look. 'And so you have. Well done.' He extended a hand. 'Nice to meet you, Detective Sergeant Marita Van Hassel.'

As they shook hands a little charge of electricity went through her skin.

'Sorry about that,' he said. 'It's all the static around here. I don't think we're falling in love.' That smile again. Soft and wicked.

'No chance of that,' she said smoothly. 'I need lightning bolts. And thunder.'

As soon as she said it, she realised she was playing with him. From the look in his eyes, he liked it.

'I've got to say you don't look like a plain-clothes cop,' said Barbie.

'What do I look like?'

'You could pass for a model – and I'm not trying to flatter you. I know what I'm talking about. My wife's a model.'

'So I've read – and seen. Women's magazines can't get enough of her – and you.' Now who was using flattery?

Barbie gave a polite laugh and gestured towards the studio door. 'We can talk in my dressing room.' He turned to the make-up girl. 'I'll clean myself up, Candy. I don't want to be disturbed.'

They walked down a broad linoleum corridor to a room with his name on the door. He ushered her in and offered her a chair. As Rita sat down, she crossed her legs and the hem of her skirt rode up her thigh. She caught his look as he turned and seated himself in front of the brightly lit mirror to remove his make-up.

'Kelly Grattan,' she said abruptly. 'Why did you pay her off?'

For a split second it seemed like his hand trembled as he held a cotton pad to his cheek, but then it steadied and he continued wiping off the powder.

'That's a strange way to put it,' he said.

Rita leant forward in her chair. 'How much did you give her?'

'The figure's confidential. But you'd be right to assume it's substantial.'

'Enough to keep her out of the country for a long time.'

'I don't think that's the point.' A bead of sweat had risen on his temple and he brushed it away. 'It was a business transaction. What she does with the money is up to her.'

Despite his coolness, Rita could sense his discomfort. 'You call it a transaction. A transaction for what?'

'I don't see what you're driving at,' he said, then hesitated before continuing. 'The transaction – to give it a name – was her severance pay. The early termination of her contract. As you may know, my software firm is on the brink of an extremely important and sensitive deal. For personal reasons, Kelly needed to leave the company. For professional reasons, including strict commercial secrecy, I needed to ensure Kelly's continued loyalty. Hence the "pay-off", as you put it.'

Rita eased back and said, 'These "personal reasons" – you saw them for yourself when you met her to agree on the money?'

'I saw she'd been injured and heard her explanation about the unfortunate mishap.'

'But you know she was brutally attacked?'

He blinked twice, and Rita knew he was about to lie.

'I know nothing of any attack. And if she didn't want to tell me, it's none of my concern. What we discussed was purely business. I don't think I can help you in your inquiries,' he said, then turned back to the mirror and picked up a fresh pad to dab around his mouth.

This man was going to be hard to catch out, thought Rita. He was a very good liar. Almost in the class of women. That's when Rita realised he was removing a thin layer of lipstick. For some reason she found it amusing, and vaguely sensual.

'What shade do you wear, Mr Barbie?'

The question startled him more than the others.

'Oh, um . . .' He fumbled around for the lipstick tube. 'Baby Pink for today's shoot.'

'Hmm,' she said. 'Nice and modest. You don't wear lip gloss?'

'People on the box shouldn't wear gloss. It's like drooling for the camera. Their lips look permanently wet.' He gave a low laugh. 'For location shots I wear Nude.'

'I'll bet you do.'

'Can I ask you one thing? Call me Martin, Marty, Mart or even just Barbie. But never Mister. The day people think of me as Mister my career in showbiz is over.'

They were looking directly into each other's eyes. He was hitting on her, and she knew it. It was clear he knew that she knew it and was pleased that she didn't protest. The erotic nuance hung between them like a scent in the air.

'I think I'll call you Barbie,' she said. 'It reminds me of girls' dolls and toys.'

He grinned.

They were playing a game and it was on several levels. He was obviously lying and she wanted to find out how much. She was probing into his secrets, and she could see he was pretending to cooperate, but he also seemed to fancy her. From what Josh had said, Barbie was a womaniser and a risk taker, and it might appeal to his speculative instincts to flirt with a policewoman who was pursuing him. She too was being manipulative, deliberately using sex appeal to draw him out. But the question was how far was she prepared to go?

Just then her mobile rang.

'Excuse me,' she said, taking her phone out of her bag as Barbie resumed his work in the mirror.

It was Strickland on the phone.

'Drop what you're doing,' he told her. 'Homicide want you at a crime scene right now.'

'Homicide? Why? What's happened?'

'Another prostitute's been mutilated. But this one's dead.'

43

Rita peeled off her jacket and unhitched her skirt inside the scene-of-crime van and pulled on the plastic trousers and top. Then she slid on gloves, stepped out of the van, walked into the apartment block and climbed the stairs to the second-floor flat. As she entered the bedroom the first thing she noticed was the smell, followed by the body on the bed.

'Ah, Van Hassel. I hope you can give us something on this.' It was the head of the Homicide Squad, Detective Inspector Barry Mace. 'I'm told you've already started a profile on the guy who blinded the first prostitute.'

She nodded. 'You think it's the same man?'

'I do. There's already a prints match. And we've got a second girl mutilated – this time the ears. And she's another street hooker. Nadine McKeever, only twenty-one. Looks like your reporter boyfriend was right about a serial attacker.'

'He's not my boyfriend,' she said, frowning, as she began to concentrate on the crime scene.

'Will you make sure I get a full set of photos and a copy of the video?' she said.

'Of course,' said Mace.

'And if a card with Plato's Cave on it turns up, I want to be told straightaway.'

'Okay.' Mace was a big man, broad-shouldered and with a tough face that would have looked at home in a boxing ring. But he was also astute. 'I heard what happened to you – the carpeting by Nash. In my opinion you were dropped in it unfairly. But it's no good getting personal with Kavella. It'll only get in the way if you've got a hard-on for him.'

'I haven't,' said Rita tightly. 'But if another card turns up it's crucial evidence.'

'Fine,' he said. 'Now get me something to work with. We've got a real psycho-freak on the loose.'

Rita got out her notebook and moved past the evidence techs to where the pathologist was bending over the body, which was spread-eagled on the bed. Thin, pale and rigid. Limbs clasped in bondage restraints. The victim was young. The quilt she was lying on was dark with stains from the blood that had poured from her ears. There was also congealed blood that had spilled from her mouth and down her neck. Her glassy eyes stared at the ceiling. The lividity of the corpse showed that this was the position she'd been killed in. On surfaces around the bed, six candles had melted down into pools of wax. Her severed ears, circled in chalk, were lying on the floor.

'What did he do to her?' asked Rita.

'As well as the obvious mutilation, he gouged out her eardrums with a steak knife,' said the pathologist, gesturing to the weapon on the rug beside the bed.

'That's what killed her?'

'Not exactly. I'll need to get the body back to the lab to be sure, but I think in the process of inserting the blade he severed her carotid artery. An internal wound. Looks like she drowned in her own blood.'

Rita made some notes then said, 'So he may not have meant to kill her. The murder might have been a consequence of his need to mutilate.'

'Well, that's conjecture.'

'Yes, and conjecture's my job. What else did he do?'

'He had violent sexual intercourse with her.' The pathologist pointed to bruising of the vagina and thighs. 'And it was unprotected. Even before we take a swab you can see the traces of semen.'

Rita nodded. 'What else?'

'She was hit with a heavy object. Look at the split skin and contusion on her temple. Could even be a fractured skull.'

Rita glanced across to where a brass candlestick was circled on the floor. 'Is that the weapon?'

'Again, I'll need to check it at the lab, but it fits the bill.'

A few feet away another object was circled. She went over and looked at it – an unopened condom, just lying there, in the middle of the floor.

'Now that's odd,' she said as Mace walked over to her.

'Why?' He shook his head. 'A condom was the least protection she needed.'

Rita raised a finger reflectively to her lips. 'But she didn't know that before she was attacked. And it's possible she was approaching him with it at the moment she was hit.'

Mace scratched his head. 'You're not telling me she was killed because of a condom?'

'No.' She waved a hand dismissively. 'I'm trying to reconstruct how the crime was committed.'

'Well, we're all doing that.'

'Yes, but I'm doing a psychological evaluation. What type of person would do this? What's he saying? What fantasy drives him?'

'Hookers and fantasy go together, don't they?'

'True. But is he choosing prostitutes because of a fixation with them or because they're easy victims?' She rubbed her chin, concentrating. 'Where did the steak knife come from?'

'The kitchen, by the look of it,' said Mace. 'Other knives match it. You'll get the forensic report when it's ready.'

She sighed, flicking the notebook irritably against her ribs. 'This guy's a contradiction.'

'What do you mean? What are you seeing that I'm not?'

Rita was silent, preoccupied.

'Look,' said Mace. 'I'm not one of those stick-in-the-mud arseholes who thinks there's only one way to solve a case. If your profiling can give me evidence, believe me, I'll use it.'

'Thanks for the vote of confidence. I mean it.' She gave him an appraising look. 'But it doesn't work like that. Profiling won't provide evidence. It doesn't nail anybody. All it can do is suggest a possible suspect. To be honest, it's closer to art than science.'

'Yeah. Okay. You want to explain that to me?'

'What I'm looking for is his mind trace. His crime signature, as distinct from his MO. What he does that is unnecessary. His extra touch.'

'Like beating his victims senseless then mutilating them.'

'Exactly. The crime is the canvas on which he projects himself. The way he does it says something unique to him. That's what I mean by fantasy. It's very, very important.'

'You said he's a contradiction, but you didn't say how.'

Rita gestured at the room with a sweep of her hand. 'This crime scene is random and sloppy. Disorganised. It doesn't fit with the way an intelligent, socially competent, serial offender would behave. There's a lack of control. Weapons lying around. DNA, fingerprints. The body just left there. It points to someone of low intelligence and a social failure.'

'So where's the contradiction?'

'The description of the man who blinded Emma Schultz. He's the complete opposite. All the hallmarks of a slick professional. Well dressed. Driving a smart convertible. Someone in control of the situation.'

'Are we talking split personality?'

'Not quite a technical term.' She gave a low chuckle. 'But I think we have someone struggling to cope with pressure that's pulling him apart. A professional man who has to vent his sexual need and inner violence. He plans and controls his pick-ups, and at the point of sex loses his self-control. He doesn't bring weapons, he improvises. The same goes for props, such as the candles here, the fire at the first crime scene. And that well-worn bondage gear looks like it belonged to the girl.'

'That's right,' said Mace. 'It's from a set in her wardrobe.'

'So the offender begins with a straightforward pick-up and the intention of recreating his fantasy of the cave. But as he does so, he extemporises and loses control, maiming his victims and leaving a blood-stained mess littered with evidence. It points to a form of breakdown. Something in his life has triggered a fundamental change. He won't be able to stop.'

'Where did you get all that from?'

'Just a leap of logic.'

'Right,' said Mace dubiously. 'But I agree with you about one thing. These mutilations have only just started. We'd better get ready for the next one.'

He was interrupted by one of his detectives.

'Look what else we found in the wardrobe,' said the officer, brandishing a Plato's Cave T-shirt. It was black and red, with the trademark design of the nightclub.

'Well that settles it,' said Mace. 'We now have a common link in both attacks. I don't care what Proctor says, we need to pay a call on Kavella's club and turn over a few rocks. See what crawls out.'

44

As Rita and her fellow detectives were examining the scene, news of the murder hit the media in a flurry of agency snaps. It wasn't long before the apartment block was besieged by reporters, photographers, TV camera crews and satellite vans. They were all jumping on the angle of a serial attacker on the loose, and now they had a title for him. Some injudicious cop patrolling the crime scene perimeter had mentioned the mutilation of the victim's ears. Putting that together with the first victim's injuries, the reporters came up with an appropriate nickname: the Hacker.

The clamour for a statement was finally satisfied when Mace emerged and answered questions to a cluster of microphones in the glow of arc lights, cameras flashing. It was all that the assembled journalists needed. Although Mace spoke briefly and was circumspect in his comments, there was enough information to hype the story to the hilt. And when crime correspondent Mike Cassidy glimpsed his ex-girlfriend on an upstairs balcony, it handed him a little scoop on the side.

Cassidy's TV channel broke into its lunchtime show with a news flash.

> *We interrupt our normal programming to bring you breaking news on the gruesome discovery of a murdered woman, believed to be the second victim of a serial attacker. We're now crossing to our crime correspondent, Mike Cassidy, who's reporting live from the murder scene.*

Cassidy began his report: *Police hunting the man who blinded a prostitute in a vicious attack early last week believe he's struck again, this time killing his victim. The body of a young woman, also said to be involved* in sex work, was discovered this morning in the apartment block behind me. This second victim fell prey to a savage assault, during which she suffered mutilation injuries. While the girl last week had her eyes gouged out, this second girl was apparently stabbed through the ears. The nature of the wounds in both cases has led tabloid reporters around me to dub the maniac behind the attacks 'the Hacker'. It's not yet clear when the woman was killed, with police only confirming that it was sometime in the past few days. The investigation is now being headed by the Homicide Squad's Detective Inspector Barry Mace, who spoke to us a few moments ago.

Video of Mace: *What I can confirm, at this point in time, is that we are investigating the death of a young woman. The body was discovered after our attention was drawn to her apartment this morning by a phone call from a concerned neighbour. I can also confirm that she suffered a violent assault that led to her death. Forensic officers are still examining the crime scene as the evidentiary process continues.*

Voice of Cassidy: *Is it true the victim was a prostitute who was stabbed through the ears?*

Video of Mace: *It's our understanding that the young woman was a street worker, yes. As to the type of injuries inflicted, I'm not prepared to go into details.*

Voice of Cassidy: *Will you confirm you're linking the murder with last week's blinding of prostitute Emma Schultz?*

Video of Mace: *At this stage each investigation will stand alone, with the forensic analysis ongoing. However, the nature of the crimes indicate to us there may be a connection.*

Cassidy to camera: *Fears that a maniac is on the loose now prove to be justified, and it's clear that his violence is escalating. Women in the sex trade have already been warned that they're targets, and now people living in this area admit they're frightened.*

Video of local woman resident: *It's bad enough what we put up with around here. You see the hookers, most of them junkies, plying their trade from here to Carlisle Street, pulling over the motorists. And if they don't take them back to their homes, they do it in their customers' cars. It's disgusting. Now we've got this lunatic prowling the streets. It makes you worried about walking out your front door.*

Cassidy to camera: *Of course, it's not just a worry for red light districts, although these seem the most likely hunting grounds for this predator. As if to underscore police concerns, I can exclusively reveal they've again drafted in criminal profiler Marita Van Hassel, who is analysing the crime scene behind me as I speak. That seems to indicate no solid leads have emerged, and detectives are no nearer to catching or even identifying the Hacker. At this stage officers are unable to give us any further details of the man who perpetrated these horrendous crimes, so he remains at large. Now, back to the studio.*

The tabloid press followed suit, making the most of the nickname attributed to the killer. The first front page of the afternoon exploited it neatly with the lurid headline: HACKER CUTS DOWN HOOKERS.

The coverage was the last thing the crime squads needed, and with some of the macabre details in public circulation their job had just become harder.

45

Rita and Erin Webster joined around two dozen detectives from the Homicide, Organised Crime and Sexual Crimes squads as they filed into a briefing room and took their places at a long white table under the fluorescent strip lighting.

'This reminds me of detention at school,' whispered Erin.

'I'm sure you had plenty,' said Rita, 'and deserved it.'

At the head of the table, Barry Mace and Jack Loftus sat together, hemmed in by a bank of filing cabinets, flip charts and a row of whiteboards. All the relevant information from the two attacks had been gathered and displayed on the walls around them. The graphic images of crime scene photos had been arranged alongside arrowed street maps, forensic science reports, evidence lists, timelines, interview records, clipboards and even Rita's preliminary profile. Newspaper front pages with Hacker headlines had been tacked to a corkboard. The accumulated data generated by the two cases loomed over the detectives settling into their chairs as Mace got to his feet.

'It will be obvious to you why we're here,' he began. 'And you can forget what I told the media earlier today about two separate investigations. We're hunting the same perpetrator in both cases and he won't be easy to track down. We're dealing with an anonymous offender, no prints or DNA on record, someone who appears to strike at random. He's intensified his attacks from mutilation to maiming and murder, and so far we've established no direct link with his victims. You can all see the type of investigation we're facing, as well as the workload and potential duration. That means we had to make a decision. The result is the gathering in this room. We've decided to set up a dedicated taskforce to focus on these two cases, and any further ones the Hacker hands us. We're calling it Taskforce Nightwatch.'

Mace bowed his head and leant forward on the table, before continuing. 'Now, you may feel we've been here before. In fact, some of you have. A year ago we used the same room for the taskforce hunting the Scalper. I've heard the speculation, so let me make a few things crystal clear. Although the file on the Scalper is still open, he hasn't come back to plague us. It's definitely *not* the same offender. The DNA, prints, crime scenes and victimology are emphatically different. Having said that, we do face an odd coincidence – the same make, model and colour of car, a black Mazda MX-5. It means we have to go through the same process of trying to eliminate all the owners of such vehicles. That process is well in hand thanks to Detective Senior Constable Matt Bradby. How far along are we, Bradby?'

Bradby straightened up in his chair. 'When you mention we've been here before,' he told the gathering, 'it's more like a nasty case of déjà vu. We've hit roughly the same barrier total as in the Scalper case. Let me give you the background. The Mazda MX-5 is the best-selling two-seater sports car of all time, according to the *Guinness Book of Records*. It's got a global cult following and worldwide sales heading towards a million, with Australia's share approaching fifteen thousand. When factors such as car colour, region and driver age group are taken into account, we still can't get the potential suspect pool below three hundred. We're about halfway through the list, checking out a lot of the same young guys we did a year ago, and so far – zip, nothing to give us the Hacker. We need to narrow the field by getting additional specifics about the car. Either that or conduct a mass mandatory DNA test of Mazda owners.'

That got a laugh.

'It would certainly mean fun and games with the civil liberties lobby,' commented Mace. 'Anyhow, it shows the sort of thing we're up against. But that's just one line of inquiry. The pathologist puts the time of death at two nights ago and we've started the process of interviewing the dead girl's neighbours and fellow hookers. As yet, we've got no witnesses, so there's nothing to add to the suspect description.'

Mace took a deep breath, raising himself to his full height. 'However, we do have a new focus after establishing a common link between the two victims,' he said. 'It turns out both were regulars at the Plato's Cave nightclub, which is a popular pick-up joint for prostitutes. It's also frontline turf of the city's gangland, so we're going to have to tread carefully.' He paused, directing a fierce frown around the room. 'Now I can't emphasise this strongly enough: it's the *customers* we're looking at, not the club's owner, Tony Kavella. I don't want anyone to approach him. Leave that to me or Jack Loftus. But with or without Kavella's cooperation, in the next few hours we're going to start questioning his Friday night crowd – any customer who fits the description of the Hacker provided by Emma Schultz. It's tricky ground because of our recent history with Kavella, so I want everyone to behave with the utmost professionalism. That's about all I've got to say at this stage. Jack?'

Loftus nodded and stood up. 'I want to underline the point that we need to be patient,' he said. 'As with the Scalper case, it looks like we're facing a high frequency of attacks, not much more than a week apart. But we mustn't feel compelled to prevent the next attack. If we overreact to time pressure, we'll only make things worse. With patience, with methodical work, with detailed examination of the evidence and by building a profile, we'll home in on a prime suspect. He may seem like a phantom at the moment, but we *will* catch this killer.'

Loftus glanced around the faces at the table. 'That's all for now,' he added. 'There'll be fuller briefings later as we finetune the operation. In the meantime, if you can clear the decks of any case files that are less than urgent, it will help.'

As the detectives began filing from the room, Mace drew Rita aside. 'You heard what Jack just said about a profile,' he told her. 'We see that as your primary role with the taskforce.'

'Okay,' she said.

'Much as I fancy the club for this, I don't want it to be our only line of attack,' Mace went on. 'For a start, if the Hacker's smart, he won't go back there. So I want you working the flank, finding out as much about him as you can, psyching him out.'

'You know I can only type him,' she reminded him. 'I can't name him for you.'

'That's a pity,' said Mace.

'But there's something I've still got to do,' she said. 'Revisit the crime scene, now that things have calmed down there. I need to go on my own – at night. I might pick up on something I've missed.'

'I remember,' put in Mace, patting her on the shoulder. 'Getting the mind trace.'

'Exactly.'

As Mace walked away, Loftus asked her, 'How'd you go with Martin Barbie?'

'As far as I could,' she answered. 'He was friendly, cooperative and, just as with Kelly Grattan, I got nowhere. I'm convinced they're both plausible liars, but I have to admit there's nothing to show they have any bearing on the investigation, or even a crime. If they're both covering something up, it's well and truly buried.'

46

It was late at night and Rita was parked outside the apartment block where the young prostitute had been killed. There were no lights on in any of the flats, no sign of police presence other than the crime scene tape, no sign of any activity at all. Residents of the neighbouring flats had made other arrangements and moved out for the night. She could hear the sea at the end of the road, and the tinkling sounds of the marina, the moored yachts riding the swell, the rigging playing tunes upon the masts. She could hear the splash of waves and smell the brine coming with the onshore breeze. No one else was around. It felt peaceful.

She picked up her mini-disc recorder, got out of the car, climbed the stairs to the upstairs flat and pushed aside the police tape. After letting herself in with the key she turned on the lights and went to the bedroom. Then she pressed Record.

'You picked her up locally and she brought you back here. How far did you intend to go? You don't arrive with a carefully planned program of attack. But you need aggressive, unprotected penetration and you make sure you get it. So why go further? Why the symbolic mutilation? It's because something takes over – the need to inflict a ritual payback or tribute or conquest. That's why you permanently damage them. Only this time you went too far. It makes you a killer now. But, of course, that's only in your secret life. It's like having another identity, one in which you lose all restraint and vent your fury. The more you let go, the more you lose yourself, the more difficult it is to focus on who you really are. It still begs the question, though. What has triggered it? What has fractured your sense of reality?'

She switched off the recorder, a niggling doubt in her mind. Her analysis was drawing her away from the conclusion that the Hacker was a calculating psychopath – a theory her police colleagues had automatically embraced. Instead, she was seeing him as intelligent but deluded – possibly a paranoid schizophrenic. Perhaps she was assuming too much. It was late and she was tired.

She locked up the flat and went back to her car, feeling that her brain needed a rest. She turned the ignition, switched on the lights and drove off. When she reached the corner of the beach road, she stopped and listened again to the waves against the shore and the clinking percussions of the marina. The sounds were soothing and reassuring – a reminder of normality – just as the killer had heard them.

47

It was Saturday morning and a day off work, but Rita needed to update the profile with her observations from the night before. First she phoned Loftus to ask about the taskforce operation at the nightclub.

'It had an impact,' he told her. 'The place was packed with clubbers. Mace went in mob-handed with a dozen detectives and another dozen uniforms. He spoke in person to Kavella, explained it was nothing personal, even though it was conducted like a raid. I'm not sure who's more pissed off – Kavella or Proctor, who doesn't want us muddying his pitch.'

'Any suspects?' Rita asked.

'Initially, yes. About twenty customers fit the description. They were questioned, and after a bit of persuasion gave us prints and DNA. None of the prints match. But that's only phase one. Mace plans to hit the place again to check out the Saturday night crowd. He might get lucky.'

'I doubt it,' said Rita.

'I agree,' said Loftus. 'The Hacker might be insane but he's not crazy. He would have to be nuts to call on the club. Anyway, this is Mace's play. You've got the weekend off, so relax. Do something other than work.'

'I'll try,' she said. 'I promise.'

After emailing the updated profile to the taskforce team, Rita collected her gym bag, locked up her home and got in her car, which was parked out front. She sat behind the wheel, mobile in hand, wondering if she should call Byron Huxley. It was tempting, she had the whole weekend free, yet instinctively she felt the next move was up to him. She put away the mobile, her thoughts turning instead to the taskforce raid on Kavella's club and wondering what the fallout would be.

Despite her promise to Loftus, Rita found it hard to relax. She sighed, sat back and looked around her. The narrow street of little houses seemed to drowse in the sunshine. She wound down the window and caught the scent of roses blooming in a neighbour's garden. A cat sprawled in the sun on a window sill. From down the street came the high-pitched laughter of children and a dog's playful barking. Like Jack said, she reminded herself, take it easy; relax.

She started the car, pulled away from the kerb and drove through the grid of inner suburban roads until she reached the shopping strip along Smith Street. Parking, she bought copies of the morning newspapers and went into her favourite local cafe.

The decor was basic with a bare concrete floor, bare wooden tables and chairs, and rough clay-coloured walls resembling the stone interior of a cave. She often came here to decompress and get work out of her head. The only other customers were a couple of down-at-heel students who sat smoking over empty cups and textbooks. Trams clanged and rumbled through the nearby intersection. A thin stream of pedestrians went by the window – shoppers and bargain hunters, the occasional junkie looking gaunt and harassed. A weather-beaten drunk lurched into view then lurched out again. A police patrol car cruised by, the eyes of the officers hidden by dark sunglasses as they scanned the pavement.

As she ordered a light breakfast with an espresso, her mobile bleeped with a text message from Lola: *Am flying north. No strings attached. See you next Wednesday.*

Rita smiled to herself. She'd just spread the papers and was about to sip her coffee when a shadow fell across her table. She looked up and caught her breath as she saw the Duck standing over her.

'I join you,' he said, promptly pulling up a chair and sitting opposite her.

'What do you want?' she asked coldly.

'The Duck pay social call. Smooth things over. Make things clear.'

'You've been following me,' she said.

'This my neighbourhood, I live round here,' he replied.

'Kavella's put you up to this. What does he want?'

'He just want to have private chat with you.'

'Yeah, right, like that's going to happen,' she said.

'He want you stop causing trouble. Stop raids on club,' said the Duck.

'Or what?'

The Duck chuckled and the grin disappeared. 'You know what,' he said with deliberate menace. 'I come visit you soon while you asleep.'

The words made her shiver.

'I make myself home,' he went on. 'Piss in your dunny. Spit on your food.' Then he leant forward, lowering his voice. 'I do things to you. Use my knife.'

With a quick flick she emptied the cup of hot coffee onto his hands and he sprang back, yelping as if he'd been stung, his chair crashing onto the concrete floor.

'You bitch!' he shouted, and rushed through into the back of the cafe to find the kitchen, a startled waiter staring nervously after him.

There were bangs and crashes, the sound of breaking crockery, followed by the splash of running water against a staccato burst of Vietnamese curses. Moments later he came back, a deadly look on his face as he wiped his hands with a dishcloth and walked up to Rita, who was on her feet, ready for him.

'You going to regret that,' he said through his teeth, glancing back sharply at the witnesses, their heads bowing quickly.

Rita stood her ground. 'Tell your boss you delivered your message,' she said more calmly than she felt, 'and you got my reply.'

He flung down the dishcloth and stalked off.

Rita was still battling to control her breathing when the waiter came over with a fresh cup.

'You seem to have spilt your coffee,' he said.

As she thanked him, her phone rang. She snatched it up and snapped, 'Yes?'

'Hello,' said Byron Huxley. 'Have I caught you at a bad time?'

'Sorry,' she said, still breathing rapidly. 'There was something nasty in my coffee.'

'Oh, right,' he replied. 'Look, I've got the afternoon clear and I was wondering if we could meet up.'

'Yeah, why not. I'm going for a workout at midday, but I'll be free after that.'

'Good, I'll be driving back up from the Peninsula campus, so why don't we meet somewhere along the bay?'

'Where do you suggest?' she asked.

'How about the Ricketts Point tearooms? They're right on the beach.'

'Sounds charming. What time?'

'Around three?'

'See you then.'

Rita's trip to the gym was far more strenuous than she'd planned. She did the full workout – weights, Stairmaster, rowing machine, a high-speed five k on the treadmill and a dozen laps of the pool. It helped burn off the nervous tension and anger brought on by the Duck's intrusion. Feeling more relaxed, she showered and went to the massage room for her scheduled appointment, lying face down in the dimmed lighting. Environmental mood music played softly in the background and a soothing scent of aromatherapy filled the air as she waited for the masseuse to arrive.

The door of the massage room opened and closed as someone entered. Rita, lying naked under a towel, didn't look up. Not until the person spoke.

'You haven't got a gun this time,' said Kavella. 'Unless it's hidden up your pussy.'

Rita twisted around, a hollow shock in her stomach, to see him standing over her, a brutal smile on his face.

'If you're ready for your rub down, I'll give it to you,' he offered.

'Don't touch me!' she warned him, trying to pull the towel around her and sit up.

'Shut up and don't move,' he said, pushing her flat again. 'I like you in this position.'

She clutched the towel tightly to her sides, feeling utterly vulnerable, her gun out of reach stowed away in a locker.

'Where do you want it, Van Hassel?' he asked, moving behind her. 'In your twat?'

She shuddered.

'Come on, speak up!' he shouted. 'Or do you prefer it up the arse?'

She swallowed and lifted her head. 'Lay a finger on me and I'll rip your balls off,' she said. 'Even if I have to do it in the nude.'

'I'd like to see you try,' he chuckled. 'Lucky for you I haven't got time to play around anymore.'

He walked around to the front of the massage table, leaning forward on it until his face was only a few inches from hers. His voice was just above a whisper as he said, 'I sent a request for a meeting, but you turned down the invitation. That's why I've come looking for you.'

'What do we have to talk about?' she asked.

'You lied to me,' he said. 'About the Delos Club. I checked with the boys and they haven't breathed a word of it, so you didn't hear it from them. I want you to look me in the eye and tell me what you know.'

'Why should I?'

'Because you're lying naked in front of me. Because I've got a hard cock and a Glock semi-automatic in my trousers,' he said, raising his voice. 'And because I'm pissed off at my nightclub being stormed on the pretext of a rape hunt!' He was shouting in her face now. 'I want you to tell me what the fuck you know before I call Moyle in here to open your legs and hold you down!'

It was obvious she had to say something but not till she stood a chance of defending herself. 'I'm not uttering a word until you let me up.'

'Okay, get up,' he said.

Rita sat up quickly, tucking the towel around her body and dropping off the massage table so it lay between them.

'So the Delos Club really is important to you,' she began. 'I thought it might be.'

'It would be very dumb of you to take the piss right now,' he warned her.

'Okay, my guess is you've set up a virtual private network as a secure line of communication with fellow hoods, like the ones you were having lunch with at Fioretto's.'

'And why would you think that?'

'I got the crime lab to hack into contacts between you and Victor Yang,' she lied.

'But you were ordered to back off.'

'Was I?'

'Don't play games with me,' said Kavella. 'So you went after me anyway, and what did you find?'

'Some busy electronic traffic, a lot of encrypted data and a reference to the Delos Club. Putting that together with your megalomania, I drew my own conclusions.'

He gave her a hard stare.

She put her hands on her hips and said, 'Tell me I'm wrong.'

Kavella folded his arms, trying to gauge if she was lying.

'As for questioning your customers last night, that was no pretext, you callous prick,' Rita continued. 'Two prostitutes have been attacked and mutilated, one of them murdered, and both of them used your nightclub to pick up punters. What are we supposed to do, treat Plato's Cave as a safe haven for killers?'

'Okay, okay. We know where this goes,' said Kavella, looking at his watch. 'And much as I'm enjoying this chat, I've got to be somewhere else – a top-level conference of hoods!' He suddenly barked out a laugh at her. 'Arranged through our VPN!'

'I'm glad you find it funny,' she said.

'You slay me, Van Hassel. You're great for amusement value. If you'd accepted my invitation, there'd have been no need to interrupt your massage. We should try being friends.'

'That's about as likely as you getting a conscience.'

'You never know, we could make it happen,' he laughed. 'You scratch my back, and I'll massage your crotch!'

With that, he swept out of the door, which slid shut behind him.

Rita breathed out heavily, slumping against the wall.

A moment later the masseuse appeared. 'Are you all right?' she asked. 'Those men wouldn't let me in.'

'I've been better,' Rita replied.

'Do you still want your massage?'

'Somehow I'm not in the mood.'

Rita was dressed, the holstered gun on her hip, workout bag over her shoulder, when a plain-clothes detective from Proctor's Taskforce Nero wandered into the gym.

'What are you doing here?' he asked.

'Being threatened by Kavella,' she answered tartly.

'Oh, that explains it,' he said. 'We couldn't work out why he and his entourage would visit a gym on their way to a gangland summit.'

'Great,' she said. 'While you were hanging around outside I was lying there naked with that psycho breathing in my face! I want to talk to Proctor, now!'

The officer nodded, called Jim Proctor on his mobile and handed it to Rita.

'I'm having a fun Saturday,' she told him. 'So far I've been threatened twice – once by Kavella and once by one of his hitmen – and all on my day off.'

'What did Kavella want?' asked Proctor.

'To find out how I knew about the Delos Club.'

'And you told him?'

'A line of bullshit about a crime lab hack and my suspicions of a VPN.'

'He swallowed it?'

'Yes, and now he wants us to be friends,' Rita sighed. 'That's even scarier than being enemies.'

'You've done well again,' Proctor told her. 'But I'm ordering some security for you. Tonight there'll be a patrol car stationed outside your house.'

48

'I had second thoughts after I suggested we meet here,' said Huxley. 'It occurred to me that tearooms on the beach sounds old-fashioned. I don't want you to think I'm a fogey.'

'It's a perfect choice,' Rita reassured him. 'After the sort of day I've had, this is just what I need. Low-key and civilised.'

They were sitting at a table beneath white umbrellas on the teahouse decking with a view of the bay. A strand of tea-trees and coast banksia lined the beach, sand gleaming in the sunshine, waves flopping onto the shore, mothers and toddlers paddling in the shallows. Pelicans were propped along an off-shore reef. Out on the blue expanse of water yachts were rolling with the swell, sails billowing.

'So why are you stressed out?' he asked. 'Bad day at the barricades?'

Rita gave him an indulgent smile. 'You wouldn't want to know.'

Huxley shrugged. He looked completely at ease with the beach setting in his safari shirt, baggy shorts and thongs, limbs tanned, face naturally handsome in the sunlight. Rita was wearing a denim skirt, strappy sandals and a white scoop top that wasn't too sexy, her face glowing, her skin scented with expensive perfume. But she was still on edge from the confrontation at the gym.

'Get it off your chest,' said Huxley.

'No, really. I don't want to spoil this afternoon.'

'If you felt there was something you couldn't tell me, *that* would spoil it.'

Rita gave him a searching look. 'I don't want to shock you.'

'I think I can take it.'

'Well, let's order first – though I feel like I'm living on coffee.'

'Then we'll share an afternoon cream tea,' he suggested. 'Scones, jam and a pot of Earl Grey.'

'Very traditional.'

After ordering at the counter, he sat down again. 'So what's upset you?' he asked.

'Work's become a bit full-on,' she said, frowning. 'I've got involved in an operation against one of the biggest scumbags in the city. What makes it worse is that he's someone who already hates my guts. This morning I was threatened by one of his thugs, just before you phoned me.'

'So that's what was nasty in your coffee.'

'Yes, I threw it over him.' She sighed. 'That wasn't the end of it, though. After my workout I was lying on the massage table, covered only by a towel, when the scumbag himself walked in – not just to intimidate me, but to threaten me with rape, right there in the gym, and there was nothing I could have done to stop him. I was mentally preparing for the worst, and I've never felt so helpless.' She stopped, bowing her head, tears running down her cheeks.

Huxley reached over and held her hand. 'Tell me his name,' he said.

'No way.'

'I'm not afraid of bullies, only of letting them go unchecked.'

'It's not your job, it's police work.' She shook her head. 'You're a good man. I don't want you involved in any way at all.'

'Don't you realise I already am? I care about you, so anything that puts you in harm's way involves me.'

She looked up at him with a tear-stained smile. 'I can't tell you his name. It would be in breach of an undercover police operation.' She squeezed both his hands. 'Don't worry. He's another step nearer twenty years in jail, the net's closing on him.'

'I hope you're right,' said Huxley, his face creased with concern. 'But if you ever need somewhere safe to stay my place is always available. It's only an hour away, up in the hills near Olinda. No one will find you there.'

'It's very kind of you.' She wiped her eyes. 'And I feel better now I've got that off my chest.'

'Good. And just in time for our cream tea.'

The waitress delivered a tray with a teapot, cups and food. As they served themselves with scones and clotted cream, Huxley pouring from the teapot, Rita asked about his family background. 'All I know about your personal life is you were conceived in Venice.'

Huxley laughed.

'That's the only exotic thing there is to know. My parents were part-time teachers and part-time hippies. As an infant they dragged me around Europe, California, Nepal – places I can't remember – and settled down as soon as I reached school age. So my upbringing was suburban and predictable: school, university, academic career.'

'Girlfriends?'

'I've had a few flings,' he answered. 'But not so fast. Your turn.'

'Fair enough. I was born in Amsterdam then spent my early childhood among Dutch expats in Java. My parents split up when I was seven and I moved to Australia after my mother remarried. Then much like you it was school, uni and career.'

'Why the police?'

'Family connection. My stepfather's a forensic toxicologist.'

'And your natural father?'

'I don't think about him so much these days.' She toyed with a teaspoon. 'He's an executive with a pharmaceutical firm. We lived in Jakarta after he was posted there. He walked out on the family for a Javanese girl. Up till then he'd doted on me, but from that moment my life changed.'

'And it's still with you.'

'Watch it, professor. You're treading on my turf, trying to psych me out,' she said, smiling. 'What about *your* parents? Are they into science?'

'No, English Lit, both of them. They're still baffled by my passion for cyberpunk. As a kid they tried to wean me off P.K. Dick and William Gibson but I'm still hooked. And now I get to play around with all that subversive stuff in a computer lab.'

'Cyberpunk?' said Rita dubiously. 'That's how you see your field of expertise?'

'Yes, a paradigm shift in what's real – liberating and dangerous at the same time. I love it.'

'That explains why you're different.'

'Different, how?'

'You're not a conventional academic, you're a digital rebel.'

'I suppose I am. You think I should add the title to my faculty door?'

They both laughed.

As they sipped their tea, the conversation turned to lighter subjects – movies, music, sport.

Afterwards they took a walk along the beach trail.

They stood at the point, watching a container ship wallowing in the distance.

'If I didn't have a formal dinner tonight, I'd ask you out,' said Huxley.

'What about next Saturday?' Rita asked.

'I've got to do a presentation at the Windsor Hotel for a state government think tank. But I'm booked into one of the suites, so we could share some free champagne.'

'I'll let you know,' she said.

He walked her back to her car.

Instead of getting in she leant against the bodywork, put her hands on his shoulders, drew him towards her and kissed him on the mouth. His arms went around her and the kiss became more intense, his body pressed against hers, his hands sliding to the back of her hips.

At last they separated.

He opened his mouth to speak but she put a finger to his lips.

'Till next time,' she said teasingly, as she got into her car.

She smiled as she drove off, blowing him a kiss as she headed north along the beach road.

That night Rita went to bed in a positive mood, despite the encounter with Kavella. And she had no trouble drifting off, thanks to an additional sense of security – in the shape of an armed police officer sitting in a patrol car outside her front gate.

49

The compulsion was on him again, the demon in his belly. It was time to cruise the night.

Once he was out on the empty roads he felt the thrill of the chase. But as a precaution he avoided the seafront and the area around the casino. The police were alert to those because of the two she-devils he'd already put out of action. This time he decided on an ethnic precinct – the Indochinese enclave that filled parts of the old industrial suburbs. He drove past the crumbling shell of a brewery and empty warehouses waiting for redevelopment. There were derelict factories with brick chimney stacks. Industrial sites due to be auctioned. Graffiti scrawled on walls and hoardings: ELVIS LIVES, FUCK CAPITALISM. The roads and pavements were deserted. No one about. Just the lonely glare of the street lamps.

He emerged onto the main road and drove past Vietnamese restaurants and takeaways. From an all-night cafe he could hear the voices of Vietnamese women chatting. He pulled over to the kerb and waited. Within minutes one of them was tapping on his window. She was young and obvious. They agreed on a price – one hundred dollars, bondage included. She got in and they drove past tower blocks and turned into a street of little wooden houses with corrugated iron fences. She told him where to park then led him to her front door. As he stood on the step he looked at her tiny strip of garden. It was full of weeds, with a berry bush that had collapsed for lack of pruning, and a rusted iron birdbath with rusted iron birds perched on the rim.

Once inside it felt like a familiar hunting ground, another interior with female trappings. There were oriental dolls and lanterns, silk tapestries, and by the bedroom mirror a clutter of cosmetics.

After he gave her the money, she asked him if he wanted a drink. He said yes, and she came back with a bottle of clear spirit. She filled a shot glass and handed it to him. He swallowed it in one gulp and coughed hard as it burnt his throat. She gave a dry laugh and set about attaching black leather straps with metal buckles to the bedposts. Then, at his request, she lit four lanterns, arranged them by the bed and switched off the overhead lights, leaving the room full of shadows and a soft, flickering glow. He nodded with satisfaction, stripped and put on his bronze mask. He was back in the cave.

She asked him about the mask, listened to his odd answer and promptly took off her clothes. Her body was slim and petite, almost boyish, with small round breasts and large dark nipples. She massaged his penis until it was hard. As she reached for a condom he felt that familiar rush of ferocity. He picked up the liquor bottle and smacked it against her skull. She fell back onto the bed, her eyes staring at him and her lips quivering, but making no sound. He fastened the buckles around her wrists and ankles, then spread her legs wider and penetrated her with brute force. The pleasure was over too quickly for him.

Her lips were still moving soundlessly as he went looking for a surgical tool. He found a sharp carving knife in a metal sheath on her draining board. He came back with it and knelt over her prostrate body. With one hand he forced her mouth wide open and with the other he thrust the blade down into her throat. He pushed it deep, twisting and cutting, until he'd severed her tongue by the root. He held it in his hand, looking at it, then dropped it on the floor with the knife. Feeling much calmer now, he dressed and left.

As he got back in his car a figure approached along the pavement – another young Vietnamese woman. She glanced at him but he ducked his head and drove off. In his rear-vision mirror he saw her enter the house he'd just left. Good timing. The thought of her imminent discovery pleased him. It also showed his luck was holding. He'd scored his point and left his mark. It was another victory in the battle.

50

Rita received a phone call from Strickland at first light.

'We've got another victim, and forensics have matched the prints to the Hacker's,' he said. 'This time he's cut her tongue out.'

She sat up in bed, rubbing her eyes. 'Is she alive?'

'Yes, but still unconscious. I thought you might want to join me at the crime scene.'

'I will. As soon as I've got dressed and poured a coffee down my throat. Give me the address.'

As Rita made her way through the forensic science officers in her plastic suit, she could see the crime scene was a parallel of the previous two. The same type of scenario was there again, with the buckled leather straps, the lanterns and the blood-stained knife.

'Not my idea of a quiet Sunday morning,' greeted Strickland, unshaven with a blast of nicotine on his breath, 'picking through the debris of another bondage mutilation. And what's with the soft lighting?'

'The Hacker needs his imitation cave,' Rita explained, 'with a prisoner in the shadows before he inflicts the symbolic wounds.'

There was blood on the bed, on the floor, and a spray of it on the silk tapestries.

Rita bent down to a chalk circle around a stain on the floor, next to the circled carving knife.

'What was here?' she asked.

'The severed tongue,' said Strickland. 'And if that's symbolic, even I can see a common theme in his three attacks: *see no evil, hear no evil, speak no evil*. Or am I way off beam?'

'It's possible you're right,' Rita said, 'but do you really think he'll stop at three?'

Strickland shook his head, 'No. So what's his next mutilation?'

'When he wounds his victims it's an act of sense deprivation, so he'll target another sense organ,' said Rita. 'And that makes him consistent with Plato, who argued that our senses are obstacles to perceiving the real world. The Hacker has taken the point literally.'

'We're back into mad philosopher territory,' Strickland said with a groan.

Rita noticed an unopened condom on the floor.

'He gets angry if they try to take control,' she observed, squatting down to peer at a liquor bottle lying on its side. It had already been dusted for prints, and there were traces of blood and hair on its surface.

'Is this what he used to subdue her?' she asked.

'Probably,' said Strickland. 'The doctors say her injuries include a blow to the head. My guess is she gave him a drink,' he pointed to a glass, 'after which he bashed her with the bottle, bound her, raped her and cut out her tongue. I think the only reason she survived was thanks to a friend turning up almost immediately afterwards. By the way, that second girl could be a witness.'

'She saw the Hacker?'

'No, but she saw a car drive off – and it wasn't an MX-5, it was a black ute. Hopefully the victim will be able to confirm it once she's conscious.' Strickland shook his head. 'By switching cars, this psycho may have outsmarted himself. It gives us something to cross-reference.'

'The more I see of his work, the less I'm inclined to consider him a psychopath,' said Rita, standing up and opening her notebook. 'It's as if he goes in organised and comes out disorganised, almost as though he carries in one fantasy, then impulsively acts out another. I think we're dealing with a delusional offender.'

'Sorry, but I'm missing the subtle distinction,' growled Strickland, heading for the door on his way to another cigarette. 'I don't see how it helps if the Hacker's cracking up.'

51

It was late afternoon before Rita could question the victim in hospital. The girl's eyes stared at her, full of terrible fear and incomprehension. Padding protruded from her mouth. Surgical dressing was taped to her skull where the blow had split the skin and stunned her. Emergency surgery had gone as far as possible to repair the physical trauma to her throat and larynx, and stitch up the damage to her wounded lips. But microsurgery to reattach the tongue had been ruled out; it was beyond repair. The psychological trauma would never heal.

Her name was Hei Vuong. She printed it on a pad. Her friend, who'd saved her life, sat beside the hospital bed, clutching her hand. Strickland stood in the background, hands in pockets. A police artist waited with him. A doctor kept watch on them all.

Rita asked the questions patiently, and watched as the young woman wrote down the answers. It was a slow, painful process.

'What did he look like?' asked Rita.

Normal guy, wrote the girl. *Smooth, handsome face.*

'What about his hair?'

Dark. Neat.

'Did you see his eyes?'

No. He wore glasses.

'Did they have mirror lenses?'

Yes. Then he put on a mask.

'A bronze mask?'

Yes.

'What was he wearing?'

Denim shirt. Black jeans.

'What car was he driving?'
Black ute.
'Ford or Holden?'
Don't know.
'Did you notice the numberplate?'
No.
'Did he mention a name?'
No.
'An area, or a place of work?'
No.

Rita sighed and glanced over her shoulder at Strickland. So far there was little new information to go on.

'Where and when did he pick you up?' she resumed.
Victoria Street, about two o'clock.
'Did he ask for bondage?'
Yes. Then he drove me home.

'I'm going to take a guess about what happened next,' Rita told her. 'But stop me if I get any detail wrong, okay? He paid and you offered him a drink, which he accepted. He asked you to light the lanterns and switch off the electric lights, which you did. You attached the bondage equipment to the bed, and in the process of you both getting undressed he put on the mask. Then you picked up a condom. Did he say anything at any stage?'

Only when I asked about the mask, wrote the girl.

'Give me his exact answer.'

He said, 'It's my other face.'

Rita stared at the words on the pad before continuing. 'Tell me how he attacked you.'

He went crazy, wrote the girl. *He hit me with the bottle. I felt nothing but I could still see and hear.*

'So you were still conscious?' asked Rita.

Yes. But numb all over.

Rita swore under her breath, but went on. 'What did he do?'

He threw me on the bed. Raped me like an animal. Then he got a meat knife from the kitchen. I thought he would kill me. But he cut out my tongue.

Her eyes filled with tears and she couldn't go on.

Rita glanced at the police artist. The man raised his eyebrows and shook his head in disbelief. Strickland was frowning, arms folded. She turned back to Hei but the girl was convulsing, unable to get breath into her lungs. The doctor called for assistance and the police contingent was swiftly ushered out of the room as the medical staff sedated her again.

'This is going to be a slow process,' said Strickland.

Rita nodded. 'I doubt we'll get much more.'

52

Rita left the hospital in a subdued mood, carrying dark thoughts about the Hacker's mental state, and depressing images of another young life in ruins. She arrived back in the taskforce room with Strickland to add the latest evidence to the case files and to hear Mace addressing his team ahead of another visit to the nightclub. The atmosphere was tense.

'The Vietnamese victim would be dead but for the quick thinking of her friend,' Mace told the detectives, his voice edgy. 'That was lucky for her and lucky for us. It also means we now have an artist's impression of the Hacker. We're about to release this to the media but don't let that distract you. It's to keep them occupied as much as anything else. I'm not confident it's accurate. Looks like any other yuppie to me. So keep in mind it's just an impression. We'll question anyone tonight who bears even a vague resemblance.'

Mace breathed out heavily then he went on. 'Now, what I'm about to add is very important. I know you weren't expecting to be called out again tonight, but it's because of other developments. It means, initially, we'll be playing a secondary role.' His rough features were creased with a hard frown as he gazed around the faces in the room. 'For more than three months, Jim Proctor has been running a secret surveillance operation against Tony Kavella. I won't go into details, other than to say that in the next couple of hours Proctor's Taskforce Nero will be launching raids against gangland organisations around the city. A key target is the Plato's Cave nightclub, and the offices attached to it. One of the aims is to shut Kavella down – permanently. If all hell breaks loose, we'll be there as backup. If it goes smoothly, we'll follow up with another trawl through the clubbers for anyone matching the Hacker's description.' He paused to let the implications sink in. 'Okay, let's roll. And again – I don't want any slip-ups.'

Mace led the team from the room, leaving Rita and Strickland facing each other across the table.

'The shit's about to hit the fan,' said Strickland, pulling himself up from his chair. 'We might as well pack it in for the night.'

'I'll just type up some notes,' Rita told him.

'Well, don't knock yourself out. We're about to be overtaken by events. Kavella won't go down without a fight.'

As Strickland left, Rita dragged over a keyboard, logged on and started filing the details supplied by Hei Vuong. She was sitting alone in the room, elbows on the table, when Jim Proctor strode in.

'Good, I wanted to catch up with you,' he said, leaning on the table beside her. 'I assume you've heard we're going in tonight.' He glanced at his watch. 'Less than two hours to go, and we're hitting all of them at once. I've had to bring the raids forward because Kavella's very twitchy, thanks to Mace going into the club mob-handed two nights in a row.' Proctor sat down in the chair beside her. 'Anyway, that's not what I need to talk to you about. We've got Kavella on tape planning to do a runner to some secret bolthole he's got. And there's something else you have to hear.' He gestured to the keyboard. 'May I?'

'Help yourself,' said Rita, moving aside.

She watched Proctor pull a USB memory stick from his pocket, plug it in and call up a digital audio file.

'Ready?' he asked.

She nodded, he hit the play button and the voices of Kavella and Brendan Moyle came out of the speaker:

Kavella: *Why do I bother paying cops if they don't give me more warning?*

Moyle: *Deadshits.*

Kavella: *I want everything in place, in case I get the final word.*

Moyle: *No problem. They won't see us for dust.*

Kavella: *Once we're out we can take it easy – a long holiday in the Caribbean – I'm almost looking forward to it. But there's one piece of unfinished business.*

Moyle: *If you want me to do the bitch, it'd be a pleasure.*
Kavella: *I'm through with twisting her tail, it's party time. I want to fuck her over. I want to make her bleed. I want her to scream. I want her dead!*
Moyle: *I'm on it.*
Kavella: *No, you're staying with me. Get the Duck. Tell him to kill Van Hassel and let me know how he did it.*

Proctor hit the stop button and stared at her gravely. 'Of course we've got him right there on conspiracy to murder,' he said.

She gave him a grim smile. 'You're welcome.'

'I'm sorry, I bear a lot of responsibility.'

'No you don't,' she said. 'Kavella's been out for revenge since his arrest. You've just helped speed things up.'

'I've booked two patrol cars for you tonight,' Proctor went on. 'One out front, the other in the alleyway at the back of your house. That should keep you safe.'

'Thanks.'

'Now go home, lock up and wait for tomorrow's news.' Proctor stood up, smiling. 'We're about to make some headlines.'

53

Rita was overtired. She'd been woken before dawn and the pressures of the long day had worn her down. Once she'd checked through the house with the patrol officers, she saw them out, locking and bolting the doors behind them. Then she double-checked that all the windows were secure, a habit she'd developed since the anonymous guest had let himself in to watch her TV and rummage through her things. Next she tidied up a bit, straightening her books and videos, and finally, she tended to the feng shui balance of her bedroom – making delicate adjustments to the positions of the mirrors, indoor ferns, the bamboo screen, the wooden drawers. It was only just after ten o'clock, with almost an hour to go till Proctor's raids, but she was ready for bed.

She propped herself up on pillows and switched off the lamp, but she'd left the blinds partly open to let in some streetlight. The room was full of deep shadows, but not complete darkness. As her eyes adjusted she could see the outlines of the objects around her, and the glimmer of the gun on the sheet beside her. It was a Smith & Wesson .38, with a chequered walnut grip and satin nickel stock. More than once she picked it up, felt the weight, then put it down again. Its presence was reassuring. And while her rational mind told her to set aside fears of an intruder – baleful imaginings that come in the night – the glossy metal presence of the revolver felt like a protective charm, in addition to the cops on watch outside.

It wasn't long before the security of the gun, and the weight of tiredness, had her eyelids drooping. As she nodded off, she slumped down further onto the pillows, and drifted into a dreamless sleep.

She woke within minutes, bleary-eyed and wondering for a moment why she was propped up in bed. Then she remembered, and with a jolt was suddenly alert. Something – she didn't know what – had disturbed her sleep. Instinctively she reached for the gun, hardly daring to breathe. The room was no different. Solid with shadows cast by the dim streetlight. The air warm and still. No sounds in the dead of night. No traffic, no footsteps. Nothing at all. Maybe she was mistaken, letting her fears get to her. But just as her breathing started to ease, she heard it. The quiet scraping of something overhead, a possum on the roof perhaps. When it came again she realised it wasn't *on* the roof, the sound was *in* the roof. A moment later she heard the creak of the ceiling trapdoor being opened above the kitchen, followed by the groan of the loose floorboard under the linoleum. Someone was inside her house, moving slowly towards her bedroom.

She flicked off the safety catch, pointed the gun at the doorway, and held it steady, both hands on the grip. She tried to do the breathing exercises she'd been taught to allay panic, but her heart was hammering.

The first movement was barely perceptible, there and gone in an instant. She lowered the angle of the barrel. As she did, he hurled himself through the air with terrifying agility. If she hadn't been poised, gun at the ready, she wouldn't have stood a chance. As it was, she had just a moment to react. The dark shape of his body descending on her, the glint of metal from a knife. She dodged sideways, firing at point-blank range. The bullets exploding through his skull, the sound of the gunshots deafening. Smoke in her eyes. The smell of cordite. Something wet on her face. His body crashing against hers. The knife grazing her shoulder.

She twisted out from under him, sprang across the room and switched on the light, the .38 still aimed at the shape on the bed. But no more bullets were needed. Her muscles and sinews tensed as she recognised what was left of her would-be killer, the Duck, his forehead blasted away. Dark red oozing from his mouth into her duvet. Her walls and ceiling spattered with his blood, bone fragments and brain matter. More of the same dripping from her face.

She wiped it quickly with her forearm and lowered the gun. Despite her close brush with death, she felt strangely cool and self-possessed now. And though her heart was pumping heavily, her thoughts were clear. She'd done what was necessary. But the feng shui arrangements of her bedroom now resembled a slaughterhouse.

As she stood there staring at the blood and membranes, Rita heard doors banging, voices shouting, footsteps running. She was walking towards her front door when it burst in and slammed against the wall. A torchlight blinded her and all she could see in the glare was a gun barrel and a cop in uniform. Instantly she raised her hands.

'Are you all right?'

It was the urgent voice of the young constable who'd been on watch in the street out front.

'Yes.'

'Where is he?'

'In the bedroom – dead.'

Then came another loud crash, this time behind her, as the kitchen door sheered out of its frame and smacked against the sink. Heavy boots were thudding on the linoleum bringing another cop with a gun and torchlight.

'Okay, okay,' said the first officer. 'The incident's over.' He switched on the hall lights and looked at her. 'Are you injured? You're covered in blood.'

'No, it's his. I shot him in the head.'

She led them into the bedroom and they looked down at what was left of the Duck, taking in the slow dark ooze from his shattered skull, the glassy eyes, the frozen snarl of his gold-studded teeth, the knife lying harmlessly under his limp hand.

'Thank God you had your gun,' said one of the officers, while the other radioed in the police alert. 'How did we miss him?'

'He got here before us,' answered Rita. 'He must have picked a lock and hidden in the roof.'

'Shit,' said the young cop, his voice rough with emotion. 'We nearly lost you.'

54

Eleven o'clock on a Sunday night, and the nightclub was buzzing. The top celebrity guest was an AFL footballer wired to the eyeballs on coke, pumping himself around the dance floor, stripped to the waist, medallion bouncing, muscles flexing in a sheen of perspiration, his brain telling him he could bop forever. His girlfriend, a calendar model, was too far gone on high-octane cocktails to keep up and was being buffeted around by the other dancers as they heaved to a retro mix of seventies hits spun by the DJ. In the row of booths figures leant towards each other, faces shadowed, hands out of sight. This was, after all, primarily a pick-up joint. Against the cellar walls, dripping with condensation, the tables were crowded with empty bottles, jugs and glasses. Along the bar slumped older men, some in blazers, full of beer and lascivious fantasies as they peeled open their wallets for women with tight skirts and scavenger faces. Behind them the bar staff worked at a steady pace, mixing cocktails, pulling the pumps, working the tills. Above their heads, fogged in the dim, clammy, smoky atmosphere, glowed the red neon sign reading Plato's Cave.

Then several things happened at once.

The calendar model fell flat on her face, legs splayed out, skirt dislodged, exposing the fact she was wearing no panties. A man on a bar stool pointed and laughed, 'Look at the naked arse!', so the footballer went up and punched him to the floor before raining kicks on him. The bouncers swooped and hauled him off just in time to hear the crash overhead and see what looked like a regiment of cops swarming down the stairs.

As the police fanned out around the nightclub, the lights came up and the music stopped, leaving an uncomfortable hush. The customers shuffled awkwardly, wanting to leave, but they were going nowhere. If they had any guilty secrets, this was their moment of reckoning.

A few minutes later, Jim Proctor pushed through the wall of officers at the top of the stairs, radio in hand, talking urgently to Mace.

'Anyone make a run for it?' asked Proctor.

'No,' answered Mace. 'And we've got every exit covered.'

'Shit,' said Proctor. 'The computer boys are in the adjoining building but it looks like we're too late. There's been a mass delete of the programs.'

'Where's Kavella?'

'He's vanished,' said Proctor, 'which means we've got a manhunt.'

55

Rita sat with a mug of warm tea in her hand as she completed a statement to Jack Loftus back in his office. She'd showered, sealed her clothes in an evidence bag, and changed into the tracksuit and tennis shoes from her locker. The grey light of early dawn was seeping through the windows. From the far end of the office came the hum of vacuum cleaners.

The formalities over, Loftus reached over his desk and put a hand on hers.

'You sure you're okay?' he asked.

She nodded. 'Just tired. I've gone twenty-four hours without sleep. Any word yet on Kavella?'

'Wait here, I'll check.'

While Loftus went off to the communications centre, Rita switched on his office TV in time to catch Mike Cassidy mid-flow in the early breakfast bulletin.

> *... and so what happened in the club behind me overnight was part of an unprecedented series of police raids against top gangland figures. Members of the Fazio family, with their well-known connections to the Calabrian mafia, are in custody. So too is Triads overlord Victor Yang. However, arrest warrants have been issued for fugitive crime boss Tony Kavella and his chief lieutenant, Brendan Moyle, who made a last-minute getaway before Plato's Cave was surrounded and cordoned off last night. They're wanted on a long list of charges, including conspiracy to murder. The latter count relates to a hit ordered on criminal profiler Marita Van Hassel. Reliable sources tell me the police were aware of the threat, after months of surveillance by a special operation known*

as Taskforce Nero. Although the details haven't yet emerged, it's been confirmed that underworld hitman Duc Hung Long – also known as the Duck – was shot dead inside the profiler's house. How all this is linked, we're yet to be informed, but as we find out we'll update you from here at the scene. Now it's back to the studio.

Rita switched off the TV as Loftus returned.

'Well?' she asked.

'No trace of Kavella or Moyle,' he said, flopping back into his chair. 'We're facing one of the biggest police hunts in years.' He rubbed his eyes. 'But that's not your concern. You've got to get some sleep. Is there anyone you can stay with while your house is out of action?'

'Now that you mention it, I'm a bit stuffed at the moment. My parents have retired to the Gold Coast, my sister lives in Canada, and my best friend is away in the Whitsundays being wooed by a lesbian. I suppose I could ask Erin, but she's got her hands full already.'

'There are a couple of spare bedrooms at my place,' offered Loftus. 'Or we could just put you up at a hotel.'

'I'll think about it in a minute,' said Rita distractedly. 'I just realised I'd better phone my parents before they find out what happened from the telly.'

'I'll get you another tea.'

After making a call that at first alarmed her mother and stepfather, then reassured them, she was about to tell Loftus to book her into a hotel when her mobile rang. It was Byron Huxley.

'I've just seen the news,' he said, his voice full of concern. 'Are you okay?'

'I'm knackered, but I'm fine,' she answered with a smile. 'You don't have to worry.'

But he contradicted her. 'Yes, I do. Where are you staying?'

'I'll book into a hotel,' she began, but he interrupted.

'You're staying at my place, Rita. No arguments, please. And there are no ulterior motives, I promise. It's very peaceful and well away from the city, a great place to chill out. Are you at the police complex at the moment?'

'Yes.'

'I'll be there in an hour, if you agree.'

A wave of relief seemed to wash over her, along with something more tender.

'Okay,' she said.

An hour later Huxley pulled up at the front entrance in his four-wheel drive. Rita was waiting for him. As she got in beside him, she gave him an affectionate kiss on the cheek.

'What's that for?' he asked.

'For coming to my rescue,' she answered. 'My knight in a shining Range Rover.'

Ten minutes into the drive she was sound asleep.

She woke up as they reached Huxley's place outside the village of Olinda. It was built on a slope between the road and the forest. There was no garden, just a driveway, a garage and a modern split-level cottage in a space among the gum trees. The minimalist theme continued inside, with wooden walls and floors, suede furniture and little that was decorative. Not that it was needed, with picture windows and glass doors opening onto a balcony with forest views, the sunlight streaming through the foliage.

'This is it,' said Huxley. 'Make yourself at home.'

'I'm sorry, but I really need to sleep,' Rita told him.

'No problem. The bedroom's upstairs. On this level you've got the bathroom, kitchen and lounge, and downstairs is the computer den.'

'Only one bedroom?' she asked.

'Yes, and it's yours. I'll be sleeping on the sofa.'

'Are you sure?'

'Absolutely. And if you're asleep when I get back from university tonight I won't wake you. What about work tomorrow?'

'I need to get back as early as I can,' she answered.

'Okay, in the morning you take the Range Rover,' he said.

'But how will you get to the university?'

'I'll use taxis. And here,' he said, taking keys from an overhead cupboard. 'My spare set of house keys to let yourself in when you drive back after work.'

She laughed. 'So this isn't a one-night stand?'

'You stay as long as you need to. Come and go as you please. Eat, sleep, go for a walk – there's no better place to relax.' He glanced at his watch. 'But I've got to get going. I'm due to deliver a lecture in less than an hour.' He bent over and kissed her forehead. 'Catch up on your sleep.'

She squeezed his hand in thanks.

Moments later his Range Rover was crunching back up the gravel driveway before disappearing along the road.

Rita wearily climbed the stairs to a broad attic bedroom with a high ceiling, skylights and French windows level with the forest canopy. She flopped onto a king-size bed, dozed fitfully for a few hours, then got up and helped herself to a chicken salad from Huxley's fridge. After wandering barefoot around his home she decided it was pleasant enough, if rather Spartan. She tried watching TV but, unable to keep her eyes open, gave up and went back to bed before six p.m. This time she fell into a deep sleep.

56

Before the forest birds began their chorus of calls and screeches in the morning twilight, Rita was already wide awake, her sleep pattern totally disrupted. She spent an hour trying to settle again without success, and as the early grey light seeped through the leaves, she rose, showered and dressed.

Huxley was sound asleep under a duvet on his sofa. He'd left the car keys on the kitchen counter with a note saying, 'Happy motoring!' She collected the keys with a smile, tiptoed out, got in the car and drove into the city ahead of the rush hour, allowing her time to call in at her house on the way to work.

She lifted the police tape hung across her front door and let herself in. Somehow the place didn't feel the same. Even the smell of the house was different. The dead body had been removed from the bedroom, but the stains still covered the bed, and the blood spatter had left an ugly residue on the walls and ceiling. She realised no amount of redecorating would remove those marks for her, they were indelible, and in that moment she was also aware that this, sadly, could never be her home again.

Despite Huxley's insistence on her using the Range Rover, Rita had a better idea. After changing into clothes more suitable for work, she packed an overnight bag and got in her own car to drive to the office. From there she'd phone up one of the specialist chauffeur firms to ferry Huxley's car out to the university. That way they'd each have their own set of wheels.

At police headquarters Jim Proctor was coordinating the search for Tony Kavella and Brendan Moyle which, for the moment, was taking precedence over the Hacker investigation. All available officers were being drafted into the manhunt, including Rita. She was again teamed up with Kevin O'Keefe, as they waited to hear what roles they'd be assigned.

'We have to consider both men armed and dangerous,' Proctor told the pool of detectives. 'It's just over twenty-four hours since they went on the run, so we've still got a good chance of apprehending them. We moved fast enough on Sunday night to keep a watch on key transport routes, including the highways, so I'm pretty confident they're bottled up somewhere in the metropolitan area. We know Kavella's got a hide-out somewhere, but he has to emerge at some stage. Every relevant location familiar to Taskforce Nero is under observation, so many of you will be going out this morning to relieve officers who've been on all-night stake-outs.' He gave a nod of appreciation before continuing. 'This is an immense team effort and I want to thank you all for getting in so early, but let me add a final note of caution. While it's crucial to stop these two fugitives getting away overseas, they know they have little to lose by trying to shoot their way out. Keep that in mind. Now let's get on with it.'

As officers were being dispatched, O'Keefe nudged Rita.

'Okay, boss,' came his gruff voice in her ear. 'How do we get in on the act?'

'We're about to find out,' she said.

Proctor approached them, clipboard in hand. 'There must be things about Kavella you know that I don't,' he said. 'Where do you think he's likely to surface?'

'If he's planning to go into exile,' Rita answered, 'he'll try to say a personal goodbye to his family. That's his only allegiance, other than to himself.'

'Well, the homes and offices of the brothers and brothers' wives are staked out, and so is the mother's home.'

'Has anyone tried *talking* to Nina?' asked Rita.

'No, we're keeping a discreet distance from family members,' answered Proctor. 'You think Kavella's mother would cooperate?'

'Nina is the one person who holds emotional sway over him, and she's also his number one critic,' she said. 'She's never forgiven him for throwing away his academic prospects and turning to evil, as she puts it. She's quite religious and active in the local Orthodox church.'

'She knows you?'

'Yes, she poured out her heart to me a couple of times.'

'Then do it,' said Proctor. 'Go talk to her. But you two watch each other's backs. And Van Hassel, requisition another gun.'

O'Keefe was behind the wheel of the unmarked police car as Rita directed him through a Greek neighbourhood in the suburbs.

'It's just gone ten o'clock,' she said, 'so we might catch Nina at the cemetery.'

'How come?' asked O'Keefe.

'She puts fresh flowers on her husband's grave each Tuesday to mark his time of death.'

O'Keefe drove through the cemetery gates and parked.

'You wait here,' Rita told him.

She got out and walked through the mottled clutter of tombs and monuments until she reached the grave. The fresh flowers were there, but no sign of Nina Kavella.

Rita went briskly back to the car.

'We just missed her,' she told O'Keefe. 'Let's try the church, it's just up the road. She might have gone there if she's on flower duty.'

O'Keefe drove out of the cemetery, covered the short distance through the next intersection and pulled over opposite the church. It stood behind iron railings and a row of poplars, its whitewashed stone walls topped by a gold cupola, reflecting the sunshine. To either side were front gardens of suburban houses, with vans and station wagons in the driveways. The only other vehicle was a black Mercedes limousine with dark tinted windows, parked outside the church gates.

'This time I'm coming with you,' said O'Keefe.

'Okay,' agreed Rita. 'But this is a place of worship, so let's treat it with respect.'

They crossed the road and walked up the path to the church steps.

'Let me check it out first,' said Rita, 'just to see if she's in there.' She disappeared through the doors.

O'Keefe walked across the lawn to the side of the church, as much out of instinct as anything else, to see if anyone was around. He heard a cough, then saw a bulky figure in a dark suit emerge from the back of the church. It was Brendan Moyle, who was busily zipping up his flies.

As soon as Moyle caught sight of him, he turned and bolted like a runaway bull, using all his momentum to hurdle a paling fence into someone's backyard, with O'Keefe hard on his heels. The detective clambered over the fence in pursuit and sprinted after Moyle through vegetable plots of beans and pumpkins, then through a scatter of wildly clucking hens. The chase ended when Moyle wheeled around the side of a garden shed, pivoted and pulled out his gun, aiming it at O'Keefe, who stopped in his tracks.

'Enough!' shouted Moyle. 'Or I'll blow your fucking head off!'

'Don't be an idiot,' said O'Keefe, panting heavily.

The commotion brought a man in singlet and shorts out of the shed.

'What's going on?' he demanded.

'Fuck off!' said Moyle, and the man backed away.

At the same time, two old women in black shawls emerged from the house, a madly yapping poodle darting between them to race headlong at Moyle, snapping at his leg. He gave the dog a kick, but it sprang back at him, barking viciously. He turned and shot it. The dog bared its teeth, snarling, so he shot it again.

In that instant, O'Keefe lunged at him, grabbing his gun arm. Moyle swore loudly as the two men buffeted and thumped against each other, wrestling for control of the weapon, crashing through dustbins and a tangle of laundry on a Hills hoist.

Heads were appearing over neighbouring fences.

'I'm gonna kill you!' yelled Moyle, as their two bodies banged into the side of a chicken coop, the gun discharging and blasting a hole through O'Keefe's thigh.

He let out an involuntary cry as he chopped the weapon from Moyle's hand, then limped sideways, blood running down his leg.

Moyle snatched up a long-handled garden hoe. 'I'm gonna kill you then gut you!'

But as Moyle thrust forward with the hoe, O'Keefe grabbed it, yanking it towards him, bringing Moyle stumbling forward into a headlock. They twisted and swayed, their combined weight pressing against the wire cage. O'Keefe saw the flash of metal as Moyle got hold of the knife in his boot and, with a powerful jerk, he snapped Moyle's head around. There was a loud crack of bone as his neck broke. Moyle convulsed as the dead weight of his body collapsed through the wire into the chicken coop, where it lay motionless, his lungs expiring, his head flopping underneath at an impossible angle.

'I'm a policeman!' O'Keefe yelled to the residents, pulling out his radio. 'I'm calling for backup, but I've got to get back to my partner.'

He shouted instructions into the radio, hobbling away as fast as he could, leaving a trail of blood through the vegetable garden. Kavella must be inside the church, and Rita would be at his mercy.

Rita was talking to Nina Kavella in the nave, where the elderly widow was arranging flowers in front of the Byzantine images of the altar screen. The walls around them were decorated with icons and murals, the smell of incense hanging in the air.

'I don't really want to know what my son has done now,' said Nina. 'It's too disappointing. He's been a lost soul since his father died.'

'He'll try to escape overseas because this time his lawyers won't be able to stop him going to prison,' explained Rita.

'He shames our community,' said Nina, with a nervous glance behind her. 'Like he has for years.'

'I think he'll try to say goodbye to you.'

'You think so?' said Kavella, stepping from behind the altar screen, gun in hand.

'Tony!' protested his mother. 'It's desecration for you to enter the sanctuary.'

'I didn't have much choice,' he said, edging through the Holy Doors, his gun aimed at Rita's chest. 'Where did you think I was hiding?'

'It's sacrilege,' said Nina.

'I'm sorry if I interrupted your last farewell,' said Rita.

'I'm not,' returned Kavella. 'Because now I can take care of some unfinished business.'

He raised the gun to fire.

'Tony, no!' shrieked his mother.

As Nina raised her hands, begging him to stop, Rita flung herself behind the woman, pulling out her .38 as she did so. Kavella was jostling to get a clear shot when he lost his footing on the white marble steps. Rita stood up straight, gun held steady in both hands, and while Kavella propped himself up to fire, she shot him through the throat. Even as the first spurt of blood sprayed from his neck, a second bullet, fired by O'Keefe leaning in the doorway, hit Kavella full in the chest. To the sound of the gun blasts, and the screams of his mother, Kavella crumpled to his knees, blood pouring from his wounds, his body pitching forward to smack against the marble floor, where it lay contorted in death, bleeding over the altar steps.

Within minutes, the church, its grounds and the neighbouring gardens were swarming with police and crime scene officers. The surrounding streets were cordoned off, with traffic diverted and eyewitnesses herded towards patrol vans.

A priest was trying to comfort a hysterical Nina on the pavement outside the church, while an ambulance arrived to carry O'Keefe off to hospital, his leg treated by medics as he gave a verbal statement to a fellow detective. Rita did a detailed walk-through of the shoot-out with Proctor, who nodded gravely, staring coldly at the corpse lying in a vast pool of blood. It wasn't the conclusion he'd hoped for.

'Okay,' Proctor said at last. 'I've got a clear picture of what went down.' He looked at his watch. 'But it's past midday and we're about to hit a feeding frenzy by the media. I want you out of here.'

'What do you want me to do?' she asked.

'Head straight back to the office, give your report in writing to Jack Loftus, then go off duty. There'll be some internal flak over this as well.' He put his hand on her shoulder. 'It's best for you and O'Keefe to keep your heads down for the next day or two. So if there's anywhere you can lie low, I suggest you go there.'

'There is,' she said. 'And I will.'

It was mid afternoon before Rita was able to leave police headquarters.

'This will keep the bureaucrats at bay for now,' Loftus told her, patting the printout of her detailed report. 'Time for you to head for the hills.'

'Thank God,' she said. 'I feel completely knackered.'

'By the way, the crime lab's retrieved the burnt remains of smartcards from Kavella's fortress, so we might have unearthed a link to the Hacker after all.'

'I hope so.'

'This Huxley chap . . .' he said as an afterthought. 'How serious is it?'

'I'm not sure myself,' she admitted. 'But if you're hinting at what I think you are, the answer is he's been a perfect gentleman.'

'Well, that's a rare species these days,' grunted Loftus. 'You certainly need someone who's caring and thoughtful after what you've been through the last couple of days.'

'Thanks, Jack. You're not too bad at it yourself.'

'Call me tomorrow when you've recuperated a bit.'

As she got into the lift to go down to the basement car park, she called Huxley.

'Was your Range Rover delivered to you?' she asked.

'Yes, thanks,' he answered. 'It's parked outside my lab.'

'Good. I've finished for the day and I'm about to drive up to Olinda and crash out again. You have no idea how blissful that seems.'

'Why?' he said. 'What's happened?'

'Don't ask,' she replied. 'Just watch the news and decide if you still want me as a house guest.'

'You needn't doubt it for a second.'

57

They were taking his wife's BMW to the airport because Barbie didn't want to park his Lamborghini there. He was driving. Giselle was in the passenger seat talking about her catwalk assignment in Japan. She was flying out to Tokyo for a one-day fashion spectacular, being shown live on television. He was taking the Cityflyer service to Sydney for a series of business meetings.

'What styles will you be modelling?' he asked.

'A lot of high hemlines by the sound of it. The latest thing seems to be full-on sex appeal – bolted stilettos, thigh-high stockings, tight corsets and micro-minis. Lots of micro-minis.'

'Pussy helmets,' said Barbie dismissively.

Giselle gave him a sideways look. He seemed on edge. 'What's wrong?' she asked.

He didn't answer straightaway, just gazed ahead at the strip of airport freeway unwinding through a fringe of fields, gum trees and giant billboards. His own grinning face mooned back at him from one of the hoardings – an ad for his TV game show.

'Business hiccups,' he said at last. 'That's all.'

She knew he was understating the problem. 'Are we in financial trouble?' she asked pointedly.

He looked at her quickly and said with a bleak smile, 'Not yet.'

She frowned. 'You had a phone call before we got in the car. Jojima again, was it?'

'Yes.'

'Is he the hiccup?'

He let the question hang there for a moment. It was a reminder of why he'd married her. Despite appearances, Giselle was not just arm candy, as one dyspeptic columnist had described her. She was observant and smart, with a perceptive grasp of the crude and mercenary forces that shaped the social life around her. As well as being decorative, she was a valuable ally.

'Jojima' – Barbie pronounced the name as if it referred to a venomous species – 'is in a position to do us damage.'

'How?'

'He's threatening to pull the plug on a very big deal I've been working on. The new VR game. I don't know if the threat's real or it's just brinkmanship ahead of Friday's deadline. The whole thing's up and running at last but the software research has cost a fortune. If the Japanese don't sign now, I'm left with a cashflow problem. That's why I'm flying up to Sydney. There's a takeover bid for the first production company. I'd been hanging onto it for sentimental value. Now we need the money.'

'Well that's more important than sentiment,' she said, giving him a sceptical look.

He nodded and accelerated past a line of trucks.

'Can't you sell to someone else?' she went on. 'The Americans?'

'Timing.' He shook his head. 'Just the process of trying to set up another deal.'

'And our personal finances if Jojima says no?'

'Tight.'

She didn't like the sound of that at all. It had a nasty ring of austerity. 'What's he really like, this Jojima?' she asked. 'I've only met him once at that black-tie dinner when the state government was touting for trade. He seemed quite pleasant.'

'Don't you believe it. He's commercially ruthless. Hard as nails.'

'Yes, but what's he like away from the office? What sort of man is he?'

'Pretty cold from what I gather. Precise. Formal. No emotions. I've tried getting round his defences – but no luck so far. It's like playing chess with a grandmaster.'

'Married?'

'No.'

'Gay?'

'Definitely not. He uses women prostitutes on a regular basis.'

'Japanese or western?'

'Western, as a matter of fact. He has a thing about them. Why do you ask?'

This time Giselle didn't answer, turning to look through the window and watching a 747 climbing from take-off.

'How important is he to us?' she said at last.

'Extremely important,' he said with a sigh. 'If he says no, we lose millions. If he says yes, we stand to make our first billion.'

She nodded, as if making up her mind about something. 'I think I should look him up in Tokyo. Get him to take me out – for a social drink at least. Would he do that?'

Barbie pondered the suggestion. 'He would if I asked him to.'

'I think you should. I can charm him in ways you can't.'

Barbie fell silent, knowing exactly what she meant. He had no misconceptions about their marriage. There was nothing idealistic or romantic in it – other than for public display. Like most things, it had been a pragmatic choice for both of them. And on that basis, it was consistent for Giselle to do whatever she could to seal the contract in Tokyo. With a mixture of distaste and admiration for her commitment, he nodded his assent.

He drove into the tiers of long-term parking and pulled into one of the bays. Before he turned off the ignition, his wife rested her hand on his forearm and looked him straight in the eye. She wanted her own verbal agreement. There could be no guilt, no recriminations.

'If I think I can save the deal, should I let him fuck me?'

She was offloading the responsibility. It was Barbie's decision.

He switched off the engine and sat back, averting his eyes so he was facing straight ahead at a grey concrete wall. 'A lot of money's at stake, and it might only need a nudge to get him to commit,' he said. 'Just play it by ear.'

They looked the perfect couple as they walked through the jostle of people milling around the international departures gate – Giselle sharply dressed in a black slashed top with matching trousers and peep-toe sandals, Barbie in his lightweight Italian wool suit. Smooth beige. Open-neck cream shirt. They were both dressed for travel.

Behind her she trailed her black leather Louis Vuitton flight case, while he carried an overnight bag, laptop and business suit. They stopped just short of the sliding doors. Around them people backed off a little. Smiles of recognition. Heads turning. It was something they were used to – personal rituals performed in public – but the rewards were worth it. Image was everything.

'Well,' he said. 'See you on Thursday.'

She nodded, but in her eyes there was a coldness and it spoke volumes. For the first time in their partnership she was letting him see an entirely new emotion: disappointment. He didn't like it. He was being censured for failing to maintain the basis of their marriage, unassailable wealth, and as a result forcing her into a sacrifice that few women would contemplate. The expression in her eyes lingered for a long moment, like a warning, then switched to their usual brightness as a fellow fashion model approached – her travelling companion to Tokyo.

As the two women greeted each other, kissing the air and embracing with all the sincerity of a stage-managed welcome, Barbie was frowning. Giselle's brief display of disapproval was like a shot across his bows, a potential threat to their relationship, based as it was on mutual respect, public loyalty and professional empathy. As he faced the biggest financial crisis of his career it was the last thing he needed.

They said their goodbyes and the two women disappeared through the sliding doors on their way to the executive lounge. While he stood there distracted by his thoughts a small boy approached, a shy smile on his face, autograph book in hand. Barbie signed it without a word, then turned and walked briskly towards the domestic terminal. The pressures in his life were converging. Problems were multiplying. Secrets were getting harder to manage. His trip to Sydney was shaping up as a moment of truth, and the flash of hostility from his wife was like a bad omen.

58

Every now and then the air hostess would brush by, wanting to catch his attention or fuss over him. Now she was flirting openly.

'Coffee, tea or me?' she asked with a teasing smile.

Barbie looked up from his laptop, his mind still juggling sets of figures. He leant back in the comfort of his business-class seat, took a deep breath and gave her the once-over. Slim. Tanned. Attractive enough in a fresh-faced, ingenuous sort of way. Not his type at all. No hint of the fallen woman. It was what he always looked for, the thing that excited him most: a lubricious element of vice. He was astute enough to know it was because of his repressive upbringing – and indulgent enough to pursue it. But this woman was just available. No sign of corruption in her eyes.

'Coffee,' he said with a selfless shrug. 'Triple espresso.'

She gave a mock sigh and went off to get it. Too bad. But that's all he wanted from her. Caffeine. Lots of caffeine. He was flying into battle and needed his wits about him. The three business meetings that lay ahead would all be tough ones.

Far below the lazy course of the Murray River wandered through a dry brown landscape, where wide open farmland stretched towards the crumpled ridges of the mountains. From twenty-three thousand feet it all seemed bled of moisture under the harsh exposure of the sun. Dry paddocks. Dry roads. Dry dusty towns. The odd homestead baking in the heat. While other passengers peered through the windows, Barbie was too busy on his laptop with his calculations. When the stewardess delivered his coffee he didn't notice her at all.

•

A chauffeur-driven car collected him from Sydney Airport and drove him into the city. He checked into his favourite harbourside hotel, with its five-star service, marble lobby and views over The Rocks and Circular Quay, and rode the lift up to a suite on the twenty-fifth floor. He changed into a fresh shirt, tie and business suit, ready to do battle with a team of bankers in half an hour – the first of his meetings. But before leaving he took a moment to pause and clear his thoughts and adjust his mental geography. This was the place where he'd gained his first taste of liberation and had begun to explore his own hidden depths.

He crossed to the window and gazed down over the broad blue sweep of the harbour. The glittering water was dotted with ferries and launches and white sails – the billowing arcs of the Opera House on one side of the quay, and the giant metal arches of the Harbour Bridge on the other. Lines of cars and trucks swarmed over the freeway network far below, and on the crest of the bridge he noticed a column of tiny figures – a tourist party – like a file of insects trying to crawl into the sky.

Barbie had always been unimpressive at field sports but he was adept at psychological games, among them stud poker. That was something else he'd learnt in this city, as a cadet reporter on the *Sydney Morning Herald*, during late-night sessions in the rambling old rabbit warren of a building in Ultimo. Card games in a back room under clouds of cigarette smoke, excitement fuelled by booze smuggled in under the jackets of rheumy-eyed hacks. It was his first job, fresh out of grammar school. It was also his first whiff of freedom from the archangels of fear that towered over his formative years. He smiled at the memory as the taxi took him from the hotel to the central business district. Yes, he'd treat the meeting with his bankers like a game of stud. That way he had a better chance of winning.

He was into the bank for millions upon millions of dollars. The total amount scared even him. Much better to think of it as so many chips around a poker table. The dealer would raise the stakes so he'd raise them even more. And as in seven-card stud, the others in the game couldn't see all of his hand. Some of the cards were face down. Just as well, given what he was hiding. Tokyo threatening to pull the plug on his VR deal. Police knocking on his door. The concealment of a sex crime. And the next meeting on his schedule with the TV network's head of programming. He had a nasty feeling his reality show would lose its prime-time slot due to a recent slide in ratings. Of course the bankers must know none of this. Instead they'd be treated to a carefully delivered bluff.

He got out of the cab at Martin Place and strode purposefully across the plaza, oblivious to his surroundings as he psyched himself up for the negotiations ahead. Ignoring a *Big Issue* seller he entered the sombre chamber of an old bank, its heavy presence redolent of a century of tradition, prudence and serious money. In the lift he checked himself out in the mirror, anxiously playing with his tie. Getting out on the third floor, he walked down the corridor to the boardroom. He glanced at his watch. Right on time. The door was open, waiting for his arrival, so he went straight in.

At the far end of the deliberately imposing boardroom sat the same three bank executives who'd grilled him during the winter – a trio of formal, uptight bureaucrats called Garvey, Rosenberg and Fisk. In front of them were documents, sheets of paper, files and laptops. To their right was a fourth man, whom Barbie didn't recognise. To their left was the same woman who would take the minutes and slip him shy smiles when the financial going got heavy. She was the only one whose sympathy he could rely on. Unfortunately it counted for nothing.

They all stood up as Barbie walked along the length of the table, exchanging handshakes and conventional greetings. Just as on previous occasions, Rosenberg, as the most senior manager, was in charge of proceedings. He seemed to distrust Barbie instinctively. The feeling was mutual, as was the underlying antagonism.

Rosenberg introduced the fourth man, whose name was Theobald. Barbie took him in as they shook hands. He had a new suit, a brutal haircut and ambitious eyes.

'He's just been promoted,' explained Rosenberg. 'I hope you don't mind if he sits in and learns the ropes.'

'No problem,' Barbie said and sat down on the opposite side of the table from the rest of them.

Rosenberg looked up from his files and frowned. 'I notice you haven't brought any documents with you,' he said.

Barbie nodded. 'I didn't need to.'

'But if we're to review your financial position –'

'I know exactly what my financial position is,' interrupted Barbie.

Rosenberg sat back, a mixture of concern and suspicion on his face. 'When we met over six months ago, you agreed to certain economies.'

'They were aspirations – not fixed limits.'

'According to our information, you haven't met any of them.'

'There are good reasons,' said Barbie firmly. 'Sound business reasons.'

'And there's a pressing argument, from the bank's point of view, to consider you a liability.'

Barbie had been waiting for this – the first threat. He folded his hands in his lap and asked, 'Is this a review or an inquisition?', his tone calmly aggressive.

Rosenberg observed him carefully then tapped a black folder on the table. 'We've done a risk assessment on you,' he said coolly. 'Would you like to see it?'

'No thanks,' said Barbie. 'All I want from you is an assurance of the bank's continued support while I develop my investment projects – principal among them, my software company.'

'Ah, yes,' said Rosenberg grimly. 'The computer game. If I read the financial profile correctly, it's drained off all your liquid assets.'

'The R&D is expensive.'

'R&D aside, you've just arranged a bank transfer of two million dollars to a private account in Malaysia. What was that? A gift? A personal donation?'

Barbie cleared his throat as if to dislodge the memory of rape, blackmail and bribery, along with the sour taste of revenge inflicted by Kelly Grattan. 'It was a necessary expense to ensure confidentiality in a very sensitive market.'

'Where you have no guaranteed buyer.'

'A contract is being negotiated, but I can't disclose details.'

'"Being negotiated"?' repeated Rosenberg dubiously.

'At this very moment,' said Barbie, a disturbing image – his wife submitting to Jojima – flashing into his mind. It unsettled him and he looked away to where a shaft of sunlight poured through a tall leaded window to fall on the grey marble hearth of an antique fireplace.

'That's all well and good, but have you got any working capital left?'

Barbie sighed. 'That's why I'm in Sydney. Tomorrow I sign on the dotted line. I'm selling my first production company. It's not making much money but it holds some lucrative rights. The sale will be worth a clean ten million to me, which will offset my cashflow problems.'

The bankers exchanged looks.

'But one other thing, gentlemen,' Barbie said, then paused, standing up, leaning forward on the table and giving them a cold smile. 'You've done a risk assessment on me. Be careful, though. If I dump this bank, and do it publicly and eloquently – which I would be very good at – you might want to consider your own reputational risk. Do I make myself clear?' He looked from one to the other and, getting no more response than a set of startled looks, said, 'Good. Meeting over.'

As he turned and strode from the boardroom the only sound was the slap of his shoes on the floor and the faint echoes from the high gilded ceiling.

59

The bluff had worked. As Barbie cut briskly through the streams of pedestrians and dodged through the traffic on George Street, he felt a new spring in his step, confident he'd coerced the bank's continued support – for the time being at least. And that was enough. It would have been nothing less than disaster if Rosenberg and his dreary colleagues had yanked the rug from under him before he could clinch the software deal with the Japanese. So much was riding on that now. Not just his investments but his entire financial future, his marriage and, more importantly, his image. Trying to bounce back from bankruptcy and the stigma of failure in the full glare of the media spotlights was not a prospect he relished. Such a nosedive would stick in the public's mind and permanently tarnish his celebrity status. He brushed that worry aside for the moment. His luck might be riding on a high-stakes gamble, but he was still in the game and the prize was a stake in the new multimedia galaxy. It was worth the risk.

He passed the Romanesque structure of the Queen Victoria Building, with its copper dome and ornate stonework, as he headed towards Darling Harbour and his second business appointment of the day – one likely to be even more problematic than his showdown at the bank. He needed to psych himself up for this one as well and, with a few minutes to spare, he sat down at a cafe table, loosened his tie and ordered a triple espresso – his third for the day.

He couldn't afford to relax. After going through his strategy for the next meeting, he drank down the rest of his coffee, straightened his tie, got up and walked towards the TV network office among the buildings looming over the harbour. As he strode up the slope the metallic whirr of the monorail zoomed overhead.

He'd been summoned by the network's head of programming – media super-bitch Curtis Cole. Most people in the industry knew her only by way of poisonous gossip, but Barbie knew her intimately as well as professionally. It was a daunting privilege and a burden. She was one of the reasons he'd switched his career base back to Melbourne.

They'd met when they started in television together on a children's program – he as showbiz reporter, she as producer. They were both in their early twenties and their professional relationship quickly became something more. They'd tried living together but couldn't settle into conventional roles. It had turned out to be no more than a volatile fling ending in a salvo of recriminations. She was too bossy and demanding, accusing him of being too detached. She behaved like a bully. He treated the relationship like a game. That was over ten years ago, when they were at the bottom of the heap and little more than overgrown kids. Now they were both at the top and thoroughly adult-rated.

Curtis's appearance belied her reputation. She was slim and petite, with dark curly hair, gypsy-black eyes, full lips and the face of an angel – though what came out of her mouth was hardly angelic. Verbal abuse was one of her strong points. She packed a literal punch, with Barbie on the receiving end more than once. Like the time he made a joke about her westie background and called her a bogan. She'd replied with a left hook that nearly dislocated his jaw. After that he chose his words carefully, which was just as well given her rapid rise through the corporate ranks. She was now tipped as the TV channel's next chief executive, and no man dared put a glass ceiling in her way. She'd blow a hole in it with a bazooka.

Curtis interested Barbie in a compulsive sort of way, like watching an executioner in action. She had a frightening combination of looks, perception, mental certitude and the instincts of a hammerhead shark. She'd devoured her way to the top by adhering to the agenda of the tyrant – motivation by intimidation – and by outspending her rivals in the ratings war. She was a living embodiment of the dynamic of aggression.

Barbie sat patiently in her office suite while Curtis aimed her rancour down the phone, apparently at an interstate line manager, telling him variously to 'get a grip', 'find your balls', 'stop being a softcock' and 'sack the dickhead'. She was wearing a salmon pink suit opening on a red silk top, and Barbie wondered what sort of statement she was trying to make with it. As the one-sided conversation dragged on, it became even louder and more irksome. Barbie got up, strolled to the window and took in the view over Darling Harbour. Life was so much less stressful down there.

The sound of Curtis finally slamming down the phone pulled him back from the window.

'For Christ's sake, Barbie, stop hovering and sit down.'

He did as he was told and waited.

'You know why you're here.'

'Ratings?'

'Well it's not to play tonsil hockey. Of course bloody ratings. You're not delivering. Why not?'

'It's summer, Curtis,' he said, smoothing down his jacket.

'Fuck that!'

'You have another explanation?'

'No wow factor. Your show's gone stale.' She thumped the desk with her tight little fist. 'As presenter and producer that's down to you.'

Barbie sighed. 'Have you got me here just to have a fight?'

'Not *just* a fight, no. But that's top of the agenda.'

'As long as I don't end up with more bruises,' he said, his face calm and patient.

'Don't count on it.' A hint of humour played around her lips, but then her already dark eyes darkened further. 'My spies in Melbourne tell me the show's on the slide because you're playing hookey on me. Not putting in the time. Too busy with other enterprises. Don't forget, I've got personal experience with your lack of commitment,' she said, waving an admonishing finger at him.

'I'll bet you rehearsed that one,' he said, thoroughly unimpressed. 'But it's not true. Your spies are fools.'

'I'm getting feedback direct from your studio floor.'

'Tittle-tattle from toadies.'

'Nothing gets past me. I'm fed information from everywhere in this industry.'

'Unreliable sources.'

'Don't try to bullshit me. I'm the gatekeeper. I know who you are.' She slapped the top of her desk, making her black paperclips jump, then reached for a file of photocopied cuttings. 'Have you read what the critics are saying about your show? Look at the headlines. GOLD RUSH GOES DOWN THE PAN. Wonderful publicity. And this one: YOU-REEKER!'

'That's quite clever.'

'Not for the network it isn't!'

'Then the network's paranoid.'

She threw the file at him.

He batted it away with a deft backhand, then said, 'Calm down, Curtis, before you wear out your batteries.'

She stretched forward on her desk, face flushed with anger. 'You won't be so smug if you lose your prime-time slot. And I'll do it, too,' she warned. 'And don't bother threatening to switch networks.'

'I'll leave the threats to you.'

'Good. Because you're one step away from being rescheduled, cost-cut and held to contract. Fancy spending the next two years in late-night oblivion?'

'You know what your problem is and always was?' he asked rhetorically. 'A lack of faith.'

She gave a derisory laugh, 'Faith in you gets a girl nothing but broken promises.'

'It could never have worked. Trust me.' Then he went on dispassionately, 'We're not real people, you and I. We don't live in the real world. We inhabit a consensual fantasy. Like the line from the song. We broadcast our images in space and in time. And we're experts at it. The best. You as a commodity broker. Me as a brand name.'

'What's your point?'

'My show is my shop window. Me as product in the spotlight. To suggest I'd let myself be degraded is ridiculous.' He glowered at her. 'I'm telling you now, *Gold Rush* is still a winner. The contestants are one week away from turning on each other. It'll be dog-eat-dog. The viewers will love it. The critics will swallow their words. The network will be full of self-congratulation. You can doubt me on anything else, but not this.'

'You've got till the end of the month,' she snapped, before picking up her mobile phone and putting it in her handbag. 'I knew it was worth hauling you here for a face-to-face.'

'Does that mean our fight's over?'

'Yes,' she said. 'Now let's go eat and get drunk together.'

She'd booked a table at Doyles, so they took the company launch across the harbour. The water was choppy, the wind whipping up spray as the prow slapped against the waves. In their wake lay the Opera House, the late gleam of the sun brushing its arches with a tint of dusk. Behind it rose the Harbour Bridge and the city skyline, the angles of the buildings burnished in the light.

'You should never have left Sydney,' she told him, to which he didn't respond.

The launch dropped them off at the Watsons Bay pier. Clearly a favoured customer, she'd been given an outside table for two under the awning. The significance wasn't lost on him. It was where they'd shared their first date more than a decade ago. But why had she brought him here? Nostalgia? To make some sort of point? Revenge? If he didn't know what she wanted, it was harder to negotiate – and with her there was always a transaction involved.

As they sat down Curtis ordered a bottle of vintage chardonnay. The waitress filled their glasses and Curtis raised hers for a toast. 'To old times.'

'Is that why we're here?' said Barbie, deadpan.

'I thought we'd revisit our roots.'

He spotted the glint in her eye – and the double entendre – and their glasses clinked like the soft chime of a bell to ring in Round Two.

It was dangerously familiar. The restaurant had the same seductive old charm. Mostly couples at the tables. Languid conversations. The tang of seafood. And opening out beyond the stretch of sand, the vast rippling sweep of the harbour.

'It's a special city,' he said as he looked out over the water. 'Scene of my liberation.'

'Whatever happened to your father?'

His jaw tightened and he put down his glass. 'He died. Just over four years ago. Why do you ask?'

'He beat the shit out of you as a kid, didn't he?'

Barbie took a short, sharp breath. 'Yes.'

'Nasty old bugger, wasn't he? Served the Nazis in Estonia. Some sort of war criminal.'

Barbie answered slowly, an unnatural heaviness in his voice. 'He was investigated. But there were no proceedings against him.'

'Not enough evidence,' she said glibly.

As he wondered where this was leading, the waitress returned. Curtis ordered oysters as a starter for both of them and lobster for her main course. Barbie asked for the barramundi.

'So,' she resumed. 'Tell me. How bad was it? As a kid.'

He rubbed his eyes, feeling suddenly tired. 'It was bad.'

He gulped down the rest of his wine and observed the sunset casting a blood-red glow over the darkening harbour.

She watched his cheek muscles harden as he struggled with his inner demons. 'Go on,' she said.

As Barbie's eyes fell on her he realised she was the only person he'd ever bared his soul to. He could do it because of the unbridled intimacy they'd shared and because her soul was as debased as his. He refilled his glass, drank some more and stared into the middle distance. 'The bathroom was where he did it. Like a ritual. Marching me into the punishment chamber.' He was speaking in a monotone now, controlling the flow. 'The first beating I can remember, I must've been three years old. But it got worse as I got older. He was still doing it when I was at grammar school, using his belt with the big metal buckle. He was a devout churchgoer by then. A fundamentalist. He'd make me strip off while he thrashed the wickedness out of me and recited the Bible. "Thou shalt not take the name of the Lord thy God in vain." Old Testament quotations. "Wound for wound, stripe for stripe." "Honour thy father –"' Barbie's voice trailed off. He turned and looked at her, a deadness in his eyes. 'I had to wipe up my own blood afterwards.'

Then the oysters arrived.

They tipped them into their mouths and drank more wine and watched the night swallow up the view, leaving a scattering of lights to dance upon the water. Gradually he recovered his composure.

'How's your wife?' Curtis asked, deliberately changing the dynamic.

'Fine, thank you,' he said, wary now.

'What do you see in her?'

He thought for a moment and said, 'Dependability.'

'You make her sound like a four-wheel drive.' Curtis had never met the woman but she hated her anyway. 'Give you much of a ride?'

'We have a rewarding marriage.'

'That's a "no" then.'

She smiled to herself as she slid the last of the oysters down her throat and ordered another bottle of wine. He drummed his fingers on the pale blue tablecloth and wondered what she was after. It wouldn't matter so much if his economic position weren't so precarious. As if to underscore the problem his mobile phone bleeped and he pulled it from his pocket to find a text message from Jojima, saying there was no change yet in corporate thinking about the VR game. No change meant no deal. Great. The bank, the TV network and now Tokyo. One after another they were threatening to pull the support from under him, leaving him financially exposed like a tightrope walker with no safety net.

When the waitress delivered the main course he'd lost his appetite. He picked at his fish while Curtis cracked open her lobster with relish.

'You've got a wife who's *dependable*,' she said sarcastically. 'So where do you get your kicks?'

He shrugged off the question, but she went on. 'I know your secret vices. I helped you find them. You and an honest marriage just don't go together – like wanking at Sunday school.'

'Charming.'

'Still got a thing for prostitutes?'

He bent forward on his elbows. 'I'm a respectable married man.'

'Know what I think? I think your marriage is just another commercial production. And why not? Like you said, that's what we do. Project the fantasy. We're the best in the business.'

He didn't bother to disagree, but asked, 'What about you? No husband on your running order?'

She laughed and wiped her mouth on a napkin. 'Can't find a man whose cock's as good as yours.'

'Curtis, that's years ago.'

'Big deal. You pressed the right buttons.' She flicked back her curls, reached over, laid a hand on his and looked into his eyes. 'You and I are two of a kind.'

That's when he realised what she was after – what this evening was really about. She wanted sex. With a smile of relief he took hold of her hand, dipped forward and brushed it with his lips.

When they'd finished their meal and their third bottle of wine she got out her phone and ordered a water taxi.

'I've got a beach apartment in Manly,' she explained. 'More relaxing than going back to the city.'

As they strolled down to the jetty, the vibrancy of the night around them, the lights on the water, the waves hissing along the shore, he peeled off his jacket and hooked it in his hand over his shoulder – just as he'd done on their first date over ten years ago. Despite his misgivings he felt strangely calm. It seemed he could be more honest with Curtis – in a warped kind of way – than with anyone else. Between fights, they clicked. She was a cruel bitch and he was an ineffable bastard, but in their occasional moments together it didn't matter. Nor did the decadence of the world they lived in, where fathers could torture their sons in the name of deliverance, and daughters could indulge in backstreet fornication. They were both at home with corruption and perhaps, in the end, they would stroll with one another to damnation. As the water taxi pulled up, waiting patiently like the boat of Charon, the thought didn't bother him at all.

They climbed into the glassed-in speedboat and it carried them surging through the waves to the far side of the harbour. From there they took a conventional cab to the rocky headland that rose from the northern point of the ocean beach. Her apartment was on the seventh floor of a block overlooking the Pacific, but the view was the last thing on their minds. She closed the door behind them and slumped back against the wall.

'You've got years to make up for,' she said, an accusing tone in her voice.

He pressed against her and bent down to kiss her neck, his hand loosening her red silk top and sliding down over the slim curve of her abdomen.

She took hold of his arms and eased him back, breathing more heavily now. 'I'll get the lubricant,' she whispered. 'Then I'll tell you what you're going to do to me.'

They were using her customised sex stool. The narrow, oblong surface was upholstered in black leather, with the legs and handgrips made of chrome. It stood on the rug in the middle of her lounge room among the overstuffed armchairs and sofa with their red ochre coverings. Aboriginal paintings decorated the walls – a series depicting the rainbow serpent. They hovered in the shifting glow of candles, the flames flickering in a breeze that slipped through the open balcony doors, fanning the curtains and wafting the smell of incense from a pair of joss sticks on her coffee table. From outside came the roar of the surf and the shouts of drunken teenagers enjoying a beach party. Inside, from her music system, came the soft, plaintive sounds of Gaelic mood-song – while from the centre of the room, where the two of them heaved and strained against each other, came much more animal noises.

The stool rose to groin height for an easy angle of penetration, which Barbie, naked and sweating, was delivering with rhythmic force.

'Faster,' she said.

He ignored her and continued pleasuring himself at his own pace.

Curtis lay on her back like a contorted nude, her body doubled up, her legs over her shoulders and her thighs pressing onto her stomach. Her grunts and gasps were as much from the pressure on her torso as from him pushing deep inside her – a taut expression on her face as he pinned her to the leather contraption, her black curls shaking, her small breasts bouncing, and her eyes dilated with a feral intensity. But he wasn't looking at her face. His eyes were on the tight cheeks of her buttocks, cupped in his hands like an exquisite sin.

'Harder,' she said.

He had a flashback to her power trip in the office that afternoon, when she'd played the unscrupulous vixen and hurled a file at him. The thought heated his blood and he thrust as hard and deep as he could till she cried out with pain. From the open balcony doors came a burst of shrieks and laughing from the beach party below, but her cries drowned them out as she started to orgasm.

When he woke next morning, still tired from his exertions, she was already dressed. Sun was streaming through the windows. The heavy rollers of the Pacific were thudding along the beach. The smell of fresh coffee was in the air. He got up out of the bed and walked naked into her lounge room. The glass doors were still open onto the balcony, but the chrome and leather stool had been packed away out of sight. She gave his body a look of approval, poured two cups of espresso and handed one to him.

'I've got a meeting with a bunch of spineless accountants to go to. But you're welcome to stay here as long as you like. Spend the day. Make yourself comfortable. I could get used to you again.'

'The offer's tempting but I've got a meeting myself this morning. Some final haggling over figures before a deal's clinched. I'm signing away my first production company.'

He sipped his coffee and padded barefoot onto the balcony, taking in the slightly vertiginous view – though that was probably due to last night's drink and sex. Below lay a great swathe of sand gleaming in the morning light. The bodies of sunbathers, tanned and oiled, stretched out in the heat. The muscled torsos of the lifeguards. The shrieks of beach volleyball. Surfers in wetsuits bobbing on their boards as they waited for the big waves to roll in. And lining the promenade, the tall fringe of Norfolk Island pines.

She sidled up to him and said, 'I know we've got our differences, but we're on the same wavelength. We've got a hell of a lot in common.'

He grimaced. 'Hell being the operative word.'

'So what? A boring, peaceful life – who needs it!'

'Let's face it,' he sighed. 'We're bad people, Curtis. We each need a steadying influence in our lives. Together we become too destructive.'

She pressed against the balcony rail. 'But I miss having you around – even just for a fight. Everyone else is such a pushover.'

'You'll soon be CEO. That'll keep you occupied.'

'And what about you, Mr Millionaire? You've come a long way since your first attempts to crack the business side of the media. It used to give me a buzz listening to your evil plans. Have they all paid off?'

'Nearly all.'

'What about Plato's Cave?' she asked.

He gazed out over the ocean to the dark blue rim that curved along the horizon. 'Plato's Cave,' he said cryptically. 'Of all my plans, that was the killer.'

60

It felt like she was emerging from hibernation. After sleeping uninterrupted for fifteen hours, Rita awoke feeling relaxed and refreshed. It was what she needed after living on caffeine and adrenalin for the best part of a week in which she'd confronted the worst violence of her life. Now she could put it behind her.

It was after nine a.m. as she drank orange juice in Byron Huxley's kitchen, with its view into the depths of the eucalypt forest. He'd come and gone last night and this morning without disturbing her, his hospitality faultless in his effort to provide a quiet haven. It was a type of devotion she hadn't experienced before, and if this was the beginning of a relationship she had to think carefully about what happened next. Whatever developed, it was essential to maintain her independence, and with Lola due to return today that meant moving back into town. Rita sent her best friend a text message.

Then there was work. As much as she was enjoying a well-earned rest, she needed to stay up to speed, so she phoned Jack Loftus.

'Don't come in today,' he told her. 'It's chaos.'

'What about the fallout over Kavella and Moyle?' Rita asked.

'That's what I'm talking about,' said Loftus. 'The media's all over it and everybody's getting in on the act, from the Commissioner down. I don't know if I'm coming or going.'

'Don't you need O'Keefe and me on deck?'

'No,' insisted Loftus. 'I've told Nash I want the pair of you to keep a low profile today, and he agrees. When you get back tomorrow we'll start going through all the legal formalities. For today, your initial reports are enough.'

'That's good, I'm enjoying the break. It means I can catch up on some sleep,' she admitted. 'What about the Hacker taskforce?'

'That's on the back burner till next week,' said Loftus. 'There's nothing new to work on, no fresh leads and no viable suspect who owns both an MX-5 and a black ute. Anyway, the decks have been cleared to deal with the aftermath of Proctor's raids.'

'Any more smartcards turn up at the club?'

'What's left of them, yeah. And the computer boys say Kavella's electronic fortress was definitely rigged for a virtual private network, accessible globally, but most of the data's been trashed. He actually installed a floor of satellite-linked studios in there. He wasn't setting up a city-wide consortium, he was going international.'

'Jack,' she interrupted, 'any Plato's Cave cards?'

'That's what I'm getting to,' he explained. 'The crime lab people have been going through a basement incinerator full of burnt discs, molten silicon and God knows what. Looks like Kavella had a bonfire to cover his tracks. They've retrieved the remains of smartcards with Delos Club on them, but that's it. It's possible any Plato's Cave cards may have been reduced to a pool of melted plastic. Anyway they're doing their best to analyse what's there.'

'Damn,' said Rita. 'If they could just partially identify one card, it would narrow the search for the Hacker.'

'Forget the Hacker for the time being,' Loftus advised her. 'You won't be able to work on the case properly till next week. In the meantime, I need you and O'Keefe back on board tomorrow, focusing on what went down in and around the church. I need statements, reports, interviews, all clear and consistent. I don't want any comebacks from the family lawyers waiting in the wings. Have you seen the coverage this morning?'

'No, and I think I'll give it a miss.'

'Probably a good idea,' agreed Loftus. 'So what will you do with your day off?'

'Something I haven't been able to do for a while – just chill out.'

'Good for you,' he said.

Rita showered, dressed in jeans and a T-shirt, and wandered into the village, past wooden shopfronts and craft centres, till she found a restaurant with outdoor tables. She was eating a breakfast of pancakes when she got a phone call from Lola, who'd just flown in.

'I've been reading all about you on the flight down!' Lola shrieked. 'I can't believe what a hero you are!'

'So they don't get any news up in the Whitsundays,' said Rita.

'You've got to be kidding, they're too busy partying. I swear I was drunk for four days, but I'll tell you later. Where are you now?'

'I'm having breakfast in Olinda.'

'What are you doing in the Dandenongs?' asked Lola. 'Have you gone bush?'

'I've been staying at Byron Huxley's place.'

'I can't believe it's all happened while I've been away!' Lola was beside herself with excitement. 'I'm dumping my things and driving up to see you.'

They arranged to meet at a tourist cafe in the forest.

After finishing breakfast, Rita strolled back to Huxley's cottage, got in her car and drove to the cafe, arriving with time to spare. She decided to stretch her legs.

It was peaceful to walk here, therapeutic, the scent of eucalyptus heavy in the air among the gum trees and towering stands of mountain ash. The ringing calls of bellbirds chimed against the raucous sounds of the kookaburras and the squawking of parrots that dived in flocks of crimson shapes, flashing among the branches. The occasional scuttle of a lizard rustled the undergrowth on the forest trail strewn with bark and overhung by the fronds of tree ferns. In the musty quiet of a fern-lined gully, she stopped to lean on the wooden rail of a footbridge, gazing distractedly at the muddy water of a creek, before strolling back to the cafe in time to see Lola arrive.

They sat on the wooden verandah and chatted over coffees. Rita was reluctant to talk about her recent brush with violence – she'd be doing that officially over the next couple of days – but what details she did reveal simply horrified Lola.

'I can't believe you're so brave!' she said, clasping Rita's hand. 'And I wasn't even here for you. I was too busy being chased around a sundeck by a randy lesbian.'

Rita laughed. 'So tell me, how's your new girlfriend – I thought she was supposed to be hot?'

'Hot, flash and mad as a fruit bat,' said Lola. 'Whenever we were alone I spent most of the time fending her off.'

'Successfully, I hope.'

'To tell you the truth, I was so paralytic a couple of nights, I can't actually remember what, or *who*, I did!'

Rita chuckled. 'So you might be a designer dyke?'

'How the fuck do I know?' said Lola, tossing back her long hair. 'I'd rather not think about it.' She put a cigarette in her mouth and lit it. 'Let's change the subject. Enjoy the scenery. Watch the parrots crap on the tourists.'

A coach had just pulled up, spilling out a party of Japanese sightseers, cameras clicking. Right on cue, a flock of rosellas descended on the picnic tables, with sulphur-crested cockatoos waiting in the wings.

'What's far more interesting,' resumed Lola, 'is what you've been getting up to with the hunky professor. Have you had sex yet?'

'No.'

'Oh my God, you cold-hearted bitch! You've been sharing his bed without letting him bang you!'

'He's been on the sofa,' Rita explained, 'while I've been in his bed alone – *sleeping!* Lots of sleeping.'

'Well, I suppose you've got an excuse.'

'Thank you. But you're right, I've imposed on him enough.'

'I hope you're not thinking of going back to your house,' said Lola, blowing out a stream of smoke. 'Not after what happened there.'

'No,' sighed Rita. 'I'll put it on the market.'

'Good. Then you're moving in with me.'

'I was counting on that,' said Rita. 'And it should be an interesting experiment. We're complete opposites.'

'Don't worry about that,' Lola said, flicking ash on the wooden floor. 'I'll leave a mess, you'll tidy up. We'll be perfect flatmates!'

As Lola drove back to the city and a belated return to her duties at the magazine, Rita headed back to Olinda and the cottage she now thought of as the Byron Huxley Retreat. She packed her bag, left him an effusive thankyou note and took a leisurely drive along the freeway to Lola's place in South Yarra.

The apartment was in a converted Victorian house set in a garden among hibiscus plants and old oak trees, with a view down a steep road to the river. It had two bedrooms, a spacious kitchen and an old-fashioned parlour strewn with magazines, fashion accessories, bags, shoes and more shoes. Despite the chaos, Rita felt at home straightaway. Within hours of moving in, her bedroom was the tidiest space in the apartment.

'Bloody hell, you're anal,' was Lola's comment when she got home that night.

They opened a bottle of wine and slumped down on the sofa, gossiping busily, not paying much attention to the news program on the TV until the late-night preview of the next morning's first editions.

'My God!' screamed Lola, grabbing the remote and boosting the volume. 'Look at that!'

Rita stared at the TV screen to see a photo of herself – a provocative full-length shot in a purple bikini – filling the front page of tomorrow's tabloid under the headline POLICE SIREN.

She was speechless.

But Lola wasn't. 'How on earth did they get hold of that?' she shouted.

Rita found her voice. 'From Mike Cassidy,' she said hoarsely. 'It's from our holiday last year. I'm going to kill him.'

61

Rita turned up at police headquarters next morning in a sober grey outfit, making a vain attempt to counter the image of her in a bikini plastered across the front pages. Kevin O'Keefe arrived in camouflage pants and on crutches. They sat next to each other outside the office of Superintendent Gordon Nash, waiting to be summoned inside. A secretary sat at a desk, tapping placidly on a keyboard beside a vase of cornflowers and a murmuring TV monitor.

'I've got to admit it,' said O'Keefe, a twinkle in his eye. 'As bosses go, you're a bit of a beach babe.'

'Don't even go there,' Rita warned him.

'I assume your ex did the dirty on you.'

'He's an odious prick, but don't get me started,' she growled. 'How's your leg?'

'The bullet tore a hole through my flexor muscles and buggered my hamstring,' O'Keefe grumbled. 'It could wreck my swimming style.'

'And let's face it, that's more important than your career.'

'Too right,' said O'Keefe, as Mike Cassidy's face appeared on TV. 'Speak of the devil.'

Cassidy was standing outside court buildings, with a 'Breaking News' caption flashing across the screen.

Rita swore under her breath as she stooped over the secretary and turned up the volume.

In the latest dramatic development over the death of crime baron Tony Kavella, his family have announced they're suing the police. Lawyers acting for his younger brothers, Theo and Nikos Kavella, claim detectives were operating a shoot-to-kill policy in one of the state's biggest-ever manhunts for the high-profile fugitive. I spoke to the Kavella family solicitor, Clayton Pearce, a short time ago.

Video of Pearce: *If we set aside the sensational headlines, there are clear grounds for filing a lawsuit. The post-mortem examination shows Mr Kavella was hit by bullets discharged from weapons held by two police officers, even though he didn't fire a shot. The fact that he was gunned down in front of his mother, inside a church, only adds weight to evidence that he was the victim of an execution-style killing – or, as his brothers put it, the target of a police assassination.*

Cassidy: *Senior officers at police headquarters are yet to officially respond, although a spokesman for the Police Association has dismissed the accusations as 'cynical and groundless'. Lawyers acting for the sister of gangland figure Brendan Moyle are also preparing to take legal action, claiming his neck was broken and his body dumped in a chicken coop after he'd been disarmed. Meanwhile, the Kavella family have announced plans for one of the most ostentatious underworld funerals likely to be seen in this city. In a final irony, the funeral will be held in the same church where Tony Kavella was baptised, attended services as a boy, and lay bleeding to death after being shot. Now back to the studio.*

Rita turned down the volume as the bulletin moved on to other news.

'Your ex has got a brutal way with words,' observed O'Keefe. 'Maybe I should wring his neck as well.'

'That's too good for him,' she said. 'You know what all this means?'

'We've got a long, gruelling day ahead of us.'

'And instead of being heroes, we're going to face an inquisition.'

Rita and O'Keefe sat in front of Nash's desk while he regarded them over his steel-rimmed glasses. To their left sat Jack Loftus, to their right a three-man team of legal advisers. The atmosphere was heavy with accountability.

'I toyed with the idea of suspending both of you but I was talked out of it,' said Nash, throwing an accusing glance at Loftus. 'As it is, you're going to spend the next two days dotting every "i" and crossing every "t" so those predatory lawyers won't get to first base with any court action. At the same time we've got to go through our internal procedures. That means by tomorrow evening I want all reports – witness, crime scene and ballistic – formal statements, interview transcripts, the lot, processed, triple-checked, finalised and on my desk. Understand?'

They nodded.

'That means,' he continued, 'your sick leave doesn't resume until Saturday, O'Keefe. And you, Van Hassel, are off all other duties until next week. While I'm sure you acted courageously, if precipitously, out in the field, I don't want either of you to get carried away with feelings that you're not accountable. The reputation of the force has taken a battering recently, and it's down to both of you to make sure the lawyers, the press and the Office of Police Integrity don't have any fresh ammunition to fire at us. Am I making myself clear?'

'Yes, sir,' they both said.

'And we could do without this!' he snapped, tossing the morning newspaper onto his desk. 'With the sort of tacky publicity you've been getting lately,' he fixed Rita with a glare, 'your career as a profiler could become untenable.'

She decided not to argue. 'Point taken, sir,' she said.

'All right. Now both of you, get on with it.'

They stood up and left Nash's office, closing the door behind them.

'Mike Cassidy's arse is grass,' Rita muttered as she headed towards the lifts, O'Keefe clomping along on his crutches beside her.

'You know how we blew it?' he said. 'We made the wrong call.'

'In what way?' she asked.

'We should have let the bastards kill us!'

62

A full twenty-four hours had elapsed since Barbie's return from Sydney and he was feeling tense. Giselle was overdue from Japan, having phoned from Tokyo to warn of delays. There'd been an underwater quake off Honshu causing structural damage, scores of injuries, disruption to flight schedules at Narita International and a tsunami alert.

'Sounds serious,' he'd said, though it was structural damage to his business plans that really concerned him.

With the deadline for the VR deal now only one day away, Jojima's failure to say whether it was on or off was driving Barbie into a state of nervous agitation. When he'd asked Giselle about her time with Jojima she'd said, 'It was like a field trip in anthropology.' He couldn't tell from her tone if that was good or bad and she'd refused to go into details over the phone. Now he was on edge, with her return flight due in the early afternoon. He was in no mood for the office, nor could he bring himself to eat. Breakfast was chilled orange juice. Unable to settle he wandered around the house, finally forcing himself to sit down on the sundeck by his swimming pool. There he went through the morning papers.

To his continuing amazement Marita Van Hassel was still front-page news. Monday's headlines about her deadly duel with the Duck had been sensational enough, allowing the nation's tabloids to express their sentiments over the killing of the hit-man with customary zeal: DUCK SHOOT and QUACK QUACK, YOU'RE WHACKED! Yesterday's coverage on the aftermath of the Kavella shoot-out went further – HOLY BLOODBATH and DEATH RITES IN CHURCH – while a sober-minded broadsheet noted GREEK TRAGEDY. This morning, though, her page-one image capped the rest, showing her in a brief bikini that exposed her copious charms under the inspired headline POLICE SIREN.

To anyone in the publicity business it was awe-inspiring. From heroic crime-buster to pin-up within three days. What a scoop. And what an opportunity. Any PR agent who got her on his books would be laughing.

He skipped the rest of the news, flicking through the pages to the TV reviews, and punched the air in triumph. 'Yes!'

Just as he'd predicted, the spite now being displayed by his reality show contestants was grabbing attention. It had become a must-see spectator sport. The viewers were hooked, the critics were back on board. GOLD RUSH STRIKES A VEIN – THE JUGULAR! Barbie read it all with glee. Finally the cards were starting to fall in his favour after all.

By mid afternoon it was too hot to sit outdoors. The northerly wind was shaking the trees and buffeting the houses, like the draught from a furnace. It sent leaves clattering over the eaves and loose doors banging. Even hardy blooms in the garden plots were wilting from thirst as the parched lawns around them turned a coarser shade of desiccated brown. The local streets were as arid as dry riverbeds, the heat shimmering off the bitumen, and along suburban shopping strips pedestrians battled from door to door, the gusty conditions snagging their hair and flicking up dresses. High overhead a dirty-coloured film was seeping into the sky turning the sun to a vicious ball of red, while in the air hung a faint scent of burning, the ominous sign of bushfires.

Barbie skulked indoors in his air-conditioned refuge, waiting impatiently for his wife's return. Nothing else mattered except the decision in Tokyo. But before he could press Jojima for it, he needed the intelligence Giselle was bringing. What had happened? Did her visit make a difference? The suspense was infuriating. To concentrate on anything else was impossible. He'd occupied his time by taking a long shower, changing into a white tennis shirt and shorts, then forcing himself to eat a light lunch even though he wasn't hungry.

By the time her car arrived from the airport he was pacing up and down the parquet floor in a lather of anticipation.

He was hovering at the open front door as she walked through the pillared archway of the porch, looking cool and elegant in a mauve silk top, matching skirt and shoes, and dark glasses. In her wake came the driver, lugging her cases.

'I need a drink,' she said.

Barbie followed her into the kitchen where she mixed herself a vodka and tonic with lime and crushed ice. She drank it swiftly then put the glass down on the breakfast bar between them.

'That's better,' she said, staring at him unemotionally.

'For God's sake,' he said. 'What happened with Jojima?'

Giselle opened her handbag, took out a thin pad and dabbed at her lips. Barbie watched each move intently, trying to read clues from her behaviour, but she was too good an actress for him – indecipherable. He gave up, went to the fridge and pulled out a can of cold lager, slamming the door shut.

'There's no need for petulance,' she said evenly.

He accepted the rebuke, flipped open the ring-pull and sat facing her on a high-backed stool. 'Okay, no problem,' he said. 'Let's talk about the modelling.'

She gave him a frosty look. 'You don't give a damn about the fashion show.'

'I would normally, but it's a bit hard to concentrate with a deal worth hundreds of millions of dollars on the line.' He wasn't happy with the way this was going. It was unlike them to squabble.

She took off her dark glasses and laid them on the counter. 'At least that's a flattering sum for prostituting myself.'

Barbie didn't dare say anything. He filled the pause by lifting the can to his lips and swallowing a long, slow mouthful of beer. It was pleasantly refreshing.

'As for the modelling,' she went on matter-of-factly, 'I had to cut short my appearance. I told the designers I was ill.'

'But you weren't.'

'No. But I was certainly indisposed.' She sighed, sat down on a breakfast stool and threw him a look that could have decapitated him. 'What you want to hear, I'm only going to tell you once. Then we'll never speak of it again. And tomorrow our lawyers will draw up a new set of contracts, giving me a fifty per cent financial interest in all your companies. Do you agree?'

He raised his eyes to the ceiling as he swallowed another mouthful of beer. This one nearly stuck in his throat. There was no choice, though. If the deal was off, he was bust anyway. If the deal was back on, it was Giselle who'd swung it.

When he looked at her again he said, 'Agreed. It's a fair bargain.'

'Good.' She sank forward on her elbows, eyes downcast. 'It lasted all night. Jojima couldn't get enough of me. As a western fashion model I fulfilled all his wet fantasies. He pretends to his colleagues he's into heavy *manga* – brutal comic book stuff, animated films – where women are reduced to sex objects.' She closed her eyes and massaged her temples. 'But what he's really into is self-abasement, water sports.'

Barbie put the drink aside and clasped his hands as if in prayer. 'I need to know some specifics.' His voice was quiet and patient. 'Logistical details, like where and when. For example, did he take you out to a restaurant? Were other company executives present?'

'At the start of the evening, yes. It was all agonisingly polite and correct. Jojima and two other executives. After the meal he escorted me to my hotel room. That's where we fucked. From there he drove me to his private retreat outside Tokyo. I've kept the address.' She folded her arms and hugged them to her chest. 'I had to play along while he indulged himself. There was a lot of begging and spanking. I had to chastise him while jerking him off. Finally he stuck his tongue up my arse while I pissed on him. It was dehumanising. I've never been so humiliated in my life.'

'When you last saw him, what was his attitude?'

She thought for a moment and said, 'Very humble and solicitous. He implored me to say nothing.'

Barbie flopped back with a pensive expression on his face, fingering the cold beer can distractedly. 'Excellent,' he said at last. 'I think it's time I had a chat with him.'

Barbie sat in the padded comfort of his computer den, the stern face of Kenshi Jojima on the video link in front of him. As usual they'd greeted each other with bland niceties, before Barbie added another nicety with barbed edges.

'My wife has told me how you devoted so much time and attention to her in Tokyo. You shouldn't have, Kenshi. I would hate your work life to suffer.'

From the screen came silence as Jojima's jaw stiffened. He knew he'd been threatened – his career, his reputation, his honour were in jeopardy. He didn't say anything, just sat waiting for the inevitable question.

'So?' Barbie continued mercilessly. 'What is your decision on my new game? Is the deal on?'

Jojima swallowed his pride. 'Your sample software has been tested with excellent results,' he replied. 'The level of input is extremely impressive. The 3-D perspectives, death graphics, action sequences and erotic images are all compelling. The visual realism is the best we've ever tested. My team and I fly out tonight. Congratulations, Barbie-san, the deal is on. We will sign, as scheduled, tomorrow.'

As the call ended with ritual pleasantries, Barbie could hardly contain his joy. With Giselle's help he had risen from the brink of bankruptcy and the pit of failure to turn his fortunes completely around. He could relax at last. The future was rosy. His triumph was secure.

63

Two days passed in a bureaucratic blur for Rita and O'Keefe. Never before had they produced such a range of crime reports that were so lengthy, intricate and meticulously formulated, on top of being interrogated over every aspect of events surrounding the confrontation at the church. Each time the legal advisers went through the reports they had to be revised, and each time an internal interview was conducted, a new set of minor details was probed. The process was officious and agonisingly repetitive. Finally, when all the required documents had been checked, approved and delivered to Nash by Friday evening, they both felt the need for a drink.

'I would have thought twice about shooting Kavella if I'd known it meant two days of paperwork from hell,' said Rita.

'I'm just fucked,' added O'Keefe. 'I don't know what aches more, my leg or my brain.'

Loftus met up with them in the squad room. 'Here's how things stand,' he told them. 'The status quo remains while the legal process moves forward at the usual pace.'

'So we could still be hung out to dry?' asked Rita.

'Not on my assessment. I've gone through your reports, and the way you both responded in the field was completely justified. If you'd acted in any other way the consequences would have been much worse.' He grimaced. 'That's my reading of it, but you both know what the legal system's like.'

'Unreliable,' said Rita. 'Especially when dealing with Kavella, alive or dead.'

'That remains to be seen,' said Loftus. 'But it's not something you should waste time trying to predict, either of you. O'Keefe, you can now go back on sick leave. That'll keep you out of mischief for the immediate future. Van Hassel, you've got the weekend to forget about everything to do with Kavella, Proctor's Taskforce Nero and the late lamented Delos Club. In my opinion, it's distracted us from an equally pressing investigation.'

'But there's an obvious overlap with the hunt for the Hacker,' Rita objected.

'Obvious, maybe. But what if there was no real overlap, and we merely assumed it?' He put a hand on her shoulder. 'Anyway, don't think about it now. Come back with a fresh mind on Monday when Taskforce Nightwatch will be getting back up to speed.' He waved them off. 'And don't worry about your positions here.'

'As soon as a manager tells you that,' grumbled O'Keefe, 'it's time to polish up your CV.'

They made their way to the nearest pub. Rita held open the door while O'Keefe hobbled through. She bought two beers and carried them to a padded booth where O'Keefe was sprawled sideways, his crutches propped against a table.

'What are you doing this weekend?' she asked.

'I'm at the mercy of the missus,' he said. 'I'll try to get comfortable and watch the sports channel, but I'll be a captive audience to her nagging.'

Rita laughed. 'It's funny how even the strongest males are pushovers when it comes to sexual politics.'

'Yeah, hilarious,' said O'Keefe. 'What are your plans?'

'I'm having a night out on the town tomorrow with Erin Webster and my friend Lola. We're going to some trendy new hotspot.'

'Sounds dangerous.'

'Maybe not as dangerous as the alternative,' she said with a sly smile. 'I've also been invited for free champagne at the Windsor.'

64

The Hacker wasn't the name he'd chosen for himself. Yet it had a ring to it, with a suggestion of accessing the forbidden and disposing of enemies. Although he didn't object to the title, his true persona was less prosaic, belonging to the pantheon of Platonic warriors. Originally he'd seen himself as the Light Seeker or Fire Tracer, but now he knew he was the Shadow Maker, the dark creature of the cave. But for the purpose of the greater game, the Hacker would do.

In the end it didn't matter what they called him. Being aware of his presence was acknowledgement enough. Though even that was less important than his own self-awareness – allowing him to view the human spectacle objectively and see it for what it was. The ability to *stand outside it* – and *stand outside himself* – was the true meaning of the word *ecstasy*. And that's what he felt as a performer, a player.

And why?

Because the *game* was *real*.

But people didn't know it. They walked around in their daily lives ignorant of the roles they were playing. They confused conformity with reality. They mistakenly believed the social noise surrounding them was meaningful. And they took the artificial images imposed on them at face value. More fools them. So many in the game of life were losers. He had no intention of joining their ranks.

And yet there were moments of clarity when he questioned what he'd become. More than once he was unable to explain why he'd surrendered control to his dark fantasies, why they had become so intense, so irresistible. Perhaps he'd been under too much stress recently. Or maybe the timing was accidental and his fate had been lying in wait, like a trap to fall into. Perhaps it was inevitable. The cause probably lay in his childhood, feedback from the past, his own voice in his ear, his own urges. But what had made him act on them? What had triggered the move from imagining extreme violence to perpetrating it? Such desperate thoughts opened a new horror. Along with his victims, he'd mutilated the person he used to be. His innocence was lost forever. He was damned. The abyss opened below him. Suicide became an option.

Fortunately the mood of self-destruction lifted quickly, allowing him to focus again on the state of play, with its most intriguing development, a rival player. Unlike the she-devils he'd dealt with so far, this woman was a warrior like him. She, too, was deadly, with her victories splashed all over the media, just like his. Her presence in the field, hunting and killing in real time, made it much more interesting, even though they were operating on different levels. While he cut and thrust his way through demons, Van Hassel was dispatching monsters. Good for her. At this stage he could admire her progress, blowing off one head after another, although the time would come when she would recognise him because they were two of a kind. Ultimately, of course, they would face each other in a duel to the death. Those were the rules of the cave. In the meantime, he would applaud her from a distance.

Now for more immediate sport.

Friday night. Time to play.

Like anything you did, the more practised you became, the better you were at it. Your observation was sharper, your reflexes more attuned. To his trained eye they stood out from the others, like a different species of female. Something in the way they dressed, the way they moved. But more obviously, in the way they looked at you – straight into your eyes, daring you – provocative and alluring at the same time. Their eyes questioned you at first and then, if they held your attention, they drew you in. You felt excitement rising in your belly – the primeval thrill – and you wanted to follow it, even though you sensed the danger. Even though you knew they were acquisitive and destructive. These creatures had no conscience. They were out for themselves. And if you let them, they'd chew you up and spit you out.

Let them try. The huntress could also become the hunted. And then how the tables would be turned. The predator might find she was pursuing her own nemesis. Instead of procuring her prey and feasting on his ruin, she was herself destroyed.

He could see her now, poised among the shadows of the tavern. Her companions were talking to her, but her eyes keep drifting back to him as she flicked her hair and sucked on a straw. Their mutual recognition was part of an unspoken language – a non-verbal invitation. It was just a matter of time before she got up from her chair and walked over to his table.

He watched her approach.

Her voice was low and inviting, her intentions clear.

The game plan was decided.

They drove to her lair. Once they were inside his heart beat faster. The chase was reaching its climax. She agreed to his demands without hesitation, attaching metal cuffs to the head and foot of the iron bedstead, and lighting a fire in the tiled hearth in her bedroom while he undressed and pulled on the bronze mask. The sound of her voice was sweet and beguiling as she talked to her pets and fed them – a scene of disarming innocence. It was a ploy to weaken him, trick him. He excused himself and went to urinate and select a weapon, then waited for her to strip off.

Armed with a metal club he confronted her. Naked, she tried to fight him off. He beat her on the hands and the arms and the skull. She was defeated. He fastened her hands and feet to the bed and claimed his prize by exerting his power over her body. The experience was one of release. Time to mark his victory. He found a sharp knife and returned and stood over her, studying her face. Then he bent down, placed the blade against the bridge of her nose and cut down hard against the bone.

When the job was done he dropped the knife.

'That will put a stop to you,' he said.

He washed the blood from his hands and left the arena.

Game over.

65

At last, after all the financial angst, Barbie's gamble had paid off. The deal had been finalised. Tokyo had bought the software, the prototype hardware, the global rights to the game, the multimedia strategy and the marketing profile. The whole damn package.

Coming after months of negotiations, it was liberating – like a rite of passage. The thing he'd nurtured, which had gobbled up so much investment in time, money and nervous energy, had turned into a groundbreaking new product and was no longer his. He was on his way to becoming a billionaire. The exhaustive process concluded with everything formally signed and countersigned late Friday. Now it was Saturday night, and there was nothing to do but celebrate. He raised a tall champagne glass to his lips and sucked down a Bellini.

Across the table from him, Kenshi Jojima pondered a glass of shochu.

'You look worried,' said Barbie.

'You misinterpret,' said Jojima quietly, picking up his drink and downing it in one. 'This is my meditative expression.'

Barbie wasn't sure if that was Nipponese irony. Then again, he was never sure of anything about Jojima. The man was an oriental sphinx. He sat there stiffly, in his business suit, wearing an air of formality and self-containment. By contrast, Barbie was smart casual and wickedly playful. Once all the documents had been processed and filed, he'd felt like a new man. Tonight he could shed the protocol. It was time to enjoy himself. He sat back, legs crossed, looking dangerously relaxed in his white linen suit and black silk shirt, open at the neck.

They were between courses in the city's funkiest Japanese bar and restaurant. It seemed an appropriate place to celebrate. As usual it was crowded. At the far end was a bare brick wall, lined with every type of liquor on the market. Jojima's underlings were ranged there on bar stools, drinking as if on some alcoholic kamikaze mission. The bar was partitioned from the restaurant by cedarwood lattice screens. There was also a lounge area with low leather sofas, delicate bamboo plants and dim lanterns. Above the babble of voices, a DJ was spinning an exotic mix of Edith Piaf and urban rap on his chrome-plated designer decks.

'Meditation.' Barbie beckoned to the cocktail waitress. 'I took a course in that once.'

Jojima folded his hands. 'You studied Zen?'

'Yes. I needed a relaxation technique. Unlike you, I'm not a Buddhist.'

Jojima leant forward a little, his face sharp and earnest. 'It's true I had Buddhist training, but I have no religion. I have faith only in my own judgement.'

Barbie gestured to the hovering waitress for another champagne cocktail and another large shochu. 'No wonder you drive such a hard bargain,' he said. 'No self-doubt. No moral hesitation.'

Jojima gazed back at his host studiously, letting him know he could recognise a backhanded compliment when he heard one. Barbie smiled, feeling at liberty to speak his mind now that the multi-million-dollar deal had been completed.

'In whatever one does there are always ethical considerations,' said Jojima.

'What about war?'

'Even in war one needs a personal code of honour. Without it, a man's no better than a beast.'

Barbie's eyes met his. 'So you have a strong sense of honour?'

The question was loaded, and Jojima knew it. He'd been waiting for something of the sort. It was because of the unspoken pact between them – an unholy transaction involving Barbie's wife. The way both men had used her was anything but honourable. Barbie had made her services available in return for a business contract, and Jojima had been unable to resist the bribe.

'I try to be worthy of my ancestors,' he said hesitantly, then gave a polite shrug and glanced down.

Barbie smiled to himself. This was something else to savour. He'd not only clinched the deal, he'd also subverted the toughest negotiator he'd ever dealt with in the process. Never mind he'd used the tactics of a pimp. Moral corruption didn't bother him much at all. If anything, it amused him. All the better if it served his purpose. As for Giselle, he couldn't help admiring her dedication to material success. In practical terms, she'd actually strengthened their marriage. And what was that, ultimately, but just another contract?

Jojima again downed his drink in one gulp and placed the empty glass in front of him. 'And what about you, Barbie-san?' he asked. 'What do you believe in?'

His host thought about it for a moment, then answered, 'I believe in original sin.'

Jojima frowned. 'That's a Judaeo-Christian concept I find difficult to grasp.'

'It's quite straightforward really,' said Barbie, gesturing at the people around him as if indicating a riot of hedonism. 'Think of it as genetics. Original programming – the animal drives embedded in our brains by millions of years of evolution. Peel away our layers of social convention, and there it is – primal instinct. Freud called it the id.'

Jojima nodded. 'And that's the idea behind the game you've sold us.'

'Exactly. No VR game on the market is as vivid. None comes near it for sensory experience. There's nothing like it for stimulating the pleasure centres of the brain. Hardcore horror meets erotic violence. It's like plugging into the devil's playground. Audiovisual cocaine. The whole world will get hooked.'

Barbie laughed. The laugh wasn't quite manic, but it wasn't restrained either. It was the triumphant laugh of someone making a mockery of virtue. That too was a strong theme in Judaeo-Christian culture.

•

After the first bottle of sake, Rita could feel it loosening the grip of her self-control, dislodging the frustrations that had built up during her two days of paperwork and formal interrogations.

'You're *so* in the mood to party,' said Lola.

'How can you tell?'

'Your outfit,' said Lola, waving her chopsticks at her friend's low-cut top, slit skirt and stilettos. 'Complete giveaway.'

'Then we've come to the right place,' said Erin as she slid a rice ball into her mouth. 'Tarts' corner.'

'Talking of tarts,' Lola huffed, 'my lesbian admirer's more persistent than any male who's pursued me.'

'Serves you right,' said Rita.

'Sometimes she calls me every half hour and we end up having screaming rows over the phone.'

'One woman in a relationship and you've got a high level of emotion,' Rita pointed out. 'Two and you're talking volatile, explosive.'

'But I'm usually so fucking cool!' shouted Lola. 'I never have to explain myself!'

'So what exactly does she see in you?' asked Rita.

'She loves my tits.'

'Don't we all?' put in Erin. 'I once got called a "diesel dyke" by a sergeant in the Fraud Squad but I made him eat his words.'

'You look like sex on a stick,' came a male voice from behind Rita.

She looked up to find Martin Barbie standing over her, his eyes moving lazily from her exposed thigh to the open sway of her breasts. Next to him was a stern-looking Japanese man.

'Kenshi Jojima, let me introduce Detective Sergeant Marita Van Hassel, who thinks I'm something of a villain.'

Jojima looked alarmed, but gave a curt bow.

Barbie beamed around the table at her companions. 'And your friends are . . . ?'

With a sigh, Rita introduced them, amazement on their faces as he shook Erin's hand and kissed Lola's, his celebrity image glowing like an aura. They were both instantly charmed.

He turned back to Rita. 'I'd love to stay and chat, but we're heading off to the casino. Champagne celebration.' He pulled a business card from his pocket and handed it to her. 'This has my mobile number on it. Come and join me later. We can party together.'

Just like before, in the television studio, she felt that flush of excitement in her stomach. She couldn't tell if it was despite his smooth, sexual arrogance or because of it.

'What about your wife?' she asked.

'Ah, my wife.' Barbie couldn't help glancing at Jojima, who dropped his gaze – an exchange that left Rita wondering. 'My wife is otherwise engaged. So come along. Undercover, if you like. Though with what you're wearing, I hesitate to say it.' He smiled at one and all, oozing sincerity, and with a regal wave escorted Jojima from the restaurant.

Rita threw back a shot of sake, then dumped the wet glass on top of his business card. 'Arsehole.'

'You've got to be kidding!' gasped Lola. 'You've just been asked out by the hottest guy in town. You can't turn down an invitation like that!'

'I don't trust him. And he's already half pissed.'

'So what?' said Erin. 'So are you! And how on earth do you know Martin Barbie?'

'Like he said, because he's bent – though in what way I don't know. I questioned him over a line of inquiry to do with the Hacker, but it got nowhere. It's not on file.'

'Oh for God's sake.' Lola shook her head in exasperation. 'I swear, if you don't take the card and call him, I will. I mean it!'

Alarm bells were ringing in Rita's mind, warning her not to go to Barbie's party. Wealthy businessmen indulging themselves were dangerous territory with their monstrous egos and powerful connections. Not only would she be out of her depth, but it was the sort of social event where a woman's reputation – not to mention her career – could be compromised. No. Bad idea. But somewhere inside her head a seductive whisper was urging her on.

For one thing she had unfinished business with Barbie. Police business. Tonight would be a golden opportunity to catch him off guard. He might let slip something about the disappearance of Kelly Grattan, and the truth about that could have crucial implications. On the other hand, there was Huxley's open invitation for champagne at the Windsor. She sat in the glow of paper lanterns trying to make up her mind while the DJ did an experimental mix of Japanese dreamscape music and Kylie Minogue.

'The DJ's definitely gay,' said Lola. 'And you, Rita, need to let yourself go.'

Erin interrupted Rita's thoughts with a sisterly hand on her arm. 'You have a choice between a champagne party with a millionaire media star or a predictable evening of gossip with us.' She shook her head. 'No contest.'

She knew they were right. In the same way that the wheel of fate is right. Somehow it felt like she was meant to encounter Barbie tonight. For good or ill, she was also meant to follow through.

66

Rita took a taxi to the casino complex. As she walked into the hotel lobby she was in the mood for battle, the heels of her stilettos tapping emphatically across the expanse of black marble floor. If Barbie wanted to be cute, she was ready to match him.

Stopping, she punched up the number of his mobile.

'Hello?' he answered, nearly drowned out by a rowdy background.

'It's Marita Van Hassel. I'm in the lobby.'

'Fantastic.' He sounded genuinely pleased. 'I'll send someone down to get you.'

As she waited she looked around at the opulent glitz, a cross between a marble palace and Las Vegas. A grand staircase swept up through the galleried lobby. Immense chandeliers dripped from the ceiling and lights played on indoor fountains.

A hard-faced man in a dinner jacket came up to her. He had a buzz-saw haircut, thick neck muscles, and a radio earpiece. Security. Ex-army probably.

'Miss Van Hassel?' he asked.

She nodded.

'If you'll come with me, I'll take you up to Mr Barbie's suite.'

As Rita and the hired muscle rode the lift high up into the hotel tower she was already having second thoughts. What exactly was she walking into?

She found out as she passed another heavy-jawed security guard and entered Barbie's suite. The broad curve of the windows was filled with a spectacular night view over the city. Skyscrapers gleamed in the darkness, their reflections shimmering on the surface of the river far below. In the suite, the lights had been dimmed to heighten the dramatic effect. Champagne buckets were everywhere. Corporate executives, bow ties undone, created a loud din of conversation, high-class callgirls waiting to attend to their needs. So it was that sort of party. Decadent chic. In front of the centre window, Barbie was holding forth to men she recognised as state politicians. Much nodding, laughing and mutual toasts. Maybe it was true. Maybe the city was his for the taking.

He saw her and gestured her over. Hesitating, she was just wondering if she could make a quick retreat when someone touched her arm. She turned and found herself facing Josh Barrett, looking uncomfortable in a dinner jacket, champagne glass in hand. Behind him were his computer colleagues, equally out of place.

'What kind of weird party is this?' said Maynard with an adolescent grin. His hired suit didn't fit properly and served only to make him look more gangly. 'We've got hookers, karaoke and Japanese juice freaks. Now we've got a woman cop dressed to kill.'

'Shut up, you dork,' said Flynn. He too looked awkward in formal wear, trying to loosen his bow tie as he turned to Rita. 'But he's got a point. What are you doing here?'

'A last-minute invitation from your boss,' she answered. 'We bumped into each other at a Japanese restaurant.'

'That figures,' Flynn grumbled. 'Looks like everyone's been invited by the Great Barbie to help him celebrate us making him millions.'

'So when is the game being unveiled?' asked Rita.

'Like I told you before,' snapped Flynn, 'we've got strict confidentiality clauses. If we breathe a word then it's no job and no bonus.'

'He's right,' put in Josh. 'We're under contract to keep our mouths shut – commercial secrets and all that – but the timetable's now down to the Japanese. All the official announcements will come from Tokyo.'

'I'll look forward to them,' she said. 'Should I buy a new PlayStation?'

'And the rest of the kit,' said Maynard.

'Shut the fuck up,' said Flynn, cutting him short. 'Come on, time to drink up. We don't belong here.'

'We were just about to split,' said Josh, clearly wanting to add something but feeling constrained by the others. 'I guess you're staying for a while.'

'I'd better say hello to the host and thank him for inviting me.'

'Hello's about the only word you'll get in,' said Flynn. 'He's more full of himself than ever.'

Having greeted Barbie in a scrum of businessmen, Rita was standing by the window, sipping champagne and admiring the view when she was approached by a distinguished-looking man with a shock of steel grey hair, a florid face and a plum-coloured bow tie. She recognised him straightaway as another politician – though federal this time. From the expression on his face, he had only sexual politics in mind.

'Wonderful sight,' he said with a suggestive smile. 'This city's got so much to offer.'

'Yes,' she replied, glancing Barbie's way. He was circulating now. Lots of backslapping. 'Especially with the right contacts.'

The politician thought he'd caught her drift. 'It's always who you know,' he said, glancing around furtively and leaning towards her. 'So are you available tonight?' he whispered, nodding slyly towards the drunken Japanese. 'Or are you spoken for?'

Rita averted her eyes and took a swig of champagne as she suppressed the urge to tell him to go fuck himself. Then she saw the irony. The way she was dressed. The type of party it was. Maybe that's why Barbie had invited her, the manipulative bastard. Put her in her place. Include her in the company of upmarket prostitutes. And of course that's why there were no wives or girlfriends present. All the women here had the raw glamour of professional hostesses. In a crude way it was a compliment as well as an insult that this jerk thought she was one of them.

The politician edged closer. 'So, my dear. Have our friends from Nippon claimed you?'

She remembered the brothel madam's insight about the male brain. This one was shedding points from his IQ like rats from a sinking ship.

'I'm on my own,' was all she said.

He beamed at her. 'Excellent. That means you're free for the night.'

She nursed her drink, feeling a mixture of revulsion, righteous indignation and malice, then she looked him squarely in the eyes and said, 'A girl is never free.'

'Ah.' That set him back. 'What sort of figure do you have in mind?'

It was part of her job to know market rates, but how high up the price index would she pitch herself?

'Three grand,' she said, off the top of her head.

'Three . . . ?' His expression stiffened. 'That's a bit steep. Especially as the hospitality's been paid for by the host.'

'Has it now?' Maybe she should put it on file. Barbie the procurer, Barbie the pimp. 'Well he hasn't paid for me.'

He wasn't beaming now. 'I can have you thrown out,' he said, his tone threatening. 'There's no end of trouble I can cause.'

Trying to intimidate her. Wrong move. 'You're not the only one, Senator . . .' she replied.

But before she could say any more, Barbie was at her side, his hand on her elbow, smiling into the politician's face. 'So you've met the detective sergeant? Not what you expect, is she?'

The senator blanched. 'You're with the police?' His voice sounded hoarse. 'A detective? Which squad?'

'Sex crimes,' she said sharply. 'Vice.'

He began to back away. 'You realise this party's strictly private.'

'Don't worry.' Barbie's smile was like a salesman's guarantee. 'She's off-duty.'

But it was the politician's turn to be affronted. 'She's also off the leash.'

As they watched him retreat, Barbie asked her casually, 'Did you spook the honourable Senator?'

Rita drank the rest of her champagne. 'Not nearly enough.'

'I thought you'd make an interesting addition to the party,' he said, amused.

'In addition to what? The balloons and party poppers?' she replied, her voice hot with annoyance. 'The frigging karaoke?'

Barbie laughed as if nothing could faze him tonight. The battle was won. He'd conquered the world. But she was right about one thing – the noise level from the karaoke. Voices caterwauling. The screech of feedback from the amplifiers. He had to raise his voice to speak above it.

'You're far more decorous.'

She had a powerful urge to slap the conceit off his face. 'I don't know why you invited me. But if it's for a bit of sport –'

But he cut her short. 'No way. No way.' Waving off the suggestion. 'I thought it might be to our mutual benefit. A mixture of business and pleasure.'

What was he after now, she wondered. Inside information? The prospect of a bribe?

'Okay,' she said. 'I'm listening.'

'Good. But let's go where we can hear ourselves talk.'

She was sinking into the overstuffed cushions of an embroidered sofa, relieved to be off her feet and away from the noise of the party. Barbie had escorted her here, into the adjoining suite, which he used as his private accommodation. His 'haven', he'd called it, his 'urban retreat'. She could think of other names that were less edifying.

It was peaceful here after the raucous atmosphere of the celebration – seductively peaceful. The sofa was blissfully soft. She could feel her anger draining away. Her muscles relaxing. A strange sort of music was playing quietly in the background. Voices singing in Latin. Slow and moody. And in the air, a touch of incense. She was sitting in candlelight amid a sea of thick rugs, a champagne bottle in a silver ice bucket on a table in front of her, her gaze drifting across the cinematic spectacle of city lights filling the windows as she waited for Barbie to return with a pair of chilled champagne glasses.

She was still puzzling over his motives when she recognised the music. It was a Gregorian chant. For a moment, nothing seemed less appropriate to his personality. Ritual religious plainsong. How odd. And incense. Another hint of something esoteric. Then it clicked.

She'd read a background file on him. Research material. Not the sort of information in the media. It included references to his family. How his father had served the Nazis in Estonia. A platoon commander in a police battalion during the Second World War. A few years before his death, Barbie senior had been a war crimes suspect, implicated in the torture and killing of civilians, mostly Jews. He denied it and there was insufficient evidence. What was on record was his time in Australia. The man was a prosperous member of the community in Melbourne's southern suburbs, the owner of a carpet business, and a local councillor known for his right-wing views. Together with his Australian-born wife, he was a zealous adherent of a Christian fundamentalist church. In other words, a religious fascist.

This, then, was Barbie's father. And with a flash of insight, she saw the boy. The product of an authoritarian home burdened with the wrath of Jehovah, along with a secret and odious past. What had the child endured? What psychological devices had he used to survive and triumph? And religion? One way or another it would play a powerful theme in his life. Did he fear God, or mock Him? As she sniffed the ceremonial scent and listened to the haunting, monastic music, she knew it was the latter. His private retreat was sensual, profane. And her first-hand experience of his business life revealed a victory of commerce over morals. Perhaps he had none. And women? How did he use women? Was rape part of his apostasy?

Or was she assuming too much?

Her criminal profiler's brain told her he was guilty of something – but she didn't know what. Anyway, the night's infusion of alcohol was clouding her judgement. And whatever Barbie's flaws, he was certainly entertaining.

'I hope I didn't offend you earlier,' he said. 'I really am glad you made it.'

'Quite a celebration,' she said dryly. 'Complete with sideshows.'

'Keeps the customers happy. A few party games.'

'Especially the lucky dip.'

He gave a low chuckle and said, 'Sounds like you disapprove.'

'Maybe I do.'

'Personally or professionally?'

The question irked her and she let him hear it in her voice. 'I can't think of one good reason why you'd invite me.'

He paused, the champagne bottle tilted towards a glass. 'If that's what you think, why did you come?'

'To escape a girls' night out,' she quipped.

Barbie pulled a sympathetic face. 'Fair enough.' He wasn't bothered. 'Their loss, my gain.'

He filled the glass and handed it to her. As he bent forward she saw again how well he moved. Very polished. Each gesture almost choreographed. A man with great self-control, but relaxed with it. She watched him fill his own glass and place the bottle gently back in the ice bucket. He'd shed the jacket and stood there in his tailored linen trousers and black silk shirt, the top buttons undone. She noticed his firm shoulder muscles and the smooth skin of his neck and chest.

He raised his glass. 'To lucky escapes!'

'Yours or mine?'

His eyes gleamed at her. 'Both!'

There it was. The tease. He was in a wicked mood. Ready to play a sophisticated game of cat-and-mouse.

But so was she. 'Cheers,' she responded.

They both drank and looked at each other with a sort of mutual relish, heightened by the tang of champagne. As she crossed her legs, the slit in her skirt fell open on her thigh, exposing the top of her stocking and part of a suspender belt.

'Have I dragged you away from your party guests?' she asked coyly.

'You have, but I'm glad.' He eased himself into an armchair directly opposite her. 'I hope the ambience here is more to your liking.'

'It is. But the Gregorian chant's a bit of a surprise.'

'Not my style, you mean? Too celestial?'

'I've just seen you playing host to the seven deadly sins – complete with vice girls. I'd say your style's more devil than anything else.'

He chuckled sardonically. 'If I'm the devil, who are you?' His eyes moving over her body. 'Jezebel?'

'No. I'm definitely on the side of the avenging angels.'

Barbie took a sip of champagne, eyes gleaming as if he wanted to arrange her fall there and then. 'I mentioned before there's something I want to put to you.'

'If it's a proposition,' she said, 'I've already had one from the senator.'

He waved that aside. 'I don't mean this in a suggestive way, but how satisfied are you?'

'What do you mean?'

'Your job. Your career.' He was being amiable. 'Your aspirations.'

'Somehow I don't see you as a headhunter.'

'You'd be surprised. I know, for a start, you have an honours degree in psychology. But it seems wasted in your current job.'

'Comes in very handy, thank you.'

'But is your ability recognised? Or are you frustrated?'

'By what?' she wanted to know.

'Institutional prejudice. Bureaucratic inertia.' His expression was earnest now. Conviction in his voice. It was unsettling. 'Are you fulfilled in your work?'

When she answered, 'Of course,' they both knew she was lying.

He sat forward, very serious now, the glass dangling from his hand. 'Come and work for me.'

She just looked at him, a startled expression on her face.

'The media's the real power in the world now,' he went on. 'We shape opinion. Create the future. That's why we need the most dynamic people. It's something I feel passionately about. We need people like you.'

'Me?'

'Absolutely. With your intellect and drive. And of course your looks.' He flourished the glass at her in admiration. 'And now your public profile . . .'

'Okay, slow down,' she said with a nervous laugh. 'What exactly are you talking about?'

'You're front-page news. We've all read about what you did.'

'That's not a profile. That's criminal casework. Last week's headlines.'

'Oh, God!' He threw back his head in disbelief. 'How wrong you are.'

'Look,' she said defensively. 'I think I'm good at what I do . . .'

'So am I.'

'. . . but I'm not in the marketing business.'

'Well I am. And I'm the best. Believe me, your publicity is priceless. A woman cop who blew away a hitman in her own bedroom – who outgunned one of the city's worst gangsters in a church shoot-out . . .'

'That's not strictly true.'

'Nothing ever is. It's how you sell it that counts. The tabloids, TV, have given you an image – and image is reality. Like it or not, you're now a celebrity. Make the most of it. Come and work for me. I'll pay you ten times what you're earning.'

For a moment she was speechless, the idea swimming in her head along with the alcohol. Then she blurted out, 'Doing what?'

'Presentation. You're a natural.'

'I don't think so.'

'Then whatever you like. Production, research. Take your pick.'

The offer was bewildering. And very tempting. But despite his plausible sales pitch, she knew that it – like everything else about him – was deceptive. And the more she observed him, the more she realised how clever he was. That was the answer. That was how he'd emerged from a harsh childhood to achieve so much success. He had a grasp of human frailty because it was beaten deep within him. Moral corruption was his Tree of Knowledge. It gave him insight. He understood the power of greed and glamour. He knew what buttons to press.

'So you don't have any particular role lined up for me?' she asked.

'I just want you on board.'

'What sort of job security would I have?'

'A five-year contract. If you went early, you'd get a very big payout.'

'As much as Kelly Grattan?'

The name hung in the air between them. Along with the quiet chant of monks. But in that instant, the room went cold.

Without a word, Barbie put down his glass, got up, and walked over to the broad curve of the window. He stood there, his back to her, hands in pockets, looking out over the urban nightscape like an offended monarch.

Rita watched him with a new clarity. Now she knew why she'd accepted his invitation. Saturday night drinking and personal demons aside, there was another reason. It was to do with her sense of justice. No matter whether she was on leave or off-duty, it would always nag at her. Like the sight of Kelly Grattan, propped up in a hospital bed. A smart attractive woman reduced to a victim – bruises on her hands, face scratched, skull fractured – and refusing to talk about it, because of the man who now stood a few feet away. The same man who was offering an extravagant, career-altering bribe to keep Rita's mouth shut. Whatever his crime, he must be desperate to keep it hidden.

'Kelly was one of my most trusted employees,' he said at last, his back to her still. 'And whatever happened, that's why I paid her a lot of money. No matter what you think.'

'I think you know exactly what happened to her.'

Barbie didn't respond immediately and didn't turn around. He stood quite still in the muted glow of the candlelight, staring out through the sleek towers of the skyline to the darkness beyond. 'Then you're wrong,' he said, composed now. 'I hope the subject's closed. And I should get back to my party.'

'Of course.' She finished her drink, put the glass down on the table and stood up. 'It's been very interesting.'

'The job offer's still there.'

She shook her head. 'Thanks. But I can't accept.'

'Pity. There's a lot more to you than a policewoman. And if you could get past your hostility, you'd see we have something.'

'Like what?'

'A rapport.'

'Are we still talking business?' she asked. 'Or have we moved onto pleasure?'

'Let's call it emotional intelligence.'

'And what's on that agenda?'

He thought for a moment then said without humour, 'Love thy enemy.'

67

As she left the casino complex there was only one person whose company Rita wanted – the man who was due to be wrapping up his think-tank presentation at the Windsor about now. She hadn't told Byron Huxley whether or not she'd drop in on him, but after her encounter with high-level corruption he seemed more decent, considerate and attractive than ever. Sexier, too, though that could have something to do with her alcohol intake and the way Martin Barbie had aroused her animal emotions.

She arrived by cab at the grand old hotel as state government advisers were dispersing towards limousines. Once inside the conference room she found hotel staff dismantling the sets from the presentation. Huxley was nowhere to be seen, and Rita hurried to the reception desk and asked for his room number. He'd been booked into one of the Victorian suites, so she climbed a sweep of staircase and knocked on his door.

As he opened it, a broad smile lit up his face. 'You made it after all,' he said, delighted.

'A girl can't resist an offer of free champagne,' she said, brushing past him into the suite.

'Just as well I kept a bottle.'

He was still in his dinner jacket, but his bow tie hung loosely from his collar, and the top buttons of his white shirt were undone.

'A great pad you've got here,' she observed.

'Designed for royalty,' he said, waving a hand at the antique furniture, lush fittings and gilt-framed paintings. 'For us to enjoy at the taxpayers' expense, I might add.'

She nodded her approval as he popped the cork of the champagne bottle, the fizz of bubbles spilling over the glasses.

'I have to warn you I've knocked off a few drinks already,' she told him, 'so I'm not entirely sober.'

'Then I'll try to catch up.'

They clinked glasses. As she tasted the bubbly she noticed it was cheaper than Barbie's, but a lot easier to swallow.

'Are you going to show me around?' she prompted.

'Of course,' he said, leading the way. 'Separate reception room, dining room – with table for eight guests – and sitting room. Through here is the marble bathroom, and there are two bedrooms: the guest room' – he opened the door and she poked her head through – 'and the main boudoir.'

She followed him, champagne glass in hand, into a spacious room with double bed, soft carpet and heavy curtains. Lights from the street filtered through the nets on the windows.

'I think you should close the curtains,' she suggested, putting down her glass on a polished dressing-table.

He went over to the windows and drew the curtains, cloaking the room in semi-darkness. As he walked back around the bed, she took his glass from him and put it down.

'We should make the most of taxpayers' generosity,' she told him, grabbing hold of his shirt and undoing the rest of the buttons.

Huxley couldn't get his jacket and shirt off quickly enough, flinging them onto the floor. As Rita ran her hands over his bare chest, he bent down and kissed her neck, then, when she rolled her tongue over his nipples, he threw his head back with a gasp.

'Where did you learn that?' he groaned.

'Never you mind,' she answered, raking her fingernails down the middle of his back with one hand, while the other slid into his trousers, clamping him in a groin hold; his penis was already hard.

He pulled her mouth up to his and kissed her until she pushed him back onto the bed, laughing.

While he struggled out of his shoes and pants, Rita stripped off, tossing her clothes onto the floor beside his. Her body was impressive – strong and athletic, with full breasts, her slim buttocks smooth and glossy in the dim light.

She bent down to him, her voice husky, close to his ear. 'I'm going to fuck your brains out.'

'You're bad,' he said with a wolfish smile.

'You'd better believe it.'

And that's where the conversation ended as she got astride him on all fours, lowering herself till the pointed tips of her breasts brushed his cheeks. She kissed him again, her lips and tongue gliding softly over his. Then she sat up, straddling his thighs, his erection rigid and straining inside her. As he pushed deeper, she arched her spine and tossed back her head, running her fingers through her hair. It was a moment of intimacy worth waiting for, letting herself go and moaning freely, as her body responded to the erotic rush.

68

They sat in white bathrobes on either side of an antique dining table, eating a late breakfast in Huxley's hotel suite. The full menu, including fried courses, toast and coffee, had been delivered on a silver service by a waiter in a frock coat. Rita sipped juice and picked at a fruit bowl as she watched Huxley tucking into a plate of sausages, bacon and hash browns.

'I'm ravenous,' he explained.

'I've noticed,' she said.

He finished his fry-up and yawned. 'Would you pour me a coffee?' he asked.

'Yes, dear,' chuckled Rita, filling a china cup and pushing it across to him.

'This is an unexpected surprise.'

'Enjoy it while it lasts,' she told him.

He stretched, yawning again, a contented smile on his face. 'We seemed to have a lot of sex last night.'

She threw some grapes at him. 'We were at it like rabbits,' she chided.

'We must do it again soon.'

'Then finish your coffee,' she said, standing up, loosening her bathrobe and letting it drop to the floor. 'How about now?'

Huxley didn't need any further encouragement, flinging off his robe and chasing her as she ran, naked and shrieking with laughter, to the bedroom.

It was late morning when Huxley pulled his Range Rover into the driveway of Lola's apartment block to drop off Rita.

'If I didn't have a damn postgraduate barbecue to go to I'd spend the rest of the day with you,' he complained. 'But I'm guest of honour.'

'That's okay, you've worn me out enough already,' she said.

As she opened the door to get out he took hold of her hand.

She turned and looked into his eyes.

'I need to see you again soon,' he said, expression serious.

She stretched towards him and kissed him softly on the lips, before getting out, laughing happily. 'I think that can be arranged.'

Rita walked into the apartment to find Lola groaning her way through a black coffee, head in hands, elbows on the kitchen table, a loose silk robe covering her.

'Oh God,' moaned Lola. 'Why did I mix my drinks?'

'You seemed fine when I left,' said Rita.

'Yes, but then Erin ordered some cab sav. We got through two bottles of it.'

'Sake and red wine? Bit of a funky mix.'

'Erin's got the palate of a petrol can. It's *her* fault,' said Lola, letting out another groan. 'And what have you been up to, swanning back home the next day with a smug look on your face?'

'Well I drank champagne for the rest of the evening.'

'If you ended up shagging Martin Barbie I owe Erin a hundred bucks.'

'Your money's safe,' said Rita. 'But guess what?'

'What?'

'I spent the night at the Windsor.'

'Thank God – at last! You got it together with the hunky professor. I knew you were made for each other.'

Lola was interrupted by Rita's phone ringing. The call was from Jack Loftus. Nothing urgent, he told her – he just wanted to come and see her. He'd be there in half an hour.

By the time Loftus arrived Rita had changed out of her evening wear, pulled on jeans and a T-shirt, and cleaned up after Lola, who'd withdrawn to the bathroom, thrown up and taken to her bed.

As Rita filled the kettle he sat down at the kitchen table, pushing aside the empty coffee cup.

'So,' he said. 'How're you feeling?'

'I'm fine. Ready to get back to profiling the Hacker. Why do you ask?'

'It worries me that, because of the bedlam of the past week, you didn't get to talk through things with a counsellor,' he said, frowning.

'I don't need a counsellor.'

'Maybe a counsellor could tell me that.'

'Jesus, Jack. *I'm* telling you – as a cop, as a psychologist, as a hard bitch who's had her share of personal traumas – *I'm* telling you I'm okay. And the only way I'll go nuts is if I *don't* get back on the Hacker case first thing tomorrow.'

'Yeah, well I just needed to hear it from you.'

She put her hands on her hips and looked at him, sitting there in his scruffy weekend casuals. A frayed tartan shirt and brown cords. He was a different person out of his formal office wear. There was a spray of sawdust on his sleeve and a smear of paint on his trouser leg. Eggshell pink.

She gave him an affectionate smile. 'Interrupted your hobbies, have you?'

'Redecorating the dining room,' he said. 'Forced labour. I bloody hate it. You're my excuse for a break.'

It made her laugh, how often women got their way. No matter how tough a man was outside the home, inside they were often pushovers, Loftus and O'Keefe being perfect examples.

Rita poured a mug of tea and handed it to him.

'Okay, Jack. Anything new?'

He spooned in some sugar and said, 'I don't think you'll have Nash to worry about. He's been ticked off himself. The Chief Commissioner's pissed off with how you and O'Keefe have been treated, calling it heavy-handed. And the lawyers are convinced neither of you have a case to answer over the deaths of Kavella and Moyle. They say there's a powerful argument of self-defence in both cases.'

'Excellent!' She gave him a gleeful hug. 'And just when I was getting other job offers.'

'Like what?'

'Never mind.' She clapped her hands. 'Any more fallout from Taskforce Nero?'

'Yes, Jim Proctor's turned over a couple of dirty cops who were in Kavella's pocket – both constables, one from Homicide.'

'Just as well we stopped him when we did.'

'Yeah, and that's largely down to you rattling his cage – and nearly getting yourself killed in the process.'

'I told you I'm okay. What about the crime lab – are they any further on the smartcard?'

'No.' He drank some of his tea. 'But as I hinted on Friday, I'm thinking we should start from scratch with the Hacker case. If our assumptions were wrong then Kavella, his associates and his customers had nothing to do with it – and his nightclub has no bearing at all on the case. Which begs the question.'

'Exactly.' She reached over to her handbag and slid out the glossy Plato's Cave card. 'I've been carrying this thing around with me for weeks.' She brandished it in front of her face like a black and silver laminated riddle. 'It's like one of my accessories. I shuffle it in and out of my wallet. I put it down on cafe tables. I contemplate it. I turn it over. I tap it against bottles of water. I flick sugar cubes with it. I even tried to put it in a cash machine by mistake.' She pursed her lips and tossed the card onto the kitchen table. 'What I can't do is crack its secret.'

Loftus picked it up, looked at it and put it down again. 'I've done some follow-up checks of my own. The brothel. The academic fellowship. Like you, I can't find a connection. At the moment, it's got me stumped.' He finished his tea and pushed away the mug. 'On that note, I'd better get back to my bloody decorating.'

'Think of it as therapeutic,' she said.

'I don't want to think of it at all.' He got up to leave. 'By the way, after I spoke to the guy from the fellowship he wanted to tell you something about Plato.'

'Phillip Roxby?'

'Yes.' Loftus was feeling in his pockets for his car keys. 'But I wouldn't let him talk to you on Friday, you had enough to think about.'

'Did he say anything else?'

'He asked if you could call him over the weekend. I only said maybe.'

She called Roxby straightaway but he wouldn't talk over the phone. He wanted to meet.

'Why?' she said.

'Plato's Cave,' he answered. 'You want to know about it?'

She bit her lip and wondered. Was he toying with her? Or did he really have something to say? And if so, what? She had to find out.

'Okay.'

'Great. Let's do lunch.'

'Where?' she asked.

'There's an old Edwardian pub in Abbotsford. The Retreat.'

'I know it,' she said.

'I'll be there in fifteen minutes. I'll get a table in the snug.'

She hung up abruptly and bowed her head. This was an unexpected date. But what exactly was he up to? Perhaps just another mind game.

When she arrived he was sitting there, looking urbane in his blazer, blue cotton shirt and neat navy trousers. She was still in T-shirt, jeans and tennis shoes. The place had the quaint, cosy atmosphere of a bygone age. Lunches in the dining room. Couples chatting over glasses of beer. Sunday drinkers propped on stools along the curving bar with its serving hatches, brass rail and beer pumps. Stained-glass windows and glazed tile walls. Framed photos from the horse and buggy era.

He stood up as she came in. 'I'm glad we could get together,' he said, waiting for her to get comfortable before resuming his seat. 'Last time we met was a bit alarming. I didn't respond very well.'

She gave him a level look. 'What do you want to tell me?'

He held up a finger and said, 'First, let's order lunch.'

He went for nachos and a glass of chardonnay. She asked for a lime and soda.

'Isn't it nice to have a rendezvous here?' he went on wistfully. 'I once brought my ex-wife to this pub way back when we were courting. Long before the divorce turned my life to shit.'

'Is that so?'

The sentiment drained from his face. 'Another strange paradox, isn't it, how love can turn into hate. How we build our lives on illusions. How nothing we take for granted is real.'

She tried to interrupt, 'What specifically –'

But he kept on. 'How fantasy dominates our minds. How people who appear to be rational, and function perfectly in society, are objectively insane.'

She moved uneasily in her chair. 'I don't need a lesson in psychology.'

'You want to know about Plato's Cave?' he said sharply. 'Well, I'm telling you.'

She couldn't guess where he was leading. 'What are you saying?'

'I was less than candid when you came to see me on campus. You asked me a question but I didn't respond appropriately.'

She sat back, her pulse beating a little faster. What was coming next? 'Go on,' she said.

'I had trouble collecting my thoughts. Doesn't happen very often.' He blew out a sigh. 'Just around certain types of women.'

She caught the accusation in his eyes, and the self-pity, then looked away.

'I read about you in the papers.' His voice more subdued. 'How you shot dead the man who ran the nightclub, the man we spoke about, and how the hunt's still on for the guy maiming hookers. I realised then I could've been more helpful. Given you a straight answer.'

'To which question?' she asked.

'You asked me the meaning of Plato's Cave. That question.' He took a deep breath, and explained, 'Your question is about the foundation of western thought – back there, among those ancient Greeks . . .'

'Am I about to hear one of your lectures?'

'Bear with me,' he insisted. 'Plato says the citizens of the cave believe the fake images projected around them are real. Well that still applies today. If anything, it's more valid than ever in our media-saturated, celebrity-obsessed, consumer-driven mass culture. We all inhabit the cave. We're all deluded, believing the cinema-screen version of reality – unless we can get up, and turn around, and see the projector.'

A thought struck her. Something Barbie had been going on about. She said hesitantly, 'And he who controls the projector . . .'

'. . . controls social reality.' He nodded. 'Projecting phoney images onto the walls of our collective mind. But I don't want you to get the wrong idea. Plato gives us a way out.'

'I've read *The Republic*.'

'Which tells us we can crawl out of the cave and into the dazzling light of truth.' Roxby gave a sniff of satisfaction. The same as when he delivered a punchline to an auditorium full of students, no doubt. 'And there's one other thing. That card you showed me. I've been thinking about it. Have you worked out what it represents?'

'If you can tell me,' she said soberly, 'I might not put you on file.'

'What an offer.' He scooped up some spicy topping with a tortilla chip and waved it, as if to tantalise her. 'You've been looking in the wrong places. The club, the brothel, the fellowship. It's not a business card. It's a token. A talisman. An emblem of private membership. Like a key that unlocks an exclusive fantasyland.'

'Don't suppose you can point out which one?'

'Sorry, I'm giving you a philosophic profile. The geographic one I'll leave to you.'

'For the sake of argument,' she said, 'let's assume you're right. Now there's a basic premise of profiling – decipher what the serial offender is dreaming when he indulges in ritualistic violence and you know where he's coming from. You can formulate his background, his motives and his strategy.'

'And what you've stumbled on, Detective Sergeant, is a secret dreamland.'

'So, logically, the Plato's Cave I'm looking for has no sign over the door, no phone number, no website, no public face,' she said, 'which is what I have to assume with Kavella's operation apparently ruled out.' For all that she disliked him, Roxby was pointing her in the same direction as Jack Loftus, the same direction now of her own reasoning. 'And while that makes it harder to find, it doesn't alter a basic fact that shows this case is different in a fundamental way.'

'Okay, I'll play Glaucon to your Socrates,' said Roxby. 'What way?'

'The context of this killer's dreaming is somehow outside his own head. It's external. It's objectively real, my dear Glaucon,' she surmised. 'It has a smartcard as a key.'

69

It was late Sunday morning and Flynn could hear church bells ringing when he got the summons from Barbie.

'I'm sending a limo to pick you up. It'll be there in half an hour.'

As Flynn put down the phone he couldn't help smiling. Despite the fractious relationship between them, he'd been expecting an invitation from his boss to receive his reward for delivering the game. After shaving and showering, he dressed in smart chinos and a blue silk shirt as befitted such a meeting on a bright and sunny morning. He was ready when the chauffeur-driven limousine arrived at his apartment block. The drive to Brighton took little more than ten minutes, but instead of delivering him to the beachfront mansion the chauffeur dropped him off at a cafe-bar nearby – the Half Moon. This was where Barbie went on Sundays when there was no urgent business to attend to and he felt like a holiday from his professional image.

He was sitting at a window table looking as relaxed as a post-coital lizard, lounging behind a bacon and egg breakfast, knife and fork in hand, wearing beach shorts, sandals, a faded Eagles T-shirt and a pair of Clooney sunglasses. A Sunday newspaper was spread open on the table. Flynn immediately felt overdressed. This wasn't the reception he'd anticipated. Not when you were in line for a big bonus – and the kudos you deserved.

Barbie gave a lazy wave towards the chair opposite. 'Thanks for coming at short notice,' he said. 'But I thought I should tell you in person.'

'Tell me what?'

'Xanthus. I'm shutting it down.'

Flynn couldn't believe what he was hearing. 'Why, for fuck's sake?'

'It's done its job. I got the deal I wanted. Time to move on to frontiers new.' Barbie cut a piece of fried bread and chewed on it. 'I'll retain various rights, of course – and the profits. But the assets will be sold off. I'll make the announcement next month.'

'What happens to me?'

'I'll buy out the rest of your contract, of course. Then it's back on the job market – like everyone else at the company.' He brushed a crumb from his lip. 'But the experience you've gained will be invaluable – as long as you don't breach any commercial secrets or copyrights.'

Flynn read the threat with disgust. 'You mean *keep my mouth shut.* What about the recognition? What about the bonus I deserve?'

Barbie put down his knife and fork. 'There was never any mention of a bonus. Besides, you're just one member of a changing line-up. Over the past three years, fifteen different faces have filled the core team and, while I appreciate your contribution, it was the work of my project manager, Josh Barrett, that ensured we met the deadline. And let's face it, your histrionics tended to get in the way, so I feel I've done more than enough for you. I'm the one who carried the entire burden of risk, so I reap the rewards.'

'Hog all the credit, you mean.'

'Yes, well, don't let it bug you,' said Barbie, sipping from a glass of cranberry juice. '*Sic gloria transit mundi.*'

'Sick is right. I should be in line for an ex gratia pay-off.'

'Get real.' Barbie took off his glasses so Flynn could see the look in his eyes. 'You can't afford to be bitter, my friend. I don't want to deal with any repercussions, if you see what I mean.' He swallowed the rest of his juice and stood up. 'By the way, don't have anything to do with that woman cop. I saw you talking to her at the party. She's dangerous. Sees beneath the surface of people. I don't want to have to deal with her either.' He picked up a Sunday paper and turned to go. 'I'll send in the chauffeur to drive you home.'

Flynn didn't say anything. When the chauffeur came in he told him, 'Get lost.' Then he ordered a large whisky and drank it neat. Then he ordered another and sat there contemplating his plight, trying to pinpoint the blame. It wasn't a pleasant exercise.

As he drank more whisky he felt his emotions flicker back and forth between rage and anxiety. The rage centred on Barbie, who'd used Flynn's brilliance to make himself hundreds of millions of dollars. And in return? No reward. No recognition. It was unacceptable. That meant he had to do something about it – and that's where the anxiety kicked in. It centred on Detective Sergeant Van Hassel. She could be used for revenge – but how much was he going to divulge? He was still undecided when he took her card out of his wallet and phoned her.

Rita drove along the highway, past upmarket car dealerships and turned into the leafy streets of Brighton. The houses here were substantial, the gardens fastidiously neat, the two combining to exude an air of respectability and money. Among its residents it could count one Martin Barbie – so it was intriguing to be invited for an 'off-the-record' chat with Eddy Flynn, who said he was ready to 'dump the dirt' on this epitome of bourgeois success.

Even the main shopping strip had an exclusive feel to it, with people in refined casual mode enjoying the pavement cafes or browsing at the expensive shop windows. Rita found a parking space beside the copper-steepled church and joined the promenade past fashion boutiques and patisseries, a bookshop called Thesaurus and a Victorian post office now selling Laura Ashley. The place she was looking for was opposite the railway station. She went in and spied Flynn at a window table downing a drink. He looked distracted and uncomfortable among the rest of the customers – mothers with babies; well-groomed men; immaculate women, invariably blonde.

'Okay, I'm here.' She sat at his table. 'And I'm all ears.'

'Good,' he said. 'I've got a few things to tell you about the man I've been working for.'

She'd only met Eddy Flynn twice before. On both occasions he'd been assertive if not aggressive. Almost theatrical in his managerial role. Today he was quite different. Subdued. Deflated. An intelligent young man wrestling with disappointment. He was holding it in, but not very well.

'Fine. I'm off-duty and this is off the record.'

She glanced around but no one was paying them any attention. Two infants were squawking in highchairs nearby, their mothers spooning froth into their mouths from babycinos. At other tables couples grazed over late lunches, the women flicking through Sunday magazines, the men with their faces in the sports pages. Under umbrellas outside sleek females with perfect tans and faces older than their figures exchanged gossip over salads. A man walked by with a pair of Afghan hounds on leads. The railway gates started clanging. The coffee machine growled.

'I'm not completely the arrogant bastard I seem,' Flynn began. 'Some of it's just an act.'

'I know.'

'My way of getting people's attention, motivating them.' He clasped his hands. 'Getting the job done.'

'The secret of your success,' she said.

'Until today.'

'What's happened?'

'Barbie – the evil fuck – has sacked me. At this table. Less than an hour ago.' Flynn put his head in his hands.

'Why?' she asked.

'He's selling off the firm next month. We're all getting the chop.'

The waitress came over and Rita ordered a latte.

'When I say he's evil,' Flynn resumed, 'I mean it literally. He's got everyone fooled, the way he charms the pants off people. Like the devil himself. But underneath he's got the scruples of a thug.'

This was beginning to sound like nothing more than personal resentment. She wondered if there was any real information for her. 'Is he really that bad?'

'I've accessed his private data. It shows what he's up to. He manipulates everyone. Exploits their strengths and weaknesses. Corrupts whatever he touches. His public image – fake. Business ethics – non-existent. Marriage – a sham. Private life – degenerate. And he doesn't care who gets hurt. That's why you should stop him.'

'Me? Personally?'

'You've got him worried. He thinks you're onto him.'

'About what?'

'Whatever you suspect him of.'

'I suspect him of a lot of things,' said Rita. 'What can you tell me about Kelly Grattan's sudden exit?'

'I've already told you all I know, which is nothing.'

'When you say Barbie's corrupt,' she went on, 'have you got any hard evidence against him?'

Flynn cut her short. 'That's your job. This is off the record, remember?'

The waitress placed a latte on the table as a suburban train rumbled out of the station.

Apart from confirming her opinion of Barbie, this didn't seem to be going anywhere helpful.

'Why do you say his marriage is a sham?'

'It's just about money. For both of them. That's why she whored for him in Tokyo.'

'What do you mean?'

'I don't know the details. Just that Giselle's body was part of the deal. What you'd call a sweetener.'

There was nothing she could do with this information, amazing as it was – though she wondered if it was true. 'You mentioned his private life.'

'He uses prostitutes.'

'I saw that for myself,' she said. 'At his party last night.'

'No, you don't get it.' Flynn shook his head. 'He uses them all the time. He's addicted to them. That's how you catch him out. Expose him. Destroy his reputation.'

'I'm not some sort of moral crusader.'

'You're a hotshot detective with the Sexual Crimes Squad,' Flynn interrupted again. 'We've all seen what you do – how you crack cases, deliver summary justice, blow away criminals.'

'Don't be conned by the media,' she said. 'Look, I know Martin Barbie's an immoral man with a fake image. But unless he's breaking the law, he's allowed to be manipulative. He can also be as decadent as he likes with consenting adults, including his wife.'

'What about his complete lack of business ethics?'

'Again, that's only relevant if you can prove he's breaking the law.' Rita sighed. 'In my opinion the closure of Xanthus Software is no great loss. The firm is riddled with corporate neurosis. If it wasn't being shut down, I'd recommend a team of industrial psychologists go in and blitz the place.' She drank some coffee and decided there was nothing she could act on. 'So let's be realistic.'

'Huh.' Flynn showed his contempt. 'Same fucking thing he said to me. You and Barbie have more in common than you realise. You play by the same rules.'

'It isn't a game.'

'Of course it is. Like everything else in life.' He pushed away his empty whisky glass and got up from the table. 'I've been wasting my time talking to you and I've got better things to do. Like deciding what happens with the rest of my fucking life.' With that he walked off.

Rita shook her head and finished her latte.

As she left the cafe the railway bells were clanging again, prompting a tired father in distressed denim to chase a toddler along the path, the little boy excited at the approach of the train. While she waited for the gates to open she cast her mind back to the hospital interview with Kelly Grattan. The question mark over Kelly's injuries was lodged in her case notes like an unresolved discrepancy, while Kelly's deceit, pay-off and flight overseas were consistent with the culture of angst that infested the firm. Xanthus was an investigative itch that Rita couldn't scratch, and Flynn had added nothing to alter that. As a line of inquiry, it was still a dead end.

70

It was late Sunday, around the time of evensong, when she arrived, and Barbie was wearing a gold silk robe. She walked hesitantly into his suite and gasped at the panoramic view, the gleaming lights of the skyline filling the windows.

'Very impressive,' she said, her voice rich with the intonation of old Europe.

He looked her up and down. She was a good choice, young and fair-haired with high cheekbones and sultry eyes. She was dressed in a suit that would deflect suspicion.

'Where are you from?' he asked.

'Moscow.'

'How old are you?'

'I'm twenty-two,' she said pertly. 'And I offer all services.'

'Very good, Natasha. We'll start with the oral.'

As she undressed he tossed aside the robe and sat naked on his embroidered sofa. Then she got down on her knees between his legs. Her compliance was what he needed – someone at ease with venality, no questions asked.

He'd set the scene before her arrival, scattering rugs, putting candles on the table and lighting the incense. Its pungent scent drifted through the room, adding to the strangely blasphemous mood induced by the Gregorian chant playing softly on the music system. It appealed to his sense of decadence, letting the sound of religion calm his mind while the young Russian knelt in front of him, her perfect body glowing in the candlelight. She was like a lubricious nymph – and she was at his mercy.

71

Rita arrived at the police complex on Monday morning to be called into an immediate briefing with fellow taskforce officers. As they filed into the room the reason for the urgency became obvious. An additional set of crime scene photos had been stuck to the wall. The Hacker had struck again, and his latest victim was obviously dead.

Mace was again in charge. Loftus stood beside him, expression sombre, as the detectives settled around the table, cups of tea and coffee in their hands, tight Monday morning frowns on their faces.

Mace waited for the grunts and shuffling to subside. 'The call came in just before one o'clock this morning,' he began. 'Victim number four. DSS Strickland and DSC Matt Bradby were called out to the scene. They and the crime lab people spent most of the night there or backtracking the girl's movements and waking up witnesses. They only packed up a couple of hours ago, so we've got a pretty good idea how the Hacker carried out his latest attack.'

He cleared his throat. 'To summarise – victim's name: Catherine Lentz. Known to her friends as Cathy. Age: twenty-one. Full-time student, part-time prostitute. Doing her final year in business studies at Monash. Lived in Geelong till she got a place at uni. She was sharing a rented house with another female student and supplementing her Austudy money by taking cash for sex, the deal being she only took clients back to her bedroom when the other girl was away, which was the case on Friday. Our killer picked her up at a bar, the Scholar's Tavern, around nine p.m. and drove her back to the house in Oakleigh, where the sequence of events went like this . . .'

Mace looked down at his notes. 'The chain of events we've surmised is as follows: Cathy agreed to a bondage session, attaching handcuffs to the four corners of her bed. She also agreed to light a fire in the bedroom hearth, despite the warm weather. About this stage she let in two angora rabbits from the backyard – her housemate's pets – to feed them. We assume the killer went to the bathroom at the same time. Having put the rabbit food on the kitchen floor, Cathy went to her bedroom and got undressed. Her killer came back from the bathroom with a metal towel rail that he'd dislodged from the wall.'

He glanced around at them grimly. 'Cathy tried to fight him off – we found defensive injuries on her hands and forearms. Broken knuckles, severe contusions. He was hitting her hard. Smashed her skull, front and back. He cuffed her, hand and foot, and as she lay on the bed, probably unconscious, he had sex with her. Then he went to the kitchen, found a sharp carving knife and used it to slice her nose off to the bone. She was still alive at this stage and bleeding from the external wound, but it was the massive trauma to her brain – and the internal haemorrhage – that killed her a few minutes later. When he'd finished, he dumped the knife on the floor, went to the bathroom, washed his hands and left.'

Mace breathed out a heavy sigh. 'The place is a mess. The body wasn't discovered by the housemate till after midnight this morning, and in the meantime the rabbits went berserk. They weren't used to being shut inside for so long. They panicked, tried to get out, jumped onto shelves and got at food, crapped all over the place, knocked everything off tables, shredded the furniture, and one of them impaled itself on a magnetic knife rack. At first we thought the killer had done the rabbit as well, so the pathologist had to do a post-mortem on it. Turned out to have died thirty-six hours after Cathy.'

He thumped the table with his fist. 'This freak's attacked four times in less than three weeks, leaving two dead, two maimed for life and a trail of forensic evidence. We've got his fingerprints, blood type, DNA, hairs, fibres. We have his age group and a consistent description – the man who picked up Cathy was neatly groomed and smartly dressed, wearing mirror shades. We've got so much to nail him with – but we still don't know where to look. We know he drives an MX-5 and a ute, but we've already ruled out the list of drivers who are registered owners of both types of vehicle. We've taken the prints and DNA of nearly fifty Plato's Cave customers and none of them is our man. With the club now shut, Kavella dead, his databases erased and his membership list a work of fiction, what looked like our best line of inquiry has hit a wall.' He sighed, before adding finally, 'We need to come up with a fresh approach. When you get your assignments I want you all to read through the files. We need to identify evidence, leads or people we haven't followed up. Okay, let's get on with it.'

Rita finished reading the case file updates in her office, pushed back from the desk, stretched out her legs and put her hands behind her head. Another freshly issued .38 lay holstered beside her keyboard. When Loftus knocked lightly on the glass-panelled door and walked in, she swivelled around to face him.

'Glad to be back profiling?' he asked.

'It's a welcome change.'

'So have you come up with any ideas?'

'It's the psych that bugs me,' she said, shaking her head. 'The contradictions.'

'Maybe the Hacker just flips, then panics.'

'Flips, possibly. Panics, no. His parting acts of mutilation are unnecessary and deliberate. They have deep meaning for him. He's leaving his signature. But I can't square the inconsistencies.'

'One thing I've learnt, Van Hassel, through the long and lonely years, is the universal presence of miscalculation. Not just for evildoers, but for us too.'

He tapped one of the postcards taped to the wall above her desk with his finger. It was a picture of the Mandelbrot set with a quote superimposed: 'Reality is structured chaos.'

'Are you telling me I'm way off beam?' asked Rita.

'No. I'm saying for every classification – social, criminal, psychological – there's always the odd one out.'

'But he's not on his own.' She clicked on the mouse and called up a past file. 'He makes two of a kind with the Scalper.'

'In what way? The Scalper spiked women's drinks with Rohypnol then hacked off their hair.'

'Yes, and his first two victims were scarred for life, but survived...'

'The final two,' interrupted Loftus, 'he decapitated. Then he seemed to stop. What are you getting at?'

'I wasn't here for the investigation, so tell me how it ended.'

'Funny you should ask – Mace and I were discussing it earlier this morning,' said Loftus uncomfortably. 'We seem to be reliving the same scenario. The Scalper taskforce reached a similar position to the one we're in with the Hacker – four attacks over a few weeks with two fatalities, a load of forensic evidence, eyewitness descriptions – and then nothing. With no more attacks, the case just drifted away from us, though of course the file is still open. But frankly I don't see any link. How could there be? The methods are different, the types of victim are different and, most significantly, the DNA is different.'

'Yes, different crime signature completely,' Rita agreed. 'But from a profiling perspective, the similarities are uncanny. Both killers are well-dressed and articulate. They seem to be *organised* attackers who leave *sloppy* crime scenes with plenty of evidence, fingerprints, DNA. They both inflict mutilations as part of their sexual violence. And weirder still, they're both reported as driving the same type of car, a black Mazda MX-5.'

That made him stop and think. 'A copycat?' he asked. 'If that's what you're getting at, it seems to be stretching a point.'

'I don't know if I'm making any point at all. Just kicking ideas around. Thinking the unthinkable.' She bent over and picked up her shoulder bag. 'But I won't make any progress without the mindset.'

'And where do you get that?'

'Same place as always. The crime scene.'

Rita was now familiar with the drive towards Monash University, but when she left the freeway she had trouble finding her first point of reference. The Scholar's Tavern turned out to be a low breeze-block building with a corrugated-iron roof tucked away in a back street behind the broad, windswept campus. She parked and went inside. It was hardly the classic Australian pub – more a glorified shed serving cheap meals and booze to students. It wasn't crowded. Just a few dozen sat at tables eating an early lunch, their textbooks and lecture notes stacked alongside the plates and beer glasses. She went up to the counter, ordered a lime and soda and showed her police ID to the young barman. He was a student himself, doing the job part-time.

Rita told him she was investigating the murder of Cathy Lentz.

'I was working the bar Friday night when she was in here,' he volunteered. 'Served her the usual – a couple of Bacardi and Cokes.'

'You knew her?'

'Oh yeah. She was a regular. Mostly at weekends.'

'How well did you know her?'

He caught the undertone in her question and hunched forward, lowering his voice. 'D'ya mean did I pay her for sex?'

'Did you?'

'Yeah, once. Last semester. She was a real babe. Worth the eighty bucks.'

'You went back to her place?'

'Nah. We did it in my room at the hall of residence.'

'On Friday night, did you notice the man she went off with?'

'Too right. But like I told the cops this morning, I'd never seen him before.' He ran a damp cloth over the surface in front of him. 'I assumed he was a tutor.'

'Why?'

'He was about ten years older than most of the kids in here, and his manner was different.'

'In what way, what was he like?'

'I only saw him from a distance but he was slick-looking, you know – good haircut, jeans, denim shirt, black leather jacket, designer shades. And the way he sat there, you know, a cool type of guy, confident.'

Rita nodded, then asked, 'What makes you think he was from the university?'

'That's all we get in here. Undergrads, mostly – and faculty staff when they're slumming it.'

'What about the neighbours? Local residents?'

'Avoid it like the plague. Think all students are fuckwits.'

As he slid off along the bar to serve some fresh customers, Rita realised something about the killer's background. He was familiar with this backstreet pub. It wasn't a place you found by cruising for a pick-up, because you didn't know about it unless you had a connection with the university. That tied in with the geographic profile as well. The first three attacks fell within a six-kilometre radius from the city centre, indicating he worked and lived within that area. But this last one was nearly twenty k out. What was his link with the campus?

She finished her drink, thanked the barman and left.

The crime scene was a five-minute drive from the Scholar's Tavern. As she homed in on it she could feel her pulse quickening and her lungs tightening. No surprise there. Her plan of action had worked. The mindset was returning, along with the adrenalin rush.

She pulled up outside an ordinary-looking cream brick house in a dull suburban street. No one was around. No pedestrians, no traffic. Just a few cars parked at the kerb. The sun, at its zenith, laid a scorching light and heat on road, pavement, yards and roofs, wilting the shrubbery and filling the air with a burning lethargy. The house looked like a place where only mundane things could happen, its blandness seeming to defy any notion of horrific violence. It was semi-detached, with a low brick fence, a short driveway and a front yard with nothing in it but lank, dry grass. The only sign of something sinister was the yellow crime scene tape.

Rita crossed the narrow porch, let herself in with the key and closed the door behind her. The stifling heat and pungent air inside the house enclosed her. It was heavy with something like a barnyard smell and the rooms were buzzing with flies. As Mace had said, there was mess everywhere. The lounge carpet was covered in broken china, overturned lamps, chewed-up magazines and dry rabbit droppings. The furniture upholstery was bursting through rips and claw marks.

The front bedroom had less wreckage. It had been cleared of personal items. This had been the housemate's room. She'd packed her belongings, collected the one surviving rabbit and moved back to her family home in Bundoora. Like Cathy Lentz, she would never come back here. The horror of finding the brutalised corpse would stay with her for the rest of her life.

The worst mess and the worst smells were in the kitchen. It looked like the work of mindless vandals. Smashed crockery and shards of glass seemed to litter every surface, mixed in with droppings and paw prints and spilt liquid. The room was thick with flies, and maggots crawled over rotting food. A pool of congealed blood lay beneath the knife rack where the hapless rabbit had skewered itself.

The bathroom was still intact because the killer had closed the door. The knobs were grimy with dust from where the crime scene detectives had collected more of his prints. There was only one bit of slight damage. A wall bracket was dislodged where the towel rail had been removed. Surfaces here were also smudged with fingerprint dust, along with the bathroom mirror and cabinet.

The last room she entered was the back bedroom. This was where Cathy Lentz had been murdered. The floor was bare. Sheets, mattress, bed and carpet had all been shipped off to the crime lab. But her business studies books still lined the shelves, her clothes still hung forlornly in the wardrobe and the ashes from the killer's fire still lay in the hearth. Despite the heat, Rita shuddered as she relived in her mind what had happened here. The sequence was becoming clearer.

She took the mini-disc recorder from her bag but decided it was too stuffy in here to record her impressions, so she unlocked the back door and went out. The yard had been converted into an oversized rabbit hutch with wire mesh coating the side gate and fences. There was a shed, a stack of packing crates, a lemon tree and the mauled remains of a garden plot. What had once been a lawn was now more dirt than grass, and it was pockmarked with holes and burrows.

Watching carefully where she walked, Rita took a plastic crate and set it down in the shade of the lemon tree. She sat there quietly for a few minutes, calming her breathing and letting her thoughts drift. This was something else she'd picked up from a profiler at the FBI – the value of meditation. The house and yard seemed to exhale an unnatural hush. Few sounds reached her through the torpid midday heat. No human voices. No traffic noise. It was as if the surroundings were deserted – like an outpost on an abandoned planet. Overhead a hostile sun blazed in an empty sky. Its fierce light glinted on the shed roof. The distant hum of an airliner vibrated through the air. Then, as if to reassure her of normality, the sound of a blackbird singing came from the branches of a gum tree in the garden next door. She held the microphone to her mouth, pressed Record and started speaking.

'Naked apart from your bronze mask, which is your other face, and brandishing the metal rail as a weapon, you go into her bedroom. You see her naked body in the firelight, the prisoner restraints on the bed, the flames casting shadows around the room, just as you require because these are the rules of the cave. If she screams or pleads or tries to win you over, you are implacable, you are on a mission. But your aim is not to kill her. It's to render her unconscious for sex. That makes it rape, which is what you need. Then you inflict the mutilation. Why? To punish her? Disable her? Disarm her? In a way, you're branding her. And there's nothing new in that. It's been done over the centuries by those wielding power. Marking her with an indelible stamp. Just as the Scalper did to his victims before you.'

She paused for a moment, breathless. The parallels were more striking than ever.

'Could it be that you both have a common cause? That you're following the same pattern? That you're acting from the same template, as it were? Is it possible that you both draw your inspiration from the same secret dreamland?'

Rita clicked off the recorder, a savage look in her eyes, startled at her power of empathy. Where did that come from? Some fugue into her own zone of otherness? Not that it mattered. Because now she had found a fresh approach that was desperately needed. To narrow the focus on this killer she needed to look more closely at the trail left by another.

72

The first thing Rita did when she got back to her desk in the squad room was to call up all the Scalper files from the database. They provided details of predatory pick-ups in bars and clubs – the four victims single women, living alone, all with long curly hair. He drove them back to their apartments, rendered them helpless with a date-rape drug and hacked off their hair – along with some of their skin. With the last two, he chopped off their heads as well. Unlike the current killer, the Scalper came armed with his own weapons – cut-throat razors and hatchets. Then he performed oral sex on his victims, and left. That was all more than a year ago. No fresh attacks since. But there was also the car. A black Mazda MX-5. Just like the current killer's. Of course it could be a coincidence, as others had argued, but what if it wasn't? What if there was some undetected parallel?

She scrolled through the interview notes with the Scalper's two survivors. They described what he looked like – not a clone of the Hacker, but in the same general mould – tall, dark-haired, well-dressed, articulate, with a photofit likeness showing another smooth thirty-something. The women had outlined how he'd behaved, the way he looked, what he'd said – teasing comments, like, 'Ever hear the voices of the gods?' That sounded a little too convenient – but if he meant it, the phrase qualified him for schizophrenia. Then there was the curious line of flattery he'd used on both of them about their curly hair – 'wild as a hatful of snakes'. At the time the women had laughed. Afterwards it haunted them. The words had been a psychotic warning, but they'd ignored it.

To her profiler's mind the two sets of crimes committed by the Scalper and the Hacker were like separate configurations from the same puzzle. But Rita needed to prove it one way or the other, not least to herself, even if it meant spending the rest of the afternoon going through all the evidence boxes, hard-copy files and paperwork generated by the Scalper taskforce.

For the next two hours she sifted through printouts, stacks of notes, crime scene photos – much of the material summarised on the database – without finding anything to confirm her suspicions. But as she scanned a handwritten list of names, something jumped out at her. She stared at it, confounded by what she saw. It didn't appear on the computer file because it was next to a name that had been crossed off the list. It read: 'Ormond Keppel (Xanthus Software) – Deceased'.

As Rita looked at the words her brain went into hyperdrive. The odds against Xanthus Software appearing by chance in the Scalper hunt must be astronomical. It also raised the possibility that Barbie's company concealed more than one dirty secret, and that Martin Barbie was himself more degenerate than she had imagined. She could certainly believe it. Beneath that polished persona was a twisted soul she'd seen at first hand. Add to that Flynn's outburst over moral corruption, and Josh Barrett's heavy hints of the same, and perhaps she'd underestimated just how evil Barbie was.

The thought made her gasp. She sprang up from her desk. One way or another she had to find out. She had to know if she'd uncovered a link to serial crimes, or if it was nothing more than a huge coincidence. The initials on the list were Bradby's. She rushed across the squad room to his desk. He was on the phone, talking in a bored monotone. She paced up and down in front of him until he got the message and cut the call short.

'Okay. What's up?' he said.

She thrust the piece of paper under his nose and demanded breathlessly, 'Tell me what you know about Ormond Keppel.'

'Hey, slow down.' He scanned the list without immediately recognising it. 'What is this, anyway?'

'It's from the Scalper files, a year ago. You compiled this list of people to question. But Keppel's name isn't on the case file in the computer.'

'Obviously because I didn't question him. Like it says here: *Deceased.*'

'Come on, Bradby,' she said impatiently. 'Don't you remember anything about him?'

He sighed and thought for a moment, then clicked his fingers. 'Shit. Yeah. He was the guy who drowned.' He spun around to his screen and did a search on the name. One item came up from the database – a conviction for a minor assault on a female clubgoer. It was from three years ago. 'That's right. He pleaded guilty. The court decided there was an element of provocation. The victim was high on ice. Keppel got a suspended sentence.'

'That's why he was on your list?'

'That and he was a Kiwi. Came over here to do a university course . . .'

'Which university?' she snapped.

'Hell. Um . . . let me think.'

'Monash?'

'Yeah, that's right. Why? What have you got?'

'I'm not sure yet. What else do you remember?'

'Well one of the Scalper's victims thought she'd detected a New Zealand accent. I checked with the Auckland cops and sure enough Keppel was known to them for beating up girls as a teenager. Nothing serious, but he sounded like a promising candidate. That's as far as I got. I didn't have his current address, just his place of work. When I phoned they broke the news to me. He'd drowned in a rip off Portsea. What the stupid mullet was doing I don't know. People on the beach saw him being dragged out but by the time a rescue attempt was made he'd vanished. Body never recovered. If he was our boy then he was shark bait. So I had a name – but no one to question.'

'And no body – no DNA,' said Rita quietly. Then she asked, 'This is important: did he drown before or after the last Scalper attack?'

Bradby put on a cheesy smile. 'I was just thinking the same thing. It was definitely after.' Behind the smile was a searching look. 'So why are you digging into another case? What's pulling your chain about Keppel?'

'Xanthus Software,' she said distractedly.

'What about it?'

'Sounds like a very bad place to work.'

She left Bradby with a puzzled expression on his face, hurried back to her desk, grabbed her mobile phone and called Josh Barrett's number.

As soon as he answered she said, 'It's Detective Sergeant Marita Van Hassel. What do you know about an Ormond Keppel?'

'And hello to you too,' Josh said sarcastically.

'Josh, please. He worked for Martin Barbie till a year ago.'

'I know that he drowned.'

'Did you work with him?'

'Hardly. I'm the guy Barbie hired as a replacement.'

'Shit.'

'But I could ask Maynard and Flynn –'

'Don't mention this to anyone,' she cut him short. 'I just need to check out his background without going through Xanthus. Maybe the university can help.'

'As I was about to say before I was so rudely interrupted,' Josh came back at her, 'Maynard and Flynn were fellow recruits with Keppel. Barbie headhunted half a dozen of the best postgraduates out at Monash. They were doing research for a professor they all hero-worshipped.'

A sinking feeling hit Rita in the pit of the stomach as she asked, 'What's the professor's name?'

'Byron Huxley.'

73

Rita sat at her desk, hesitating, with Byron's phone number displayed on her mobile's screen. She realised there was so much she didn't know about him – the man she'd contacted for expert advice, the man who'd become her lover, the man now linked to a murder investigation. She'd put her trust in him, and yet his entire background was unknown to her. When she called him this time, it would be to question him formally about what he knew.

She clicked on his number.

'Rita, hi!' he answered, whispering. 'Can't talk at the moment, I'm in the middle of an honours seminar.'

'Byron, I've got to ask you something. It's important.'

'Okay, go on.'

'What's your connection with Xanthus Software?'

'The computer games company? I don't have a connection, apart from it poaching some of my best students.'

'Have any of them been out to Monash recently?' she asked.

'Only Bruce Maynard. Look, I've got to go,' he insisted. 'I'll call you later.'

Maynard was the gangling nerd with an unhealthy interest in sex crimes. Rita got his home number and called it. His mother answered. She said Maynard was at a comic book convention and wouldn't be back for a couple of hours.

As Rita hung up the phone, an alert flashed onto her computer screen from the live message service. She clicked on it automatically and read the greeting:

shadow maker says:
Hello at last!

She frowned at it, mystified, but decided to respond:

van hassel says:
Who are you?

A moment later came the reply:

shadow maker says:
I'm the one that you want!

It looked like a wind-up but, her curiosity aroused, she continued with the online dialogue:

van hassel says:
Is that so?

shadow maker says:
Yes, the man in the mask.

van hassel says:
What colour mask?

shadow maker says:
Bronze, of course. It's my other face.

Rita yelled across the squad room, 'Erin! Erin!'
Erin Webster dropped what she was doing and rushed over. 'What?'
'I've got the Hacker online!' she shouted. 'Get the computer mob on it, now!'
'Shit!' said Erin, scrambling for the nearest phone.
'I'll keep him on as long as I can,' said Rita.

van hassel says:
So who is behind the face?

shadow maker says:
At first I thought it was the Fire Tracer or Flame Stalker, but now I know it's the Shadow Maker – someone just like you!

van hassel says:
Why am I the Shadow Maker?

shadow maker says:
Because you're a killer.

van hassel says:
Is that what it means?

shadow maker says:
The Shadow Maker is a death warrior. His touch is the touch of death. He takes life from those he cuts down and in their place leaves only shadows. Just like you.

Erin rushed back, breathless. 'They've traced him,' she said. 'He's in an internet cafe at the southern end of Elizabeth Street.'

'The nearest cops are in Flinders Lane,' said Rita. 'Tell them to seal off the cafe, let nobody in or out. I'll keep him online.'

van hassel says:
How can you compare our actions?

shadow maker says:
Because I've sensed an empathy between us. I feel at home in your personal space.

van hassel says:
So it was you who broke into my home. Why?

shadow maker says:
I needed to be sure about you, and fate has proved me right. We are Platonic heroes sending the shades of the dead to the Underworld.

van hassel says:
You're talking about Plato's Cave, aren't you?

shadow maker says:
Of course.

van hassel says:
Where is Plato's Cave?

shadow maker says:
Everywhere. The world we inhabit. It's where we live, work, play and die.

van hassel says:
Then why does it need a smartcard to access it?
(shadow maker cannot answer because he appears to be offline)

'Damn it!' shouted Rita.
'They're on their way,' said Erin.
'He'll be gone before they get there.'

The Hacker eluded capture by five minutes.

By the time Rita joined detectives and uniformed police at the cordoned-off internet cafe, it was obvious that he'd slipped the net. The customers and manager were all checked and eliminated as suspects. None of them had paid any attention to the person who'd used the terminal in the corner, other than to say he looked like a nerd in his hooded black anorak and mirror glasses. The cafe's grainy CCTV footage confirmed the description without providing a clear view of him, simply showing a stooped figure shuffling in and out with his face averted from the camera.

The terminal used by the Hacker was isolated, and crime lab scientist Dale Quinn dusted it for prints.

'Yep, they're a match,' he said.

'We nearly got him,' Rita breathed. 'Any chance of enhancing the video footage?'

'We'll do our best,' said Quinn. 'But I doubt you'll get a clear shot of him. He's deliberately disguised his appearance. What about his email login? Have you got onto the internet service provider?'

'The Computer Crime Squad's already done that,' she answered. 'The name supplied is fake, and the address given is in Abbotsford.'

'Isn't it worth checking?' asked Quinn.

'I don't have to. The address is mine.'

74

Rita commandeered Quinn and his crime lab van, asking him to follow her as she drove to Maynard's address. She took the freeway that skirted the southern edge of the inner city and crossed the Bolte Bridge high over the docks before driving past the wholesale markets lining Footscray Road. As she headed away from the city she went through a mental checklist of what she knew about Maynard. He certainly had the prerequisites for a personality disorder. There were signs of maladaptive behaviour, the characteristics of a social isolate and a brief display of unhealthy interest in the mutilation of prostitutes. She remembered that from her first encounter with him. On the other hand, to describe him as well-dressed and articulate would be a stretch.

Maynard's mother's house occupied a corner plot at the end of a side street. It was a drab postwar home that was a brick-and-tile clone of its neighbours. Rita parked outside, waited for Quinn to join her with his kit, and walked up to the porch. It took several rings of the doorbell before a middle-aged woman answered. She had red cheeks and beer on her breath.

'Mrs Maynard?' Rita asked.

'Yes?'

'I'm Detective Sergeant Marita Van Hassel and this is my colleague Dale Quinn. I phoned a while ago. Is Bruce here?'

'No,' she answered. 'The useless drongo's still blowing his dough on comics and cowboy boots. What's this all about?'

'A routine inquiry, but I need to check Bruce's fingerprints in order to eliminate him. If you let us in now we don't need to get a warrant.'

'Fair enough,' said Mrs Maynard, throwing open the flyscreen door. 'Try his bedroom. No one else goes in there and his grubby paw marks are all over it.'

They followed Maynard's mother through a kitchen, past a table laden with empty beer cans and full ashtrays. Dirty plates were crammed in a gaping dishwasher. Dirty pans were piled in the sink. There was a faint smell of burnt food in the room, and an overweight labrador lolled on the floor.

'His room's at the end of the hall,' gestured Mrs Maynard. 'Thinks he's bloody fancy with all that computer stuff in there. Flash as a rat with a gold tooth.'

Rita led Quinn down the passageway into Maynard's room. It was far more juvenile than she'd expected for a man of his age. Yet she wasn't surprised. The movie posters, the collection of comics, the childish duvet and pyjamas spoke volumes about Maynard's personality – indicative of someone with social problems. But she was looking for signs of a psychotic killer – not the escapist fantasies of a pubescent adult.

'How old is this guy?' asked Quinn.

'About twenty-eight going on seven,' answered Rita.

'His keyboard's the best bet.'

As Quinn began dusting the computer, Rita went through Maynard's drawers and cupboards, but found nothing more than a jumble of clothes and the accumulated mess of an arrested childhood – toys, puzzles, comics, infantile scrapbooks. Nothing sinister – just immature. Then she sat on the unmade bed and perused movie souvenirs papering the walls till her eyes came to rest on a poster for *The Matrix*. The film carried the subversive message that people are imprisoned, without knowing it, in a false reality, but now she realised the idea dated from the fourth century BC. Maybe it should also have carried a credit to Plato.

Quinn double-checked his print analysis and comparisons through his microscope, before turning to Rita.

'You can rule him out,' he said. 'Bruce Maynard is not the Hacker.'

75

Quinn put the lab kit back in his van, slid the door shut and asked Rita, 'Why are you homing in on Xanthus Software?'

'Because it fits,' she answered. 'I'm sure I was right about Kelly Grattan – a former executive now out of reach overseas – she fought off a rapist. That incident was the stressor for the man who attacked her. It tipped him over the edge, triggering a cyclical pattern of extreme violence, turning him into the Hacker.'

'And this woman knew him?'

'It could explain how she pressured Martin Barbie into a seven-figure pay-out,' said Rita.

'My God!' exclaimed Quinn. 'You think Barbie's a prime suspect?'

'He's certainly a candidate, one of several who match the profile. Everyone from the firm has lied to me, from Kelly onwards, and they've all got the software connection that's a crucial element of the case.'

'You're talking about the smartcard,' said Quinn. 'Don't tell me you've cracked the Plato's Cave link.'

'Not quite, but I'm getting there,' she said. 'So stay within reach tonight. I may need you again.'

'No problem,' said Quinn, his enthusiasm obvious. 'I'm your man.'

A change was in the air as Rita headed back into the city. She was driving fast. A southerly buster was blowing up masses of dark grey clouds that were piling over the bay. The wind was bringing the end of the March heatwave and much-needed rain. The light in the sky cast a dirty bronze tinge into the basin of the port as streams of homeward-bound commuters filed across the bridges above the docks. As she neared the freeway exit the traffic slowed to a crawl.

She got out her phone and called Barbie's mobile. It diverted her to his office number and a distinctly unhelpful secretary.

'He's away from the office and can't be contacted.'

'What, never?' demanded Rita.

'For the rest of the evening. He's in a private meeting.'

'What's he doing after that? I need to see him urgently.'

'He has no more business engagements that I'm aware of. Later tonight he's due home. His wife's holding a cocktail party, but attendance is by invitation only.'

Rita ended the call abruptly then tried Josh Barrett's mobile. It was switched through to voicemail. She left a message telling him to call her back urgently. But when her mobile rang it was Byron Huxley on the line, and he was apologetic. 'Sorry I couldn't talk before.'

'Thanks for calling back,' she said. 'I'm not being rude, but I'm pressed for time and I've got questions.'

'Fire away.'

'Ormond Keppel. Tell me about him.'

'Brilliant student, excellent postgrad researcher, a natural at software design,' Huxley replied. 'But that was three years ago. I lost touch with him after that.'

'Would you say he was psychologically stable?' Rita asked.

'He had his problems. At times he felt the world and certain individuals in it were against him.'

'He was paranoid? Delusional?'

'If you want to be brutal about it, but most of the time he was very positive. His drowning was a terrible tragedy.'

'Those he thought were against him – did they include women?'

'Mostly women. How did you guess?'

'It's a theory I'm working on,' she answered. 'Now you said Bruce Maynard was out at Monash recently.'

'At the start of summer, yes. He wanted to test some games software.'

'From Xanthus?'

'Yes. New-generation virtual reality. Maynard was worried about side effects.'

'Why?'

'He thought the input was too powerful, even hypnotic.'

'What sort of tests?'

'Brain scans,' said Huxley. 'We got a few volunteers, put them into VR and did some PET scans on them.'

'And?'

'An odd combination of the frontal lobe and amygdala kept firing, not something associated with hypnosis.'

'What *does* it indicate?' she asked.

'A sharp focus of attention and arousal of strong emotion.'

'And the content of the game?'

'Very violent and pornographic. It's full of nymphs, warriors and monsters.'

'The warriors,' said Rita, her pulse racing, 'do they have names like Shadow Maker, Fire Tracer and Flame Stalker?'

'That's right,' Huxley answered. 'And there are others called Light Seeker, Echo Chaser, that sort of thing. But I don't know what the game's called.'

'Well I do,' she said. 'It's called Plato's Cave.'

As the traffic merged it began flowing again. Once Rita left the freeway she drove straight to Xanthus Software.

When she pulled up at the security gate the guard emerged from his cabin and walked over, slowing down as he recognised her.

'The place is almost deserted,' he said.

'Where is everyone?' she asked.

'The techies are on holiday. Threw a big party after signing a deal with the Japs then pissed off.'

'Where are the VR studios?' she asked.

He scratched his head. 'The basement. Only the design team's allowed down there.' Then he hesitated. 'Look, there's no one to show you around and I'm due to lock up in half an hour.'

'I'll show myself around,' she told him.

'Suit yourself.'

She drove onto the empty forecourt, parked and went into the building. The place had an abandoned feel, just as the security guard had told her. No one around. She walked through reception and pushed open the door into the ground-floor office. Leftovers of a celebration littered the desks and computer terminals – streamers, balloons, the spray of party poppers. Dozens of empty champagne bottles lay stacked in cartons – tokens of Barbie's benevolence. A gesture of thanks for making a rich man even richer. But at what hidden cost?

Then she heard a movement and called out, 'Anyone there?'

No answer.

She walked past the rows of work stations till she found what it was – a loose printout flapping in the draught of a desktop fan. She reached out and switched the fan off. The room fell silent. Then she went to the stairwell, walked down two flights of metal stairs to the basement, and found herself in a dimly lit passageway.

The air was stale down here, and there was a breathless quiet. The floor and walls were of bare concrete, like a subterranean tunnel, and along the ceiling twisted the fat tentacles of cables. The only sound was the hum of a faulty fluorescent lamp that flickered overhead. Both sides of the passage were lined with steel doors. Then she saw, with something like delight, that smartcard pads were mounted beside them. Her heart thumped against her ribs.

She got out the smartcard she'd been carrying from the start of the investigation and tried the doors one by one. It was like the final tease in a puzzle. At last, one of the pads gave an electronic click as it responded to the card. The door slid open on a deep, shadowy studio filled with computer hardware, strange metal frames and mock-up background walls. Untidy strands of wiring snaked around the floor. The only lighting came from the dance of pixels on screens and the glow of task lamps.

She stared at it and said under her breath, 'The entrance to Plato's Cave.'

As she walked inside the door slid shut behind her, closing with an airtight hiss as if she were being sealed in a vault. The thought was unnerving. The possibility of being stuck down here was not appealing. She checked her mobile. No signal. Hopefully she wouldn't need it.

Moving cautiously she picked her way forward through cables and equipment that made little sense to her. It looked like a series of control decks and monitors plugged into accessories. She could only guess at their functions. A full body suit was hanging like an empty skin from one of the large frames, which she assumed was a virtual reality device. Its silhouette cast a dark shadow on the concrete wall. The outline bore an uncanny resemblance to a torture victim on a medieval rack. It added to her feeling of unease. There was something inhuman about the surroundings down here.

That's when she heard a sound from the depths of the studio. A low moaning.

'Who's there?' she called out.

There was a thud and the moaning abruptly stopped.

Reaching carefully under her jacket, she unholstered her gun and removed the safety catch. With the .38 held steady in a double-handed grip, she pointed it to where the sounds had come from and edged forward. But she could see no one. Just more machines and empty chairs and the glimmer of graphics. Then the sound came again – that chilling moan – but closer this time. Again there was a thud, and it stopped.

Rita stood motionless and waited and listened, the gun outstretched in front of her. She could still see no movement. No sign of anyone's presence. It crossed her mind that she'd been reckless and unprofessional to come down here alone. Her line of investigation might be more successful than she realised. Right now the sex killer might be within a few feet of her, hiding, ready to stun her as she approached. She tightened her grip on the gun.

It came again – the moan – louder in her ears. Again it was cut short by a thud.

With her back against a mainframe, she slid slowly sideways until she could see around a corner of the studio. She found she was aiming her gun at a bank of screens. They were filled with computer graphics – exotic images from Greek mythology. Most of them were static. But one screen in the middle was on a loop. As she watched, the hideous, moaning figure of a Gorgon approached, its head writhing with snakes. Then came the slash of a sword and the beast was decapitated, its head dropping with a thud. The screen froze. After a minute or two, the loop resumed and the monster repeated its death ritual.

Rita lowered the gun and her breathing eased. She may have picked a disturbing way to do it, but she'd tracked it down at last – the *secret dreamland*. Displayed in front of her, in vivid detail, were scenes from a game that exploited the violence of mythic fantasy. And somehow it inspired real bloodlust and murder.

76

It was mid evening when Rita pulled up outside the beachfront mansion. All the lights were on and the sounds of party voices and laughter drifted from the upstairs balconies. She sat there for a minute in the darkness, collecting her thoughts, then she got out of the car and strode to the black and gold iron gate in the two-metre high whitewashed stone wall. When she pressed the security buzzer a maid answered and released the lock only when Rita said she was from the police.

The garden path, lit with lanterns, took her across an expanse of lawn, landscaped with fountains, rockeries, fish ponds and palm trees. A broad driveway led to a four-car garage on one side. On the other was a glass-domed outdoor pool and spa with a tennis court beyond. A porch of polished granite curved along the entire front of the house, which was ribbed with bay windows and French doors, and framed in white pillars. She walked through the central arch as the maid opened the front door.

Rita told her she had to speak with Martin Barbie immediately.

The maid replied that he wasn't at home, but if Rita would wait in the reception hall she'd fetch his wife.

'Damn,' Rita muttered, as the maid headed upstairs.

As she paced around she noticed the interior of the house was as palatial as its setting. The hall was long and wide and two storeys high. The decor was traditional chic. Chandeliers, gold-plated fittings, parquetry floors and a solid walnut staircase. She was already starting to feel uncomfortable, when Giselle made her entrance down the stairs, her hand lightly skimming the banister, her gold leather shoes tapping each step, her deep V-neck purple satin evening dress clinging to her body like a second skin. With her pale complexion, slim figure and striking face she was a contemporary goddess of elegance. Rita, in her favourite linen suit, felt almost grubby in her presence.

Giselle walked up to her with a formal smile on her face. 'Can I help you?' she said.

'It's your husband I need to speak to.'

'He left the party a few minutes ago.'

'I can't get him on his mobile.' Rita was feeling more awkward with each sentence. 'Did he say where he was going?'

'Business. That's all he said.' Giselle's smile slipped a little. 'You're from the police, you say. Do you have any identification?'

'Of course,' said Rita and fumbled in her jacket pocket, dropping her ID and having to bend down to pick it up. She was blushing as she stood up again.

Giselle studied it carefully. She had a strange aura of control, like a priestess in her own temple. 'How do you know my husband?'

'I had reason to interview him – about a case involving one of his employees.'

'But you've got his private and confidential phone number?'

'He gave it to me.'

'Is that so?' Giselle's smile had withered away. 'When?'

'On Friday. But that's not the point. I need to see him urgently about some serious crimes.'

'What crimes?'

'I can't go into that with you.' Rita felt uncharacteristically defensive. She was on the receiving end of an interrogation. 'I just need to talk to him.'

'Absolutely not.' Giselle stood her ground in her vast hall. 'Unless you tell me exactly what this is about, you won't make one further move to contact Martin. I can walk straight over to the phone and call a senior officer in the police force – Superintendent Gordon Nash. He's a friend of ours. I can have him here in ten minutes. Do you want me to do that?'

Rita swallowed. 'No.'

'And as for your association with my husband, I suspect it's less than professional.'

'Unlike yours,' Rita blurted out before she could stop herself.

The expression on Giselle's sculpted face turned to stone. But she was the type of woman who couldn't be flustered. 'If anything, that proves my point,' she said evenly. 'You were there, on Friday, at his celebration, weren't you? Along with the other girls.'

'Yes I was.' Rita's voice was rising with her temper. 'And what do you think about that, Mrs Barbie? Your husband procuring prostitutes?'

'I don't think about it at all.'

'What about other crimes – like assault and rape?'

'If you're implying my husband is involved in anything of the sort, our lawyers will eat you for breakfast.' Giselle moved closer and ushered her towards the door. As she did, she whispered in her ear, 'Even if it were true.'

Several minutes later Rita was still sitting in her parked car, listening to the party noises from the balconies. She thumped the steering wheel with her fists. 'Fuck it! Fuck it! Fuck it!'

Then she paused for breath, staring through the windscreen at the night. There were pulses of lightning on the horizon and the sea was rough with a storm bearing down on the city.

She picked up her phone and called Strickland at the office.

'I haven't tracked down anyone from Xanthus yet,' she told him. 'I'm outside Barbie's house but he's not here.'

'Seems like we've been over this ground before,' said Strickland. 'You're sure you're right this time?'

'Absolutely. The smartcard is also a key card. It opens the studio doors at Xanthus, and everything the Hacker has said and done points to someone who's intimate with the new computer game.'

'I've got taskforce officers doing checks on company personnel,' put in Strickland. 'There are nearly fifty people on the books.'

'But only a fraction of them would have direct access to the game,' Rita pointed out. 'And one of them is a killer.'

'Just a friendly word of caution,' said Strickland. 'Don't overstep the mark with Barbie or it could all blow up in your face. I've got a feeling you're right about this and we're closing in on the Hacker. But we can't make a move till we have positive identification or it could cause a real shit-storm with Barbie, as well as landing us with another bout of bad publicity. In the meantime, dig up what you can and I'll back you when necessary.'

'So I'm flying under the radar with your blessing?'

'Don't push it, Van Hassel. Where are you heading now?'

'Next on my list is Eddy Flynn.'

'Call me with an update.'

She tried phoning Flynn but got no answer, so she started the car, pulled out onto the beach road and drove towards the inner suburbs.

77

Flynn lived in an upmarket apartment block overlooking Albert Park. It was a modern white building set behind a stone fountain, a fringe of birch trees and a crescent driveway. Rita parked at the entrance, got out and pressed the buzzer for his apartment. No answer. This was getting frustrating. She looked at her watch – nearly nine-thirty. She noticed a buzzer for the caretaker and pressed it.

'Yeah? Who's there?' came the response.

'Police,' she said, holding her ID up to the security camera.

'Orright. Hang on a tick,' came the reply before the door clicked open.

As Rita crossed the entrance lobby, the caretaker emerged from his ground-floor flat to meet her. He was brawny and square-jawed with bleached hair flopping across his forehead – the type of man who looked at home on a surfboard. He was wearing baggy shorts, an Eminem T-shirt, a pair of thongs and an inquisitive grin.

'I wish this bloody weather would break,' he said amiably. 'So what's up?'

'I'm trying to get hold of one of your residents here,' she said. 'Eddy Flynn. Do you know if he's around or away on holiday?'

'Nah. He wouldn't tell me anyway. Keeps to himself. But I noticed one of his cars was in the garage this mornin'.'

'Okay, thanks.'

'Is he in trouble or somethin'?' asked the caretaker.

'I just need to ask him some questions,' she said.

'You're the first cop who's ever turned up here,' he went on. 'But it doesn't surprise me it's about that Flynn character.'

'Why do you say that?' she asked.

'Well, y'know. Real narkie bastard. Ignore you for months, then chuck a berko over nothin'.' He shook his head. 'Just a matter of time till he got in a blue.'

'Is that right?' she said.

'Yeah, and the rest. Reckon he's got a cocky loose in the rafters.'

She had to smile. 'Interesting diagnosis. Any particular reason for it?'

'I dunno – somethin' shonky about him. Always on his own. Never has any mates visit. And the hours he keeps – in and out in the middle of the night, buzzin' around in that noisy ute of his.'

'A ute? What colour?'

'Black.'

'You said it was one of his cars. What else does he drive?'

'A bloody little sports car.'

'What type – a Mazda?'

'Could be. But all those little bum-bouncers look the same to me.'

'Okay,' said Rita, the smile gone from her face. 'I need to get into his apartment now. Do you have a pass key?'

'Yeah, sure.'

He went back into his flat and returned with a key ring. 'There y'go.' He handed it over. 'It's on the fourth. Help yourself.'

'Thanks.'

'No sweat. Turn the place over for all I care.'

Her heart thumped as she rode the elevator up to the fourth floor, wondering what she'd find. The door to Flynn's apartment was at the end of an empty landing. She let herself in and switched on the light.

It was cool, air-conditioned and spacious – a neat, well-furnished residence. There were leather chairs and sofas, colour coordinated curtains and cushions and rugs, hi-tech fittings, imitation Art Deco shelving and sliding glass doors that opened onto a balcony with a view over the park and lake. She did a walk-through from lounge to kitchen to bathroom to bedroom and back again, then stopped, a little perplexed. It was a startling contrast to where she'd been during the afternoon – her visit to Maynard's place. This was the complete opposite – a perfect specimen of a single pad. And yet, something wasn't quite right.

It took her a while to spot what it was. Then she realised. It was too perfect. This apartment was straight out of a brochure – not just fastidiously tidy, but also impersonal. She could see no family photos on display – in fact, no photos at all. There were no books anywhere, no magazines scattered around. The CD and DVD collections stood in their racks in pristine condition. And the shelves were sparsely decorated with minor objets d'art that could have come out of a catalogue. As she surveyed the rooms, just one thing stood out – one item that betrayed some wayward individual taste. It was a picture on his bedroom wall – a framed print of Gustave Doré's *Red Riding Hood*, with its sinister image of the wolf, its claws exposed, in bed with the little girl. As she stared at it, a cold sensation crept down her spine. She felt like she'd missed something.

It was right in front of her.

The picture was mounted on walnut panelling. But the central panel wasn't just part of the wall. At waist height there was a recessed handle. The panel was also a door. She reached out and opened it. Inside was a small adjoining room – used as a computer den.

She walked in and gasped at what she saw. There were screens and keyboards and electronic decks, with VR accessories of goggles and gloves. Like the rest of the apartment, it was neat and spotless. But unlike the other rooms, this one had photos on the wall – maybe a hundred of them – tacked in rows to corkboards. They were all explicit, hard-core and illegal – a nauseating gallery of child pornography. Lining the shelves below were hundreds of labelled discs with numbered references from Kidophiliax, a paedophile website that had evaded law enforcement agencies around the world. Rita appeared to have walked into its production room.

It was now imperative to find out what was on Flynn's computer. She slotted in the Plato's Cave smartcard and tried to log on. The system immediately recognised the card, responding with a series of security steps, but these were beyond her limited hacking skills and the system denied her access.

She phoned Strickland and told him what she'd found.

'Right, I'll send one of the computer boys straightaway,' he said. 'I'll join you there later when I've got a search warrant. We don't want to trip up over procedure.'

Rita left the computer den and went and stood by the balcony doors, giving her a clear view of the driveway.

She watched and waited, counting off the minutes as the first heavy spots of rain started slapping against the windows. Lightning flickered intermittently. Her eyes scanned the late-night traffic for any sign of either of Flynn's cars heading towards the apartment block. His return now would be bad timing. But within ten minutes an unmarked police car arrived, and moments later she let an officer from the Computer Crime Squad into the apartment, directing him towards the secret room.

'Gross,' uttered the officer, taking in the mass of images. 'This guy is one sick bastard.'

He sat down, slotted in the card and bashed away at the keyboard, while Rita returned to the window to keep watch. It wasn't long before he emerged, shaking his head.

'It's no good,' he told her. 'The card gives entry to the system all right, but there's a sophisticated set of security protocols. I could take all night and still not be able to hack into it.'

'Shit.'

'Is there anyone you can ask who's familiar with the system?'

'Maybe there is,' she said, pulling out her mobile and trying Josh Barrett's number again. This time he answered.

'What's up?' he asked.

'I'm at Eddy Flynn's place,' she said. 'I need you here. Now.'

He could hear the urgency in her voice but was mystified. 'I don't understand.'

'I'll explain when you get here. Do you know where he lives?'

'Actually, no.'

She told him the address and said, 'As quickly as you can.'

The computer crime officer returned to the den while Rita resumed her position by the window.

78

Rita was still watching when a black Falcon ute pulled into the driveway below. It stopped at the front entrance.

She swore under her breath. At any other time it would have been a welcome sight – the arrival of the type of car identified at the scene of the Hacker's third attack. It was like another piece of the jigsaw slotting into place. But right now it complicated things. She was busily working on a cover story to explain her presence in the apartment when a figure got out of the car and glanced up at the building. With a gasp of recognition, she forgot any idea of pretence.

He looked sleek and trendy in his black leather jacket, black shirt and chinos, his hair slicked back. He moved with a casual sureness that she'd seen in him before. How could she have miscalculated so badly? The figure who'd emerged from the car wasn't Flynn at all. It was Josh.

This changed everything.

Her mind was racing as he pressed the buzzer downstairs. She released the security lock and spoke to him through the intercom, telling him to come up. Her voice was calm, though she felt anything but. She opened the apartment door, leaving it ajar, and backed off a few paces. Then she unclipped her holster and told the computer crime officer to stay where he was and keep out of sight.

Josh strolled into the apartment, a pair of dark glasses hanging from his pocket.

She told him to close the door behind him.

He pushed it shut and said, 'So this is Flynn's place?'

She pulled out the gun and pointed it at him. 'Get down on your knees. Put your hands behind your head.'

He looked at her dubiously. 'Is this some kind of sex game?'

This time she shouted at him. 'Do what I tell you!'

With a scowl, he knelt obediently and asked her, 'Have you gone barking mad?'

She brushed that aside. 'That car you're driving. Is it yours?'

'It's a company car.'

'You're lying. I checked the Xanthus records. No utes on the books.'

He swallowed nervously. 'They're not registered to Xanthus.'

'Why not?'

'Barbie keeps them on the books of a loss-making firm he bought.'

'Why?'

'Some accounting dodge he's up to.'

'What firm?'

'I can't remember the fucking name. Some poxy software business in Wodonga. He bought it, asset-stripped it and flogged off the bits he didn't want. And when he took over Xanthus he swapped around some of the stock – including a bunch of utes. Satisfied?'

It sounded plausible but she wasn't convinced. 'What about Mazdas?'

'He pulled the same rort with them. They're registered to a mothballed company in Ballarat.'

'How many? And what models – what colours?'

'Four black MX-5s.'

'Who drives them?'

'They're shared out – mostly among the design team.'

'Flynn?'

'He's got one.'

She was still holding the gun on him. 'What about Ormond Keppel? Did he have one?'

'Yes, so what? Is it a fucking crime to drive a Mazda?'

'Some people might think so.' She lowered the gun, holstered it and smoothed back her jacket. 'Sorry, Josh. But you gave me a fright.'

He got up off his knees and brushed himself off. 'Well I'm pissing myself.' He shook his head. 'I just don't get it.'

'You're about to.' She beckoned him to follow. 'Come with me.'

She led him through the bedroom and into the computer den, where she introduced him to the computer crime officer, who got up admitting, 'Sorry, still no luck.'

Josh saw the photos on the wall.

'Weird.' He frowned. 'Is this why I'm here – Flynn's into kiddy porn and you want me to help bust him?'

'No,' she said.

'What then?'

'I want you to hack into his computer.' She ushered him into the chair. 'We've got the smartcard but can't get past the security checks.'

Still frowning, but without a protest, he swivelled around and examined Flynn's computer set-up.

It didn't take long.

'Okay, I'm in. What are we looking for?'

'Plato's Cave.'

'He won't have the game here. Barbie would kill him. And how do you know about that anyway? It's supposed to be an industrial secret.'

'Never mind. Just look.'

He did a search and got an immediate answer. It filled the column. 'Well, bugger me,' he said. 'He's downloaded the whole damn thing. And he's got a program running on it right now.'

Josh snatched up the cyber-gloves and strapped on the goggles.

Rita watched impatiently as he wiggled around in the chair, his head wobbling, his sensor-stimulated hands manipulating the air as he negotiated his way through virtual reality.

'I'm in the game,' he said. 'And I've found the program. Not one I know. It's called Shadow Duel. Some kind of chase sequence. Must be his own hack-and-slash groove where he –'

Then he froze. 'Shit.'

Slowly he removed the goggles and peeled off the gloves.

'What is it?' she asked.

'You better take a look for yourself.'

He got up to make way for her.

She sat in the chair, pulled on the gloves and tentatively fixed the goggles over her eyes, slotting the headphone attachments into her ears.

They blotted out everything else.

The 3-D images were slightly blurred but they immediately adjusted to her eyesight – and she was inside the game.

She felt a rush of vertigo as a different world opened around her. Turning her head to either side she found she was looking around a vivid nightscape, on a seashore under a dazzling moonlit sky, the sound of waves crashing in her ears. But there was something else, too, above the receding hiss of the water. Voices; not singing exactly, nor chanting. It was almost like a wailing, charged with emotion. Eerie but somehow erotic. What strange mythic scene had she dropped into? On her left was the sea, foaming with rocks and driftwood. On her right were craggy pinnacles rising above a gorge filled with olive trees stretching into the distance. Ahead of her she could make out a figure moving away along the pale swathe of the beach – the sand ribbed with the bleached bones of skeletons. In one hand she could feel the weight of a sword, its blade stained with blood, in her other hand she carried a shield, and on her head was a helmet.

She loosened an earpiece and asked Josh, 'What am I supposed to be looking for?'

His voice came back, 'Someone else on the beach. A female figure. You're hunting her.'

'I can see a figure in the distance.'

'That's the one. You need to catch up. Use the control pad.'

She could see the small transparent icons to the left of her visual field. She tapped them with her free virtual hand and zoomed in on the figure. The nearer she got, the louder the mad, seductive wailing was in her ears, drowning out the sound of the waves. She realised the voices emanated from the fabulous female creature. Approaching from behind it was an impressive sight – a statuesque woman, naked under the moon, her curves smooth and elegant, shoulders bristling with white feathered wings. The vision was lurid and fascinating, but clearly dangerous, because it too was armed with sword, shield and helmet. In her right hand, Rita tested the weight of her weapon. She raised it to strike. As she did so, the figure turned and looked at her. The sound of the voices was now overwhelming. Rita dropped the sword. This was beyond anything else she'd experienced. As she stared at her adversary, she found herself looking into her own radiant face.

She threw off the goggles and gloves.
'Are you okay?' asked Josh.
'I've felt better,' said Rita. 'How has he put me in the game?'
'He's created his own avatar,' he explained. 'The game lets you do that. He scanned you in from your front-page photo.'
'Great. And what's he turned me into?'
'You've got the bronze sword, shield and helmet of the Shadow Maker.'
'One of the warriors of the cave.'
'Programmed for a duel to the death.'
'I need you to explain how something relates to this game,' said Rita, arms folded. 'Cutting off sense organs.'
'It's the challenge of the demon level,' said Josh. 'To defeat she-devils you remove their ability to inflict sensory torment – the Gorgon's eyes, the Siren's tongue, the Harpy's claws, and so on.'
'Tell me the sequence of levels.'
'In ascending order there's the Abyss, Warriors, Prisoners, Demons, Monsters, the tower of Hades, Escape and Light – all drawn from Greek mythology, and consistent with Platonic symbolism.'
'There's something else it's consistent with – but in *descending* order,' Rita sighed. 'Role-play, compulsion, addiction and psychosis.'
'That's a depressing thought,' said Josh. 'But I suppose that's another thing about games – you end up back at the starting point.'
'And bronze masks – how do they come into it?'
'Part of the promotional kit, bronze-coloured latex rubber, easy to wear.'
They were interrupted by the arrival of Strickland, search warrant in hand, followed by Bradby and crime lab scientist Dale Quinn, all crowding into the computer den.

'So this is it?' said Strickland, scanning the photos and discs. 'Who'd have thought by hunting the Hacker we'd stumble onto Kidophiliax. This is amazing work, Van Hassel. How did you put it all together?'

Before she could answer, she found herself looking straight at Eddy Flynn.

He was standing on the far side of the bedroom, a fresh pack of DVDs in his hand, an expression of horror on his face.

As everyone saw him and lurched forward at the same time, Flynn ditched the DVDs, stepped backwards through the door, hitting a wall button as he did so. The door slammed shut with a loud electronic click.

Strickland and Bradby rushed over and tried to open it, but they couldn't force the lock.

'How the fuck did that happen?' Strickland exclaimed. 'The bastard's locked us in!'

79

By the time the door was forced open Eddy Flynn was long gone. Strickland was already on his phone, ordering a state-wide alert, with taskforce officers scrambling in response, and photos of Flynn being downloaded for circulation to police stations and release to the media. With Strickland in charge of the crime scene, Rita was ordered back to the office to help with background intelligence for the manhunt.

The rain was coming in uneven bursts as she got back in her car. The trees by the lake were thrashing around in spasms, shaken by gusts of wind sweeping through the night. Sheets of lightning were flashing overhead. Peels of thunder were rolling in on top of each other. She watched Josh Barrett drive off, and after a final look around she started up, following the road away from the park with a mixture of anticipation and anticlimax. She wanted a hands-on role in the capture of the Hacker – instead she was retreating to the sidelines.

She drove slowly at first, still keeping a lookout for Flynn's vehicle and trying to calm her sense of impatience. The image of herself as the Shadow Maker – that surreal experience in VR – had fired her up into a state of manic alertness. The vision was still with her: confronting her own transfigured form endowed with feathered wings, a wild expression and voluptuous nudity. She was yet to get her head around it – being turned into a program by a psychotic killer. And the thing was still running, not just in cyberspace but also inside his mind. Whatever else unfolded in the coming hours, she knew there'd be no sleep for her tonight.

•

Back at police headquarters, members of the taskforce were thin on the ground, with most of them out on patrol or stake-outs trying to track down Flynn. Rita still felt restless. After a debriefing session with Loftus and Mace, she wandered into the near-deserted squad room, pacing up and down. With nothing else to do but review what she'd uncovered across the day, she found herself strangely dissatisfied with the outcome. It wasn't just that Flynn had escaped arrest; she now saw a glaring inconsistency.

Loftus found her at a window, contemplating the night, a dark frown on her face.

'What's wrong?' he asked.

'I'm wondering if we've jumped to the wrong conclusion.'

'You've got to be kidding!' said Loftus, stunned. 'You've identified Flynn as the man behind the attacks, no doubt about it, caught him virtually red-handed. You profiled him accurately, followed the evidence, located his secret base and exposed his sex crimes background. That's brilliant detective work. What's more, the crime lab's confirmed the Hacker's prints are all over his computer. I'm beginning to wonder myself if sometimes you're just perverse.'

'Thanks, Jack.'

'Okay, that's unfair, you've had another long day. There's not much point in hanging around here. Why don't you go home?'

'I think I will,' she said, shouldering her bag.

'Wait a minute,' Loftus relented. 'Tell me first what could possibly make you doubt that Flynn's our man.'

'He's a paedophile, Jack, but the Hacker isn't. It doesn't add up.'

'You're basing your doubt on textbook psychology, that's why.'

'Well it's not going to hurt to double-check some evidence,' she said, picking up the nearest phone.

'Who are you calling?' asked Loftus suspiciously.

'Dale Quinn at the crime lab,' said Rita. 'Then I'll go home. Promise.'

80

He was on the loose again. Living a split-level existence. But the shock of the confrontation this evening had pushed him further than ever before. It was as if his identity had slipped from his grasp. Only the bronze mask he was wearing was keeping him intact.

Despite his insomnia and his aching brain he'd achieved a dualistic clarity. In the virtual game he'd dispatched dozens of opponents. In the game of reality he'd decommissioned four – two scarred for life, two dead. Now it was Van Hassel's turn. The duel was imminent.

He knew she was a fellow warrior, another Shadow Maker, and between them he'd sensed a mutual respect. The more she examined his exploits, the more she would appreciate his skill and power. Now he realised she was positioning herself to subvert and destroy him. In truth, she was the most dangerous opponent of all and he couldn't risk leaving her defeat to improvisation. She symbolised a higher level of challenge. That's why he'd designed a special program, allowing him to stalk her in two worlds at once.

The other casualties, in the lower levels of the blood sport, had been easy. Compliant creatures who'd conspired in their own destruction as he gouged out eyes, ears, tongue and nostrils. But he'd left those levels behind, working his way up from the nether regions of the Underworld, through the circles of hell, to the precincts of the vast underground city. This was where the duel would be played out. This was where Van Hassel would endure her fatal end.

The oracle had whispered in his ear, telling him to go into combat armed with a meat cleaver. The sequence was already keyed in. He'd render her helpless, lying there at his mercy. And when he'd forced his way into her body and vanquished her, he'd mark her with the stigma of defeat. Something suitably extreme to disarm her. Something time-honoured. Yes. Cutting off her hands would do it. Though of course he couldn't leave it at that. Her defeat would be followed by the coup de grâce. That too was decided. He would chop out her neck.

He reminded himself.

The game was real – and the real world was the game.

As he manipulated the controls, he sped like a projectile through bronze forests and neon canyons and parabolic causeways. Geometric structures streamed across his retinas in a vortex of lights, the colours of emeralds and rubies and white phosphorus. Flickering symbols. A delirious rush through a maze of icons. But it was too fast. Too precipitate. He altered his trajectory. Slowed down. Through a crystal channel now, with dim illuminations. Past shadows in alcoves. Dark figures in the night. Metallic fingers pointing the way. Aliens. Human holograms. Designer cavemen and women.

He homed in on the target and stopped.

Focused.

Approaching carefully now.

Storm FX kicking in. Strobing veins of electricity. Tectonic rumbles.

And there it was – an open portal.

He accessed it.

Followed the gloomy passageway.

Entered the chamber.

His fist tightening on the hilt, he held the meat cleaver aloft and advanced.

The first blow severed an artery.

Blood spraying into his face as she started screaming.

But his enemy had tricked him. She'd morphed into somebody else.

He didn't recognise this woman at all.

Rita could hear the screaming as she pulled up outside Lola's apartment. As the horror hit her, she realised it was Lola herself.

She hurled herself from the car and all but collided with a figure sprinting from the garden through the rain. She fell to her knees, rolled over and scrambled along on hands and knees, and got to her feet just in time to see a figure in a bronze mask bolt into a black Falcon ute. It was there, in front of her, under the streetlamp. As she chased after him, whipping the gun from her holster, he was already revving away from the kerb, tyres squealing. She ran, lungs heaving, but he was accelerating off. She stopped, took aim and fired – one, two, three, four shots – the bullets punching holes through the bodywork, the door and splintering the side window. The car veered violently under the impact – she must have hit him – but it straightened up and sped away.

The screams were worse than hysterical. What had he done to her?

She was drenched and out of breath as she burst into the apartment, slipping on a thick trail of blood. It led from the bedroom to the bathroom. She rushed there to find Lola, in terror and uncontrolled panic, blood on the tiles, the walls, the mirror, the ceiling – unable to stop the arterial spray from a deep wound in her forearm.

She was shrieking, 'Help me!' as Rita pushed her back, sat her on the toilet seat, yanked the cord from her friend's robe and used it as a ligature, twisting it hard around Lola's upper arm.

The tourniquet worked. The blood stopped squirting. There were no other injuries.

Lola was sobbing now. There were voices outside. Alarmed neighbours coming inside. Rita shouted at them to call an ambulance. It arrived as the full force of the storm was breaking. A downpour after the lightning and thunder.

He sped through rain-slicked backstreets and alleyways, every shortcut he knew, blood streaming from his cheek wound, the sound of her gunshots still reverberating in his ears. Despite his close call with death – her last bullet had come within an inch of killing him – his hands were steady, his reflexes fluid, his brain hyper-alert. The game wasn't over. It had just moved to the ultimate level.

The car thumped over rail lines at an empty level crossing and he accelerated into the next suburb. His enemies were multiplying by the minute. Keeping to side streets, he drove across one main road after another until he reached the park. He sped around the lake through torrential rain, his wheels slapping through leaves scattered by the storm, the wipers slashing against the windscreen. With time running out, he couldn't lose momentum, couldn't falter or hesitate. His game plan would work if he maintained focus – and kept ahead of his opponents.

As suddenly as the rain began, it stopped. He headed for the warehouse entrance at the rear of Xanthus. Using his access key, he drove straight in, the gates clanking shut behind him. The gash on the left side of his face was already congealing, as were the pock marks from glass splinters. He threw away his shirt and used the warehouse washroom to wipe the smeared blood from his neck and rinse the stains from his jeans. Fabric plasters from the first-aid kit were enough to cover the gash on his cheek. Having cleaned himself up he broke open lockers and pulled on someone's jungle green army shirt. Then it was time to deal with tactics and logistics.

He took the back stairs to the shadowed clutter of the office. Without switching on a light, he logged on, checked the time and went to work. The first task was to prime a cluster of crippling viruses. Once that was done, he keyed in a countdown and launched them at their targets. Next he triggered a phone search – all the numbers listed to Barbie. The one that was answered – 'Hello, this better be important' – gave the location. Next he accessed the online home security system that he'd installed. The multiple screens showed most of the rooms were unoccupied, apart from those hosting the cocktail party. He checked the alarms were off, made sure they stayed that way, then reprogrammed the system to go into a loop over the next hour. That would give him time enough. He logged off and jogged back down the stairs.

The bullet-scarred car had to be abandoned. One of the firm's white vans was much more suitable in any case. He got the keys, opened it and loaded it with more than a dozen cans of petrol. His plan was falling into place – in line with the art of guerrilla warfare. Evading capture. Commandeering transport. Improvising weapons. The stakes were higher now but the goal was still the same. To win.

As he drove away from Xanthus a police helicopter swept through the sky above him, its searchlight probing the streets below. But in the lanes behind the firm there wasn't a police car in sight. The van threaded a course to the highway where it joined the late-night traffic heading towards the suburb of Brighton.

Rita sat beside the hospital bed, head in hands, tears running down her cheeks. Lola lay there bandaged, sedated, weakened by a loss of blood. But she was strong, and first aid had been applied in time. The violence and the trauma of the attack would leave her with one ragged scar on her arm, and a deeper, invisible one in the reaches of her mind. Her fate could have been a lot worse. With that thought in mind, Rita wiped away her tears. Then, leaving her sleeping friend to the care of the nurses, she drove back towards the police complex.

Jack Loftus was pacing up and down the communications room when she arrived. He was listening to incoming calls, waiting for news from the manhunt. Every available patrol officer was out on the road and the helicopter was extending its search radius. Flynn's apartment was among the places staked out, should he put in an appearance there. A squad car was discreetly parked opposite the front gates of Xanthus, but so far there'd been no sign of him. Local police in the Latrobe Valley were keeping a watch on his family home in case he was making his way back to his roots. The longer he was on the loose the wider the search would become. Uniformed police had taped off Lola's apartment, where the Hacker had left perfect impressions of his shoes. The soles were neatly etched in her blood. And detectives had bagged the weapon – the meat cleaver that had been embedded in her arm.

'If he's smart he's lying low somewhere,' said Loftus.

'He's more than smart.' Rita was leaning on a desk. 'He's acting with a lucid intellect.'

'That makes him unpredictable.'

'Not necessarily. He's also violently ill. That's why his crimes are so grotesque. And because his actions are compulsive they can be predicted.' Her mind was searching for clues. 'All we need to know is which part of the delusion he's following.'

'Is there anything Flynn said?'

'It's not Flynn we're hunting,' she corrected him. 'It's the Hacker.'

'How does that help us?' asked Loftus.

'Because he plays by the rules of the cave.' She pulled herself up from the desk. 'Jack, I need to get into the Xanthus building.'

'Now?'

'Yes.'

'But it's got a squad car out front. If he turns up they'll grab him.'

'I need to get inside,' she insisted.

'We'd need a warrant.'

'There's a quicker way. Get Nash to tell Giselle Barbie to tell her husband to call you immediately. He's on a private line somewhere.'

'Why Nash?'

'They're pals.'

Loftus picked up the nearest phone and put in a call to Nash. He was finishing his coffee when the call came on his mobile, Barbie saying, 'I'm always happy to help the police. No explanation needed. My security guard will be there in ten minutes to open up the place.'

Loftus thanked him and turned to Rita. She was already heading for the door.

'Don't go in alone,' he called after her.

He dimmed the lights and pulled off the road, parking in a street lined with oleander bushes. There was no sign of pursuit. He was still ahead of the game. The wind had died away and the storm's retreat had left a humid calm in the night air. Already the water from the downpour was draining away. From nearby came the sounds of laughter and excited chatter. The cocktail party guests were enjoying themselves. Good for them. They'd soon have something shocking to talk about.

Senses on high alert, he climbed the side gate and dropped into the broad back garden of Barbie's mansion. There was no one around. Crossing the lawn, he skirted the swimming pool and went inside through open patio doors. The room he wanted was at the end of the hall. He let himself into the study and closed the door behind him. Inside was the locked wooden cabinet he remembered that contained Barbie's prized collection of imported hunting rifles.

Using the heavy base of a television award statuette, he broke open the lock. The rifles stood in their rack like a small arsenal. He grabbed a lightweight .308 with a fibreglass-reinforced synthetic stock and black rubber recoil pad – a Remington 700 ADL. The stock and metalwork had a non-reflective black matte finish – just right for night hunting. He lifted it out and felt its comfortable weight. Yes, this was definitely the one. Collecting a box of bullets, he slipped out of the house as invisibly as he'd arrived, gun under his arm. Not even the security cameras would record his visit.

Before he could start the endgame he needed to gauge the heaviness of the trigger, feel the recoil, and check out the scope. He drove to a deserted point on the foreshore. Here, lying among tea-trees with waves foaming against rocks below, he fired off three shots. His target was the door of a brightly coloured bathing box under a distant light. As he peered through the sights he could see the neat pattern of holes. It boded well for what was coming. How gratifying it was going to be to use Barbie's rifle as an assassin's weapon. What a deadly irony.

The manhunt was fully operational when the communications system at the police complex malfunctioned, with radio interference, jammed phone lines, computers going off-line. A virus attack was coming in waves. Clearly someone was blitzing the system from outside. Chaos ensued as engineers grappled with the problems.

Loftus stomped around his office swearing with frustration. At its most crucial point the investigation was becoming uncoordinated and in danger of unravelling. He was losing contact with his officers. Detectives weren't responding. Patrol cars couldn't call in. Even the helicopter was out of reach.

As the problems escalated Mace burst into his office. The Homicide chief grabbed a chair and sat down heavily.

'He's blinded us electronically,' said Loftus.

'Have you come across anything like this before?'

'No.'

'So what's he up to?' Mace ran a hand through his hair. 'Is he covering his escape?'

'I don't think so,' said Loftus. 'I think it's gamesmanship.'

'What do you mean?'

'He's planning something nasty. And he doesn't want us getting in the way.'

Rita stood in the Xanthus storage area with the security guard and two squad car detectives, in front of them a black Falcon ute with blood and bullet holes in it. Lockers had been broken open, petrol cans removed, and the guard told them a white van was missing. A discarded shirt lay where it had been tossed, the stains showing where he'd bled down the front. A packet of medical dressings lay open in the washroom.

'You scored a direct hit,' said one of the detectives.

'Superficial,' said Rita, distracted.

'How'd you know he was here?' he asked.

'Guesswork.'

'Based on what?'

'On hints he dropped,' she said, glancing at the shattered windows of the car. 'And because he's on a mission.'

She turned abruptly and walked towards her car, punching in Loftus's mobile number. Busy again. She tried his direct line but that was busy too, as was the switchboard. She gave up and sat in her car thinking it through.

When her phone rang it was Dale Quinn on the line.

'Thank God I've got hold of you,' he said. 'I can't raise anyone at police headquarters. The system's crashed.'

'That figures,' Rita groaned. 'We're up against the best in the field.'

'But I've got to tell them!' Quinn shouted. 'They're completely wrong!'

'You did what I asked?'

'Yes, I went back to Flynn's apartment to double-check like you wanted me to. I dusted the DVD pack he threw down when he bolted, and you were right – the prints aren't a match. Flynn is definitely not the Hacker!'

'That means it can only be one person and he wrong-footed all of us,' said Rita, her heart pounding. 'He's the brightest of the lot – and genuinely insane. I've got to stop him.'

She knew where to go because he'd told her – you end up back at the starting point. It had to be the casino, the location of his kerbside pick-up, the spot where Emma Schultz was collected on her way to becoming the first victim.

Rita turned the key in the ignition and sped towards the casino complex. Arriving, she left her car in the tower forecourt and ran towards the riverbank promenade, dodging crowds of people as she did. Again she tried to phone Loftus. Again she couldn't get him. Then, at last, her mobile rang.

'Jack?' she breathed into the phone.

'No, it's Martin Barbie.' His voice was unfriendly. 'I'm calling you because I can't reach anyone at police headquarters.'

'The lines are jammed,' she said, scanning passers-by while she spoke. 'Where are you?'

'My suite. The one you visited.'

'I tried to get hold of you earlier.'

'I was otherwise engaged – with private business.'

'Spare me the details.' She didn't have time to waste. 'What do you want?'

'To report a threatening phone call. From Josh Barrett.'

She stopped abruptly. 'When did he call?'

'Five minutes ago.'

'Tell me what he said.' She kept looking around. 'Exactly.'

'He told me I'm about to get publicity for my new game. That I can see it for myself if I look out the window and watch the next flame show along the river.' Barbie grunted. 'It's the way he said it. As if I'm about to get a cruise missile up my arse.'

359

'Did he say anything else?'

'Called me the Great Satan and rang off,' he huffed. 'I don't know what he's up to but the next show is due in a few minutes. So if there's anything you can do –'

'Shit!' Rita exclaimed, breaking into a sprint as she spotted a white van parked on the bridge by the casino. A lone figure stood beside it, apparently with a gun in his hand.

She tried to call for backup. No luck. Lines still out. Streaking forward, she reached the bridge. Light traffic sped in either direction. Below, on the river walkway, people spilled in and out of the casino. As she neared the van she splashed into some liquid. At the same time there was a strong smell of petrol.

Her .38 was in her hand, the safety catch off. And there he was, directly in front of her, standing by the parapet, a black rifle resting on his shoulder, the bronze latex mask covering his face.

'Excellent,' he said, turning to look at her. 'Now both my opponents are here for the finale.' Then he shook his head. 'But don't bother pointing your gun at me.'

Her hand held steady as she looked down nervously.

'That's right,' he said. 'We're standing in a large pool of petrol.' It was still seeping from a collection of cans in the rear of the van. 'One spark from the muzzle will ignite it.'

Rita controlled her instinct to flee and took a deep breath.

'Let's take it easy for a moment,' she said. 'We can discuss it rationally, Josh.'

'Your ploys won't work. Josh isn't here anymore. There's no way out – for you, me or the devil in the tower.'

'Okay, okay. So tell me something. Why is he the Great Satan?'

'Because that's exactly the role he plays in all our lives. That includes the drooling fans who don't even realise they're being sucked in and brainwashed.' His voice was growing increasingly shrill. 'Right now he's up there in his tower feasting his lust and gloating over his stockpile of corrupted souls.'

'And what about me?' she asked. 'Who am I?'

He stared at her through the mask. 'You know very well who you are. The yin to my yang. Under the pretty blonde exterior you've got a mind like a scalpel. That's why we're so simpatico. Shadow Makers in a duel to the death.'

Petrol flowed around them, pooling onto the road surface. Cars were driving through it. All it needed was a spark and it would all go up.

'That's not who we are,' she said. 'Remember what I told you earlier tonight, how the effect of the game is psychosis – a schizophrenic crack-up. Listen to me, Josh, I can help you. Take off the mask, put down the gun and step out of the game.'

That made him laugh. 'But surrender was never in the program so there's only one course open – the destiny of the warrior. Kill and be killed.' He glanced at his watch. 'Go out in a blaze of glory.'

'Josh, the way you're looking at things – it's not real. It's a delusion.'

'If that's what you think, just watch. You'll soon feel how real it is.'

He checked the time again, lined up the rifle and took aim through the sights. It was trained on an upper suite of the tower.

She raised her gun higher, pointing it at his upper torso, holding it in both hands.

'Put it down,' she told him. 'What do you think you're doing?'

'Just like Josh Barrett did in the country,' he grunted. 'Shooting vermin.'

Rita tried to swallow but her throat was dry.

'And there he is at his window – Hades in all his glory,' he said. 'Lord of the Underworld.'

She couldn't let him shoot – but if she opened fire she could incinerate them both. 'Josh!' she pleaded.

But it was too late.

'Bye-bye, Barbie.'

As his finger tightened on the trigger she shot him in the shoulder, her body turning as she did so. She was sprinting for her life as he swung around groaning, the rifle discharging and falling from his grasp, the bullet firing into the petrol and igniting it. The loud crack of the gunshots distracted a driver. His car skidded and swerved wildly as he braked and slammed into an oncoming taxi. The screech of tyres and the crunch of buckling metal added to the chaos.

Then the Shadow Maker's moment arrived.

The spectacular flame show burst into action, lighting up the city skyline. As the furnace-like flares shot up from the pillars lining the riverbank, Josh's body was engulfed in fire that rippled in rapid waves across the surface of the road. Van Hassel ushered the dazed motorists to the far side of the bridge just in time to escape the blaze and get them away from the burning vehicles. Then all she could do was watch.

Josh's insanity had found its ultimate expression – a synchronised vision of hell. The giant flames belching from the pillars formed a thematic backdrop as he turned into a fireball, his screams echoed by horrified onlookers. He got as far as the parapet but his clothes, skin, hair, mask and face were gone. He crumpled and fell, spinning like a catherine-wheel, into the river. Then the van exploded, followed by the car and taxi in quick succession. As Rita turned and shielded herself she saw her shadow, and those of the rescued motorists, cast in black silhouettes against the structure of the casino complex. The sight was stark and lurid. Somehow it captured – in a stilted instant – the meaning of the night. Fire glow, contorted shapes, shadows on the wall. Plato was right. It was an image of unreality and madness.

And then it was over.

The flame show stopped. The fire on the bridge was dying down. The vehicles were burning less fiercely. People crowded the path outside the casino, craning their necks for a glimpse of the human torch. But Josh was gone, in his place the flashing lights of patrol cars converging on the bridge and emergency vehicles with their sirens blaring. Rita got out her phone and put a call into headquarters. The lines were clear now. Things were back to normal.

Up in his private suite, Barbie turned away from the window, his face expressionless. The self-immolation, though inconvenient, would have to be used to advantage in whatever way he could devise. Josh had promised him publicity for the game. Now he would have to deal with it.

81

The hours that followed saw the story played out in the media. From the first snaps on the wires and flashes on radio, the news pushed aside everything else on the agenda. By the time the newspapers published their early-morning editions the headlines were jubilant: HACKER DELETES HIMSELF! And with a pastel sunrise colouring the sky in the background, crime reporter Mike Cassidy walked across breakfast television screens, retracing the death scene on the bridge:

> *Behind me are the charred remains of three vehicles caught up in the spectacular suicide stage-managed by the serial killer dubbed 'the Hacker'. Police have confirmed the identity of Josh Barrett, described as a brilliant software designer in the computer games industry. It seems that Barrett also designed his own endgame by flooding the bridge surface here with petrol and igniting it with a gunshot, timed to coincide with the riverside flame show. The result was witnessed by hundreds of people pouring from the casino. They watched in horror as the maniac responsible for a series of mutilations and murders walked to the edge of the bridge, wreathed in flames, before plunging into the river below, a victim this time of self-immolation...*

Detective Inspector Barry Mace called a mid-morning press conference to provide details about the successful outcome of Taskforce Nightwatch. He outlined how painstaking detective work had narrowed the list of suspects to a group of software engineers, and told reporters that as the net closed in on Barrett, the killer felt cornered, panicked and chose the easy way out. While Mace himself would have preferred the case to have concluded with an arrest and prosecution, at least the public could now feel safer.

As the facts emerged, Martin Barbie called his own press conference to express his personal shock, and fan the flames of publicity for Plato's Cave. He described Josh Barrett as un-Australian and announced he was shutting down Xanthus Software out of respect for the Hacker's victims.

By lunchtime Lola was suitably dressed and groomed in her hospital bed, her arm in a sling, smiling for the cameras. She'd signed a deal with a national magazine that would keep her in expensive shoes for the next couple of years. She hoped the publication of her exclusive would help with the recovery process. But while the effects of the trauma would gradually recede, she knew she would wake up crying from nightmares for years to come.

At police headquarters, Rita walked from the taskforce room where the crime scene photos were being peeled from the walls, and the accumulated material from the investigation was being packed away into boxes. Tired from a lack of sleep but still riding an adrenalin surge, she at last filed her completed reports on the night's events and took her leave of Loftus.

'In the end you were the only one who was right,' he admitted.

'I could have had Josh at Flynn's apartment,' she said. 'But he was very clever.'

'How did he pull that off, the switch?'

'He used the smartcard's VPN access to download his own program onto Flynn's computer. And he did it right under our eyes.'

'How cool can you get?'

'No, he was far from cool,' said Rita, shaking her head. 'It was the final stressor for him. When the effect kicked in, I think he was irretrievably insane.'

'You feel sorry for him?'

'It's tragic all round.'

'By the way, we've just got word from the cops in Gippsland and they've nabbed Flynn,' added Loftus. 'It marks the end of another career paedophile.'

'No wonder he ran.'

'Well, it's all over now.'

'Don't be too sure, Jack.'

She left him with a puzzled look on his face, took the elevator down to the lobby, nodded to the desk sergeant and walked out to a waiting Range Rover. The door opened and she climbed inside to the waiting arms of Byron Huxley.

She gave him a bleary-eyed smile as he kissed her cheek and stroked her hair.

'I'm so sorry I never made the connection,' he told her.

'You weren't to know.'

'I feel it's my fault you were so much at risk. And last night I nearly lost you. It doesn't bear thinking about.'

'Don't worry, no one's breaking us up,' Rita reassured him. 'So just drive me back to Huxley's haven in the gum trees. I feel I could sleep for a week.'

82

By the time Josh Barrett's inquest was formally opened and adjourned the media interest was dying away. Rita went on to write a report for the coroner as well as compiling a double case study on the Scalper and Hacker. She'd just finished putting it all together and submitting it to Loftus when she got an unexpected call on her mobile.

'Are you at police headquarters?' a woman's voice asked.

'Yes,' Rita answered. 'Who is this?'

'Kelly Grattan. I'm just passing and called on the off-chance.'

'If you want to talk, come up,' said Rita.

'No, I'll meet you over in the park – by the Shrine,' said Kelly, before ringing off.

Rita found her standing by the eternal flame.

'I read the news while I was in Singapore, which is where I'm based now.'

The women exchanged a look that said everything.

'I owe you an apology,' Kelly continued uncomfortably. 'But more than that – I want to thank you.'

'For what?'

'For getting the man who tried to rape me. I'm glad he's dead.'

'Tell me what happened.'

'It was just as I got home from work. In the basement car park.' Kelly took a sharp breath. 'He tore my clothes and got me down on the concrete. It was terrifying with those chains and that bloody mask he was wearing, but I still recognised him.'

'But you fought him off?'

'I kicked and punched like crazy and got away from him.'

'How did he react?'

'I saw him running off to his car, stuffing the mask in his pocket.'

'You were lucky,' said Rita. 'A few hours later he picked up Emma Schultz and raped and blinded her.'

'I didn't know that when I saw you in hospital.'

'He went on to carry out his series of attacks. You could have stopped that.'

'Maybe,' said Kelly with a sigh. 'Maybe not.'

'What do you mean?'

'He was protected. By Martin Barbie.' Kelly took off her sunglasses and leant on the metal rail surrounding the flame. 'I phoned him before I admitted myself to hospital. I told him I wanted Josh handed over to the police for what he'd done to me. Barbie wouldn't hear of it. Told me to calm down. Josh was too important because of the game. Without him, Barbie would run out of time. The deal would fall through. He stood to lose hundreds of millions.'

'So you blackmailed him?'

Kelly bowed her head. 'If he wanted my silence, he could compensate me.'

'How much?'

'Two million. I think I earned it.'

'And five other women paid the price. That makes it blood money,' said Rita. 'Do you think he was aware Josh was attacking prostitutes?'

'I don't know,' said Kelly, shaking her head. 'I don't know how far his lack of scruples goes.'

'You could help bring a case against him.'

Kelly gave a brittle laugh. 'I've had my revenge,' she said, looking at her watch. 'And I've got another plane to catch.'

'Before you go,' said Rita, 'I want to ask you about someone else you worked with at Xanthus. Ormond Keppel – was there ever a problem with him?'

'The other project manager? No. Mostly pleasant and witty, not always comfortable with women. Terrible what happened to him, drowning like that. We were all shocked.' Kelly pulled a slim mobile out of her handbag and phoned for a cab. 'It's a funny thing,' she went on. 'Part of me hates Barbie. Yet in a sick sort of way he's interesting. Not like other men. But get on the wrong side of him and you see his true nature. It's as if his whole personality – and he's got loads of it – is just a front, and deep inside something's missing.'

'What exactly?'

'Emotion,' she said, and put her glasses back on. 'He's as cold as hell.'

Down below, a taxi pulled over and waited. Rita watched Kelly walk down the slope, get in and wave briefly as the car drew away from the kerb. The cab crossed to the centre lane and did a U-turn, before joining the flow of traffic towards the city and the airport beyond. Kelly could fly away to her new life, bought with hush money, and leave behind her qualms of conscience. That's why she'd wanted to meet. Not just to say sorry, but to ease her complicity in Barbie's corruption and pass on the unfinished business of his evasion from justice. That burden now sat on Rita's shoulders as she pressed against the rail and watched the shifting tongue of the eternal flame.

Loftus sat at his desk running a hand through his greying hair as he read the two documents Rita had produced for the coroner. There was no problem with the first. It was her substantive account of the events immediately preceding Josh Barrett's death. But as he read the conclusion of the second – a supplementary report – his worry lines deepened.

> The crimes of Josh Barrett should not be looked at in isolation, but in the context of a new game that appears to trigger psychotic episodes in susceptible people. Research indicates the technology produces intense neural stimulation in structures such as the frontal lobe and amygdala. By implication it also affects the dopamine pathways associated with schizophrenia. The risk is clear for those with medical or psychological weakness in this area. The receptive mind adapts the content of the game to personal delusions that are magnified and acted out in the real world. There is a rapid progression to paranoid aggression, culminating in a schizoid breakdown and suicide. To put it simply, the game can induce accelerated insanity.

Loftus rubbed his temples slowly as he read it. He could feel a headache coming on.

> There are two cases on police files: (1) Josh Barrett has been identified as the Hacker; (2) DNA tests on hair taken from the personal belongings of Ormond Keppel prove that he was the serial offender known as the Scalper. In the light of these parallel cases among a small group of people intimately connected with the game, there can be little doubt that it was instrumental. If it is released on the open market the result could be psychosexual violence, murder and suicide on an epidemic scale.

When Rita entered his office, Loftus was standing with his back to her, hands in his pockets, looking through the window. She knew what that meant.

'Sit down,' he said solemnly, which she did.

'What you've done is a brilliant piece of detective work. You've effectively closed two cases for the squad. But as far as the inquest goes, the supplementary document exceeds your remit. Only your first report will go to the coroner.'

Rita folded her arms and said nothing.

'I know it's disappointing after all your hard work,' Loftus began.

'Jack.' She cleared her throat, trying to keep a lid on her anger. 'You don't think I've been objective?'

'I think you've been clever. Too clever. You want to turn the inquest into a platform to launch a consumer crusade and discredit Martin Barbie.'

'The game should be stopped and Barbie should be prosecuted.'

'Under what laws? You've got a well-argued theory with a strong coincidence, a touch of melodrama and no criminal evidence.'

'He paid Kelly Grattan two million dollars to keep her mouth shut about Josh Barrett.'

'Will she testify to that?'

'I knew you'd do this,' she said bitterly. 'Thank me and file it away.'

'I'm being pragmatic.' He sat down at his desk. 'Apart from a lack of evidence against Barbie, there's another reason to let it rest.'

'He's friends with Nash. The old boys' network.'

'That's how the world works,' said Loftus wearily. 'You and I may not like it, but we have to deal with it.'

'Sounds like a sell-out.'

'Wrong. The worst thing I could do for you is release this report. It's the ammunition Nash needs to go after you again. He'd use it as proof you're a loose cannon. As for the game, it's way beyond our jurisdiction.' He looked at her with something of a hangdog expression on his face. 'I'm just protecting you. And I hope we can agree on keeping your second report confidential. What do you say?'

'The whole world's a sell-out. And Barbie is the salesman.'

Barbie was escaping retribution for the time being, but someone else wasn't. Mike Cassidy sat rigid in his TV newsroom, a sour look on his face, while colleagues mocked him mercilessly. On his desk lay a late edition tabloid with a picture of him on its front page. The photo, taken by Rita while they were still together, showed him in costume for a private Rocky Horror party they'd attended. He was wearing Rita's stockings, suspenders, high heels, knickers and black camisole top. Above the raunchy pose, in large bold print, was the headline: BUTCH CASSIDY! With a sense of the inevitable, he realised the image would stick to his reputation like a perennial joke, and he'd spend the rest of his career trying to scrape it off.

83

Martin Barbie stood in the building that housed the old Gothic bank feeling strangely at home. The extravagant interior was a product of the 1880s land boom when speculators celebrated being rich, dishonest and vulgar. The place where he was standing – the vestibule to the original Stock Exchange – was known as the Cathedral Room. It was obvious why. Columns of grey granite were capped by carved white limestone, with elaborate arches vaulting to a groined roof. The walls, clad in polished French marble, were also fitted with Gothic tracery windows and stained-glass panels. The floor was laid with mosaic patterned tiles. The style was ecclesiastical rather than commercial. Or, as Barbie decided, a profane use of religious symbols. Very gratifying. It could be his spiritual home.

He was there because of Van Hassel. She'd rung him on his mobile – interrupting his business conference to call him a prick and insist on a face-to-face meeting. When he said no, she said, 'Plato's Cave – meet me or I blow the whistle.' It was an invitation he couldn't refuse. The Cathedral Room was the nearest neutral turf he could think of.

It wasn't long before the tap of her heels sounded ominously along the inlaid marble of the entrance hall. When she entered the room she found him propped against a pillar, in an obvious pose, inspecting a stained-glass window. She stopped beside him, hands on hips, her face glowering. But he didn't avert his eyes from the window, where a panel depicted a bare-breasted woman, shouldering a mallet.

Still admiring the image, he said, 'That's you up there, Van Hassel.'

Curiosity got the better of her and she looked up. 'So that's how you see me?'

'Absolutely,' he insisted. 'Topless, full-bosomed, strong and with a dirty great hammer slung over your shoulder – ready to beat the crap out of someone.'

'Always the flatterer,' she said.

'Even the face is yours. Attractive and tough at the same time.' He turned to her with a flawless smile. 'You could have been the model.'

'I'll take that as a compliment – because she represents honest labour.'

'Is that so?' Barbie smoothed down the jacket of his pale grey tailored suit. 'She looks just like a female cop to me.'

'You know why I'm here?'

'Because you can't resist my charms.'

'No, you arrogant prick. Because your game is lethal.' She brandished a folded sheet of paper at him. 'Plato's Cave is a killer, and you're putting it on the open market.'

'That sounds like a wild allegation. Where's your proof?'

She thrust the sheet of paper at him, but he wouldn't touch it.

'Sorry, but I only accept documents from my lawyers.' He strolled away to the centre of the room and stood on the glass floor prisms, craning his neck to look up at the old skylight. 'What exactly do you think you've found?'

She followed him and waved the paper in his face. 'This is a copy of my report. Giving details of two software engineers who suffered violent schizophrenic breakdowns because of the game.'

'Why would that be?'

'The new-wave technology you're using. It's too powerful. It has a direct effect on the brain.'

'It's revolutionary. I can't argue with that. The most realistic VR to date. And the most stimulating.' He adjusted his mauve silk tie. 'I'm even told it can produce a cerebral orgasm. What a selling point.'

'It deranges people.'

'If that's the case' – he frowned as if perplexed – 'why hasn't everyone who's entered Plato's Cave gone nuts?'

'How do you know they won't?' Now she poked him with the printout. 'And don't you care that such a high level of criminal insanity is associated with your product? What happens when millions of people start using it? It'll be like unleashing hell on earth. Is that what you want?'

'Actually, Van Hassel, it's out of my hands now.' His eyes looked directly into hers, and in that moment she saw what Kelly had seen. A coldness at his core. A dead place, where there was no emotion. There was a chilling edge to his voice as he added, 'If you've found a problem with the game, you'd better go tell the Japanese. It belongs to them now.' He straightened up. 'Now, I must be getting back to my conference – unless there's anything else you want to ask me.'

She looked at him in silence, a tightening knot of disgust in her stomach. If she fought him, she'd lose. He had power and influence on his side. She didn't. Like Loftus said, it was the way of the world. She'd gambled on provoking him but it hadn't worked.

'Well then,' he said with an affable nod, 'I'll be on my way.'

As he turned she asked, 'Why that title for the game? Why Plato's Cave?'

He stopped, shook his head whimsically. 'It's a tribute to the father of western philosophy, who invented the idea of virtual reality. It's there in *The Republic,* along with a description of universal nerds immersed in their own light and shadow technology – the realm of illusion we inhabit in our daily lives. Except he called it a cave.' And for a moment it was there in his eyes – a profound disappointment with existence. 'Get the picture?'

'More than you realise,' she answered. 'It fits in perfectly with your psychological profile.'

'Does it really? And I thought I was just being clever. I had the idea years ago, when I was young and living in Sydney. The first carefree days of my life. Between work and debauchery, I read the classics. Plato's cave seemed the perfect model for a computer game – and a metaphor I could relate to. Seeking enlightenment. Climbing out of hell.'

'And did you?'

He shrugged. 'Do any of us?'

She stood beside one of the grey granite piers and watched him walk away over the marble inlaid floor, beneath the series of smooth arches, down the steps, then pause at the carved wooden doors. The electronic glass barrier slid open, and he walked out into the bustle of the street as if the world belonged to him.

EPILOGUE

After months of preparation in Tokyo, everything was ready. Jojima and his fellow executives popped open bottles of the most expensive vintage champagne and drank a toast to their success. It was the eve of the game's global release. The publicity campaign had guaranteed that the first delivery of stock to stores around the world would be sold within twenty-four hours. Advance orders alone were worth more than $1 billion. It was a marketing triumph – the must-have product of the year. All the mainstream news media were running the story, with TV camera crews staked out at computer shops to provide live coverage of the midnight release.

The only other big news in Tokyo was that the Samurai had struck again – his fifth attack in as many weeks. The serial killer picked up young women at bars and clubs, then drove them to isolated areas outside the city where he beat them unconscious, raped and beheaded them. His predatory presence had added a buzz of paranoia to Tokyo nightlife. Newspapers had come up with the name after forensic scientists identified the type of weapon used to kill his victims. It was a samurai sword. Police had built up a profile with the help of witnesses who'd seen him with women he'd picked up. He was in his late twenties, smartly dressed, well-spoken and worked in the software industry.

Jojima's top team of software engineers had been too busy with every aspect of testing, formatting and overseeing mass production of the game to take much notice of the news. All, that is, except one of them – Kazuki Hasegawa. For him the sensational reporting of the case was deeply disturbing. The more he read about it, the more trouble he had coping. The story pressed in on him like a living nightmare. And while his colleagues joined in the champagne celebrations, Hasegawa made his excuses and went home.

He closed the door behind him and walked through his apartment to the bedroom. That's when he caught his reflection in the bamboo-framed mirror. He stopped and stared at it in horror. There, in the mirror, he could see his own face and the other face inside it. It was the mask of his insanity. At that moment he knew that while he lived he was damned.

Before the resolve could leave him, he undressed and laid his clothes neatly on the bed. Then he knelt on the rug by the window and bowed his head. Clutching the samurai sword he'd used to decapitate his victims, he gritted his teeth against the searing pain and ripped the blade through his lower abdomen, disembowelling himself. As he lay there, feeling his life blood drain from his entrails, a coldness dulled the agony and a drowsiness eased his mind. Finally it brought a sense of relief. It was his only way of escaping the shadows of Plato's Cave.

ACKNOWLEDGEMENTS

Exploring the dark labyrinth of Plato's Cave has been a collaborative effort over six years, with invaluable help from a number of people.

Top of the list is BBC Assistant Editor Deborah Sims, my beautiful wife and frontline reader. Her encouragement, constructive criticism and storyline inspirations have played a crucial part in shaping the book, as has her patience while I walked around with my head in another zone.

Others I owe particular thanks to include: criminal profiler Deb Bennett of the Victoria Police for her advice on the role and application of profiling; computer expert Ziad Haidar for his input on the cybernetic background; Professor Ray Nichols for sharing his observations on two and a half thousand years of politics and philosophy; London Broadcasting executive Peter Thornton for his humanist critique of consumer society values; David Wilsworth for his reflections on literary themes and social psychology; TV journalist Sylvia Lennan for her insights on the dynamics of sexual relationships; Essex nature poet Mervyn Linford for elucidating primal moods and motifs; BBC radio journalist Duncan Snelling for his informed views on the crime genre; Channel 4 correspondent Simon Israel for his analysis of the media and institutional bureaucracy; Nikki Davies for initiating the process of developing the novel and seeing its potential when no other agent did; publisher Louise Thurtell for her guidance on the plot and structure of the book; copy editor Ali Lavau for her uncanny attention to detail and engaging so thoroughly with the text; and finally my parents for their unstinting support always.

Note on quoted material: p. v, *The Bible*, Book of Psalms, Psalm 107: 10; pp. 146ff, Plato, *The Republic*, bk 7, 515a–518d*; p. 153, Friedrich Nietzsche, *The Gay Science*, bk 3, sect. 108; p. 175, Lord Byron, *Don Juan*, canto 15, st. 99.

* For dramatic purposes, passages from *The Republic* have been adapted to produce a streamlined extract. An authoritative version from the nineteenth century, by Benjamin Jowett, is still widely available, including on the internet. Among the modern translations, the one by Robin Waterfield (Oxford University Press, Oxford World's Classics paperback, 1998) is a thoroughly readable rendering of Plato's text.